Tom Morison's Golden Christmas
and Other Lost Australian Goldmining Stories

Edited and introduced by Tanya Dalziell

Obiter Publishing

Published by Obiter Publishing
PO Box 5133
Braddon ACT 2612
info@obiterpublishing.com.au
www.obiterpublishing.com.au

A catalogue record for this book is available from the National Library of Australia

ISBN: 978-0-6481742-7-1

Cover design by Giraffe
Design by Karen Downing
Printed by Ingram Spark

'To Be Continued ...'

Series editor Katherine Bode

The 'To Be Continued ...' series publishes fiction discovered by literary scholar Katherine Bode and bibliographer Carol Hetherington. They used new digital methods to search the National Library of Australia's *Trove* database to uncover over 21,000 stories published in Australian newspapers between 1828 and 1914. Although fiction is a rarity in newspapers today, prior to World War One Australian newspapers routinely published fictional works, and in the nineteenth century, were the main source of fiction for colonial readers. Some of the stories discovered in this project are short, amounting to only one or two columns on a newspaper page; some are lengthy novels, published over multiple newspaper editions.

Fiction in Australian newspapers came from around the world: from Australia, Britain and America as well as France, Germany, New Zealand, Russia, and beyond. All of the titles discovered – with an interface for readers to interact with *Trove* to discover new stories and correct the newspaper text – are available at http://cdhrdatasys.anu.edu.au/tobecontinued.

The 'To Be Continued ...' series focuses on Australian fiction not previously published beyond the original newspaper pages. It thus uncovers lost pieces of the nation's literary heritage enabling new understandings of the way Australian literature developed and how early Australians understood themselves and their world.

"Sketches from the Queensland Diggings"
Wood engraving published in the *Illustrated Australian News*
Melbourne: David Syme & Co., 22 January 1879.

Contents

Publisher's note

'Tom Morison's Golden Christmas' appeared in the *South Australian Weekly Chronicle* in 1882; 'The Widow Blane' appeared in the *Australian Town and Country Journal* in 1884; 'Gold-Quest' appeared in the *Queenslander* in 1885; 'The Adventurer' appeared in the *Australasian* in 1896; 'Thompson's Claim' appeared in the *Brisbane Courier* in 1881; 'The Chistmas Reef' appeared in the *McIvor Times* in 1893; 'Gold Thirst' appeared in Rockhampton's *Morning Bulletin* in 1899; 'The Surveyor's Ghost' appeared in Sydney's *Sunday Times* in 1898; and 'The Baby Saved Them!' appeared in Sydney's *Dawn* in 1890. No changes have been made to the original formatting apart from obvious typographical errors.

An important note on the text

Readers are advised that some stories in this collection contain offensive late nineteenth-century stereotypes, prejudices and words.

Striking Gold, Writing Gold

Tanya Dalziell

Goldmining is so ubiquitous in settler-Australian history and literature that Ralph Martindale's first impressions of the mid-nineteenth century goldrushes in colonial Australia will feel familiar to many readers. In Lancelot Booth's 'Gold-Quest: A Christmas Tale of the Early Digging Days' (1885), the protagonist Martindale writes at some length to his family in the snowy English Midlands, informing them of both "the Australian bush" and the motivations that have driven him and many other men to the goldfields:

> It was impossible to resist the temptation to go
> to the 'diggings.' Every day there are fresh 'finds,'
> business is at a standstill in the coast towns, and the
> bush roads leading to the locale of the discoveries
> are thronged with bullock-drays and swagmen on
> foot, pushing forward in their thirst for gold. I have
> thrown in my lot with an American named Reuben
> Grant … He is an old Californian digger, and we
> are what they call here 'mates.' We have pegged out
> a claim, and have sunk about 6ft., but no signs yet
> of the precious metal. A claim but little removed
> from ours has got some fine nuggets, and we are in
> hopes. Oh, it is a fascinating quest—this gold quest!
> There are 4000 men here, and the cry is 'still they
> come.' And what a *pot pourri*!—lawyers, doctors,
> even clergymen, habited in moleskins, shirts and
> slouch hats, baring their arms and blistering their
> hands delving for gold. There are storekeepers who
> reap a richer harvest than the goldseekers. There

are loafers, idlers, blackguards, and the scum of
time-expired convicts. … Police protection is perfectly inadequate; brawls are of hourly occurrence
… Every man is armed, for life and property are
not safe … I anticipate trouble. These are common
episodes in this great canvas town. Men bent on
getting gold, and not a woman's softening face in
the mass.

As a newcomer to the diggings, Martindale is perfectly positioned to relate the clamour and excitement, as well as the perceived danger, of the lure of gold tugging at men from all classes and from across the world. And trouble does indeed come when he and Reuben Grant's otherwise unimpeachable plan to transport their discovered gold to Melbourne in the skins of black swans is disrupted by a gang of marauding bushrangers. Yet, by dint of Grant's wily ways that are held up as resolutely right in this lawless place—it is revealed that he once intervened to prevent a man's lynching—the gold is saved and then sold, with the proceeds taken back to England just in time to relieve Martindale's father from unexpected insolvency. Further, the man rescued from the noose is promised reconciliation with his ill and impoverished wife and child, who had coincidentally come under the care of the benevolent Martindale family after he turned to drink and deserted them. And a woman's softening face is Martindale's reward: he marries his cousin who has been awaiting his return home. This neat tying up of events is not for Grant, however. His narrative trajectory is one of adventure rather than melodrama. "Rube," as Booth tells it, "could not stand a life of inactivity." Rube says to Ralph, "Guess I'll try Australia again. You're married and settled, and got your profession … But I can't keep still; must keep moving." Grant's departure also holds out to contemporary newspaper readers the tantalising possibility of another tale of future transnational adventures.

Booth himself had travelled from England to colonial Sydney (and then Brisbane), via New Zealand, in the mid-1870s to gain experience and make money—not in the goldfields but on the stage and the page. In addition to acting, he wrote plays, poems, children's tales, short stories and, into the twentieth century, he published two popular novels. He therefore knew the worth of a good story and like so many of the writers in this volume who were looking to find paying publication in colonial newspapers, he saw in gold and the goldfields an enduring narrative pull.

The gold fever in the south-eastern colonies in Booth's story had lessened somewhat by the time Booth arrived in Australia. The rushes began with the discovery of gold near Bathurst in April 1851; the metal was found in Victoria soon after in the same year. Another gold boom started in Queensland in 1867; gold was unearthed in the Kimberley region of Westralia in 1885, and then east of the colonial capital of Perth in Coolgardie (1892) and in Kalgoorlie (1893). These discoveries immediately drew prospectors from the eastern colonies that were experiencing the economic bust of the initial gold boom; it was later that they captured significant writerly attention. Both Katharine Susannah Prichard and Randolph Stow produced important Western Australian goldmining literature with their respective works, *The Goldfields Trilogy* (1947–1950),[1] and *Tourmaline* (1963),[2] whose messianic-like diviner has an unlikely antecedent in James Crozier's story in this volume.

So, Ralph Martindale is not quite the eye-witness he purports to be. What he attests to most vividly is the idea that this volume of stories evidences: mid-nineteenth century gold finds fired both economic *and* literary imaginations well into the late nineteenth century. As gold rush historians Benjamin Mountford and Stephen Tuffnell have recognised,

---

[1] *The Goldfields Trilogy*: Katharine Susannah Prichard, *The Roaring Nineties: A Story of the Goldfields of Western Australia* (London: Jonathan Cape, 1946); Katharine Susannah Prichard, *Golden Miles* (London: Jonathan Cape, 1948); Katharine Susannah Prichard, *Winged Seeds* (London: Jonathan Cape, 1950).
[2] Randolph Stow, *Tourmaline* (London: Macdonald, 1963).

"Nothing set the world in motion like gold. Between 1848 and the turn of the twentieth century, the global rush to find and extract the precious metal from the earth in previously unimaginable quantities inspired a dramatic burst of moment and energy, affecting the course of world history."[3] The events and sights breathlessly relayed in Martindale's letter certainly had an extraordinary part to play in the reshaping of the world and the making of Australia; not only "its roads, its railways, its ports, its towns and its cities,"[4] but also its mythology.

When the influential mid-twentieth century historian, Russel Ward, wanted to understand and explain white Australia, for example, he looked back one hundred years and found the emblematic figure of the gold digger.[5] For Ward, the gold digger was a symbol of the abiding socialistic mateship that had, he thought, its origins in colonial pastoral workers and which was constitutive of "the Australian Legend." Ward's claims have been subject to scrutiny: his legend leaves out women, indigenous people, children, migrants—all of whom were also present on the goldfields—and sidesteps any number of other significant, and indeed insignificant, historical moments and Australian 'types.' But a glance at this collection's stories makes some sense of Ward's emphasis. Mateship between men is certainly apparent in these tales, and is periodically put to the test. In 'Thompson's Claim,' for example, one of the story's central characters, Joe, looks after his dying mate "like a woman would have done." And his grief at his friend's death is excessive, even by the codes of friendship that bind mates on the north Queensland goldfields. Yet, it turns out that Joe's grief is also for himself; the deceased friend had written floridly to Joe's daughter in England, on Joe's behalf, so that she

[3] Benjamin Mountford and Stephen Tuffnell, "Seeking a Global History of Gold," in *A Global History of Gold Rushes*, eds. Benjamin Mountford and Stephen Tuffnell (California: University of California Press, 2018), 3.

[4] Malcolm Knox, "What the Boom Won't Leave Behind," *The Monthly* (December 2012/January 2013): 69.

[5] Russel Ward, *The Australian Legend* (Melbourne: Oxford University Press, 1958).

might believe her father is a gentleman of learning. Joe's relationship with his daughter is also a potential casualty of his mate's death. In 'The Surveyor's Ghost' (1898) by 'Spinifex',[6] mateship extends beyond death. Harry Gifford, the "tent mate" of Simon Price on the Coolgardie gold-fields pledges to make good his friend's dying request. He is killed before he is able to carry out the entreaty, but true to his word—"I'd come back from the grave to straighten things"—he haunts his murderer until the assassin is apprehended and the gold-money intended for Price's family is recovered. What Ward's emphasis on mateship can be understood to highlight, and what this volume confirms, is the role of gold in constituting the (selective) stories Australia tells of itself.

As historians Geoffrey Serle and Weston Bate have shown, the emergent goldfields in colonial Australia attracted significant writerly attention during the mid-nineteenth century.[7] With gold already discovered in California, the world was alert to new finds. And within a decade of the first rush to Victoria, a flurry of books written in many European languages told of the Australian diggings; these were in addition to the volumes that British publishers produced and the reporting about the goldfields included in widely-circulating magazines such as Charles Dickens' *Household Words*.[8] All of these texts catered to an international curiosity about the discovery of gold in the British colonies.

Among them were narratives that put paid to Ralph Martindale's observation in Booth's story that women were absent from the diggings, including Ellen Clacy's stylistically eclectic *A Lady's Visit to the Gold*

---

[6] Pseudonym of the editor of *The Goldfield Courier* and *The Coolgardie Miner*, Alfred Chandler.

[7] Geoffrey Serle, *The Golden Age: A History of the Colony of Victoria, 1851–1861* (Melbourne: Melbourne University Press, 1963); Weston Bate, *Victorian Gold Rushes* (Fitzroy: McPhee Gribble, 1988).

[8] See Margaret Mendelawitz, ed. *Charles Dickens' Australia: Selected Essays from Household Words 1850–1859. Book Four: Mining and Gold* (Sydney: Sydney University Press, 2011).

Diggings of Australia in 1852–3 (1853),[9] Catherine Helen Spence's *Clara Morison: A Tale of South Australia during the Gold Fever* (1854) with its early fictional female 'witness' to the diggings and gold fever in colonial Adelaide,[10] and Fergus Hume's best-selling book, *Madame Midas* (1888), whose titular protagonist is a canny entrepreneur; she picks herself up from an unhappy marriage, sinks a shaft in Ballarat, and "proved herself to be a first-class woman of business."[11] Stories in this volume suggest the presence and proper role of white women on the goldfields, too, such as the store-owning 'Widow Blane' in N. Walter Swans' story of that name. Carl Feilberg's 'Thompson's Claim' (1881), however, initially pictures the diggings as bereft of the cultivated qualities white women were thought to represent and extend. Feilberg was not unaware of what 'civilising influences' meant in colonial Australia. The Danish-born Feilberg was a well-known and well-liked author in his time. Among other papers, he published in *The Brisbane Courier*, which he oversaw for a time as editor-in-chief of the *Brisbane Newspaper Company*, and his reputation was such that the by-line of 'Thompson's Claim' could read 'By the Author of "Dividing Mates".' Feilberg would be best remembered by his contemporaries for his political journalism that targeted the assumed 'civility' of frontier colonial projects and policies in Queensland, which resulted in the deaths and displacement of Aboriginal people.[12]

If the stories gathered here adhere to the notion of white women's refining influence, many of them additionally tell of gold-seeking as a masculine adventure, as suggested by the titles alone of John Arthur Barry's story 'The Adventurer' (1898)—published in *The Australasian*,

---

[9] Mrs. Charles Clacy, *A Lady's Visit to the Gold Diggings of Australia in 1852–3: Written on the Spot* (London: Hurst and Blackett, 1853).

[10] Catherine Helen Spence, *Clara Morison: A Tale of South Australia during the Gold Fever* (London: J. W. Parker and Son, 1854).

[11] Fergus Hume, *Madam Midas: Realistic and Sensational Story of Australian Mining Life* (Ludgate Hill: The Hansom Cab Publishing Company, 1888), 20.

[12] Carl Adolph Feilberg, *The Way We Civilise: Black and White, The Native Police / A Series of Articles Reprinted from the Queenslander* (Brisbane: G. and J. Black, 1880).

the weekend companion to Melbourne's *The Argus* newspaper—and John Westgarth Ellerman's 'Gold Thirst: A Queensland Tale of Adventure' (1899), which appeared in the lesser-known *Morning Bulletin* based in Rockhampton, Queensland.

Barry was a journalist and author who wrote books and published serialised fiction. He has been remembered by Australian literary history as a "prolific if superficial writer,"[13] a judgment that might have been made on the evidence of stories that are replete with surprising storylines and neat resolutions, of which 'The Adventurer' is one example. Ellerman has left fewer traces; he may have been the son of a Belgian immigrant who, rather than heading to the goldfields mid-century, grazed sheep in Antwerp, Victoria—but gold-seeking lends itself more easily to narratives of escapades and exploration than the leisurely pace implied by sheep-grazing. Both these stories undoubtedly take their cue from the contemporary genre of adventure romance, which enjoyed significant readerly interest in the colonies during the last decade of the nineteenth century.[14]

These adventure novels routinely had compelling story-lines that also confirmed colonial claims: their protagonists uncover fortunes in unknown places populated by exotic races, which were oftentimes regrettably or forcibly extinguished before the spoils were taken back to civilisation. The genre was revived and expressly yoked with gold most memorably in 1920 with the publication of Conrad H. Sayce's *Golden Buckles*,[15] which tells of remarkable gold finds in the Australian desert, and then again in the early 1930s by Ion Idriess and his best-selling Depression-era novel, *Lasseter's Last Ride* (1931).[16] This book offered a highly

---

[13] H.P. Heseltine, "John Arthur Barry (1850–1911)," *Australian Dictionary of Biography* Vol. 7, 1891–1937, eds. Bede Nairn and Geoffrey Serle (Melbourne: Melbourne University Press, 1979): http://adb.anu.edu.au/biography/barry-john-arthur-68.

[14] See Robert Dixon, *Writing the Colonial Adventure: Race, Gender and Nation in Anglo-Australian Popular Fiction 1875–1914* (Melbourne: Cambridge University Press, 1996).

[15] Conrad H. Sayce, *Golden Buckles* (Melbourne: A. McCubbin, 1920).

[16] Ion Idriess, *Lasseter's Last Ride* (Sydney: Angus and Robertson, 1931).

fictionalised account of Lewis Hubert Lasseter's ruinous quest in 1930 to rediscover a gold reef to the west of the MacDonnell Ranges that he had supposedly found in 1897. But, in an example of life mimicking art, this 'discovery' would seem to have had its truer origins in the improbable plots of late nineteenth century adventure romances.

The narrative arc of the quest, which structures the adventure form, is well-suited to newspaper serialisation, the format in which many of them were originally published. The two in this collection add some twists to the familiar narrative. The apparent death of one digger in the South Australian goldfields in 'The Adventurer,' for instance, sees another steal his identity in order to access the former's inheritance in England. The ruse is so successful that even the dead mate's mother falls for it. Yet, suspicions are raised; the interloper confesses the deception to his would-be sister, Isabel, with whom he has inconveniently fallen in love; and he returns to the diggings to give his mate a proper burial. In quick succession, he finds not a body of bones but his mate miraculously alive and stumbles across a gold reef. Both happy accidents allow for his redemption in the eyes of the story's moral compass, Isabel, and his reward is the promise of marriage to her in England.

'Gold Thirst' concludes far more unsettlingly. It is an especially curious and indeed disturbing story that admits more than it might intend; a reader today might view the story as an allegory and critique of settler colonialism and the troubling part that the rush for gold played in its development. The story's opening scene (it has the air of a play) is one of ruthless and violent betrayal, a theme that continues throughout. A gold escort, accompanied by "four black troopers," is ambushed and the stolen gold is lost, only to be discovered years later by a "half-caste" girl. Lizzie uses its value to contract a white kangaroo shooter into marriage before both are pursued by the earlier gold thieves lately 'freed' from a prison island.

Among all of the stories in this volume, it is this tale that strikingly makes whiteness visible, draws attention to the violence committed against Indigenous Australians as part of the colonial project, and underlines the anti-Chinese sentiment in both the goldfields and its fiction. In Ellerman's story, the race of the white troopers is as apparent as that of the "black troopers," with both indigenous and non-indigenous characters said to be united in their distaste for "the Chinaman." This characterisation of the Chinese is persistent in late nineteenth-century fiction; it registered widespread xenophobia in colonial Australian society.[17] The economic value of gold drives the story's white men to commit heinous crimes, including the cold-blooded slaughter of an Aboriginal man, Paddy, who is briefly 'employed' as a tracker and whose wasting shocks even the murderer's accomplice; earlier in the story, Paddy is presciently but grotesquely tied to a corpse as punishment for his refusal to do the bidding of a white trooper. It is perhaps no coincidence that the character who most troubles racial categories also dies, but not until Lizzie's worth is admitted in romantic terms. "Curse the gold," her lover cusses as Lizzie's last breath fails to communicate the whereabouts of the precious metal she has hidden. Ultimately, the gold is withheld; the story ends with a final image of Lizzie's deranged lover searching fruitlessly for the metal in shifting sands, a damning appraisal of all that has come before.

If some of the stories in this collection pose as 'adventure' narratives, they and others also turn on an abiding idea of gold as a puissant sign of the moral value in which narratives trade. When a naturalist in Louisa Atkinson's novel, *Cowanda: The Veteran's Grant* (1859) stumbles onto a New South Wales diggings site, readers are left in no doubt about the temptations that lie therein. This place is filled not only with the promise of gold but also "pleasures and sins."[18] Gold readily lent itself to imagina-

---

[17] See J.B. Hirst, *The Chinese on the Australian Goldfields* (Bundoora: La Trobe University, 1991).

[18] Louisa Atkinson, *Cowanda: The Veteran's Grant* (Sydney: J.R. Clarke, 1859), 121.

tive speculations about life in the colonies and the proper ways in which it should be led.

This purposing of gold is apparent in Maud Jeanne Franc's (Matilda Jane Evans) 'Tom Morison's Golden Christmas' (1882). Franc was a productive writer, publishing fourteen novels and many articles and short stories. And the religious tenor of that work, which accorded with Franc's beliefs—she was a Baptist Church deaconess—are apparent in this gold story. Tom Morison is recently and unhappily exiled from England with his family, thanks to the Long Depression of the late nineteenth century, and he views his new environment with some disdain. Ray, Morison's sister, sees their surrounds in distinctly Romantic terms; she expressly evokes the poetry of Leigh Hunt to describe them. By contrast, her brother is largely dismissive of the land until an epiphany grips him and he declares: "These rocks—these very rocks that I have despised so much … are doubtless rich in minerals, and only want discovering. Why should not I turn some of them to account? Gold even has been found in less promising places. Why should not I find gold?" With this revelation, the text shifts register. No longer Romantically imagined, the rocks are regarded as untapped economic resources, an outlook that is divinely confirmed. A heaven-sent lightning bolt ultimately exposes the intuited gold and Morison's mother agrees that it is "God's gold": "with eyes fast filling" she says, "we will take it from Him, and be thankful." Where the Morisons take the proceeds of their gold fever is England; they have more than enough money to repurchase the home they had left behind. What remains is a "creek with its broken rocks" and a future time of further despoliation that goes by the name of progress—"life and energy and enterprise."

This religious aspect of gold is also a theme in Crozier's 'The Christmas Reef,' although the tone in this tale is much lighter than that of Franc's earnest writing and registers the emergence of alternative spiritual beliefs that were finding expression in late-nineteenth century colonial Australia.[19] This story is unusual in the context of the wider volume in that its first-person focalisation centres on a sixteen-year-old 'city' girl, Millie Watson. Millie sees herself as a new type of woman that was making an appearance in fiction in the form of 'the Australian Girl,' claiming that "we *fin de siecle* girls are an improvement on the 'sweet sixteen' of the beginning of the century."[20] Millie has pluck and a sense of adventure—she travels alone on a train from Melbourne to Maryborough in the Victorian goldfield region and later rescues her would-be-lover from a mine shaft—and so is a spirited narrator. When she is recognised by a father and son "who belong to the cult of theosophy" as spiritually elected to find gold by means of rhabdomancy in order to fund the pair's charity works, she hardly hesitates. Her calling is confirmed by the prognostications of "Cagliostre's Crystal," a transparent ball bought relatively cheaply by the theosophists but which carries in its name a history of literary and philosophical debate over occultism and charlatanism. Her effortless divination of gold sits in contrast to the physical labour of gold acquisition in other stories, and her 'Australian Girl' attitude comes to be curtailed at the story's conclusion as the narrative slips into a romance register and casts Millie as a woman, and wife.

The role of gold in distributing moral value is also apparent in 'The Baby Saved Them' (1890), which sees a bushranger get his come-uppance when he bungles a gold robbery. This story, by an author whose identity has been lost to history, was published in Louisa Lawson's monthly, *The Dawn*, the first journal in colonial Australia to be expressly directed at a female readership and which notably promoted the cause of white female suffrage and social reform. Given that Lawson wrote much of

---

[19] See Jill Roe, *Beyond Belief: Theosophy in Australia 1879–1939* (Kensington: University of New South Wales Press, 1986).

[20] See Tanya Dalziell, *Settler Romances and the Australian Girl* (Crawley: University of Western Australia Press, 2004).

The Dawn's content, she may well have penned 'The Baby Saved Them.' Lawson herself had first hand-experience of the New South Wales goldfields, not least when she, her Norwegian husband who had first travelled to Australia to try his luck on the goldfields, and their five children, joined the goldrush in Gulgong in 1871. Her son, the author Henry Lawson, would later tell of the vicissitudes of the diggings in his stories and poems including 'The Golden Graveyard' (1901)[21] and 'Eureka' (1889).[22]

'The Baby Saved Them' largely involves a conversation between a married couple on the goldfields who have made a modest sum and are preparing for a life elsewhere with their baby. The woman's awareness of the physical dangers of the goldfields is maternal; Tess fears the young child might fall into an open shaft. And her role as a help-meet for her digger husband is apparent, with Tom expressly commenting (with more than a hint of the potential violence embedded in the uneven power relationship this gendered domestic arrangement entails), that: "To think that these little fingers that I could crush up in my hand, made and washed the diggers' shirts." Yet, the idea of 'family' that the couple and their child represent, their shared toil and future ambitions and their claim to the gold, are all rendered worthy in light of an attempted robbery. The bushranger figure, which vies with the gold digger for a central place in Australia's (white, masculine) mythology, certainly comes off second best in all of the short stories in this volume. And in this sketch, he deservedly receives a bullet in the leg.

The presence of gold in fiction established moral standards for its characters (and readers), but its pragmatic and political treatment in mid-nineteenth century publications is also worth noting. Many early books on gold served the practical purpose of providing information to would-be diggers about the emerging goldfields, as Ralph Martindale's

---

[21] Henry Lawson, "The Golden Graveyard," in *Joe Wilson and His Mates* (Edinburgh: William Blackwood, 1901), 157–75.

[22] Henry Lawson, "Eureka (a Fragment)," *The Bulletin* 10, no. 472 (2 March 1889): 12.

experiences do in Booth's story. John Capper's *The Emigrant's Guide to Australia* (1853), for example, laid out what was in store for prospectors at this far-flung part of the British empire and reminded gold seekers of their legal requirement to obtain "gold licenses and claims"[23] at the behest of Crown Mining Acts, which were rapidly imposed across the colonies. This was an obligation routinely side-stepped. Goldfields entertainer Charles Robert Thatcher carolled this recalcitrance "with deafening applause … at the Bendigo Theatre" in his song "Where's Your License".[24] In so doing, Thatcher musically registered a deep political complaint that culminated during early December 1854 in the Eureka Stockade, an event that resonates in the stories in this collection and into present day Australia.

As is now well-documented, the rebellion culminated following a protracted period of unrest and civil disobedience. Miners in the Ballarat goldfields in Victoria took up arms against colonial forces in response to both the excessive licence fees imposed on them and the violent methods used to police them. The Eureka rebellion also protested the miners' lack of suffrage. While the uprising was brief and quickly defeated, it nevertheless set in train a wider demand for legislative reform that, together with miners' rights, was implemented in the following year. Tellingly, however, these concessions were not extended to either the Indigenous custodians of the Wathaurung land on which the conflicts took place or the Chinese workers, for whom immigration restrictions were, in fact, tightened.

One hundred and sixty-five years later, the Eureka Stockade continues to have a contested hold over the national imagination. It has been variously understood as an anti-imperial protest, a rally against government impediments to the workings of free enterprise and as a working-man's

---

[23] John Capper, *The Immigrant's Guide to Australia* (Liverpool: George Phillip & Son, 1853), 121.

[24] Charles Robert Thatcher, "Where's Your License," (Melbourne: Victoria Press, 1854).

revolt. And the scores of men who died,[25] and those with stories of being miraculous saved from the violence, have troubled Australian literature. Rolf Boldrewood's (Thomas Alexander Browne) *The Miner's Right* (1890), serialised in the *Australian Town and Country Journal* in 1880, for example, has characters haunted by the bloody battle of the rebellion. Such ghosts are also glimpsed in N. Walter Swan's 'The Widow Blane: A Tale of the Times' (1884) in this collection.

Nathaniel Walter Swan ventured to the Victorian goldfield from Glasgow in 1854, and later pursued a career in colonial Australia as an admired journalist, the editor of the *Ararat Advertiser* and a successful author. Likewise published in the *Australasian Town and Country Journal*, a regular outlet for writers in Australia from 1870 until after the First World War, his story 'The Widow Blane' would seem to have little to do with the Eureka rebellion at first blush. It is a romance, which begins when John Grant, a digger on leave in the city, comes into possession of an ordinary box with hidden secrets. These revelations eventually lead him both to a union with the titular character—who is not who she seems to be but is nevertheless morally faultless—and also to a subplot. Mrs. Blane runs a store on the diggings and brings to the place the 'softening' effect Ralph Martindale in Booth's story imagines women of a certain type to possess. It is revealed that she is a grass widow, a phrase helpfully parsed by Ellen Clacy as a "mining expression" that denotes those women left alone, and usually "in town," while their husbands' infatuation with "nuggets" leads them to the goldfields.[26] Mrs. Blane's husband went to the diggings and there he was led to drink, and then suicide-by-drowning, by a ruffian who turns out to have a long record of treacherous activity. Not only does he steal the gold Mrs. Blane keeps safe in her store and nearly murders Grant in the process; he is revealed to be none other than

---

[25] Claire Wright also suggests that one woman died in the battle. Claire Wright, *The Forgotten Rebels of Eureka* (Melbourne: Text, 2013).
[26] Clacy, *A Lady's Visit*, 115.

"Ned Groves … the man who was agitator and leading conspirator of the misled diggers of the Eureka Stockade … and who suddenly disappeared with £500 when the fight was over; and finally, the man who acted as a spy on behalf of the Government." Groves is clearly overdetermined, and intended to be thoroughly unlikeable, but for the fact that he also claims to have saved Grant's life during the Eureka battle. It is by this grace that Grant demands of Groves the return of the stolen gold rather than a more punitive solution to the problem at hand. Curiously, the miners living at Boulder Point seem to have implicitly learnt from the rebellion the need for compliance; they wait with as much patience as they can muster for the newspapers to tell them of "new prospecting rules," before putting in pegs and "markin' off" their "patch."

While the men in Swan's story are waiting for signs in the newspaper to begin their diggings, their wives are interested in reading the stories these publications carried. Dick asks Mrs. Blane for a copy of the paper as, "This is Wednesday, and the wife, she thought, as having time, she might finish the story": a story of the very sort this volume brings together and which enticed readers to buy the next newspaper. The discovery of gold that these readers' husbands are hoping for certainly enlivened both newspaper business models and local writing culture. As Elizabeth Morrison has suggested in her study of mid- to late nineteenth-century country Victorian newspapers: "Slow to start, the new goldfields press had a spectacular, if erratic, growth from 1855 [… with] the peak of press activity occurring from 1855 to 1858, which was the period of highest goldmining yield for Victoria."[27] If the newspaper industry underwent a corresponding boom with the discovery of gold, Elizabeth Webby has also noted how the gold rushes had a hand in creating Melbourne as the new literary capital of Australia. By Webby's estimation, before 1850

---

[27] Elizabeth Morrison, *Engines of Influence: Newspapers of Country Victoria 1840–1890* (Carlton: Melbourne University Press, 2005), 74, 75.

Hobart and Adelaide enjoyed "relative prominence … in early Australian periodical literature," a distinction that dissipated as the gold rushes saw the populations of these cities move to Melbourne and the Victorian goldfields.[28] It was in Melbourne that magazines such as *Melbourne Punch* and the *Australian Journal* emerged and the city could claim literary credentials for itself.

All facets of literary culture, then, have been shaped by the discovery of gold in colonial Australia. In turn, stories about gold have given the metal meanings and values that say less about the substance itself than the life and times in which it circulates. As this volume attests, gold narratives serve as a point at which the histories of print culture and gold discoveries meet, and what they relate is the complex interactions of imaginative and material forces that helped produce ideas of the emergent nation of Australia that continue to be debated today.

---

[28] Elizabeth Webby, "Before the *Bulletin*: Nineteenth Century Literary Journalism," in *Cross Currents: Magazines and Newspapers in Australian Literature*, ed. Bruce Bennett (Melbourne: Longman Cheshire, 1981), 15.

Tom Morison's Golden Christmas

Maude Jeanne Franc

Chapter I: Rocky Nook

"I pity the man who can travel from Dan to
Beersheeba, and cry, 'Tis all barren." — Sterne

"It's very lovely, Tom."

"Lovely? Oh, lovely enough; but unfortunately it's a kind of loveliness that won't pay. I can see that with my little experience of things of the kind. None but an artist could turn a red cent by it; and there are no artists that I know of in our family—at least, not so far as practical results go."

"But the land has borne crops in the last owner's time."

"So it is said; but what kind of crops or how remunerative rumour saith not. To my thinking the virgin soil, what soil there is, would have been better—though to be sure this has the advantage of being cleared ready to hand."

"Ah! but what I mean, Tom, is this—if the soil will bear wheat at all, why not for us?"

"Well, my dear Ray, for precisely this reason—I don't believe farming can be taken up without an apprenticeship, more than anything else. Father knows nothing beyond the mere theory of farming, and he is too old and too delicate to take to it practically. I am still worse, for I am not only unfitted for it, but I hate and detest it, and shall only take it up because I am forced to it, having nothing literally to do now that my last chance of a profession is gone and every decent vacancy in Adelaide is filled."

The brother and sister lapsed into silence after that last outburst, Tom whittling away at a small stick he held in his hand, his sister looking far out into the quiet evening with a sad and thoughtful expression in her dark grey eyes.

It was a lovely spot, whatever else might be said about it. A few acres of arable land lay nestling away in the very heart of great rocky boulders which cropped out of the earth in all directions in a variety of quaint and grotesque forms, as though thrown together in the old time "when there were giants in the land." Some of these masses of rock, grey with moss and lichen, were grouped together like the ruins of ancient castles; others stood boldly up like pillars, raised indeed by no human hands—here an immense mass barely balanced on a smaller; and here the whole ground one series of rocky points half-covered by grass and herbage.

Two smooth slabs thrown down at the base of a monster boulder formed a comfortable seat for both brother and sister, all the more pleasant because two or three young wattles, taking advantage of a bit of good earth at the side, had thought fit to grow luxuriantly and throw a cool shadow over the spot, though their blossoms were all gone.

"There's one thing certain," said Tom, emphatically, after a long interval of silence, during which the thin chips of bark fell round him, and the upper end of the stick was artistically carved, "we cannot live altogether on milk, fruit, and eggs; and it will be months before we can plough or sow—still longer before we can reap. It is a good thing certainly that you have been offered this school, that the people all seem so eager about, though where all the scholars are to come from I am at a loss to say, but I suppose they know. It's rather a different life to that we had shaped our for ourselves, Ray, but we must make the best of it."

"Oh yes, Tom, and we will," said his sister, sitting suddenly up, and brightening considerably. "It won't be for always. We will make the best of it, and get all the good out of our 'freehold' that we can. I am sure if any have reason to complain it is papa and mamma; it must come harder on them, you know, Tom; they are no longer young."

"It was such a complete crash—so unexpected—such a rascally piece of business," said Tom angrily. "The only wonder is that we got enough out of the wreck to come out to South Australia and to buy this bit of land. We could not have done it had it not been a rare bargain."

"Yes, and with a pretty fair home on it, too. It's a nice little house, small as it is; and though only built of logs and mortar, neat and clean inside; and I'm sure the outside is picturesque enough, with its verandahs and climbing plants, and garden of fruit and flowers. I think we were very fortunate to hear of it."

"So we were, as circumstances went," said Tom, rising and stretching himself; "but, unfortunately, a pretty house and garden, and even a cow and fowls, as I said, won't keep us, though it may go some way; and I am afraid it will fall rather hard on you and Ellie and the mater to get along without a servant, and that is a luxury not to be thought of for the present. As to myself, I seem a mere drudge in the market—I'm worth nothing."

"Oh, no, Tom; it won't always be so. Your turn will come. We couldn't do without you as it is. Oh, we shall get along somehow, never fear," and, rising, she prepared to follow her brother home.

Home they were learning to call it already, though everything was new and strange. It was not a trifle to be suddenly hurled from a position of elegance and competency, to one of comparative poverty. Yet the long voyage had in part inured them to the change, and had prepared them to welcome joyfully any spot of green earth they could call their own. Perhaps this was more especially the case with Mr. and Mrs. Morison. The sudden reverse had fallen most heavily on them, but the "bit of freehold" of which Tom so contemptuously spoke was an ark of refuge that they had gladly entered; and after the restricted space and many disagreeables on board ship—which in past days were more frequently experienced than they are now—the cosy little home among the rocks, small as a nutshell as it was in comparison with their old luxurious home, was a positive pleasure to them. If the rooms were small they were so much better fitted for the limited amount of furniture they had contrived to bring with them, and the arranging of these home treasures had been a task that both Ray and her sister Ellie had thoroughly enjoyed.

It was the latter end of September when they arrived in the colony— balmy, lovely spring weather, with fresh showers and glorious sunshine. Almost too hot, it seemed to them, coming from a less genial climate, but to South Australians all that could be desired. It had not been Mr. Morison's intention to have left Adelaide if they could have obtained a house of their own at a reasonable price, and some congenial and lucra- tive employment for himself and son. But at that time there was nothing available, every situation was filled, while the applicants far exceeded the demand. There was positively nothing to occupy them that promised a living. Their funds were rapidly melting as funds will melt, and the little family were almost reduced to despair, when chance threw into their way this tiny homestead and farm among the hills, at so ridiculously low a price—the owner leaving the colony under peculiarly pressing circum- stances which permitted no delay—that Mr. Morison closed the bargain at once, and the freehold became his.

There had been no time for the inspection of the property before the purchase; the departure of the owner by the next homeward bound vessel, and their own need of a house and some provision, or prospects, for the future were so imperative that they could not be scrupulous; they had to trust to the honour of those who had the property to sell. They expected to find it very rough, and that it proved far better than their expectations was a matter of gratulation to them all.

The previous tenants had evidently been careful of their property, careful of their little rough house, and especially so of their garden. Even the small barn and cow-house were in perfect repair, for the Morisons having taken possession so immediately after the departure of the owners there had been no time or opportunity for the despoiling of the premises.

It was a cosy enough place to live in provided the business tact was there. The land had been left fallow for a year, possibly because its owner thought of leaving. There could be nothing done, as Tom said, for many months. There was very little money left after their removal and the purchase of some necessary stores, but to this they added their garden produce, a large number of fowls, and a cow. It was clear, however, something else must be done. Ray had been fortunately asked to open a school one mile from "Rocky Nook," as their place was called—that would bring in something. Ellie's services would be needful to her mother in the house; Ernest, a youth of fourteen, still studying with his father, was learning to be useful in other ways. In the garden among the fruit they soon found him invaluable, and a neighbor's boy had taught him how to milk, so that this difficulty with the cow, which at first seemed insurmountable, was at an end. Mr. Morison had appropriated one of the six small rooms as his study. He was engaged in writing lectures which were to be successfully given in the future. It kept him amused and occupied during the months of waiting, at any rate, and made him feel he was doing something, though Tom privately gave it as his opinion that the subjects he had chosen were not likely to be popular in Australia.

Poor Tom himself seemed to have no settled purpose. Cut short in his academical studies without a chance of their renewal he seemed to care very little what became of his future. There was little at present he could do, and he laughed sarcastically at his white hands when he thought of the plough-handle and the spade-work that alone lay before him. Meanwhile he went listlessly roaming about, gun in hand, sometimes bringing home a brace of pigeons or a rabbit as his contribution to the table, but too thoroughly disheartened to take any pleasure in the sport.

Chapter II: Rocky Creek

"With spots of sunny openings, and with nooks
To lie and read in, sloping into brooks."
— Leigh Hunt

A little creek went winding in and out among the rocks, now so narrow that a child's foot might span it, now wide and deep, affording a shelter to innumerable frogs, and overshadowed by teatree bushes, and bubbling over the stony bottom or rippling down a sudden declivity like a cascade in miniature.

Behind the house it had hollowed itself into a deep bed, and went softly on its way, giving life to some young cresses, that grew on its margin, and so clear was its flow that every stone it wandered over was visible.

From the back of the garden, creeping through a hedge of roses that divided it from the farm, it wandered on and on past the fallow land till it left Rocky Nook altogether, turning abruptly to the right, and running through a more level reach of country, till it presently passed the little rude school-house where Ray Morison had taken up her onerous duties. It was but a slip of a creek here, flowing between very low embankments. A little further on it widened again, and the children passing to and from school in that direction had thrown across it a neatly constructed bridge of bark; further on still it went rushing and tumbling over rocks and boulders, till it finally lost itself among the hills.

Ray had already been installed two months in her new duties with complete success. The neighborhood was not a large one, and she had only twenty scholars, but the boys and girls, rough and untaught as they were, soon learnt to respect their young teacher, and not a few to love her.

The Morisons had felt it sufficiently hot in September—November proved exceptionally so—and their inexperience of the climate made it all the more trying. The delicate mother, so differently nurtured all her life, found it most difficult to bear, and, to spare her as much fatigue as possible—indeed, to render her aid scarcely necessary—the girls and their brothers were up during the greatest portion of the week in the fresh morning hours, thus leaving a breathing space in the middle of the day. All but Ray enjoyed this resting time, and she in her cool dress, broad hat, and large white sunshade went off to her daily teaching, a little tired perhaps, but all the happier for the knowledge that her mother could rest.

Tom had as little to do as anyone in the house. He could not find a niche for himself. Sometimes he lounged half the morning, book in hand, under the shade of a large peach-tree in the garden, but he was almost too restless to study; he was dissatisfied with his life; he wanted some genuine employment; he had found nothing to his taste in Rocky Nook, and thought it impossible that he could ever bring his mind to the ploughing or reaping of land, which in its best aspect he did not believe could ever prove remunerative. What to do then? Teaching had been suggested to him, but he scouted the idea with derision. Better till the ground, unpromising as it appeared to him, than those unkempt human brains that were given up to the tender manipulations of his sister. There was certainly a breathing time for him—nothing particular for him to do, and he did it. One thing he diligently studied, and that was the weekly paper. The Chronicle was seized with avidity when it was handed to him from the post, but it never contained anything hopeful. There was no doubt about it for the present he must remain satisfied with his dog and his gun, and his books when inclination led to study.

One lovely morning—hot in the sun, but tempered very pleasantly with the sweet breeze that blew from the hills—he stood waiting at the white gate for his sister in order to escort her to the little school-house. His dog lay at his feet, eagerly watching his movements, and ready to bound forward at a word. It was a small black-and-tan terrier of a pure breed, and he valued it very highly, not only for that reason, but because he had brought it from his English home. A fine young fellow was Tom Morison, little past middle height, but with a pair of square built shoulders, and a well-set head of curly brown hair upon them. The Australian sun had not yet robbed him of his English complexion.

"It's a shame you should have to go out in the heat," he growled, as his sister came out in all her dainty freshness, swinging her little luncheon basket in her hand, and spreading her large white sunshade with its green lining as she walked along. Bright and merry she was as if she had not been as busy as a bee since six o'clock in the morning, and had not now from four to five hours' teaching before her.

"Now, Tom, don't be cross," she exclaimed, laughing, "it's as lovely as it can be this morning. Hot, you say? Yes, it is: but with such a soft breeze, full of all sorts of perfumes. And look at my flowers—these exquisite creamy rosebuds and their splendid green leaves. It ought to make you cool to look at them."

"You ought! You are a great deal too pretty, and too refined a little creature to have great unlettered boys under your training. It's not right, and I should say must be awfully distracting to them."

"Tom, Tom, you are incorrigible!" said Ray, laughing merrily. "The great unlettered boys, let me tell you, sir, are as 'docile' as wax. Don't be afraid, and cease paying compliments, or I shall think you don't mean all you say."

"Ray, I'm sick of it all."

"I've heard you make that remark before," said Ray, dryly. "What are you going to do today, Tom?"

"Oh! the old game, I suppose, lounge in the shade till even that deserts me."

"But what book are you reading, and where are you going to read it? Because I have lunch enough for us both here; something better than usual, and if you don't go too far away I'll come here at twelve and we'll share it together."

"I am not going far away—it's too confoundedly hot—I shall stay just down by the creek among the rocks at the edge of the farm. It will be cool there if anywhere. I shall be there when you come—that is, if this geology proves as interesting as I think it will."

"Are you studying geology?"

"Restudying it with practical illustrations," replied Tom, laughing. "I have an idea in my head."

"I'm glad of that; I had an idea that yours were very few and far between—lately. But, Tom, you need go no further. I see a bevy of my scholars coming to meet me, 'big unlettered boys and all'," she added saucily, "and here are your rocks, 'sunny openings' and 'nooks to lie and read in,' even the very brooks or creek at your feet—such as Leigh Hunt would have envied. So good bye, expect me at twelve o'clock," and with a gay wave of her hand she leaped across the creek and went on her way.

He went on his—not far though, just under the shadow of a huge mass of rock, where a grassy slope of peculiar richness invited him to rest, and a large teatree bank added to the shade and the seclusion, while the creek at his feet went bubbling on its own musical way, cool and pellucid enough in its rippling to suit any dreamer.

Tom opened his books, laying them out on the grass at his side—he had brought more than one volume to refer to. He sat with his back against the great rock, and his feet just above the rippling waters. It was pleasant and cool, there was no mistake in that; but he might have found cooler places nearer home if he had only needed that. For a little while his books remained unopened; he was studying the great book of nature and her pencillings among the rocks. A wild yearning desire was taking possession of him, the offspring of the idea that he had only recently entertained.

"These rocks—these very rocks that I have despised so much," he said to himself, looking round him, "are doubtless rich in minerals, and only want discovering. Why should not I turn some of them to account?

Gold even has been found in less promising places. Why should not I find gold?" And then for a little while he fell into a day-dream of what he would do if he was the happy finder—how everything should be changed, and even the old home might be repurchased.

He might have gone on dreaming much longer had not the croak of a frog disturbed his reverie, and taking up his book he was soon deeply absorbed in his study, occasionally referring to the rocks around for illustrations, or rising and breaking off pieces of the said rocks for example and comparison with other geological specimens at home. So much interested was he that he never noticed the lapse of time, and was thoroughly startled when Ray came round the corner, swinging her little basket, and sitting down at his side, roguishly asked him, "If he was too deeply engaged in his study of the earth to partake of its productions."

"Try me," he answered, closing his books and throwing them aside with amusing alacrity, as she spread her little white cloth between them, and laid upon it some particularly white rolls and little fruit pies of which she knew he was very fond. There were delicate slices of ham between the layers of roll, and a small glass each for the rich milk the bottle at her side contained.

"A luncheon for a king," said Tom with gusto; "and one of the Graces to serve it."

"Take the good of it while it is cool, my dear boy, then you shall give me the benefit of your idea. I've been wondering all the morning what it could be."

"Ah! I thought I should rouse your curiosity. And after all, really there's not much to tell—it is only an idea."

"But what is the idea?"

"Has it never occurred to you that these rocks may be very rich—in mineral wealth, I mean?"

"No—but of course it's possible," said Ray, turning rather grave.

"I've been studying the subject lately—used once to be excessively fond of it. I've gone into it again since the idea came to me," said Tom, lowering his voice as though the rocks would hear. "And do you know, Ray," he continued still lower, "I've come to the conclusion from certain indications that there is gold here about."

"Gold!" said Ray, in an awed tone of voice, growing grave with the immensity of the idea.

"Yes, sis, gold!; and what's more, I mean to find it!"

Chapter III: Among the Rocks

"One master passion in the breast

Like Aaron's serpent swallowed up the rest."

— Pope

There were no more listless days, no more unoccupied evenings for Tom Morison after that. A change had come over him for which neither his parents nor Ellie, or Ernest could account. Ray alone held the key to the mystery, and she went about with it burning in her bosom, ready at any minute to betray itself, only she had promised Tom, and resolutely holding her breath in times of temptation, was silent.

"If you would only let me give them a hint of what you are doing," said Ray one morning as they went off side by side to their separate employment.

"Oh! that will never do," said Tom, impatiently; "don't you see, if there happens to be a failure you and I will be the only disappointed ones; but if it is a success, why then it will be all the better surprise. I want to have a glorious Christmas, Ray, and I think I shall."

"Are you any nearer realising?" asked Ray anxiously, for she was beginning to believe in the chance herself, and was studying every rock she passed over in her daily walk.

"I believe I am. There was something hopeful; a few specks of the right sort in the specimens I assayed last night. It has put me at any rate on a new track. I never thought when I went in for analytical chemistry and assaying in general at home to what purpose my knowledge would be turned. It saves me a world of needless trouble, for I have no need to take my specimens to Adelaide to test them."

Christmas! that was coming on apace—difficult matter as it was to imagine a Christmas all sunshine and heat, with its fruit and flowers—no snow, no ice, no fog! It was coming, and would Tom's expectations be realised by then? Was it really possible that the whole would not prove:

"Like the baseless fabric of a vision—

Leaving no wrack behind?"

Ray thought it over as she went on her way to school, leaving her brother wandering up and down the creek, a small geological hammer in one hand, a pickaxe in the other, while his leather bag for mineral speci-mens was slung across his shoulder by its strap. She thought of it all day long—as she went through the lesson or the multiplication table with her heterogeneous class of scholars; and while they added up their rows of figures, or subtracted, or divided, or what not, she found herself more than once engaged in mental calculations such as this—Given, a certain quantity of gold-dust, how long would it take to repurchase an old English home? She got no result for her calculations, however.

"Tom's old taste for minerals and analytical chemistry has apparent-ly returned in full force since we have come among the hills," said Mr. Morison to his wife one day, as for a moment they stood together at the window watching their son and daughter as they went off together after breakfast. "It's a pity that he does not take greater interest in farming, and study up that subject."

"Oh, perhaps he will, when the land and the season is ready," replied his wife gently. "Do you know, dear," she added, "I have been thinking it such a good thing that the poor boy can take interest in anything. It has been such a bitter disappointment to him to give up all his studies and expectations when they were so nearly completed and accomplished. There is no doubt with his knowledge and taste his collection of minerals will bring a good price if he intends to sell them. I am so thankful to see him earnest in any occupation now."

"Perhaps you are right," replied his father, turning off to his own writings, with a heavy sigh. But meanwhile they neither of them guessed how one 'master' passion was swallowing up all others in Tom's mind— that for the time being even his loved and broken off academical studies and his blighted hopes were forgotten, or that night and day his one thought was—Gold!

Poor Tom! how little they knew what a feverish ordeal he was going through as day after day he went off among the rocks, never returning till the shadows of evening were lying thickly around him. It was becoming very hot in the sun, too hot for Ray to join him at noon. She packed up his luncheon in his mineral case, and though they went off together in the morning they did not meet again till she returned from school in the afternoon. Then she often went out of her way to find him, notwith-standing the heat, and sat quietly upon a prostrate boulder by the creek watching as he pursued his eager search. She scarcely dared venture to ask him what success had attended the day's work. His hot, flushed face, his bright excited eyes, or his clouded brow were sufficiently significant.

"Look here, Ray," he exclaimed one very sultry afternoon, as she slowly came up and languidly took her seat under the shade of a teatree bush. He was groping in the bed of the creek, the waters of which were dwindling away, and becoming narrower and narrower with every fresh day of heat. As she seated herself, he came up the sloping bank with his hands full of specimens, and threw himself down beside her. "Just look at these," he said; "there must be more where there is this. Here's a rich specimen—look at the bits of gold that stud the surface of this piece of quartz, and tell me if I have not plenty of reason for belief in ultimate success? It's my opinion that there must be a reef somewhere below these rocks, such as they have in Victoria. I've not a shadow of a doubt that there is—but that I must leave for others to find. What I want is surface gold, and I know it is here, and that I shall find it! It's only a question of time. Only I had made up my mind to have a Christmas gift—a golden Christmas gift for father on that day."

"Oh, never mind that, Tom," said Ray eagerly. "I'm so glad we've said nothing about it; they haven't an idea of anything of this kind. They only think you are collecting minerals to sell."

"Yes, and that is why I spent the time I so sorely grudged in fitting up those cases. When I get the gold it will be a good excuse to go to Adelaide for the sale of the minerals. Ah, well! it wants a fortnight to Christmas yet; but these specimens, Ray, are really fine—they are the best I have found yet."

"They are beautiful," said Ray; "but, Tom, you have not touched your luncheon. If you get ill, it will put a stop to everything."

"Oh, it has been too confoundedly hot to eat. I dare say you have done no better yourself."

"At any rate I have tried," said Ray, laughing, as she remembered where the greater part of the contents of her lunch basket had gone.

"Well, to tell you the truth, I forgot all about it. I'll take a bit now, while you are here, for I shall not leave this till I can see no longer. One never can tell what the next result of a stroke with the pick maybe."

"Only don't make yourself ill, Tom," she said, with a beseeching look in her grey eyes, as she spread out his forgotten luncheon as temptingly as was possible, after its lying all day in the grass at the foot of the rock.

"If only he would take it more quietly and not get so excited about it," thought Ray, as she slowly pursued the homeward path. Excited, indeed! was it any wonder that he should be so, when her own cheeks were glowing and her poises quickening at the remembrance of the beautiful lump of white quartz, rich in golden specks? Of course she believed in it now. How could she do otherwise? For where that came from there must be more to find; and if anyone could find it Tom could.

"I am afraid, my dear child, that this teaching is too much for you. You are sadly flushed this afternoon," said her mother, as she entered the little sitting-room, which with its open doors and windows and white matted floor looked cool and inviting after the heat of the sun.

"Oh, no, mother dear," said Ray, cheerfully. "It has been very hot today, but I am not much tired; and you know that Christmas will soon be here and the holidays. I shall have plenty of time to rest then."

She ran off to her room to lie down in its seclusion and think. Christmas had another meaning besides holidays for her now. She was fully partaking of her brother's "gold fever," and was almost as sanguine of ultimate success.

As to Tom, he was losing his appetite if not his energy; he could neither eat, drink, nor sleep. He was up late at night assaying his golden specimens. By early dawn he was off again to the rocks, returning reluctantly to a nominal breakfast, till at length even that seemed too great an aggression on his precious time. In future he snatched a breakfast of some kind before he left the house—not even waiting for his luncheon. So Ray on her way to school made a detour each morning and took it to him.

He was out of sight of the main road track now. The rich specimens he had displayed to Ray were discovered in a part of the creek round which the rocks clustered and stood up almost perpendicularly from the water's edge. It was on their own land, and no one had occasion to trespass—no one thought of doing so. He worked on, and dug in perfect security from prying eyes. He had it just all to himself, and no one had a right to interfere. It was rather a long round for Ray to take in the heat of the morning sun; but she thought nothing of that. Tom must be kept strong and encouraged in his work if he was to succeed. It was a great encouragement doubtless to him, the visit of his little sister and her belief in the ultimate results of his efforts. He always worked more cheerfully and hopefully after her visit, and looked for her return in the evening, especially if he had any fresh indications to show her, with an eagerness which he could not disguise.

But for all that the days were wearing away, Christmas was drawing nearer and nearer, and instead of the specimens with their golden specks increasing in number he at last wrought for four-and-twenty hours without a single sign.

He came home at night languid and weary, with clouded brow and heavy eyes. There was nothing to do that evening—nothing to assay. Ray saw how dispirited he was, and was not sorry when, complaining of headache, in answer to his mother's anxious enquiries, he did what she knew was the best thing for him to do—went quietly off to bed.

Chapter IV: The Rift in the Rock

"Nothing's so hard but search will find it out."
— Herrick

For some days the weather had been sultry in the extreme, the heat intense, and the whole sky glowing with its fervor. As night came on it brought with it but little change of temperature. There was no sun, to be sure, but the atmosphere was dense and suffocating and storm-charged, but with the dawn of each day the clouds had vanished, leaving the intense blue of the heavens unflecked by a single snowdrift; and the sun, a great golden ball of fire, daily rose, burning up the grass and herbage with its fiery beams, and drying up the creek wherever the shallow waters lay most exposed to its rays.

In such weather, and under such a sun, Tom Morison had worked with pick and hammer, and felt little of its power. His "master passion" for the time being had overthrown every other feeling and desire. Gold, and the craving for it, was burnt into his brain. He held up bravely, as long as that pick of his turned up gold flaked specimens, but that evening, after two days' steady work, had brought no sign or colour, his throbbing head warned him that rest was needed, and that if he hoped still to continue his work, rest he must take. So he quietly went to bed—and sleep, that balmy restorer, graciously closed his aching eyes, and stilled his beating pulses, and lulled him to repose.

The whole household soon followed his example, all but Ray, and she had no heart to sleep. She had been building up a great many air castles in expectation of a "golden find." Hitherto she had so thoroughly believed in the possibility of it all; and now Tom had come home so evidently dispirited, her bright visions took the alarm, and, like timid birds, fled before his despondency.

Stealing softly out of the sitting-room that she might not disturb the sleepers, she went out into the verandah and sat down; not that the sultry air without afforded much relief, but she felt smothered by the stillness and the gloom and the closeness within, and outside the house there was at least breathing space. Yes, it was decidedly better without. All day not a breath of wind had stirred the trees; but now, what was that she felt softly uplifting her hair? A little breeze was certainly rising —it was sultry yet, but that breeze might portend a change. She went out and stood beyond the trees at the gate. Ah! that was it. The last hour a deep embankment of ebony clouds had sprung up all round the horizon. Every moment they were rising higher and higher. They were angry-looking clouds, lurid with the heat, and charged with electricity; great masses flecked with salmon colour, and between these masses flashes of lightning were already playing, for a moment lighting up hills and trees and rocks with vivid phosphorescence, leaving them in deeper darkness by the contrast.

A low muttering of distant thunder, and then large drops of rain came pattering down on the leaves above and around her. Oh, how refreshingly the earth sent forth its fragrance in response to those few drops! A few more moments and she retreated hurriedly to the house. The long-threatened storm had come in earnest, and heavily rolling thunder —peal upon peal—mingled with vivid lurid flashes of lightning, shook the little house again and again. Down fell the welcome rain in torrents over the thirsty land, cooling the air in spite of its thunder-charged clouds—down fell the hail, rattling on the roof as though it would force an entrance; and Ray, at last, in response to her father's call, securing doors and windows against the violence of the storm, crept to bed with a thankful heart that they were all safely housed.

Tom slept through all the noise and clamour of thunder and hail and heard it not. The blue lightning flashed again and again on his face as it lighted up his little room, but failed to rouse him from the heavy slumber into which he had fallen. Towards morning the storm passed away, leaving only its blessed influence behind it. And when he at last arose, refreshed by his deep sleep, and struck by the pleasant change of the atmosphere, looked out from his bedroom window, the east was already purpling with the rising sunbeams, and so bright and clear and fresh was all around, that it seemed a new heaven and a new earth in comparison with the sultry skies and burnt up soil of yesterday.

"Had there been a storm, and could he have slept on oblivious to it all?" He hurriedly dressed, and quietly opening the back door went out. "A storm, eh, and a heavy one," there were evidences on every side; the wet ground, the drops glittering like gems on the leaves, broken branches of trees scattered everywhere, and the little birds rejoicing over the glorious change in a glad chorus of praise from every bush.

Ray came out presently and stood at his side.

"Oh, Tom!" she softly exclaimed, "such a storm, and such a glorious morning after it."

"I never heard it," said Tom. "Never slept so soundly in my life. I must have been fairly done up; could scarcely believe it, excepting for the unmistakeable signs all about."

"And just listen to the creek at the bottom of the garden; there's a perfect flood," said Ray.

Tom started. "Who knows?" he exclaimed, in sudden excitement, and with a bound he cleared the garden fence, and rushed off wildly in the direction of the spot where he had left his pick and spade on the previous evening, too utterly disheartened and weary to bring them home.

"What now?" cried Ray, as for a moment she stood in amazement, watching his head-long pace as he leaped over every impediment in his way. Another moment and she had snatched her hat and followed, one thought making her heart beat and her head throb.

"He has an idea, and so have I, and we may be right: who knows, indeed?"

Over the wet grass, over the fallen branches, over the pools of water left here and there among the rocks, over the very rooks themselves went Ray with light and rapid footsteps; one thought burning in her heart which she scarcely dared whisper even to herself—the storm, the storm, and its revelations!

Her brother had gone out of sight by this, but she knew well enough where she should find him. She had only to follow down the creek, now tumbling and foaming and rushing along with a hundred turns and twists, brawling as it went in petty fury pretty to see. No stagnation there, all rapid motion, the very air was full of its glad singing.

There were the rocks, among which so despairingly he had thrown his pick the evening before. But where was he? The next moment she saw him striking across the creek waving his handkerchief high above his head in a state of the greatest excitement.

"Tom! Tom! What is it?' she gasped out, exhausted by her long run. She came up at last and sank down on the bank above him.

"Hurrah!" he shouted; "Hurrah! Will you believe me now, Ray?" And as she sprang down to his side he took her by the shoulders and turned her face to the rock. What a sight met her view. There, where only yesterday had stood a solid mass of stone, a great rift appeared from the top to the bottom, shivered and shattered by the mighty influence of the storm. In the very midst of the riven mass, with its handle burnt and splintered to the hilt, lay the forgotten pick, whose bright points had attracted heaven's electricity, scattering right and left and breaking off huge pieces of the rock, and strewing the swollen waters of the creek with their fragments.

But in the midst of that riven rock lay the brightness—the glory and wonder of all—specks, nuggets, pockets of gold, as Tom pronounced them to be in true diggers' phraseology—the terms were not new to him if the actual things themselves were. The early morning sun glinted down upon the newly-discovered wealth, and Tom and Ray sat down upon the big boulders at its side with clasped hands and closed lips.

"There it is, Ray, at last," Tom faltered out, "the beginning of it—and I haven't the strength of a baby to take it. It seems too good after all to be true or real. Am I, in fact, awake or dreaming?"

"Wide awake, Tom, no doubt of it," she answered, merrily, waking up herself to the reality, and giving him a pinch to prove her words. "Oh, Tom, set to work at once, there's a good fellow, and I'll bring you the nicest breakfast I can get you—to give you strength—so you need not come home."

"Come home, indeed, and leave all this treasure to the public gaze! Not I! Not if I starved for a month," answered Tom, springing up and resuming strength and spirits both. "Yes; bring me some coffee, Ray, there's a good little sis, I must work like a brick today, and then I'm off to Adelaide. We'll have a golden Christmas after all!"

"It's God's gold and His gift as much as anything else," said Ray to herself, as she sped away to the house, the tears in her eyes, and the precious secret burning in her breast; "we ought to thank Him for it—and oh, I do—and I am sure we shall need His help that it prove not a 'root of evil,' but a source of all good both to ourselves and others."

"The stream has brought to light some fine specimens for Tom to add to his collection," said Ray, in excuse to her mother for his absence at table. "He thinks he can complete his last case of minerals today, and take them to Adelaide either tomorrow or the next day. I have taken his breakfast to him, mother dear."

"If those minerals only realise enough to pay him for his trouble?" said his father, incredulously.

"Ah, well dear," urged his wife gently "it's such a good thing he takes pleasure in the trouble. I do not think we need regret it."

"They never will," laughed Ray, hugging herself at the thought, and thinking as well of Tom's Golden Christmas.

Chapter V: A Golden Christmas

"And there is even a happiness
That makes the heart afraid."
— Hood

"Christmas Day! Could it indeed be Christmas Day with that breadth of sun shine—that soft, balmy breeze?" Ray exclaimed to herself, as she rose from her bed very early before the rest of the household were awake, and stood at the back door looking out into the garden. The fragrance of monthly roses and mignonette came to her on the wings of the fresh morning breeze, mingled with the richer odour of orange blossoms. The low murmur of the creek still swollen by the recent storm, and the hum of insects and the rustling of the leaves of the many trees on every hand, were a soft refrain to her own glad thoughts—for she was very happy—happy in the joy that that day was to bring—the wonder, the surprise of it all was before her.

Tom had not returned—but he would—she knew he would—for he had promised that nothing should detain him. She and Ellie had been very busy with preparations for their Christmas dinner. They were to dine late, and the old conventional English plum pudding would be in perfection. The turkey, a very fine one, was a presentation from the parents of one of Ray's most promising pupils. The dessert she would gather while the dew rested on it—ripe golden apricots, rich figs, luscious white heart cherries, red cheeked apples, and a bunch or two of early grapes—all were there. She took up her basket and went slowly up and down among the trees to gather the choicest she could find, stowing them in the little dairy when she had done so, covering them up with large cool vine leaves.

"It is such a beautiful country," she thought, "and yet how strange that one should sigh for the dear old land, and even for a sight of its snow and its frost and ice!" But it was so; even the golden treasure Tom had discovered was chiefly valued as a means for an ultimate return to the native land from which circumstances had so rudely torn them. She knew well enough how hope rekindled in the hearts of their parents would reconcile them to a waiting, which, if gold was still to be found, could not be a very tardy waiting after all. And oh, how glad she was of the golden secret she held—how she looked for Tom's return, and the revelations he would bring back with him.

Now and then, to be sure, a little fear mingled with her joy; for after all Tom might have been mistaken, and the apparently rich gold might prove spurious after all. But she scouted the idea as it intruded itself. Tom was too confident to be mistaken. She was positive he had assayed his findings correctly. She would not doubt—indeed, so sure was he of his accuracy, that, instead of going into Adelaide, he would simply have displayed his treasures in their crude form, and made his revelations stand as his "Christmas gift," had he not feared that his father, not possessing the same confidence in his knowledge, would look askance at his golden findings and doubt their genuine character. To obviate this he had merely taken a small packet of gold with him, carefully locking up the rest till his return. He had no intention of selling the whole in Adelaide—that would be imprudent in the extreme. He did not wish an inroad of adventurers on their land. What he could work himself, he would keep for his family—that was right enough. The reef, if there was one, could be discovered and worked out by some company after they had left the colony. He could easily find a market for his gold in Melbourne, and nobody, not a creature in the neighborhood of Rocky Nook need be the wiser.

So he reasoned it out with Ray before he went, and she fully acquiesced in all his plans. She only rather anxiously urged his speedy return, so that, laughing at her, he exclaimed—

"Why, my dear Ray, I would not be absent from home on Christmas Day for the world. I want it to be a perfectly Golden Christmas to us all."

In the strength of that promise Ray passed the morning, keeping down her excitement as best she might, and making herself as busy as possible that it might not become too apparent. She was down at the gate, though, many times through the morning, eagerly watching for the first sign of his coming.

"It would be no Christmas without Tom," said Ellie gloomily, after one of these peeps had been taken, and without result. "It seems a pity that he could not have waited till after Christmas. I don't see why he was compelled to go; the money was not immediately needed; the minerals would have sold just as well next week."

"Ah, well, he thought no time like the present, I suppose, Ellie;

Tom likes to do things at once, you know, when he is interested in the doing," said Ray, turning to entwine a straggling tendril of honeysuckle, and to hide her own laughing eyes, which might have betrayed her at the same time.

"It will be no fun at all though, Ray, if he does not come soon!" cried Ernest, half indignantly, looking up from the ground where for the last hour he had been luxuriating with a book. "I'd take a run to the turn of the road myself if it was not too hot for anything but lying down."

"Then pray remember that poor Tom has some distance to walk after he leaves the mailcoach," said Ray reproachingly, "we must give him time. I'm sure he will keep his promise if no accident occurs to prevent him."

Accident! that she had never thought of before; there might something happen—a hundred untoward things to hinder his promise-keeping. And as the time went on she became nervously restless; she could neither sit nor stand, but went so constantly backwards and forwards to and from the gate that even her mother anxiously asked—

"Is it not rather strange that Tom is not here?"

"Not at all," answered her husband, "the mail may be delayed—that is nothing new here—or he may not have effected a sale of his minerals," was the cool reply. "My dear, you are needlessly alarming yourself."

Ray had never thought of that, the possibility of no purchase, not indeed for the minerals; but the gold! And the heart sank low indeed. There were so many chances that he would not be home, and that his "Golden Christmas" would not come off after all.

The afternoon waned, the sun sank farther towards the west, leaving the setting moon in the cool shadow. Ray and Ellie had brought out all their home treasures of silver and china and damask napery to do honour to the day. The roses in the centre of the table, the fern branches on the walls, the heap of green boughs in the fireplace, the cool fragrant fruit in the baskets on the little sideboard all looked their welcome. Everything was ready but Tom, and without him Christmas festivities were at a standstill.

"Oh! he will be here; I know he will," said Ray in desperation. "Let us wait a little longer. He said he would come, and he will."

"Ray always does believe in Tom and in everything he says," replied Ernest with a boy's incredulity.

"Ah, does she? And why should she not, my fine fellow," exclaimed a laughing, merry voice at the garden gate, and Tom, heated, dusty, and tired, burst in among them.

"Here I am!" he cried, lustily; "tired and hot enough, but true to my word. What have you to say against that, Mr. Ern?"

"Poor fellow! I am afraid you are terribly tired and hot," said his mother as he bent down to kiss her. "We would not have dined without you, my boy, for anything. You need not have hurried so."

"I would not for anything have missed this day, mother dear," replied Tom; and as Ray hurried him off to his room where she had placed everything for his refreshment—cool water, brushes, and a fresh suit of white clothes included, he managed to whisper in her ear—

"It's all right, sis, as I knew it would be. We must try to keep our secret till after dinner when the cloth is removed."

Ah! what hard work to those concerned in it, it was though. They were in extravagant spirits—far too much so to do justice to the excellent viands provided. Ellie and Ernest, uninitiated as they were, were quite willing to follow lead, and perhaps the necessity for recalling to order now and then, and a little wonderment at the elasticity of the young spirits, prevented the recollections of past Christmas days in brighter circumstances from proving too overwhelming to the elder ones, who more soberly presided at the feast.

What a time it seemed before the ordeal of that dinner was over, and the cloth fairly carried off. The time went at last—as the longest time will eventually pass—the dishes were packed away till the morrow at Ray's suggestion, and the table again beautified with fruit and flowers. No question had been asked of Tom hitherto concerning his journey; but as they gathered together again at the open windows, or in the doorway, with the fragrant coolness of the evening stealing in among them, Mr. Morison, turning to his son, exclaimed—

"I suppose you have been successful in disposing of your minerals, Tom, as you seem in such excellent spirits?"

"No; but I have left them there for sale—there is no fear of their not selling," said Tom. And suddenly rising and approaching the table where his father was quietly peeling an apple, and turning perfectly white in his excitement, he added in a husky voice, "I have something to confess, father. Ray and I have had a secret; it was hard to keep, but we have done it, and here is the result." And as he spoke he emptied a small bag of sovereigns before his father's astonished gaze—at the same time opening another packet, in which the pure gold lay, nuggets of gold, some encrusted in white quartz just as he had picked them from the rift of the rock—a goodly, a wonderful display.

"What does this mean, Tom?" said Mr. Morison, hurriedly rising, and looking in bewilderment from Tom to Ray for explanation.

"It means, father, that all this is yours—these sovereigns are only a fourth part of the present gain, and there's plenty more to get by looking for it," answered Tom, flushing now with joy and pride, as he had before with excitement.

"Oh, father!" said Ray, excitedly, "it means that Tom has found something better than mineral specimens—he has struck gold!" And throwing herself into her mother's arms she burst into such tears of happiness as she had never shed before.

"Hurrah, hurrah for Tom!" shouted Ernest, as soon as in his amazement he should find his voice.

"I meant it should all come out this day," continued Tom. "I intended to have a golden Christmas. I had assayed the gold myself, and knew it was the right stuff, and so it has proved. They really wanted to get out of me where I got it, but I knew better than to tell them. I will take the rest to Melbourne with your permission, father. And now," said Tom, fairly exhausted by his hurried walk, his excitement and revelations, throwing himself along the sofa, "you need not regret leaving England, for, please God, we'll all go back again someday."

A wonderful revelation indeed it was to them all. What a tale he and Ray had to tell, and how happy they were in the telling. Now all was explained. Tom's pertinacity and energy over his geological researches, and Ray's devotion to him day after day, daring all the heat and the weariness, and the watching. It was like a fairy tale to them all, almost too good to be true, only that the indisputable gold was before them, in solid cash, and beautiful nuggets. They sauntered out in the cool of the evening along the creek to the scene of Tom's labours. Standing at last before the riven rock against which the attractive pick with its burnt and splintered handle still leaned, Ray with her head on her mother's shoulder, gently whispered, "It's God's gold, mother dear!"

"Yes, love, it is," she answered, with eyes fast filling. "And we will take it from Him, and be thankful."

"You might have let me into the secret. I could have helped ever so much, Tom," said Ernest, regretfully, as they walked home through the gathering shadows.

"You shall help me now, and welcome," replied Tom; "there's plenty of work—good hard work—yet before we can make up our pile and go back to dear Old England."

What an evening that was! How they sat together in the still, dusky verandah, watching the moonlight as it silently stole between the branches, and threw its soft silvery radiance over rocks and hills, talking of the past and of the future that was so wonderfully opening up before them!

Ray was very quiet in her happiness. It seemed enough for her to sit and listen to the rest.

"Tom," she said, softly, as they stood a moment together late that night before they retired to their rooms, "I do think I have never been so happy in my life—so happy, that I feel almost afraid!"

"Afraid!" echoed Tom, cheerfully. "Why, my dear child, there is nothing to fear. Yes, it has been exceedingly jolly; we've had a thoroughly 'Golden Christmas Day' in every sense of the word!"

Chapter VI: Finale

"All's well that ends well."
— Shakespeare

There were many Christmas Days that the Morisons enjoyed together in the old land after this, but none that were so long remembered as Tom's Golden Christmas in South Australia. They had by no means come to an end of their fortunate findings with the rich yield of the riven rock, though they never again happened on such a grand revelation of earth's hidden treasures. It would not do to awaken the curiosity of the neighbors, so their land was ploughed, and their wheat sown, and Ray went on with her school as before. But Mr. Morison wound up his course of lectures abruptly, being too deeply engaged in studying the best and easiest means of blasting the rocks about him, and Tom found an eager assistant in Ernest, who gladly threw aside his books in his search for the hidden gold. They were well repaid for the search. Tom's visits to Victoria "on business" became more and more frequent, and were certainly rather mystifying to those around them, but they kept their own counsel, quietly banking the produce of their golden creek, and laying by for the future.

By degrees the golden vein seemed to have exhausted itself, even specks of gold became rarities, their blasted rocks had no further revelations to make.

And at this moment, most fortunately for them, came news from the old country that their old home was in the market at a very low figure, and that it would be purchased and held in trust for them, if they liked to return. There was no longer reason for delay. Rocky Nook with all its golden reminiscences passed into the hands of other tenants, and the Morisons, who were little adapted for the roughness of a bush life, with glad and grateful hearts set sail for home.

The creek with its broken rocks and locked up treasure, is still in existence, waiting for other fortunate discoverers to reveal. Not a doubt of it, as Tom Morison said, a golden reef really exists in the neighborhood; but there it lies in the midst of the hills, still undiscovered, though in this day of life and energy and enterprise, it is scarcely likely that it will long remain so.

As to Tom, he had got what he wanted of its surface gold, but he always said he should never forget Rocky Nook or his "Golden Christmas Day" if he lived to be a hundred years old.

The Widow Blane

A Tale of the Times
In Nine Chapters

N. Walter Swan

Chapter I: Opening a Box

The traffic that jostles and shoulders in the city streets is often relieved by the fresh faces of visitors, who have nothing to do but good humouredly wonder at it all, from the men-women to the women-men, and the many things of glitter heaped behind plate-glass, as if there were nothing but plenty in the world, and only the luxurious tastes of the plentifully endowed were to be consulted. This might be a consoling enough belief if it were not belied by the faces of the human surge, eagerly hurrying on in some mysterious race, in which all were running, to breast a tape for prizes sought for then, or hoped for after many years. There are some exceptions to these intent faces. There are those shunted out from the hurry, wondering at the blankness and loneliness of being alone with no object to haste for. And there are of those seemingly alone who have for companionship homes that are distant and voices and faces that are beyond in the quiet bush lands, where the silence is broken by musical songs denied to streets, discoursed by choristers that are with sun and shadow, and live with the grass and flowers.

Of the latter class was John Grant, with grey in his fair hair, with sun stored in his warm face, and strength in his big figure. He jostled and shouldered through the traffic, with nothing but wonder in his blue eyes, and a lot of time on his hands that was growing irksome. In the quiet that was away beyond over the farthest hill he could see from any eminence in the city, he had promised himself a week's idleness to enjoy the sights, there were only two days run, and the time getting so heavy that he longed to be at the windlass again, and back by the water-race that washed the earth down to the creek in the shade gully, and on to the sea. The chaffer of men in shops, the cries of bellmen, the shouts of boys, seemed to him to be but a poor improvement on Boulder Point. He was contrasting, half-regretfully, the noises and features there, the plash of the earth into the water as it gurgled by, the blue overhead, and the greenness and peace on every side, when one of the crowd, attracted by his leisurely contemplation, approached and assured him, in a stereotyped tone of hurried and impressive solemnity, that a sale was just about to commence, which offered chances to a purchaser that might never occur again. The man who conveyed such an assurance had a Jewish face looking heavy with earnestness and conviction, and dark with regret at the sacrifice about to be made, of boxes and outfits, and trunks of unopened treasures about to be sold, to defray the cost of storage.

"These boxes," he pointed out, shrugging in emphasis with every sentence, "belonged to diggers' outfits, five, ten years ago; some of them had been knocked down full of such beautiful things (och! it was a shame) and sold for a song. Piff!" snapping his fingers, "two new shoots moleskins and laceups for de beggarly five and-twenty bob, s'help me!"

This was more than Mr. John Grant could stand. Here was the adventure, not to say the romance, of opening an unopened box, the owner of which might be dead, or distant many thousands of miles. There might be history below the lid, of packing by loving hands, or the confused hopelessness of broken fortunes—who could tell? When, added to this possibility, John Grant looked into the black eyes of the little Jew and saw that they were getting moist with the earnestness of persuasion and regret at the sacrifices that had escaped him, he put his broad hands away in his pockets and strolled slowly into a dark shop. It did look as if the place were of the kind in which one could expect to meet with these illegitimate bargains, with the glamour of twilight over the sale of dead or gone men's property—all the darker from the light of the sun that was in the street beyond the threshold—all the lonelier from the crowd that rolled unconsciously past it, as if the place was some long-forgotten storehouse of dead men's secrets that had no business with the outer world, and no connection with the object that hurried it. There were some half-a-dozen men inside, two of whom were speaking in whispers. The auctioneer was standing on the counter, and below him sat a decayed clerk, with spectacles which took glancings from the light at the threshold, and gave him eyes like owls'. The only part of this person that John Grant could see after leaving the street, was the owl's eyes goggling and dashing about mysteriously in the dark.

"Next lot," said the man on the counter.

The eyes moved, and went out; and reappeared again behind a heavy portmanteau. One of the whispering men bid a pound, and from some corner came a voice breaking in on them with "Thirty shillings." The voice got it, and handed over the money. Two more were disposed of in this way, and Grant's eyes, which were used to search with dim lights underground, had grown fully accustomed to the obscurity.

"Next lot."

That which the man with the spectacles handed up, and travelled over with his big eyes, was a light, homely looking box, with tarnished brass bands around it. He looked at the keyhole, and then carefully at the bottom and sides, apparently for some mark; then he whispered to the auctioneer. The auctioneer also examined and whispered back to his assistant.

"This, gentlemen, is the next lot. It does not seem to have very much inside. I don't want to deceive you, gentlemen. Shall I pass it? I like my customers to be satisfied." He held it in his hand contemptuously, as if the weight were absolutely nothing. "Shall I pass it? All right, sir." He turned and put it on the counter at his feet, saying in his quick way, "Next lot."

"Put it up," said the voice from the corner.

"Do you hear the next lot called for?" asked the auctioneer of the spectacles. "Send it up quick! Don't keep the gentlemen waiting."

The voice in the corner spoke again very deliberately.

"Put up that box at your feet, with the brass bands."

The auctioneer paused, and slowly lifted the box again.

"Thirty shillings," from the voice at the corner.

Out of the rather languid interest that all this had from Grant, he called out "Forty shillings," though he scarce knew why.

The box had lost much of its red staining, and it was chipped at the corners, but it had a homely useful look, and it seemed to have a history.

"Forty shillings," repeated the seller, in a tone of studied surprise, as his little wooden crutch hung over it for a moment, and fell. "Cash, sir?"

The digger paid two pounds and left the auction-room, with a worn box under his arm, that seemed by its weight to be half empty.

Grant had visited the shipping and the various other lines; he had wandered about the weary pavements and through the tide of people struggling and striving in every cross direction, on every conceivable purpose and errand; he had been past the rows of shops with half their stocks bulged out on the pavement and flecked with tickets; he had wandered through empty and echoing streets, through silent and reserved ones stuccoed and brass-plated and venetian-blinded; he had been where were the wretched unkempt streets, dirty and dangerous in stench and sin, hiding tragedies and shame behind the rotten walls, that gave no echo from their dead boards, muffling forlorn histories, and festering down alike on broken hearts and heroism.

Grant had had enough of city life. That great sustainer of the city pleasures and perpetuator of holiday happiness and hilarity—alcohol— had not charms for him; there was better at Boulder Point. And so he tramped up the narrow stairs of his lodging house with a sense of relief that he was out of the crowd, and, with a pleased anticipation of the enjoyment that might be forthcoming from his forty shilling purchase. His room reminded him more of home than any other place in the city. It was small, plain and clean. His own sleeping apartment could not boast of the drugget that was on the floor, or the white counterpane with its raised patterns of fluff, but he could sit down on his own bed with more ease, and he could heartily enjoy a couple of hours with that unknown box if he had it away beyond the hills at Boulder Point.

Grant looked at the purchase earnestly, and thought of postponing his curiosity till he got home again; but the roads thither were bad, and the whole history in the thing might not reach farther than a bundle of dirty clothes. He pulled the counterpane off the bed and flung it in a corner, kicked the drugget, turned the looking-glass round, placed the box on the floor between his feet, and began to smoke. He saw, while thus contemplating the box, that it was not of the kind purchased at stores. The red staining had been laid on over what seemed a dark heavy wood. The manner in which the brass binding was let into the lid and sides, wherein curves and flourishes of the metal lay like tracery work, the engraving of what seemed to be cabalistic symbols in the brass, the delicate patterns on the bosses surrounding the lock, and the peculiar inward curve of lid and sides, showed that it was of Indian manufacture. Grant took a strong new chisel from his pocket, laid it beside him, then divested himself of his coat and threw it on the drugget, smoking thoughtfully the while. He knelt down, and was about to insert the blade beneath the lid, but paused, as if overtaken by a second thought. While in this position he laid the chisel back on the bed, and took from his pocket a small bunch of keys. These he tried carelessly one after the other, placed them on the bed beside the chisel, and carried the box to the window. On examining the lock he laughed silently and had recourse to his pocket knife. Just the point of its blade touched the spot where the lid and body seemed to meet, and ran along it, showing that the securing junction was not there. At this the digger from Boulder Point laughed again and, drawing a chair to the window, he nursed his purchase with a curiously mystified and amused expression. The lock and junction of lid were both false. He turned the puzzle over carefully and shook it. There was the slight rustle of paper, and the dull evidence of clothing within. With his strong fingers he kneaded the sides, and ran along the bands, but the box might have been a carved block of wood for any change it showed. He took up the chisel again, but gravely shook his head, and put it thoughtfully back. Acting on another thought, he left the room for a short time, and returned with a saucer full of whiting, and with this he proceeded diligently to brighten the brasses. In an hour the room was full of tobacco smoke, the floor was stained with white flakes, and his trousers almost beyond hope from brushing, but he worked and smoked patiently.

What seemed like red staining washed away before the application of water, and the thing, which was neither box, nor trunk, nor casket, looked a curious antique. What appeared with the staining to be paint blister under the imitation hinges were two little silver protuberances carved to represent suns. With something of the turn of a carpenter or cabinet maker upon him, Grant could not help thinking the suns were the guardians of the mystery. When touched singly neither showed signs of yielding, but when the purchaser roughly measured their distances from the corners by spanning, and a thumb happened to press upon both simultaneously, there came a rapid noise along the sides, and the lid flew open, hinged on the side where the fictitious lock was placed; the box was stout and strong, showing no evidence of decay. If parts of the outside gave signs of hard usage, the inside was plain and polished, and it was half-filled with several articles of wearing apparel. There was an old military cap, the cloth of which was cut on the crown and stiff and underneath was the undress of a British officer. Moleskin trousers, with the pipe-clay thick upon them, were rolled up in one corner; in another were kid gloves, a set of plain gold shirt studs and a breast pin, in which a stone flashed that looked like a diamond. The back of the pin bore the initials J. M. Next a daguerreotype portrait of a handsome woman, and finally a lot of letters that scarcely showed the discolouration of time. The letters were tied in bundles and a roll of detached papers, widely written, lay upon them. It was growing dusk. Grant looked out and could see the warm sunset on the spars of the shipping, and farther away the low-lying hills over the contour of which the yellow light was flowing down. There was the sea, spotted with the traffic and all agleam. The digger sat with the paper in his hand so long, with a feeling tinctured by reluctance and shame, that the light had left the hills and sea and shipping when he turned to look at the clothes scattered at his feet, to wonder at their history, and to peruse the manuscript; but the room was darkening, and the man reverently placed the things back again. An hour after, when night had come and lights were in his bedroom, John Grant sat down before the little table and read—

"The last impressions of James Morrah.

"The man who reads this, whatever he may be will most likely begin by asking himself why the writer ever wrote it. When he has finished, he will most certainly again ask himself the same question. There is only one that can give the answer, that is the writer, and I, the writer, give it. I do not know. I do not know. I always disliked writing. I have never made a confession before, either to living man or dead paper. If there is anything prompting me to do this, it arises from the sort of feeling a traveller has who put down his impressions of a strange land before leaving it. I have been in all parts of this planet, and I have determined to leave it; that is, to leave its struggles and its chances, its misfortunes and its injustices. I believe that by putting an end to my existence I shall enter upon another one; whether it will be worse than this or whether it will be better, I do not know. It may be better; it cannot be much worse. I take the chances. No one ever takes an important step without some reason. The strongest reason I have for committing suicide, is that I believe I shall enter upon some other sort of life. My strongest reason for that belief is contained in the following short narrative:—Captain George Gray, the truest friend I ever had in the world, asked me to his bungalow before that Indian season came on one year, that in the part of the country where I lived is so dangerous and deadly. I could claim six months' leave of absence, and the prospect I then had of spending a happy vacation in the pure air and beautiful climate of the hills gave to me a keener anticipation of enjoyment than any holiday I had ever looked forward to. No holiday at school ever presented to me half the happiness I expected to enjoy there. I knew there was sport of all kinds to be enjoyed, and that keenest pleasure of all to be realised, the sense of vigour and elasticity from the bracing air. This to the man who has spent a term of weariness at one of the worst of the Indian stations, can only be realised by those who have felt the enervation and the lassitude of the days and nights that to me were little else than horrible. The journey was weary and difficult, and not unattended with danger; but as I got into a higher region I began to feel the return of my lost buoyancy, and before I arrived at my friend's place the cold bracing wind was blowing round me like a blessing. The hills were wild and breezy, and swaying flowers and herbage, the rustling of the trees, the sounds of the branches, had for me sounds akin to happiness. The night of my arrival was moonless and starlit, and the hour was, as nearly as I can remember, about 2 o'clock. Gray had retired long before, and I was shown my apartment, which branched off from the broad verandah. The room was furnished after the usual Indian fashion, and the short sleep that visited me was deep and refreshing. I rose at daybreak, and was soon in the verandah to watch the sun rise. Before me was a range of solemn looking hills, sharply distinct against the clear sky. To the right a narrow pass frowned over, and fortified, by layers of rock, and on my left a plain, threaded by a river. When I first saw the hill, I knew I should by turning see the defile. When I saw the defile I knew that the plain and river were to the south. The place was as familiar to my eyes as the lawn and avenue before my home in Surrey. I stood motionless and terrified. Memories that were not memories, amid dreams that were not dreams, came up and swept past me. It was a sort of dim revealment of a past that I knew not, and was yet with me. I may have stood, troubled and fearing I know not what, for a minute or for an hour, I could not tell how long. Time seemed to have left me as standing without the limit of past or future, till I heard the foot of a servant on the boards.

"Do you see that pass?"

The Hindoo, whom I found could speak English well, followed the direction of my hand, and, in a gentle way that was in itself an obeisance, said, with his bronze hands partially folded, "I was born here, sahib."

"That is, you know all this country?"

He nodded and smiled. "Every part of it."

"Good. Straight up through that pass, at a distance of five miles from the rocks, there is a lake, and at the south side of the lake there is a cave. The hand of the stone Vishnu sculptured at the entrance is broken. Is that so?"

The man smiled again, remarking, in his mild way. "Sahib has been here before. Lake and cave are there; the Vishnu's hand is broken."

Pointing to the hills. "Beyond there is a jungle belt of twenty miles."

The servant bowed.

"Oblige me by turning to that plain. Ten miles up the river there is the tower stone. By rounding the stone and floating with the back water, a hidden cliff is gained, large enough for a man's body to get through— What is the matter?"

The Indian was on his knees, watching me with a look of fear in his face and a glitter of danger in his eyes. Just for an instant I caught the passage of the evil look, and for a moment the sinister treachery that mixed itself with the appealing position was visible.

"Sahib is great and rich. He will not speak more of this river cave of the poor Indian. Sahib's God is great. Indian's God great. Sahib will not speak."

The man paused to listen. There was a sound of feet inside the house. One of the servants ran out hurriedly with his fingers interlaced, not knowing apparently what to do. He said something to the man who had just appealed to me, and both went hastily inside. Then came out three or four coolies, carrying a chair, and more in attendance. Captain George Gray was the occupant. He was senseless, and the moisture of pain he had suffered was standing on his drawn features. They spoke of cholera and of medicine; but the time for prescribing, I soon found, was past. The kind and tender light had left my friend's eyes, and the lids covered them for the last time.

When the affairs of my dead friend had been set in order, I turned my back upon the house, wholly forgetful of my interview with the Hindoo on the verandah. From the mountains and the wild scenery I had welcomed so warmly there seemed to have arisen a curse that was pursuing me. It was on the second afternoon of my return journey, just before the hour when the sudden twilight comes, that the tramp of a horse's feet came down the valley through which the road lay. At that time travelling in India was considered to be quite safe, and I was journeying to the easy motion of my wallahs, when a sudden fall told me they had dropped their burthen. Jumping out, I saw them scampering towards cover, and a single horseman making towards me with the shine of the sun a-glitter on his weapons. My pistols were empty, but I seized the sword that was inside, and, making a kind of barricade of the doolah, stood waiting. He swept past me, making a slash that would have finished my career there and then had I not managed to guard the cut. The parry I made was scarcely in accord with the rules of fencing, being half a blow; and, unfortunately for me, the sweep of my weapon fell upon the horse's hocks. The horseman was on the ground in an instant. He wore the garb of one of the hill tribes. The face was the face of the humble and obsequious servant I had questioned on the verandah on the morning of my arrival. Now it wore fixedly the passing look I had noticed. It was a face full of danger and of passion; and in less than a minute, I found that his knowledge of the weapon he held far exceeded mine. With the supple steel wrist that guided it, the blade seemed to play about me quiveringly. It glittered above my head; it seemed to hover before my breast; it was everywhere, before, cut, and thrust. I saw the expression of the face deepening, the glitter of the blade nearing me; and I knew no more, till three weeks thereafter, when I recognised my own room, and the dark attendants.

The wound in the head which I received will cause the reader of this to think that my brain was injured. He is welcome to the supposition. I can only say that, as I sit here writing now, I never felt clearer or calmer. I never before felt so perfect an assurance of another state of being. I visited a part of India in which I had never been before in this life. I knew the spot and described scenes connected with it I had not seen. What is the explanation? There is only one. I was then in another state of existence, and the Brahmans and Hindus are right. They with their civilisation and thought, that has been matured by a hundred centuries, teach the transmigration of souls. The keenest and wisest and subtlest of ancient nations taught metempsychosis. They are right. They found the truth as I found it, by indisputable evidence!

In my case the experience was such that to resist it would be sinful. The knowledge gives happiness and unhappiness; it gives a hope for another state of existence, and dissatisfaction with this. It matters not whether I enter on the new life as a flower, a bird, a beast, or a man; the state cannot be unhappier than the present. Therefore I seek the future, whatever it is to be. The future awaits me. It is in the knife that lies beside my hand; it is in the first drug I choose to purchase; it is in a leap from the window; it is below the glitter but there upon the sea; it is in all things. The future is the eternal and the real; the present is the transient. I shall know the future soon, nothing doubting. I might have been contented to wait over the years allotted to me if I had not come to Australia and here met the woman who has led me to long for the future that is so near. Through her stole upon me the longing that I am about to satisfy, and I shall travel to my next existence by the pathway that is always waiting upon the sea. The gleams of sun light it by day, the stars pave it by night. It widens into a glorious glittering broadway when the moon touches it with mystery, and beckons with its power … She married me with the sin of a dead husband upon her soul. I had forgotten there was a future waiting for me till I saw a letter from a man who had cursed her as he fled out of life. He quitted it and her as I am about to do. Her sin came to him as it came to me, and pushed him forward into the waiting and the merciful future as it is pushing me. I won gold for her, and came to tell her of my good fortune, and of hers, only to stand upon the threshold, of what had once been our home and look upon her shame. Then I knew the letter was true which she swore was false. I had come with the brightest evening time the sun could bestow on earth and sky. I left with darkest night, and I am here upon the threshold of another home, where I shall find rest. If the step I am going to take is madness, let the reader of this be judge. Whatever his judgment I shall be beyond its reach. I was mad when I forgot all things in looking at her face, and wondering at the power in her caressing eyes.

Writing as I do now, I feel clothed, and in my right mind. She is behind me. Not one particle of the treasure I toiled after in my insane love for her shall find her. She shall avenge me upon herself. She shall be her own Nemesis, raised and created by the two lives she has destroyed. It is a pleasure at this moment to know I could give her another home, such as she longed for; and that I withhold it. It is a pleasure to know that I saw a horror in her face that evening. The Nemesis has begun its work, and will be busy in its ceaseless hauntings when I am peaceful among the Indian hills or wheresoever I am allotted in the great future. I give her this life as a curse. I leave it for a blessing. The man into whose possession this box falls will judge me mercifully, and he will be rewarded. Every beat of time as it journeys on towards the grand future will but separate us the more. There will be no more meeting in the spheres made visible by death.

(Signed) James Morrah

Chapter II: Perusing a Portrait

Above the signature and apparently written in haste, but carefully marked out by repeated lines being drawn across it, was another sentence that could not be read. It was possibly an indication of the spot from which the writer would enter upon the "glittering broadway" alluded to by the unfortunate.

John Grant felt as if there were something weird in the box and in the room. The military cap with the sword slash in it, as he now knew, stiff with blood; the dull shines on the tarnished lace; the gleam of the pipeclayed trousers out of the shadow where they lay; the fantastic shape the light threw from the box to the floor, seemed to bring a presence back; and the strong digger started as the stout paper crackled and turned round his hand like a clasp. He felt as though he could not resist arriving at a conclusion, as if, indeed, a presence was there in waiting for it; and he reached it not through the turgid writing he had perused, but through the gaping cleft in the cap that was lying at his feet. It was the sword wound that inspired the confession of the mad man. How much of it was due to a disordered mind? How much of it was true? The night was warm and sleepless, and the noises had left the street, when Grant again stooped over the box. There were packets of letters carefully tied. These he lifted out gently and put away as one might treat memories that are full of sorrow. Beneath them, as though carpeting the bottom, was a square piece of parchment paper, half written, half printed. The digger looked in wonder. The form and features of it were as familiar to him as the sound of his cradle, or the handle of his pick. It was a deposit receipt for 800 oz. of gold. Grant carefully examined it with something very like a sigh of regret, but it was genuine. Then there was no escape from breaking further into the unfortunate man's history.

The letters must be read. Who was the unfortunate wife that had been left to starve, probably from some mad hallucination of her husband? How much misery might not that Indian box relieve amongst those who by right and justice were entitled to the treasure the piece of parchment represented. And so the puzzle of the open box, and its elfish shadow, and dead man's clothes, was growing.

To say that Grant was profoundly interested, would but be to represent him as any man would be under similar circumstances, and yet when he changed his position from the little dressing-table to the bed, he sat down and looked around him with an appearance of weariness and a seeming impatience. There lay a fortune before him which placed upon him a duty that was almost sacred, to find out who was or were the rightful heirs. If what they were, or what the dead man's wife was, agreed with the manuscript he had read, should he not study the dead man's wishes? If the confession, as it might be called, was but the imaginings of an aberrated mind, he must render justice and violate the suicide's last expressed desire. He shrank from the letters, but there was no other way of setting about a duty that seemed to have been thrust upon him by fate. They contained the clue, and to them he must apply himself for information; but it was so like lifting cerements and dragging back to light dead and buried sins.

While he thought thus in the silence he felt something touch his hand. Grant was a strong, firmly-nerved man, but he started, a second time that night, as though an unexpected presence had invaded the room, and he looked quickly down by his right side to find that his fingers had touched the daguerreotype which was lying on the bed beside him. With a half smile at his trepidation, he took it up and looked at it carelessly. It showed the face of a handsome woman, and Grant thought of a face he knew at Boulder Point. Somehow the association thus called up attracted him to a closer examination. He had seen the face before, and he had not seen it; again, it was like a memory that was distant and misty; again, it scorned to steal upon him, and again retreat. From the intellectual forehead the hair was drawn back in plain bands. The eyes seemed neither dark nor light, but their expression, with that of the mouth and face, seemed to hold an alliance of sweetness and strength and suffering. The portrait must have been taken at a time when the sitter had just begun to see that shadows were approaching; otherwise, in the woman thus revealed was something like a resolute devotion. Grant thought that the pose of the figure was familiar, and again he thought he recognised the manner in which a lace shawl rested on the shoulders. He moved over to the table again, where the lamp was standing, and looked steadily at it with great intentness. There was, he found, one thing in the portrait that had given the idea of familiarity—the brooch. He had seen it before, but where, or under what circumstances of his checkered life he could not remember. The dreamy recognition had become dreamier than ever. He felt no longer his old hesitation as to the papers. It was impossible for him to sleep now, and he undid the first packet and read the first letter. It was a folded sheet, bearing post marks on the back, and addressed to James Morrah, Bendigo Post-office, in a strong, plain female hand. He unfolded it with the feeling of a trespasser. This is what the letter contained—

"Fryer's Gully, August 28.

"My dear husband,

"It is now three months since I heard from you. You told me then you were in a very rich claim, and for your sake, who are so fond of money, I felt glad that the struggle we have had was likely to be over soon; but I cannot tell the reason of your long silence. I am sure you will pardon the anxiety of a wife, who, apart from the love she bears you, is likely to hold yet more sacred position in your regard, if I venture to hope that the promise you so solemnly made to me on the morning of your leaving has been kept, as you assured me it would be, 'as faithfully,' you said, as I kept my vow given you, and registered it before God at the altar. It was a solemn promise, that, and I would not have alluded to it now, but I feel the present to be solemn. There is the danger and the fear of the trial, and there is the prospect of a dearer interest and a dearer tie to life and to you. It is very lonely without you, and has been so through all the period of your absence; but today I feel a foreboding that I cannot well shake off. It is a feeling of gloom and desertion, and a shrinking as from a coming storm. You will remember the time, James, when last you gave way to excess, how terrible it was to me—the allusion about the imaginary letter, and about myself. I only name this period, upon which I look back with fear, to recall to you the words of Dr. Sharpe. They were, that another in-dulgence, reacting upon your wound, might prove disastrous. He judged that a second attack would not develop the ordinary confusion of ideas attendant upon the delirium caused by alcohol, but (his expression was) 'a panorama of connected yet imaginary events which might drive you into an extreme of happy excitation, or, vice versa, to end in a fixed determi-nation to commit suicide.' This is the skeleton that is haunting me. I am not in want of money thanks to your goodness, but I catch myself longing to have you near me again, or, failing this to know of a surety that you are well, and that my place in your heart is as secure as your place in mine.

"Our married life has been but short as yet, but it has been blessed with happiness, and there is only the shadow of the one fear upon it. I feel it would be weak and wrong of me to ask you to forsake the prospects you last described, and come home to me, but the early parting which necessity has imposed seems cruel. Could I not go with you? What matter how rough the shelter may be if it yield to us the blessing of union? Tell me what you think of the proposal. Think that I am lonely, and write. Remember that your letters carry me through those empty days, and above all things, be strong against the temptation which, yielding to it, might bring calamity to our lives.

"Your loving wife,

Margaret."

"By chance," muttered Grant, "I have read the right letter. They are arranged according to date. The first I opened was the last the unfortunate man put by. The calamity came to that poor woman, sure enough."

He took up the portrait with fresh interest, and looked at the remarkable face pityingly. Somehow the devotion of the expression seemed to have increased, and the shadow of trouble looked darker, but there was still the same flickering familiarity about the picture. The history of the trial put before him as plainly as the evidence of the confession, the military cap and the letter could, seemed to remove the probability of his having known any of the parties concerned yet farther away. He had neither heard nor read of such a story, and yet there was comparative wealth in his possession waiting for the desired wife. How should he find her? How learn that she was alive, or that she had died in the loneliness of her desertion and want? He sat surrounded by the broken links till the grey dawn crept up behind the sea.

***

The community living at Boulder Point was a scattered one. The neighbours there were far apart. Houses were perched upon the hillside, close to where the white earth from the tunnels was being emptied. Such flat ridges as were to be found upon the shoulders of the ranges were utilised for gardens, and the paths that crossed each other and ran branching off at every angle looked not unlike an irregular net-work of tapes lying on the green turf. Upon the plateau near the Point was a sort of disjointed township—disjointed because of the necessities for shade and shelter which the big trees offered. The houses were in clusters near where the trees stood, and they caught the shade when the sun was at its hottest, and nestled in shelter when the wind and rain came down from the north, and swept across the little plain. The miners who lived by what they won from the white-mouthed tunnels in the hills' breast, sluiced at the creek that hurried past the Point where the rocky boulders lay; and over from the settlement were to be seen the hills in constant snow that so often took an opaline lustre when the shine of the sun was on them. If in that little cluster of human life were all the heart-burnings and bitternesses inseparable from it, there were also the simple virtue, the persevering toil, and the indomitable heroism—none the less heroic that it was unknown, and bounded by the closer tiers of hills which circled it. Mining life there had its brightness and its shadows; it had its drunkenness and fights and vengeful feelings; but it was, on the whole, purer and more unstained than elsewhere, where there are thousands at toil, with vice awaiting a share of the gain in the huddled streets. The public interest, as the publicans called it, was represented by two hotels; and the general commercial wants of the consumer were supplied by two stores regularly visited by enduring commercial travellers, who branched from their circuits to supply the "Boulders."

The digger who entered upon the task of a new fence, a crop of cabbages, or a bed of potatoes, furnished food for gossip that, being slow, lasted many days. From the creek below there were the constant sounds of labour floating upwards. The calmness of the labouring time was seldom ruffled, and the beauties of the glen and the creek side, where the long shadows came from the rocks and the gnarled trees, were not to be surpassed.

Widow Blane kept the Phoenix store which was narrow, and high and gloomy. It boasted the most select and diversified stock in the settlement, taking for its useful purpose the wide range between Horrocks' longcloths and Chinaman's cauliflowers. At Widow Blane's emporium many little driblets of gold were weighed and bought, and diggers used to loiter in when the long nights came down, to earnestly discuss matters appertaining to the world beyond them, by the light of a tallow candle, and in the fragrance of the Phoenix tobacco. It was curious to see the widow and her customers in the twilight which the candle manufactured out of the darkness, spending a short time after the supper hour in the shop. She might have been 80 by her white hair, but was probably not more than 30 by her face, which was so fair to look at and so calm and patient a study. There were fine but indelible lines below the full brave eyes, with their dark fringes and delicate brows. It was not long before the miners by some subtle intuition, felt how different she was from them and their wives. Her reposeful look seemed to have in it a waiting and questioning of some coming time; and the rough men, with their bare arms and throats and heavy limbs wondered at her grace of movement, and the graciousness of her smile. She knew the children there, and lifted for them many of their young burdens. They, and many that were old enough to look out on life, and wonder and dream of the fruition which the days might bring, found how the widow could sustain and comfort by her hopeful words, and by the language of sympathy that her presence spoke.

The usual circle was one evening seated in the usual manner on sugar mats or cases which had once contained wares. There was a sort of gloomy indistinctness about them as they ventured to move or speak, while Mrs.

Blane, as the central figure behind the counter, looked lighted up with the single dim flame of the candle, and the frame of her white hair. Behind her was the darkness, and before, it was just dispelled sufficiently to show vague figures and faces.

"Ma'am," said one, whose beard, growing high upon his cheeks, and being of the colour of the gloom, made the dim whitish spot representing his face unnaturally small, "ma'am, I came up in hope of bein' able to borrow the paper. This is Wednesday, and the wife, she thought, as having time, she might finish the story."

"Mrs. Brown has not returned it yet, Dick but I promise you, you shall be the next to get it."

Dick thanked her, and gave his attention to a raw potato he had taken from a bag near him.

"I can tell you one thing, Dick," spoke a solemn voice that was somewhere, "there ain't no new prospecting rules in the paper. Mr. Crown did tell me so."

Another voice from a solid looking man, just within the circle of candlelight—"If Dick had them there new rules, he wouldn't a bin here the night. He'd a bin markin' off of his patch. Eh, Dick?"

"Well, lads," Dick made answer, "I don' deny it; and the sooner the better for all of us. When I git in the pegs you'll know the spot."

Another voice somewhere—"If Dick knew the rules now, he'd wait till Grant came back, and when Grant does come back he'll be no end of a swell, all full of yarns about what he see in town, and the shows and the instistushions and shops and people. He'll be a good while afore he wears himself out, and the longer the better. Jack don' forgot what he sees. What d'ye say, lads? he'll have plenty to listen to him of an evening."

At this there was a period of silence, which indicated approval and assent. One, who had smoked steadily hitherto, and who was noted for the despairing tenor of his mind, said—

"Grant'll get lost and in the lock-up, and he won't be here not when his fortnight's up. His botherin' about 'ill knock all what he sees out of his head, and he'll have no yarns."

This was Mr. Dodd; and that gentleman having once launched upon the darker possibilities of the case, was about to dwell on further contingencies when he stopped to look at the owner of a footstep that had also stopped at the threshold.

All the time Widow Blane leaned over the counter, resting on it with her elbows, and following with her eyes the direction of each speaker. She looked, with her strange contrast of face and hair and eyes, like the fanciful sketch of a spirit that was in the light, listening to the aspirations of others that were in the shadow of the darkness, she only to be seen vivid and bright, the others dim, and nearly unreal, behind the gloom. Her eyes also were upon the threshold, waiting to recognise the newcomer. Dick, who was anxious about the prospecting regulations, was the first to speak, with a startled ring of surprise in his voice—

"Durn my rags, if it ain't Jack—Jack Grant hisself! Why-wot-wot d'ye mean, Jack Grant, a comin' back like this here, an' surprisin' people like a ghost? Yer time ain't up, an' we don't expect ye."

"Well done, Jack, old son. You're always welcome," was the greeting of the others. "D'ye see much?"

Mr. Dodd.—"How often were you in the lockup, Jack; how much did ye lose; weren't yer hed bothered; come now?"

Mrs. Blane had raised herself from her position on the counter, and stood back from the light. There was the faint shadow of a flush on her face, and there was a brighter and quicker light in her eyes, before speaking.

"Whether you have fared well or ill, you are welcome to Boulder Point again." She spoke distinctly and slowly, and like the others who were in gloom before the counter, she retreated into the gloom that was behind it.

Mr. Grant received the widow's salutation with a somewhat earnest look, and his face showed pleasure when his fingers closed on her pretty hand.

Mr. Dodd, to whom the premature arrival gave newly-born hope of disaster, looked benignly at his pipe, and delivered himself again:

"Wot kind is the lock-ups in town, Jack? Did they put the darbies on? An' wot about the beaks, and the muddlin' and mixin' of everything in yer hed? Tell us all about it; we're friends, ye know."

"I don't know anything about the lock-ups, boys; but Dodd is not far astray about the muddling and mixing of things in one's head. I did not find the city life as pleasant and pleasurable as I anticipated. Everything there seems cooped and hurried and strange. The feeling of freedom and of ease quits one in the big towns. Before I was there two hours, I began to long to be at the old sluice by the creek side again. The picture it leaves is one that is filled with streets and big buildings, and a constant moving past of men and women and bright colours. One comes on gardens in the heart of the town, filled with trees and flowers as strange as the faces in the street. Everyone is so anxious and in such haste, that a man like me, with nothing to do but to stand and look round him and watch the people sweeping on, begins to feel ashamed of not having something to hurry him, too, and he is far more lonely than he was up in the hills here, putting down a shaft, or washing out a prospect. There is always a glare runs through the night, and lights burn and flare on everything. The streets are stringed with lamps like rows of beads on fire, and they are on the cabs, too, moving and rushing about like will-o'-the-wisps. In among them and outside and under them are women in silks, with flashing stones and beautiful faces, and language that no man here would use. This is the other part of the life. The hurrying people, with their care and trouble, quit the streets early when the shops are closed, and the town with its day life seems to get a spell before the night life begins. And when it does begin the faces it shows to one are more unhomely than those of the day. These are not people who look hurried or anxious. On the whole there is more glitter and pretence about them. They may be, most of them, very great people, and people of wealth, judging according to their chains and rings, and dangling things of gold and stones; but I did not see one of them I would trust half an ounce of gold with. They hang about the theatres and bars, and I felt as if their life and my life were as different as if they lived in the moon instead of at Boulder Point, and had brought their customs with them.

Mr. Dodd made himself audible from the gloom again.

"Didn't ye lose yor way, come now?"

"I nearly lost my way once. Going back to my lodgings one night, I heard a poor woman screaming in a lane. I was passing, and I ran up and saw a man beating her. When I had driven him away and saw the woman go into her house, I found about 20 young fellows, half men and half boys, round, trying to bustle me."

Grant paused, and laughed.

"Well, I never saw a crowd run so fast when the two leaders got hurt, and I don't think," continued the speaker, slowly, in the dim light, as if ruminating, "that I ever saw two men shoot so far before they touched ground. I was terribly frightened they would never get up. As for my coming home so early, lads, I just came back because I had more than enough of town, barring the sea and the ships; and I was kind of home-sick for the old gully here, and the rocks and trees, and shadows and faces that I know so well. Mrs. Blane, shall I put up the shutters?"

This was the signal for dispersion, and the diggers moved out towards their homes. Grant, as was his custom, made all secure, and bade Mrs. Blane goodnight.

"I forgot, Mrs. Blane," he said, with some unusual hesitancy of manner, "to ask how Ann is? I did not see her with you tonight."

"Ann, I believe, is well, John. She is at Morrison's, and will not be back till tomorrow. Don't look so surprised. I am not afraid to be alone," with a quick look from her dark eyes, "now that you are back. I often say that Mr. Grant is not half a call from me should anything happen in this peaceful place."

She paused, looking across the doorway upon the stars. Again, with the candle in her hand thus, she looked so strange and unfitted to the incongruous surroundings, that the miner wondered at the picture the candle gave against the black background, formed so much by her perfectly white and shining hair. Contrary to her wont, she held out her shapely hand again as she said goodnight. Jack took the hand for the second time, and, scarcely knowing what he did, gently pressed it. The faint flush again visited the widow's face, and a warm look swept her eyes, but it was so evanescent that the dim light did not show it; on the contrary, there was only evident a dignity of bearing which Grant had often seen upon her before.

"It is now late, Mr. Grant. We do not keep city hours at Boulder Point."

Still Grant hesitated and then awkwardly said: "If you have any goods to move about tomorrow, Mrs. Blane, or any alterations to make, I'll—I won't go to work, I mean for a day or two."

"I'll think over what you say."

"The flour and potatoes and sugar want stowing, and there are those drawers and that shelving to do."

"Thank you for your kindness."

"The fact is, your hands and your strength are not fitted for the rough work you set for yourself, and Miss Ann fidgets so that, well, I think you ought to take advantage of my couple of idle days."

There was no change in the lady's face. She seemed but waiting till Mr. Grant would leave, with that something of mystery about her that made her so difficult to reach.

"Goodnight. I hope to set to work early tomorrow."

"Goodnight."

Mrs. Blane put the candle on the counter, watched the strong figure turn past the corner of her store and dwelling, to his own cottage. Long after the sound of his footsteps had died away, she watched, as following him with her the thoughts. Upon the plateau round there were scattered lights. The sound of voices came to where she stood from one of the public houses. The windows of the hill-side huts gave twinkles upon the darkness, and overhead the silent stars were bright. Mrs. Blane stood thus watching or waiting for she know not what. She knew she was alone with her own thoughts, and she wondered that the courses of the years could have brought her there, with the meridian of her life scarce passed. None but herself could guess at the scenes that flitted before her in that quiet retrospect, or the voices and faces that came up with their memories. But of them all, she thought, there was not one face so strong, or so good, as that of John Grant, not one voice of them all as gave her such a sense of safety and trust. And if her face could have been seen, it would have shown that the shadow of past suffering and the cloud of present sorrow were upon it. When she went back to the dark store the candle showed that her eyes were full of tears, that the lines by her sensitive mouth had deepened, and that the graceful and dignified Mrs. Blane, with the calm brave eyes, had flung herself on the floor of her little parlour in a passion of sobbing. The candle would have farther showed that when the stained face, looking so strange, and still so comely, below some straying locks of white hair, raised itself, seemingly, from the tumult that had conquered, the widow and mother sought comfort and strength in prayer.

Chapter III: Asking a Question

Next morning, the first sound that Mrs. Blane heard was the regular chopping of her axe at the wood heap, and by the time she had opened the store, and bidden Grant goodmorning, the sun was abroad on everything. Grant, with his glowing face above the things around him, and the ringing blows he delivered, looked so masterful and homely, that he was to be admired. There was sufficient at his feet for a week's use as he stood leaning on the axe among the fragrance of the fresh wood, to return the salutation of the widow. As she spoke she noticed a puzzled look upon his face, as though there were something in hers, or in her voice or gesture, that arrested his attention.

"This seems a strange way of finishing your holidays, Mr. Grant. Chopping wood is harder work than sluicing, and you are spending your labour for another, for that which is not gain; that is, not gain to you."

"If a man will not spend a little time in assisting one who has so often assisted him when he was sick and helpless, he deserves no consideration, and he can have but a poor sense of gratitude. I told you last night, Mrs. Blane, that my holidays would not be over till the end of the week, and that I can undertake those few changes in the store you spoke of before I left."

"I thought about the matter last night," she answered, "and I am going to take advantage of your kindness."

While speaking she seemed intent upon moving a piece of bark with the point of her boot. The thick black lashes looked like fringes on her cheek, and the position of the figure, showing the rounded lines that belong to the prime of life, made Grant think, and not wrongly, that she would have seemed more in keeping with the surroundings if standing thus in the morning sunlight below the portico of a mansion. She raised her eyes quickly with a full look in them, and caught the puzzle upon Grant's face again. At this she laughed, and, flushing, said:

"Do you see anything strange about me this morning, Mr. Grant? You look as though there was something that puzzled you. I am not aware that I have changed much since you first saw me. What is it?"

As if this had been all the miner wanted, he let his axe fall amongst the wood, and strode across the evidences of his work to where the lady was standing.

Mrs. Blane did not appear to raise her eyes, but she saw this movement perfectly, and she saw that his face had become solemn and anxious, as if he were about to commence a task he had set himself to perform with some misgiving. The ordinary ease of Grant's manner had certainly deserted him as, with some degree of halting, he said:

"We have known each other a long time, Mrs. Blane, and in that time is included a period during which you rendered me a great service. I have a question to ask of you which may appear presumptuous on my part, but if you knew the reason I think you would admit that I am acting rightly."

He paused, as if waiting for an answer, and saw that a red blush had crept upon her face, and that her lips gave evidence of a tumult of feeling.

Grant went on:

"I have only to ask you one question, and it is easily answered."

There was no change in the expression of her face or figure.

"The question I desire to ask is—is your name Blane, or, you will pardon me, is Blane your married name?"

Mr. Grant had only seen the lady to whom he spoke when he met her as a friend. She had tended him as a sister might when he was ill a year before, and thereafter he never forgot the pure and beautiful eyes that had watched beside him. Therefrom his constant thought was to do her service. He was her recognised assistant in the settlement, not, indeed, without having excited the envy of others.

Now, for the first time, he saw Mrs. Blane in a new guise. The blood forsook her face in an instant; her eyes were cold and clear and glistening. She stood before him, pale to the lips, haughty as a queen.

"I am not aware, sir, that I have ever given you cause to doubt my honesty. No action of mine, so far as I can remember, ever savoured of deceit. Why should you, or your digging friends congregated in this wretched spot, presume to doubt me. In the weary years I have spent among you, have I ever given you cause to insult me thus?"

"Stay, oh, stop, Mrs,—"

"Stay you, sir; till you have heard me. You, must learn at least to know your position when I am speaking. I desire to hear no excuse. Take my word for, it—a lady's word, Mr. Grant—that it shall in future be my aim to guard against permitting that familiarity which leads to insolence."

Mr. Grant was stung, and it was with natural dignity, and some sternness, he made reply:

"Madam, you have been hasty and unjust. No one in this world could less have deserved the contempt that is in your face and manner and speech than I. You refuse to hear the reason which led me to ask the question. Be it so; but in this matter be assured that my last thought would be to give you pain, and my last thought the gratification of an impertinent curiosity. Your contempt for this place, which you call wretched, I can well understand, but I cannot understand your contemptuous allusion (contempt that was specially underlined, by your voice and gesture) to the diggers here. As for my digging friends (I say nothing of myself) I think that your experience will enable you to compare them favourably as honest and honourable men to those patricians who hold a high place in society, and are not to be spoken of as a lot of congregated diggers."

Mrs. Blane's pale face was raised proudly and her unquailing eyes were steadily on the speaker.

"I cannot hope to understand what your thoughts may be on this subject. I only know that we are unnecessarily prolonging a conversation that cannot be described as a pleasant one."

"I crave your pardon for a few more words, on my own behalf, as well as on behalf of my friends the diggers; and, as a fitter time is not likely to occur, I desire in my own name, and in theirs, to thank you for the good you have done many of them, for the many nameless refining influences you have sown, and for the kindnesses that have won for you so much love and respect. As for myself, I shall never forget your kindness; and when I have changed my place of residence I shall call up the memory of my stay at Boulder Point, as the brightest experience of my life. Mrs. Blane, goodbye."

He turned away with an air of a man who had cast everything from him, and he walked with an unmistakable expression of hopelessness in the carriage of his tall figure. The axe lay free. The morning's work was scattered at her foot. The morning was wearing towards noon, and she was alone. Deny it to herself how she might, she felt she had parted from the man she most trusted. She remembered now how, in many times of doubt or emergency, her reliance was placed on him. She could not but admit that she had driven him from her, not so much by the words she used as by her insolence of speech and gesture; but she still stood there outwardly cold and defiant, with the flashings of her anger marked upon her face. She was about to return to the store when her eye caught the sight of a printed cotton handkerchief she had sold to Grant a month before, lying near where he had been standing, and moving slowly to the place, she lifted a billet of wood, and with it, perhaps, the only memento she should over have of one who at that moment was nearer to her heart than she chose to admit. The sun was shining brightly on the neat folds of her luxuriant hair as she turned to her house; but her head was bowed, and she was angered again when she felt that a flush of shame was on her face. No reply which Grant could have given could have so completely disarmed her, and none could have showed her so fully his pride and manliness and strength. She felt she was beaten before she reached the door, and, when she flung the wood down, could scarce see the door for tears—when she flung herself upon her bed and sobbed as bitterly as she had done the night before; she realised how weak she was, and how poor the assumption of dignity she had displayed. She wearily tried to understand the reason of Grant's question, and wondered how he had gathered his suspicions, and whence they came. There was not a shred of anything within her store or dwelling to give cause to connect her with another sphere of life, and yet he put the question as one he had been brooding over. The thought braced her, and she moved about calmly again, but with the feeling of want having crept into her life. The slow hours passed, and the sounds of labour at the creek below came to her at midday. The straggling customers dropped in, and the silent hours came again, till the shadows had lengthened outside. The customary visitors came, too, in their deferential way, and sat in the store in the twilight, in the hope of hearing more of city life from Grant; but it was Dodd who put up the shutters that night, as he remarked, with a solemn satisfaction, that he knew Grant's head was kind of off; but no one would believe him.

"And look here, Missus," he added, with a sort of melancholy exultation, "it'll end in vertigo."

Tom Morrison had brown curling hair and blue eyes, and he had helped his father to dig the price of a farm and house and fences, and a few head of cattle, out of Boulder Point. By rights, it was Tom's own claim, his father used to say, for he marked it out because there was a horseshoe on it. The old man had steadily refused to leave the nearly worked-out lead, till one early spring morning the son came in as he sat at breakfast, with his dish under his arm, and, if his face and hands were stained with clay, there was joy and pride in his eyes, as he showed no less than a pennyweight of gold lying at the side of the dish.

"A pennyweight, and from two buckets of stuff! What do you think of that, father?" as he placed a hand affectionately on his shoulder. "I've moved the pegs to the size of a prospecting claim, and it makes the spot where the horseshoe was the heart of the ground where the surfacing will begin."

Then he took the horseshoe from his box where he had hidden it; and nailed it over the bark door, as he since nailed it over the door of the farm house. This was how, as the story ran, the Morrisons digged up the farm and sluiced it out by the side of the stream that ran hurrying round the boulders and past the shadows to the plains. Some of the old stockmen, who visited Boulder Point for the purpose of breaking the monotony of the bush with alternatives of whisky, used to say that it was a treat to look at young Morrison on horseback; and when he used to canter up to where the men were at work, or take a flying jump at the Point near which they sluiced, and tell them about the ground he thought likely-looking, the stay was generally celebrated by a "smoke-oh!" and if he had a newspaper in his pocket he would sit below one of the old rocks and read the news to his auditory of splashed faces and muddied beards. Tom Morrison was, to a certain extent, the child of the settlement. He had run messages for most of the men years ago, and old Dodd had saved his life one winter's day when he fell into the creek. It was all swollen and swift with the mountain floods, but the miner was strong then, and swam like a Newfoundland dog. He blamed that wetting for the rheumatics, and in consequence Tom had given him enough brandy to drive the pains out of a regiment of patients. Morrison was the pride of the miners. He was their bringing up.

"Just see him on the outside of a horse. Our Tom ain't none o' your sugee sort," was the usual bar criticism.

When Miss Ann Blane rode out with him on visits to his sister Harriet, the miners laughed in their beards, and wondered how long it would be before the widow's daughter would make her home at Rosevale farm. If Tom was their friend they gave allegiance to her grace and face, and to the nameless charm of her voice and manner; and when they rode up to the store the morning after the widow's conversation with Grant, the mother could not resist a feeling of pride intenser than that which had followed them as they passed the diggers at their work. They had stopped to inquire if Grant had returned, and Ann Blane's first question, as she entered and looked round the store, was for him.

"Where's Jack, mother?" with disappointment on her face, and her large eyes questioning the gloom.

"If you mean Mr. Grant, he has not been here since yesterday morning."

"But he is not at work. Why is he not here? He might be ill."

There was a seeming of irritation in Mrs. Blane's voice, which her daughter perceived at once, when she replied:

"You are showing scant courtesy to Mr. Morrison, and but a poor sense of hospitality, by leaving him sitting on horseback at the door, as if you had no further need of him. Ask Mr. Morrison to have a glass of wine."

She turned, radiant, towards the door.

"Tom, my mother says I am rude to you because I do not ask you in to have a glass of wine but I am going to do nothing of the kind. I don't like winebibbers. Tell Harry I'll send her the crochet cotton and the book by you when you come in tomorrow; and Tom, Nancy's withers are sore, I am sure of it. Goodbye."

She held up her pretty hand, but the comfort of the salutation was in the light and the expression of her eyes and face. Tom took it all into his heart, and squeezed her hand and rode away leading Nancy back.

Ann came back to where her mother sat, and stood behind her with a hand on her shoulder.

"What beautiful hair you must have had, mother," as she caressed it; "and to think that it was black."

The colour mounted in the face of the mother as she made reply.

"It was very black and soft, and was much admired; but it is the frailest colour when trouble comes. In six months it was grey, in a year it was white."

"Through grief?"

"Scarcely grief. It was trouble and sorrow that blanched it. It was the terrible knowledge that I was absolutely alone in the world with you, and the path before me seemed so desolate and dark, that I would have welcomed death for both of us; but trial gave me strength, and I took courage and hope, and here is a home, at last such as it is."

Out before them they could see the little houses scattered on the sides of the hills, in their garden patches of green. The sun lay brightly upon them all, and the distant sounds of the workers at the creek hut made the silence greater.

"And my father?"

"I will tell you that history someday, Ann; not now."

Ann, with her eyes upon the scene before her—"This does look the most peaceful place on earth for a home, and they are all so kind to us. We cannot think we are alone here, mother; but where is Jack?"

"I am not aware that I am Mr. Grant's keeper. If he is not here, and not at work, the inference is he is at home, always supposing he is not spending his time at one of the hotels."

"Mother, that is not like you. I am going to find him."

Her mother made no reply. She sought rather to turn her face away, for she knew there was a flush upon it again. She sat silent, turning her white fingers till the change of a rare smile came to her expressive mouth and a softened brightness to her eyes. Sitting thus, the face of Widow Blane was not the face her customers had ever seen; still less was it the face she wore as she rose from her chair, seeing that two shadows had fallen upon her threshold. The men came in presently, footsore, freshly shaved, and villainous looking. There was the look of dissipation below their eyes, and resolute strength about their mouths, and thick necks. They asked humbly for a few things, for which they found the shillings in recesses of their greasy clothes that needed constant shrugging to keep in position. While one of them pretended to examine some boots, she saw the quick glittering eyes of his companion taking a survey of the store, and resting on the scales used in buying gold.

"Much doing about here, ma'am?" inquired the other, turning round a piece of tobacco previous to biting a corner off with his big teeth. "Much gold getting?"

"There is very little gold being found just now. The best places have all been worked out."

"You speak relatively," said the older, with the garrulous fluency of a tramp. "How much, for example, would very little be?"

"You see ma'am," interrupted the first speaker, "we are two poor men searching after a 'onest living, like. We don't want to loaf. Work is wot our game is. That there three shillings that was paid you represented 'onest toil; didn't it, mate?"

"It was part of the tribute of those brows, ma'am, to the ban of labour."

"That's how my mate puts it. He used to spout at political meetings, and was a patriot once, my mate was; and—"with his hands in the laceups and the soles turned downwards—"we go wanderin' about in these, looking for 'onest labour, and when we meet a poor cove wots a digger, and he asks us where he's to go to keep body and soul together, we says (your information being encouragin') try your honest toil at Boulder Point. That's why we ask the information."

"So that the oppressed working man may find independence in this free country, instead of being ground down by the heels of pampered capital," added the ex-patriot.

Mrs. Blane said:—

"I have no idea as to relative quantities; that is, as to how much gold is to be regarded as much. You must go farther afield for your information. If by such means you seek to advance the interests of honest toil, I have no doubt, the mining surveyor, who lives over the ranges a trifle of about 80 miles off, would have great pleasure in fully satisfying you on the point, and so furthering your philanthropic motives."

The poor man shook the boots from his hands, as others might the dust from their feet, and left without speaking, followed by the patriot. Mrs. Blane watched them anxiously till they had recrossed the threshold; but when she heard them laughing a short distance away, and paying her a blasphemous compliment, she felt she was afraid and alone, and it came to seem to her that there lurked a shadow in the peace and brightness of the day.

When Ann returned she was panting under the weight of a side-saddle and bridle presented to her by Grant, as a memento of his Melbourne visit; and when Mrs. Blane had but partially examined it she went hurriedly out of the room.

Chapter IV: Robbing a Drawer

The aims and heart-burnings and toil of Boulder Point were all forgotten in sleep, and even from the hotels the last light had disappeared, and the most inveterate card-player had departed when the midnight came. It came on the occasion of which I write full of frowns and pale gleams, as the clouds sailed above it and flew battered across the moon, followed by dark blanks that blotted out the sky, and dragged after them broken fringes of silver fleece, and panoramas of crags and sea, and half-finished pictures of fairy-land. The night seemed to grow dark and sink to sleep, then awake with starts, as the moon grew clear and showed the spots where the miners slept, flashing its light on their little windows and fashioning ghosts out of the white earth at the tunnels' mouths. It gave sudden touches to the stream, and rolled out into shadows below the rocks; and it showed the face of the ex-patriot and of the man who sought for 'onest work closely observant of the houses on the plateau. From beside the tree where they were standing, nearly in the shadow, was the dark line of the irregular street, linked together by huts, and marked by the trees that sheltered them. The wind that hurried the clouds lifted the rags of their torn coats, and fluttered and flapped them silently as they had been the plumage of birds of prey, and they seem to flit fluttering from shadow to shadow, there being no rest for them in the dim light. The figures moving thus had queer, irregular outlines as the blasts flung their clothes about, and swept round them in sudden charges and mutterings. They hid and rested in the shade, and peered out and sought shade again further on, always silent and noiseless, and steadily in the direction of the widow's store. The patriot had marked where the back portion of the building had been finished with bark, and he had seen the tree that stood beside it. It had been prized for the cool shade that lodged with it, and the music of its boughs, and its shelter and screen were now used by the men, who soon sat roosting on the branches, and spoke below the sweeping of its rustling foliage.

Mrs. Blane had listened to the hushings of the old tree during many a night of the years she had been there, and its voices were all familiar; but on that night she did not detect below the cadence the undertone of danger, and the evil that was being planned in the whispers that the voices of the leaves were hiding. As the branches moaned and tossed, a figure swung from among them that was fitter fruit for a gallows-tree, and the bough swayed back, leaving the moving thing upon the roof. Another figure was similarly left, to be blended with the first as the glimpses came and went.

Is the success of sin and the triumph of good directed by the same providence? And is it so because, from the former, there always cometh blessing, though our minds cannot discern the results overruled by a power in whose purposes there is no time? Is it that the good arising from the evil may be seen on the morrow, or remain hidden in the folds of coming years? It was by the merest chance those two men came to Boulder Point. Had the gold scales been in their proper place they would not have been seen and the robbery would have been unattempted, and had a closed drawer not shown above it the edge of a chamois bag, the whereabout of the widow's treasure would have been unknown. The men seemed favoured by all things especially by the wind and the inconstant light. The bark sheet beside that on which they stood was moved aside without noise and the two faces looked down into the darkness and waited. As to those within the store, so to those without, there were only the rustlings of the boughs and the sudden hurryings of the wind to be heard. The hand of the man was a practised hand that struck a match silently on the cloth of his sleeve while he lay flat upon the bark, holding his arms in shelter below the roof; and a piece of candle was lighted, and the dim interior seen as a rope was tied in the rafter and both descended. There was a faint shine on tinware, but there was neither sound of feet or other motion, except the raspings of the leaves. Above the square opening the moon stood steady. Clouds came and hid it, but, as they passed on, the light was poured down again, and so defined was the contrast that it looked like a pillar of silver fading and lighting and trembling,

Mrs. Blane lay listening to the wind and the leaves, thinking of the history of the last two days, when she caught sight of the moonlight column above the partition separating the bed-room from the store. She lay wondering dreamily that the little apertures she knew were in the bark could admit so much light, and was wandering into dreams with a distorted picture of a shah's palace, pillared with silver, when the sound of a tinkling chain ran in upon her below the other noises, or rather through them, as though the stillness of quiet was without and within. It was not repeated, but she knew the sound came from the gold scales, and she sat up, startled by the remembrance that she had not, as was her custom, put the gold away in the place she had chosen for its safe keeping. Naturally this brought to her memory the faces of the two men she had seen in the store that day, and, rapid as her thought, she was standing like a ghost on the floor of her room. She walked noiselessly and unsuspectingly from her bedside and in a few paces had reached the store.

Mrs. Blane neither screamed nor fainted when she saw that a sheet of bark had been removed from the roof, and when was presented to her the picture of the two men she remembered as seeking after 'onest toil. And yet that picture was a very startling one. The light of the candle was full on their eager faces, and it glittered on their evil eyes. Neither spoke. One of them had had the little bag open that the other might see the soft yellow glint in the neck, and he leaned over it with a look of fierce greed. Then they looked into each other's eyes with the piece of burning candle between them, and whether the one saw the other's thought reflected, or whether the occasion and need of caution came to both, their eyes fell simultaneously. Had the ghost, with its white wrapper and white hair, that was standing at the doorway, been seen, there would have been murder done, for there was that strange wolfish expression in the faces that come to men when last has seized them. The success of the first search stimulated them to further effort, if happily another prize might be obtained. One raised the candle and looked down the store where Widow Blane had been standing, but he saw only the gloom and heard only the monotonous sweeping of the boughs upon the roof. Both stood watching thus as the candle threw big profiles on the wall behind them, that moved, rising and falling with the motion of the dull flame, as though giants, with huge features all contorted, were the invaders. The patriot put his hand upon a brandy bottle, but the weight of that of his companion pressed back his arm with sudden power, and the determination on his big face was not to be resisted. He placed it on the shelf again and resumed the search, while his companion held the flickering light, and by motion urged to haste and caution.

By this time Mrs. Blane was looking yet more ghostly and unreal in the moonlight. It's coming or going behind the clouds did not hide the moving figure that was so silent and so fleet. The gold that was in the hands of those men represented all her possessions, and in it were centred hopes of the future, not for herself but for her daughter, who slept. And if that daughter awoke and gave the alarm before Grant's hut was reached there were terrible possibilities. Her hurry and caution gave way to a haste, almost wild, and when the shrill cry of a night bird overtook her, she stood and trembled below the terrible necessity to retain thought and composure. She passed the pile of wood which Grant had laboured at some hours before, and even then his words came back with the strength he showed and the want she felt, and a thrill of pleasure at the memory of his figure and his presence just touched and left her as she saw the dark roof of the little house against the trailing clouds, and over among the coming and the going shades. Grant was asleep, but the first tones of the whispering, shaking voices disturbed him. They were familiar, as the recurrence of a dream is familiar, and he opened his eyes on the darkness with a sigh at the illusion, when the tones came whispering and in fear.

"Get up, for Heaven's sake, Jack, and help me now. There are robbers in the store. Oh! Jack, forgive me and help me."

The speaker, or rather the prayer, for it was a prayer she seemed to speak, it was so low and earnest, and yet so wild, heard a bound behind the logs, heard a moment's silent hurrying, and without noise, Grant stood by her with the moon on his face, and the moon on hers. Her voice had warned him, and he spoke low:

"What is the matter? Robbers in your store? They are strangers then. Do not try to keep up with me; there might be danger."

He left her, and ran swiftly. The woman hurried, too, trying to keep his figure in sight, and a short minute after he had disappeared through the open door she was near the threshold. Grant, barefooted as he was, walked with a peculiar, noiseless elasticity, and to those inside the silence remained undisturbed, although the miner was cautiously making his way from the store door to where they were. He did this so rapidly and so noiselessly that his powerful and set face seemed to be bending almost over them when they saw him. None of the three men spoke.

The digger with a blow of his powerful arm, struck the man nearest, and the patriot fell stunned.

He turned in the direction of the other, who had sprang back, and was just able to see, for a fraction of time, the upper part of a face as resolute as his own, the gleam of an eye upon a pistol barrel, while the man presenting it coolly held the candle in advance to assist his aim. There was no sign of tremor in the weapon and none of weakness in the face that was levelled with it.

The same glance showed him the white figure of Mrs. Blane coming through the door in his footsteps, when a sting struck him and spread through his frame like a thrill of cold, a great noise seemed to thunder down upon him, the whole place spun round, and he lay bleeding.

The searcher for 'onest toil ran to his companion, who by this time was on his feet, and between them there was a moment of irresolute pause, then a sullen word or two, and all was in darkness. The bar that secured the front entrance was lifted from its rests, and the two men were back again amongst the shadows and the lights of the deep stillness that was abroad.

Mrs. Blane saw the men, and in a dazed, confused way procured a light. When she saw Grant lying so still in the faint, that was like death, and put her light rapid hands upon his brow and upon his heart, she uttered no cry of fear, but she spoke tender words of endearment as she carried him some brandy in her shaking hand; and she lifted his head upon her knee, and forced some of the spirit between his lips. The wounded man opened his eyes, and saw bending over him the winning face, and heard faintly a melody and a meaning in her words he had never heard before.

Chapter V: Nursing a Patient

A pistol-shot at midnight on the quiet plateau of Boulder Point, was a sound that had not been heard for years, and when startled, people looked and they saw a light in the Phoenix store. Attracted to the mystery of the sudden sound, they ran to the open door, and, looking, saw Widow Blane with blood upon her night dress and hands, and wearing an affrighted look. When they came hurriedly in and saw the helpless man was bleeding, and learned the history of the night in a few short sentences (all the more powerful that they were self-possessed and clear, and in contrast to the ripple of dread and of helplessness that stirred through her words) a few carried the wounded man to the widow's bed, and the rest, with danger in their mutterings and in their attitudes, ran out in hot pursuit. Ann Blane was coming from her room in fear when she saw the bearded faces she knew so well carrying the wounded man to her mother's room. She recognised Grant's grey face, and followed them, and, when she learned that he was shot in defence of her and her mother, she brushed away the moist hair from his forehead and, kneeling down, she kissed him. There were no tears in her eyes, but the play of her lips and the sorrow on her face moved the men to a whispered conference, and in 20 minutes Jack Hart's bay mare was mounted, and her hoof-strokes beat away down past the Point to the Hinton road.

In the short term that remained of the morning before the sun rose, Mrs. Blane sat by the digger. There was no suffering revealed, except by the restlessness in his face and the sudden contractions of his hands. When the silent woman beside him looked at his broad palms partly open, showing the grip of labour and the strong man helpless, and, above all, when the kind eyes grew clouded with suffering, there came expressions to her face which, if Grant had seen and recognised, he would have deemed himself rich. More than once her cool hand rested on his forehead, and when the sun rose she was sitting wondering at the power he possessed over her thus powerless and helpless, maybe nearing the darkness of the shoreless sea.

The search for the burglars was characterised by more haste and energy than system. There was not one of those big fellows who would not have accounted it a privilege to have overtaken one or both of them single-handed, but the night was against the success of the searchers. Alex Robbie, with the muscle and presence of a gladiator, overtook one of the dark forms, busily searching and muttering curses on the men who had cast suspicion on the Boulder Point diggers.

"No word of them?" asked the figure, looking excitedly and suspiciously at every tree trunk, and at the corners, and in the shadows of the rocks. "They can't be far off, and they must be caught, if the boys are only active enough. They say they have got the widow's gold. I'd sooner lose six months' earnings myself. If you take that direction I'll take this. There is no time to spare." So speaking, the figure moved away rapidly in the uncertain light.

That day, about noon, Alex Robbie suddenly stopped the movements of his shovel in the sluice-box, and walked over to his mate.

"You were in the store last night, Tom. Did you hear anything said about the widow losing her gold?"

"Losing her gold? No."

"Did you hear any mention of it amongst the men?"

"No."

"I'll be back in 20 minutes." Robbie dug his shovel viciously into the turf, and walked rapidly from the creek to the plateau in the direction of the widow's store. Mrs. Blane came out softly.

"Excuse me coming to ask a question, Mrs. Blane. Was there any other damage done, I mean loss to you, beside the shootin'?"

"You are the first who has asked the question, Alex, and in my fright and anxiety and sorrow I had partly forgotten the chamois bag that holds the gold I buy for the bank, is gone. This was the object of their entrance."

"And none of the men know anything of this loss?"

"No; not yet."

Robbie slapped his thigh fiercely, and stood thinking, with a lowering look in the direction of the Point.

"What is the matter?" asked the widow nervously.

"Plenty is the matter, ma'am. Something must hev gone wrong with my head gear. I was as near to the coward that was walking off with your gold last night as I am to that counter. That hand, Mrs. Blane, look you, touched his clothes," and he laid his massive fist on the counter, looking at it ruefully. "He knew that gold had been taken, and ran off after the thieves—after himself like—one way, while he told me to take the other."

The wit of the patriot had disposed of Robbie's strength.

***

The doctor from Hinton had come and gone with the days. The diggers called in the morning and evening time to ask concerning Grant. It might be that the sudden ravings of delirium answered them from within, or the subdued voice of Mrs. Blane, with traces of weariful nights of nursing in her face. When the digger awoke to the world one afternoon there was a beam of level sun colouring the room, and flushing it with red, and with it crept in the whispering of leaves and the young summer air. The bed and the few pictures were strange to him. There was nothing to be seen in any portion of the apartment to indicate where he was, only that through the open window amongst the greenness and the soft swaying of boughs, he recognised the sounds of labour at the Point. The murmurs of the water were broken by the dull punctuation of picks and shovels and distant voices; but it seemed in some strange way, that he was not himself. His hands were white and wasted, and there was a dull pain at his shoulder he could not understand. The room seemed all aflame with the sunset that filled it, painting the white hangings and the dainty floor, tinting the pictures and glittering on the furniture of the table. The latter caused him to sit up painfully, for his wonder overcame other feelings. Grant had moved in what is termed good society more than 20 years before, before the grey had come to mix with his yellow hair, and fortune had tied him to the mines. The few articles of the toilet-table that were glittering back the rays at him, belonged to a station in life he thought he had nigh forgotten. The little display of silver and pearly things might have belonged to a palace; the sounds that travelled in towards them belonged to Boulder Point. He might be dreaming, and he lay down faint from the exertion. On the wall at the foot of the bed was the picture of a handsome man in a uniform, showing decorations, and below it the face that was on the daguerreotype in the Indian box at his hut. He lay staring at the face till it seemed to move and take an expression that had been beside him apparently a few hours before. The face was a strange face, and yet it had apparently been interwoven with his later life. Then came down to him from their frames a resplendent general, grey and grim, and a lady with a face entirely radiant and beautiful, who talked with him in his sleep, and carried him to lands whose light was a constant sunset, the voices of whose winds and zephyrs made wondrous harmony. When Grant opened his eyes again, the room seemed strange to him as when the sunbeam filled it. It was as little like his own as it resembled that in which the red rays had shaded all things. There were no sounds of labour, and no breath of flowers. The hangings of the bed were but faintly seen, and all beyond was in darkness, except in the immediate vicinity of the toilet-table. Beside it was a face that was not a face of picture or of dream, but one that he thought was as beautiful as it was familiar. The widow was asleep, and he saw the long lashes resting on her worn cheeks; he recognised the weariness and the gentleness and the pride of it, and earnestly looked at the contrast of the shining white hair on the low white brow that had such an attraction for him. One hand was resting on the table close to where medicine bottles stood, and the other lay passively, on her knee. He understood the situation now. She was again his nurse, and again, as before, she had watched him back from the threshold of death. It seemed to him that to lie and see her thus was all he desired. He dismissed speculation and restlessness from his mind, and his large eyes and sunken face were set against hers, hiding nothing of their strong and enduring devotion. Mrs. Blane opened her eyes with a start, and looked first at her patient. He was there, quiet, with the delirium gone out, and the peace of convalescence upon him. She caught and read the look with which he was regarding her, and a red flush mounted to her forehead. There was something like gladness in the depths of her eyes, and in the undertone of her voice when she put her hand upon his, still assuming the part of the nurse, and intimating to him that he was still her patient.

"I see you recognise me, John. You are forbidden to speak at present. You are forbidden to think or to exert yourself. You are to sleep continually, and to take what is offered you without question."

Her hand was still upon his when speaking, and somehow Grant's closed upon it, as she finished–

"Here is your wine."

"But how am I? Why are you—?"

"Drink this. It is 3 o'clock, John Grant, and I want to go to bed. No one will come near you till the morning. These are the instructions. Possibly I might answer some of your questions tomorrow. Goodnight."

He did not reply, but looked at her and watched her with an expression that made the widow's heart beat faster.

"You promised to answer my questions, Mrs. Blane," said the patient to his nurse next noon. "I am strong enough now to know that in the course of a few days I shall be able to relieve you of the care you have bestowed upon me," motioning towards the bottles and the chair she had occupied at the bedside. "My last clear remembrance is, running to your store at night, where you told me robbers were. How long is that ago?"

"Three weeks."

"It seems but last night since. I caught sight of one of them looking at me along a pistol barrel."

"In trying to assist me in the strait, you risked your life for me, and for my property, John."

"Ay, the very last thing on my mind was seeing you standing like a ghost in the doorway. Then the report seemed to make the place whirl."

"Have you no idea of the obligation you have conferred upon me, and what it is possible would have happened but for you?" She shuddered, and put her hands upon her face. "I was just dimly able to see one of the men fall helplessly below your blow, and when you turned full upon the other the noise and the smoke came—and I could see nothing but you fallen, and maybe dead. Men who heard the pistol-shot ran over and carried you in here."

"That is—?"

"That is to the nearest bed—to mine—where I might be near you. What could I do?" she asked, rather of herself than of her listener, "but watch over the life I had placed in such dread jeopardy? Yes, John Grant, I thought this world a very unjust one when I watched you fluttering on the very verge of another. There are some dark shadows in my life; but if you had died, that shadow would have been the darkest of all, and that trial the hardest to bear. Happily, by the mercy of Providence, it was removed from me, and you will soon be your old self again."

Grant lay listening with a pleasure such as he had felt on the night previous. He watched the expressions of her face, and the changes as they touched and passed it. The grace of the buoyant figure, the curve of her neck as the earnest thoughts came, and were spoken—the whole woman moved by gratitude.

Grant sat higher in the bed, and held out his unsteady hand that he might be heard.

"For every right or manful act that is done there is a reward. The reward of seeing and hearing you speak as you have done is to me so much greater than I deserve that you will scarcely credit me when I tell you I almost feel ashamed of accepting such a bounty of gratitude as you have given."

There were red flushes in his hollow face, and there was something of sadness in his voice as he went on:

"What in this case have I done for you that I would not have done for another? Surely I would not be fit to speak to you, or worthy of this situation, if I had not rendered as ready service to any man or woman situated as you were. I could have given my right hand to hear and see you speak to me as you have done, but–"

He paused and looked out of the little window into the fresh morning, The old tree was softly sweeping its plaintings against the roof on the silence that had come between them. Mrs. Blane's face had lost the brightness her thoughts had given it for a look of tremulous anxiety. She repeated his last word—

"But—"

"But I fear the dull sameness of my life is not to be broken by the lights I once hoped might fall athwart it."

He smiled faintly.

"I have always been more or less of a dreamer, and in this little settlement I have dreamed dreams so like to happiness that I thought they might come true. It was natural to be sanguine and presumptuous, and I was both. Who would have thought a man with grey in his hair would have allowed a dream to win him so, but it won me without a struggle. There was no effort to resist it, for there was no strength. I felt the awakening to be bitter, and the dream to be a dream. I dare not beg of gratitude what I had hoped to win."

Mrs. Blane's lips trembled, but there was the look of high thought upon her forehead and eyes.

"Dreams, John, are sent as warnings, sometimes as prophecies. If they give the gleam of a happiness that is distant or impossible, it may be rather to strengthen against obstacles, that one may be brave and strong, than to contrast the impossible with the real. Waking dreams is another term for aspirations. From these spring the best and noblest part of manhood and womanhood. If you have found your dream an impossible one, and have suffered in the awakening, what is it but a trial that will give you strength?"

She paused, and the expression of voice and bearing had left her when she resumed—

"This is not the kind of conversation that is calculated to soothe my patient. There are a lot of things to do, John Grant. I want the store made more secure, and I am waiting on you to do it."

The sick man's face reddened with pleasure.

"Then, please Providence, it won't be long till John Grant's hammer is at work again. Just a couple of days or so and, as my friend Dodd says, 'I'll be my own man again'."

Both felt and looked as if they had carefully put away something for future reference, and it was certain the room looked the brighter for it, and the faces in it calmer and happier.

"I have come to give you your wine, John Grant."

"And I have sat up to hold you to your promise. Did the men do any harm beyond this?" pointing to his shoulder. "I mean, did they take anything with them?"

A look of care came to Mrs. Blane's face so unmistakably this time, that Grant looked at her in great concern.

"Sit down and tell me."

"I have suffered from them possibly the severest blows that they could inflict. They nearly took a life that was exposed in my defence, and they took that away with them which to many is dearer than life. They took all the gold."

"All the gold?"

"It was in the large chamois bag you gave me, and the fortnight's washings were just over."

"That will be seven hundred pounds' worth?"

"A little more," she answered, looking wearily in the sunlight beyond the window. "But it is not so much what I lose. There is your deposit of £300, which the bank holds as security for the money advanced to purchase with. You are stricken in both ways. But the sale of the stock would realise the whole amount after paying merchants' bills. It will be some time, maybe a long time, before your gold is realised. You need have no fear; released it shall to the utter most farthing, John Grant. It is like beginning the world again; but I am strong, and I feel as brave to battle on as ever I was. There is only I—"

Mrs. Blane stopped, and another pause came between them. The digger was watching her face earnestly. She was looking out into the day.

"There is only what?" asked Grant, impatiently.

"This," she replied, softly; "but it is only a matter that concerns myself, and I should not intrude it now."

"Why not? Whatever the subject is that afflicts you, it cannot be an intrusion."

"Ann was to be married this coming Christmas time, and I thought—"

"Yes."

"That—that I could have managed to have given her £300 or £400, so that my daughter should not leave her mother penniless, neither shall she" (the high-bred expressions of hauteur on her varying face) "—and it would have been a great help to Tom, just now; but that is past."

"Where is Ann?"

"She is at Morrison's, unwitting of what is coming."

"What is coming?"

"The postponement of her marriage for an indefinite time."

Grant laughed, not an ordinary laugh. It was soft, but marked with pleasure.

There was a flash of anger and pride in her voice which she scarcely controlled.

"A disappointment of this kind may seem a light thing to you. It may even serve as a source of amusement; but I do not think even you would laugh if you could realise its bitterness, and the possibility of a life's happiness being lost (for it is possible) that is so near attainment. The bitterness that I must tell her, the bitterness that she must hear me tell her. When she knows all, the time looked forward to with so much hope will be a season of sorrow. She is as proud as—"

"As you are."

"I was going to say so; and she will never wed portionless. Better never wed at all. You need not look amused. My ideas are quite formed on this point, by passages of my own history. The sunny life of Ann will soon be made acquainted with its first darkness.

Mrs. Blane could not understand Grant. There was neither sympathy nor cloud on his face, so quick to show sympathy and concern; and a cold feeling of disappointment crept on her. She realised that, after all, she was alone, and above or beyond the sympathy of those surrounding her.

There was the battle to be recommenced, and the weary emptiness and routine of the coming days to be fought and fought—for how long? Certainly till all the brightness was out of life.

Mrs. Blane did the most womanly thing possible: she put her hands before her face to hide the tears that would not be restrained. She wept silently, but there was no sign from the bed. Then she hurriedly dried her burning eyes, and rose proudly to her feet. Grant's face was solemn, almost sad, and his voice and eyes were kind.

"Sit down, Mrs. Blane, a little while longer."

Not as a tribute to the ordinary visit of a patient, and certainly not by her own desire, but in answer to something in the voice and look of Grant that held some subtle power and strength, she at once resumed her seat.

He was now lying with his face upon his hand, with his attention fixed on some thought beyond his hostess.

"I have a favour to ask of you, and I want you to grant it before this interview closes."

"I do not know what favour I can grant you, but whatever it is in my power to do is yours by right of being won over and over again."

"If it were not in your power to grant it, I would not ask it; if I did not believe it was right that you should grant it, neither would I ask it. Have I your promise?"

" You have my promise, John Grant."

"My request is, that you make no mention to Ann of the postponement of the wedding."

"Of course, yes; but until when?"

"Simply that you make no mention of the postponement at any time."

"But you heard what I said," her eyes sparkling, "about her marrying penniless."

"Neither shall she."

"John Grant, I will break my promise just given. You have suffered enough for us. You shall suffer no more."

In the same tones she had noticed before—

"I have been moderately fortunate, and I am moderately old, and what little I can do for you or your daughter will be to me a privilege and happiness. The other day (it seems but yesterday to me) when you made me feel and acknowledge to myself how much you were above me, I only spoke the simple truth when I said, or meant to say, that the happiest period of my life had been passed at Boulder Point, because of you."

"Stop! oh, stop!" She first put her hand up to her burning face, and then upon his hand lying on the coverlet. "Do not say one word more till you tell me you forgive me. You will remember I asked you for forgiveness on that unfortunate night when the robbers came. Oh! how humble I felt before your strength and dignity."

He lifted her trembling hand to his lips, and went on:

"You have shown me, possibly without knowing it, how much of happiness is to be gathered from life, and when I think of you there comes back to me a feeling that seemed to have left me many years ago, of joyful hope, of a glad future, of present contentment. It is akin to what someone somewhere calls ecstasy of life. What great blessing of indebtedness than this?"

Mrs. Blane's face looked very bright. There was a sparkle of pride and happiness in her eyes, adding to the effect of the colour that seemed spread from neck to brow. He saw the emotion as she left the room, with the warning that he was dreaming again.

Chapter VI: Recovering Treasures

The sound of Grant's hammer soon answered all comers as to the state of his health, and the evenings came round when they met in the store to hear descriptions of Melbourne life, clearly to the direst confusion of Mr. Dodd's prophecies although that gentleman listened with grim patience for the evidences of his predictions. Grant soon found himself completely restored, and the running up of timber, the changing of the shelving, the disposing of the wares, and the general bestowal of greater security and strength upon the Phoenix store, was a proceeding that was greatly approved by the miners.

During this period, Grant's spare time was given to writing to the police department. He took the matter of the burglary in hand, had the store visited by the troopers, solemnly examined and notes taken, which were duly pigeon-holed and forgotten.

And so the beautiful lustrous days passed, full of peace, of his enjoyment of the present, and possible dim anticipations that might rise again in the future. The months crept away into the time when the fields were yellowing and the shades grew welcome. The last of the weather-boards was nearly nailed upon the standards and the lengthened-out labour was, beyond excuse, approaching conclusion, when Grant, perceiving a shadow behind him one morning, stopped suddenly and looked round upon Alick Robbie with his bare arms half hidden in his big moleskins.

"What is the news this morning, Alick? I hear you have come back to us with news that our own little corner here is the best in the district. Is that so?"

"That is so," Alick returned, sending his arms further down in his pockets by way of emphasising his deep voice. "But that is not all the news. I only got back yesterday, and I owe a kind of duty to you, and, for the matter of that, to myself. You know how near I was to the man who stole the gold that night?"

Grant laid down his hammer and looked full at the speaker.

"They told me of it many times. What of that?"

"I felt ever since I could have given a month's earnings out of the best claim on the Point to catch that fellow, and as safe as I am standing here I know where he is. First, d'ye see, his voice has stayed with me ever since. That's one thing I couldn't forget; and second, as to his height, just half a head below me, that I could swear to. What will you think if I tell you the man's not 40 miles from here?" The speaker waited for a reply.

"There were two of them."

"I know nothing about two," he answered sharply. "I only saw and spoke to one,"

"Come over to my hut, Alick."

"No need, lad, there's nobody listening. When I left here I made for Hinton, and stopped there awhile; over from there, about 20 miles, I heard of a diggings where a good deal of cradle and sluice-work was going on; and the place at first looked so likely that I thought of giving it a spell, and so, as I might learn the news, I stopped at a public where all the diggers used to come of a night playing cards. Well, dash my rags, if the very first night I did not hear a voice that I know as well as yours. It was the voice that had told me Mrs. Blane's gold was stolen, when no man in the place knew that it was, only Mrs. Blane herself; and the more I heard it, the more grew up before me the blustering night, and the shine and the clouds that kept coming and going. I stopped playing and listened, and began asking promiscuous questions, when I found he was a stranger, that he had come there just about the time of the robbery, and give hisself out a digger, and not a digger only, mind ye, but a lucky digger; that fetched me! Of course, I soon got into conversation with the chap. He had on a new pea jacket, and was regular rigged out. Sometimes he'd smoke cigars for a spell and then back to his pipe; and to hear him speak! he just spoke like a parson. Man, the words came from him just like

1 o'clock; and there I was talking to him every evening till he kinder looked for me; but nothing could I find or make out, only the tone of his voice coming in every now and then, striking on me, and mocking of me, like as if it was saying—'Do ye mind the valley of the Hinton road, and how he told you in the half darkness and half lights of the moon, Alick Robbie?' He would spend his money middling free, and always had change, never no notes. Once or twice early in the day, I noticed he got change of a pound, and the notes were always new, and always on the same bank. There's one of them I managed to get back in change for a fiver. You'll see it's on the Union Bank, just as clean as when given out." Robbie held out the piece of paper, carefully folded, to his listener and waited.

Grant, who was becoming interested, unfolded and examined it.

"Yes, that note has not passed through many hands. Go on."

"Well. Pretending not to watch him, I watched him like a cat does a mouse; but this was all the guide I could get for a long time, till one evening he pulled his handkerchief out of his pocket, and I saw something drop on to the floor beside my foot. In a minute my foot was over it, and him talking away about the rights of labour, and what he had done for the working man. After a while I shoved a card off the table with my elbow, and stooped to lift it. Then I took up what was under my feet. I don't know whether it is any good or not, John Grant, but whether it is or not, there is enough in what I told you to make you go over there and judge for yourself. I know you are looking after this for the widow, as any of us would do and I thought it best to tell you first because maybe I am all wrong, but I'll take my oath I am not. It would be easy, you see, to find out from the Union Bank. There is a branch there, and at Hinton, and one further back still at Nerrywon. That will be the place. I would not mind going with you, Grant, if only to make good the mistake I made that night."

"But you have not shown me what you found beneath your feet when you made the card fall."

"No more I have. It's here, somewhere, but don't suppose it's much, now I come to think of it."

While Robbie was speaking, he felt his ribs below his jumper, and plunged his hands into his pockets, finally drawing something forth that was hidden in his great hand.

"I thought it might have been a letter or paper, or a receipt, or something. However, that's what I found," and he showed, lying on his palm, a crumpled chamois bag.

The whole expression of Grant's face changed. His fingers were upon it in a moment, and when he held it closer to examine it minutely, and stopped as apparently at something he had been searching for, his hands were trembling, and red spots were on his cheeks.

Robbie laughed.

"That bag fetched you, like the voice and the 'lucky digger' fetched me. So, by the time we put this and that together, we'll have something to go on."

There was pleasure in Grant's face, and there was a certain dash of sternness in it too, as he held out his hand in frank acknowledgment of the service. When his grasp closed on Robbie's in a kind of congratulatory ceremony, he said—

"Let there be no word of this among the men Alick. Who can tell? A hint might spoil all. We'll make Hinton tomorrow, and on by coach. Why, man! You are nigh as close upon him as you were that breezy night at the Point yonder."

To this Robbie—"I thought I was pretty cock sure of the chap over there, and yet, when I came to think of everything separately, why, dash my rags, I thought I might have been mistook. Now you know what I know, and you are more cock sure than I was. There is something in this business I don't quite understand."

"To be sure there is, Alick. This chamois bag is one I gave to Mrs.

Blane, and that little darn in it—look! I put in myself. It was a cut I made with the point of a penknife one day the blade slipped. It was in this bag the gold was then stolen. We'll start to-morrow, by the first light, Alick."

And Alick, proudly conscious of his instrumentality—"I'll be ready lad, never fear."

When the diggers reached Belter Gully by the evening coach, Robbie showed the way to what he called the diggers' public. The evening was early, but the bar and bar-parlour were glaring with light, and busy with groups, and voices, and faces. Diggers were exchanging their experiences of the day, and mingling their ideas with tobacco smoke. Here and there some strong voices took the lead in a quiet fashion, and it was evident that customers were calmly settling down to the evening's enjoyment, consisting of the fellowship of conversation, and cards there procurable. Night-shift men lounged in their oilskins to partake of their last pint, before the whistles of the engines called them to their work, and, on the whole, the place was lively and slightly noisy, but peaceable.

One voice, not by any means the loudest, but certainly the most impressive, ran through the other voices, and kept itself connected without effort, till it won general attention. Towards the owner of the voice Robbie nodded.

"That's the voice. Who could forget it? If you listen for a while, you won't be able to get away from it. Mind me, John Grant, there is no mistaking that voice."

The 'lucky digger' was saying to his particular knot of smokers—

"Take co-operations. What is it but putting the chances all in favour of capital? Some fellow born into wealth takes his share, and signs his cheque for £50 or a £100. You fellows are the slaves of that cheque: that dash of that man's pen is a fetter on you. You work and toil and slave for that cheque; you risk your lives for it, and some of you get crushed for it. If you risk your lives putting in a set of timber, to get enough stuff to give two ounces of gold, five grains off it goes to the cheque. If you risked your life for the two ounces, so you did for the five grains that is got through your lives, and through your sweat to satisfy the rapacious man of that bloated cheque, and its bloated owner. Any way you look at it, men, you are ground down, and any way you turn it, you are slaving to make the rich man richer. He is our bane, and the almighty everlasting clog on the wheels of labour."

"Where," inquired one of the audience, whose elbows were on the table and whose jaws were in his palms, "are we to get the machinery to drain the ground, if not by the bloated cheque? That's what bothers me!"

"That," replied the patriot, flowing back into his usual voice and channel, "is altogether another department of the subject. A cheque is simply condensed labour or condensed wages. We give the labour and get the wages. Why can't we condense them on our own behalf, we who are the wage earners and the labourers? Let us say we work for three penny-weights a day—out of that the cheque giver who employs us profits by one pennyweight, or whatever his profit is. If he did not get profit he would not employ us. He wrings what we are worth out of us, and we make him rich. Why? Because we don't know our value, or how to profit by the full utilisation of our labour? There, gentlemen, the matter lies in a nutshell!"

In spite of himself, Grant became interested, not only in the fluent, ready voice of the speaker, but in his face. It seemed to him to be one with which some trouble in the past was connected. The eyes, like all the other features, were large and shifty, and his long closely shaven chin somehow conveyed a double impression of boldness and irresolution, the whole face being singularly wanting in anything like force. He was the man to stir the crowd with his quick tongue, and resign the leadership when danger presented itself. In a short time the restless eyes met those of Grant, and the man halted, stammered over a few sentences and stopped.

Thereafter, in the course of the evening there lingered a paleness round his mouth and on his long chin. The eyes of the two men met so often that Grant felt it would be unsafe to postpone his business.

He had no remembrance whatever of the face as being that of one of the men who had robbed the store, but he did not know whether his face had been seen or not on the night of the burglary. The digger from Boulder Point rose in an unconcerned manner and strolled out to ask the landlord if he could supply him with a private room. It did not matter how rough it might be so that he could have it at once, that was the main thing. And while speaking he turned in the direction of the patriot instinctively to see his large eyes shifted unto him, to mark again the paleness round his large mouth and on his long chin. Grant saw that a light was placed in the room and returned. He saw the speaker intently regarding the ground in silence. Motioning to Alick, the latter got up from his seat and came over where Grant was standing. The eyes of the stranger followed him till both stood together and took, unknown to the man himself, an expression of waiting to be called. It seemed even to Grant that it was natural he should beckon to him, much as he had to Robbie. The man rose without hesitation, but it appeared as though the thoughts that had disquieted him were intensified, as the expression of the mouth and the grey shade round it testified. Grant waited till he came up.

"I want to speak to you privately, in that room, for a moment," pointing to a light beyond an open door across the passage.

He looked hurried and furtive, but without speaking walked hastily to the open door, Robbie and Grant following. It was curious to note how quickly the anatomist of labour and capital sat down, and what little surprise he exhibited when the other two, having closed the door, stood loungingly between him and it; but it was yet more curious to note the way in which the easy penetrating voice resumed the current of talk, as though what he was going to say had been studied and thought out.

"What, may I ask, is your occupation now, Mr. Grant? It is a long time since we met!"

Grant replied slowly, wrestling with his recollection of the face.

"That is as it may appear to either of us. Sometimes a short period seems long enough to span years.

"The short period I allude to is somewhere about 20 years."

The man spoke very respectfully, almost with humility, showing a change in his manner, but none in the pale colour that rested on his face like a scare.

Grant stood looking at the speaker in puzzled silence. The speaker looked unsteadily back at Grant.

"If you can remember the period when we met, you can also remember the occasion of the meeting."

"I remember it as well as I do yesterday. The last time we had the pleasure of meeting was when I had the meritorious honour of saving your life."

Grant drew a chair from the wall and sat closer to the man. There was a flash of recognition on his face, but it was as far from expressing any sense of gratitude or cordiality as ever. He put his elbow on the table and leaned over towards the stranger.

"The pistol-ball might have killed me, or it might not. I will not deny that the weapon was in my direction, but the trooper had just leaped his horse over the stockade, and was galloping past; I certainly will not deny that you struck his arm, and that the charge lodged in the ground somewhere near the horse's feet."

A pause, in which Robbie looked from one to the other in hopeless perplexity. Grant resumed:

"So, then, you are Ned Groves?"

The man, straightening himself in his seat, and bringing his hand emphatically on the table—

"What then?"

"Your mode of reply," continued Grant, with pause but for the two words, and with an expression upon his face half stern and half contemptuous, "is that of one who awaits a charge. As I now look at you, and your face becomes the more fully impressed on me; some at least of the incidents of your career overtake my memory without effort. You are the Ned Groves remarkable once for his long beard, the man who was the agitator and leading conspirator of the misled diggers of the Eureka Stockade. The Mr. Groves, who was their secretary, and who suddenly disappeared with £500 when the fight was over; and finally, the man who acted as a spy on behalf of the Government. The charges are short, but they are very heavy, Mr. Ned Groves."

"Only the lying tongues of menials, wearing the livery of Government, could have conceived such a charge against me as that of spy. The oaths were false, and the papers forged, sir, because I was marked out for their special vengeance."

"There was no forgery about the papers I saw."

"You might have thought so, but there was, I can assure you, Mr. Grant. However, we can allow that to pass for the present. Did I act like a guilty man when I brought myself to your remembrance? The charge of my disappearance with the money, you make in a manner that admits of only one interpretation. Did it ever occur to you, Mr. Grant, that the miners actively engaged in that foolish riot scattered to hiding places all over the country, and that it was a matter of impossibility to find them, even if I had been wandering about in the search till today. Here was my list. I can remember it as well as if it had been filled up only yesterday: Lanky Jim £6, Black Harry £5, Bendigo Tom £5, Charley Yank £5, and so on, and so on. Was I to leave my money and my belongings to the troopers? I took it with me, all I could, Mr. Grant, and you would have done the same. Because it was impossible to find those subscribers, and because I was unfortunate afterwards and lost the money—who will charge me with dishonesty?"

Grant felt as if he was very nearly silenced, though far from being convinced.

"And yet you were one of the chief, and by far the most dangerous inciters of what you have yourself called the foolish riot!"

"Undoubtedly I was one of the inciters; but yours is the charge of a schoolboy. The question is—Did the surroundings warrant the action I took? Were the diggers warranted in what they did? If they were, I was warranted in what I did. They could see the situation as plainly as I could. You were amongst them, sir, and you were able to think for yourself. If I used the word foolish, in reference to that riot I was wrong. It was the means of bestowing great privileges on the digging community, and from that, I unhesitatingly assert, grew the liberty which we enjoy today."

This man, who considered the sound of his own voice the only music worth listening to, changed his position, looked suspiciously and uneasily at his audience of two, and took a fresh departure.

"Suppose I am guilty of all you charge me with; granted that I have been a spy, an interested inciter to a foolish riot, an embezzler of the funds committed to my charge—granted, in short, that I am a Judas, I would pass your presence every day, I would cross your threshold and recross it, if there was a price set on my head, with the most perfect security."

"Why?"

"Why?" The man almost shouted, as he sprang to his feet, with his eyes glistening, and with the fullest force of which his forcible voice was capable. "Why? Because I saved your life. I—saved—your—life!" and, as he tapped his breast, and held himself up straight and reliant-looking, he seemed for the time almost imposing and strong.

"That is the armour I wear against you, Mr. Grant, and you will never seek to pierce the joints."

It may not have been noticed, by the Boulder Point men, but it would have been easily seen nevertheless by any observer not so much interested, that Groves had all this time, done nothing more than repeat a task the lines of which his quick brain had already laid out. The paleness in his face did not abate at all except when he jumped to his feet to assert himself; but it returned slowly and seemed more pronounced, as though something that he dreaded was coming closer. Grant was certainly embarrassed. From the way in which the stranger had spoken, he knew the stranger was right, and that if an exigency came he would, as payment of a possible debt, have aided his escape from justice or other danger. This was the half-feeling that arose, but he pushed it from him, and said:

"I have not admitted that you saved my life, although it is perhaps possible that you may have done so on the occasion alluded to."

"If I made such a reply to you, Mr. Grant, being in your place, and you in mine, you would tell me I was shuffling and paltering. No man, under such circumstances, would require to know that the weapon was properly charged and accurately presented before admitting the obligation."

"The obligation?"

"What would you have me call it? You owe your life to that hand, and there the matter ends. If I had done the same for an American Indian he would have remembered it with gratitude all the days of his uncivilised life. This is civilisation." And the man held out his two palms to the two men. "This is the man I saved from lying dead that day, like a dog in a ditch."

"Dash my rags! If he ain't got the best of it," muttered Robbie, also taking a chair.

After a silence of almost a minute, Grant said, slightly stammering:

"There is another matter I want to speak to you about. It was for the subject I am about to speak of, I brought you into this room. I do not know what excuse you will make in this case. I only warn you," gathering sternness, "that I have not the power of accepting any excuse your ingenuity can offer."

He stopped for a reply, but the voluble man sat silent, watching the candle and waiting.

"A fortnight ago yesterday you sold 180oz of gold at the Nerrywon-branch of the Union Bank of Australia, and eight weeks before that (I have got the dates here) you robbed the store of Widow Blane, in company with another man, of a bag of gold containing 185oz. I can swear to the gold, some of it having been found by me, and some by Robbie, here, by reason of some curious pieces that happened to be in both the parcels. Here is the bag it was in when stolen, and the bag was in your possession four days ago. I purpose having you lodged in the lock-up in half an hour. The gold is not mine; the case is not mine. There is the bag," and he flung it down on the table.

Groves again looked rapidly at the men, and resumed his contemplation of the candle.

"This, I repeat, is a matter I cannot interpose in. The gold belongs to a widow lady and must be restored to her."

The blow had come. Expected as it was, it brought the beads of perspiration out, standing on the man's face. Without replying he took up the chamois bag and muttered to it:

"When I missed you, I feared the game was up."

He seemed to weigh the bag in his fingers, with his moist face bending over, as if he were weighing his thoughts with it. He looked at the candle again, forgetful of the leathern bag in his hand, and suddenly turned straight upon his accuser:

"Have you no offer to make, Mr. Grant, to the man who saved your life?" adding, as an afterthought, "I do not admit being guilty of the charge."

Grant replied:

"The case is not mine."

Groves did not seem to hear him. There were gathered knots and furrows about his brows, and his weak mouth was trembling.

"There is £100 of the money gone."

The accuser turned his face away rapidly, to hide the look of satisfaction that he felt come to it, and then set it sternly opposite to that of Groves.

"Where is the man who assisted you in the robbery?"

As nearly as a man could be expected to under the circumstances, Groves smiled. "I never saw him since that night; we had agreed to go to Melbourne by different routes, but I took care he wouldn't find me, and we had no time for a divide. I have no doubt he is making anxious inquiries about me somewhere or other."

"A hundred pounds short?" queried Grant.

"A hundred pounds short, Mr. Grant," replied the thief. "I will give you the money here now, in gold and notes, on one condition."

"That condition is that you be allowed to your escape, and that the matter be not pursued any farther; that condition is granted. Where is the money?"

"In my bedroom."

"We will adjourn to that place. Take up the light, Mr. Groves, and lead the way. You have too much good sense not to know that we are close behind you."

Groves put the candle down, and turning to the speaker, with his old assurance and fluency of manner and speech.

"I have, the more especially as there is nothing to be gained by deceiving you. Gentlemen, this way."

When they reached the bedroom Mr. Groves opened the door with a flourish, invited the visitors to enter, and in a very short time took a packet from a recess he had cunningly constructed below the hearthstone. Standing with the packet in his hand, and contemplating his visitors with his peculiar smile, he pointed to the fireplace.

"This, gentlemen, is the only bedroom in the house which boasts of a chimney. It cost me chills innumerable, and as many appeals to the humanity of the landlord, before I got it."

The chimney presented a ready means of egress, and the hearth an apparently safe depository.

"He (the landlord) turned his mother-in-law out in my favour, and I am allowed the privilege of a fire should the chills return. You will find in that parcel, Mr. Grant, the money I received for the gold, less £100. The Boulder Point gold has been the first dishonest action of my life. It shall be the last. In my final arrangements with you now, you will find honesty of purpose the leading characteristic. Honesty is the best policy."

Groves leaned back against the wall, contemplating the counting of the money, as careless as though the transaction was one in which he had no concern. He had grown tired of the anxiety the possession gave him, and of late had caught himself contrasting his present with the old Bohemian life of wandering, and its most precious privilege of hearing himself talking in season and out of season on the rights of labour and the baleful oppression of capital. Before he took part in the robbery, he could express himself fearlessly; since then the shadow of a constant fear had oppressed him. Robbie sat watching Grant, and at times stealing an inquisitive look at Groves, who stood calmly watching the men rather as an observer of human nature, and as declared enemy of the paper and coin that were being counted, than as one of the principals in that meeting of three. The two diggers sat upon the bed with the candle and the paper and the coin between them; the light cast their shadow big and dim on opposite ends of the room, and it lighted fully Groves's face as it watched the transfer, showing a look of satisfaction in his restless eyes, and the nervousness and paleness gone from around his mouth. The half-wandering, half-inquiring looks of Robbie did not in the least disturb him; he took them rather as tribute to his talent.

Grant took a scrap of paper from his pocket and looked at some figures on it.

"The money is here quite right, barring the £100; and now, Mr. Groves, we are quits. You are free to go, or to stay, as it may please you and to take whatever course you may find most consistent with the maxim you quoted a short time since. Do you consider the Eureka Stockade debt wiped out now?"

"Nay," said Groves, flowing off immediately, "that is a question for your own consideration. Who should know the value of the life saved, if not yourself? Assess that, you. Look here, Mr Grant, after this evening it is very unlikely we shall ever meet again. You have done me a favour, which I do not consider a very great one. Any searcher after stolen or lost money would have been glad to waive his claim to £100 out of a sum of over £700, to get his money back without trouble and without delay. But if you had done much more for me, if, in point of fact, you had saved my life at the risk of your own (I ran no risk), yet the debt as between us cannot be balanced or, as I should say, wiped out. Twenty years after this, if we are both alive, you would save my life if you could, or run a risk to preserve me from danger; and I, who am one of the most selfish of men, would, I think, do the same on your behalf. I have been of service to you; you have partly repaid it. You cannot but take some interest in me hereafter. So it will be with me. Sterne says—'We take a withered stick and we plant it, and we water it because we planted it.' Now, gentlemen, goodnight; I purpose being early on my way tomorrow."

Grant, rising, turned to Robbie.

"I will follow you presently, Alick; I wish to speak to Groves privately."

When the door closed, Grant resumed.

"Listen, Groves; I feel that your sayings and protestations and explanations are as hollow you always were and always will be. I believe you to be a clever scoundrel who has scarcely courage to defy the law; but that you are a scoundrel, and a most dangerous one, in the true sense of the word, there is not the shadow of a doubt on my mind. Still, you did me that service at the Stockade. And, in view of that, and because I retrieved the money so easily, I will on my own account give you something to help you on your way. There are £20." He held out the little roll of money, watching Groves' face.

Groves, carelessly—"I am not wholly unprovided for. I have some few bounds of that hundred left."

"I have supposed that from the first. I give this money on my own account."

Groves reached out his hand slowly.

"I honestly confess to you, Mr. Grant, that I don't care much about it. When my pockets are empty my brains are busy; I feel clearer and better then. Goodnight, sir. I purpose going to bed and making an early start."

Grant passed from the room and the vagabond sat down to smoke before sleeping the sleep of the just.

He had not been in this position long when a knock came. Groves gave a ready invitation to enter, and the big figure of Robbie stepped inside.

"I came back to ask you one or two questions," explained Robbie.

"Ask away, but don't be long."

"You was one of the party wot worked on that rich claim near the whipstick, at Bendigo, at the rush?"

The smoker took the pipe from his mouth and looked searchingly at the questioner. He thought for a moment over the history of that wild time, and replied:

"Yes."

"You was one of Captain Morrah's party?"

"Yes."

"It was you got him on the spree, and kept him at it?"

"He got himself on the spree, and kept himself at it; but, for the sake of convenience—Yes."

"If I had my way I'd wring your neck where you ait. That bout you got him on drove him mad. Do you know that he drowned hisself in Melbourne? If you had not cleared out when you did, you'd a bin tarred and feathered, and here's the man would hev' done it. I'd like to do it now. I didn't know till long after that he was married. Wot do you think of yourself?" and Robbie towered opposite him with a formidable look of indignation and strength.

"Look here, Mr.—, what's your name?"

"Robbie—Alex Robbie."

"Mr. Robbie, it's too late to enter upon that subject tonight. It would occupy too much time to lay that affair before you from my point of view. Be assured of this, that if I did, you would conclude in my favour, as you did in the matter of the embezzled funds a short time since." Yawning, "I am getting sleepy, Mr. Robbie, and, however much I would like to win your good opinion, I have not time to spare."

"I'll take time to tell you this: I could pass over every charge made against you tonight, pooh! just like that (snapping his fingers), but for that Captain Morrah affair I consider you to be in my debt. If ever I have the chance of getting my hands upon you, you shall pay it. You understand me!" and he let his hand fall heavily on the man's shoulder.

Groves saw the danger in the digger's eyes, and said nothing.

Robbie stood for a moment undecided, then slowly took his hand away and left the room.

Mr. Groves turned the key of his bedroom door, smoked a while longer, and retired to find sweet and tranquil sleep, unencumbered by care or conscience.

Chapter VII: Making a Bargain

Though the snow was on the farthest hills, the winds that came down from these gathered breaths from defiles, and valleys, and spans of plain, till it was laden with the testimony that spring was at hand. The soft air bore its perfume to the plateau of Boulder Point, and from thence might be seen the patches of yellow above the grass and among the trees, with many dappling spots of colour made by wild flowers that looked like blue lake pools, or scattered and gleaming like stars in the sombre of the olive woods. The morning was full of all this, and of the busy harmony and blessing given, when Grant walked in the sunlight to the store. He carried with him good news for her he loved most to think of, and he anticipated the pleasure that would show itself in her eyes and gather in her face. He knew the reason of the weariness he had seen there of late, and was he not carrying to her the joy of glad tidings?

After his couple of days' absence he felt repaid as he walked in to see the sudden look of satisfaction that was expressed, and to hear her voice bid him welcome. The calm, high look of the brow and eyes was always there, but the mouth changeful and tender gave value to her few earnest words.

"Back at last, John Grant. And has your pleasure trip done you good? You are welcome, and look almost as happy as the spring-day out there in the shine and among the trees. Come in."

He followed her to the little parlour he had half-partitioned and half-built a short time before, and she paused on the threshold with a look that awaited criticism, and an anticipated pleasure in the verdict.

There were few things in the room, but they were such as he had not seen before at Boulder Point. There were curtains of queer rich stuff, and a few ornaments that were rare; and there were little things tastefully scattered about, all of which were a refinement he could scarce have believed possible. A touch of her cunning hand here and there seemed to have done it all.

"I see by your face that you are about to flatter me. Do not say it, whatever it is."

Then with a shade of care coming—

"I have asked you in here, John Grant, respecting a promise I gave you not long ago. Sit down. It wants some hours to noon, and we are not likely to be disturbed. I could not but give you the promise you asked of me respecting my daughter's marriage, and while I could not refuse such a favour to you again now if you asked it, still I wish you would release me. I will tell why I ask that release as a special favour to myself."

The look in Grant's face changed gradually to one of amused expectation; and the lady, with her keen sense, read it with a feeling of surprise, almost of impatience.

"My reasons," she explained in a tone that grew firm, and a look in which was sadness as well as resolve, "are these. It seems to me a long time since I have known you, and, recalling as I have done every passage of your history with which I am acquainted and of which I have had experience, I find that you are as proud I am. Prouder, indeed, and more difficult to deal with in many things. You know the reason why I decided to break off the marriage, and yet you requested of me that it should not be broken off. That, with you, could only mean one of two things, either that the marriage should go under circumstances that would be very painful to me, or that you intended to supply the lost portion. Now, John Grant, I know your generosity, and I know your pride. In reference to the first supposition, put yourself in my place; in reference to the last, put yourself in my place also. If you do this honestly, and you will do it honestly, you can only say there is only one course to be pursued: the marriage must be postponed not for long. I have been busily engaged roughly taking stock, as well as I could, since you left and a year's delay will be sufficient. With a little indulgence from the banks, I am not afraid of delaying my child's prospects and wishes long, but delayed for a time at least they must be. Put yourself in my place, and agree with me."

She put her hand over, almost beseechingly, and laid it on his arm.

"Have you anything more to say, Mrs. Blane?"

She looked up with a quick expression of pain which became intensified when she saw that he showed no evidence of having been touched by her representation, which was almost a pleading.

"I could sit here this beautiful forenoon and hear and see you talk for hours together. You can scarcely imagine what pleasure it gives me. When I left Boulder Point the other day I took care to give you no clue to the business that took me away. That business, or journey, was undertaken on your behalf."

"On mine?"

"Have you no business abroad in which I might be useful?"

"I know of none," she made reply, her face clouding, "except that weary burglary affair. But that is past and gone; with me, it is dead and buried."

"You will require to bury it over, again, then. I have resurrected it."

"I don't understand you," she said, hopelessly.

"You will understand me when I tell you that Robbie and I have interviewed the thief, and," (taking a packet from his big breast pocket) "there is the value of the gold stolen, barring one hundred pounds. It is right to a fraction, Mrs. Blane. I counted it myself."

When he put the money down his countenance changed and his voice shook; his large kind eyes were moist at the feeling of gratitude and joy the lady's face exhibited. One glance flamed in her eyes for an instant. So full of thankfulness and of love, that it sank down upon his heart carrying a memory with it that was destined to remain there through all his coming life, and it visited him often after, bringing along with it the sunny day that lived beyond the window and shed in upon them the fragrance it carried. She leaned towards him, glowing warmer and brighter than the day, and put her hands upon his. Then it seemed to him that some sudden pain smote and chilled her, that the life fled out of her face, that she drew herself back shuddering and pallid, and looked at him with fear.

"Oh! My—Mrs. Blane, you are ill! what's the matter?" he asked, rising hurriedly.

She was looking out beyond him, away through and past the gladness of the day, as to a darkness that was before her. She caught for the moment the earnest concern that was in his eyes, the language of which she had learned to read long ago.

There was a struggle at her brave heart, but it gave way to tears, before suffering that shook her like a storm. He moved closer, but she looked up with her face stained, and asked him to leave her. And he stood still and almost trembling for he could not mistake the true quiver of fear that was in the entreaty.

She bent her head upon her hands, and the shadows moved silently and fitfully upon the table, trembling tenderly on her hair. The packet of money looked coarse and curled in the light half ragged and daubed and strangled with knotted cord. Between them, and to them both came many voices. The royal sunlight flowed in upon the silence between the strong man and the bowed woman. Mrs. Blane pressed her hands upon her eyes and drew them rapidly down her face, as she falteringly rose from her seat and retreated farther from the man who had served her so well, before speaking, and supporting herself with one trembling hand on the chair that was now before her, she said:

"The debt of gratitude that I owe to you, John Grant, is one of those that is not to be measured by any ordinary standard. When I first came to this place, you were the one to give me aid and the first to interest yourself in the welfare of a woman who was a stranger and utterly unknown to every person in the little settlement. It is to your exertion I owe this home, and the sense of independence it has brought to me. I owe the happiness and calmness that have marked my life since I found a harbour here. For that, God bless you! I am not a young and inexperienced girl, but a mother and a woman whom the world has tutored harshly. You know nothing of my past history; if you did, this explanation could not have occurred; neither could another scene which happened before you were wounded."

She raised her face with the evidence of resolve coming to her brow and eyes again.

"I know I am in some degree, and in the only way possible, discharging my debt of gratitude to you, when I state what, under any other circumstances, I would not dare to do. Since I came to Boulder Point I have watched and studied you. There is not a thought expressed by your face, or voice, or eyes that I cannot read; and I would be acting ungratefully towards you if I did not tell you that I know you love me. It is visible in your voice when it speaks, and in every speaking expression you wear. You are hoping for what is impossible of attainment. What my feelings are towards you, you will not ask me to say. That cannot matter, considering our relative positions."

He stood farther back in a gossamer-like shadow that fell from the curtains as if seeking some sort of shade or shelter, and his voice seemed at once to have grown thin and drawn, offering a singular contrast to her intense tones and the light of her face.

"You have spoken truly, Mrs. Blane. I have seen in you every day, from the day I first saw you at the crossing place by the loaded dray, the first and only passion of my life. I have never fought or wrestled with it, being content to regard it as a dream, and to regard you as something to aspire to but not to reach. You would not believe, Mrs. Blane, how wonderfully that feeling has softened and enriched my life, and how bare the loss will leave it. I should have told you of my love one day, but not yet. I was so afraid of what my words might bring. There was the happiness of a possible realisation sometime, maybe when your daughter was married and you were alone; and I rested on this as men will rest on a possibility that is bright but far. It was a long dream, and it was a fair one; to settle down and live with thankful hearts among the beauties and in the calm that are always here."

Mrs. Blane's hand was white with her tightened grasp of the chair, and it shook painfully, although the blush from neck to brow became deeper red. She spoke brokenly.

"John Grant, you do not know the danger. You do not know the position. You do not know your strength. Let me do you one service that will count against the hundreds you have done for me."

"Ay, if it will give you happiness."

But the manner of his speaking frightened her, and she stood giddily for nearly a minute getting the mastery of herself.

"That which will give you a calm and tranquil life, and permit the fruit of your goodness to find you with their peace and their content."

"And what is that?"

"Give me the pleasure of knowing I have made one sacrifice for you. My daughter's home and future are assured," pointing to the stained parcel. "I have often heard you say you would rather live at Boulder Point than in any other corner of the earth. Let me, for your sake, go out into the world again. There is enough there and in the store to assure my future, thanks to you. Live here, John Grant, and be a friend to my daughter, and let me go."

John Grant smiled but did not speak.

She took her hand off the chair, and in the extremity of her agitation interlaced her fingers pathetically.

"You do not know, you cannot tell, how necessary it is that we should separate. Oh! I fear for the future!" and she put her hands upon her face again.

"And why? Surely I have a right to ask?"

"Surely you have, and if you do ask I will answer the question, and answer it fully, whatever it may cost me."

She stepped over to where he stood in the slight shade, and placed her hands on his shoulders.

"It will be the only unkind, thing you have over done to me, John Grant, if you ask the question."

Her face had answered him more plainly than words could, his look brightened and his voice was full and tremulous.

"I will not ask, but I have an offer, to make that may be accepted as a compromise. I have business away from Boulder Point. There is a link in a broken chain to be picked up somewhere away from this, that I have neglected, which may indeed turn out to be a criminal neglect on my part. Again, I like that place, Nerrywon, where we recovered the gold. In short," he said, taking her not unwilling hand, "I purpose leaving you for six months, and at the conclusion of that time, learning from yourself, if my life can be crowned as I hope it may be yet, I will pack up odds and ends in some stout cases over there, and leave you the key."

She only shook her head. The beauty of the day seemed to have left it, and its brightness looked a mockery.

"Goodbye!"

For the first time he took her face between his hands and kissed it, and when she turned to look after him the assurance of strength she had relied on was gone, and the long steady stride of the man who had won her, came back on her loneliness. She sank upon her seat and looked down upon her shaking hands, upon the thin gold ring that was there; she turned it wearily round and round, and flung her hand from her—as flinging away a clasp, all the firmer that, it was not to be seen, all the more fateful and binding that it was but the ghost of another hand that was resting upon hers. She trembled suddenly before some thought that presented itself to her, as ghostly and unreal as the hand; and when her daughter returned from her walk among the huts, and the flowers that were coming up to broider the sward and touch the shades with tints, she found her mother lying forward upon the table in a swoon.

Chapter VIII: Offering a Reward

When the sun had rusted the grass, and the wind had swept its withering dust in swirls from the plains and bare hills, the baleful breath of the changeless sky was drooping the flowers shrivelling all things green at Morrison's farm with the exception of the new life that had begun there. The rambling old building, with its corners and gables, on which the vine and rose leaves turned and trembled, had had another stage attached for the life drama to be there enacted. The plash of fallen water lingered at it, and birds hovered there to greet the morning with notes, and the evening time, when the dimness fell softly on the hills, with calls.

To this place Morrison had led Ann Blane. There was no cloud upon the mother's face when she parted with her on the threshold. The light of happiness that is so subtle rested above the bride. It was in her bearing and around and upon her, and it told a story beyond the expression of speech, such as the haze of sunrise tells in the morning. But the mother, while rejoicing in the beauty of the picture she took away to be conjured up in the lonely store, felt as though she had put from her a hope in the last act she did before leaving her daughter's home. She had furnished her little toilet-table with the singularly beautiful appointments that John Grant had seen when coming back to the world from the mists of fever, and it was to her like relinquishing something to which some vague unfulfilled thought in her mind had caused her latterly to cling. She could not tell the reason why she had set them forth and silently hung the pictures on the wall when the sick man lay in his deep sleep, but she sat amongst them there, and near to him, with her heart opening towards some sunny future as flowers to the warmth. She felt it was a hopeless dream, and rose sorrowfully from her contemplation, when the tears came to her eyes, and blurred the outward signs of a possibility to be forgotten.

***

The gloom in the store was cool in the long evenings, and the bearded diggers lounged in as before. The speculation as to Grant's departure had perturbed them mildly for a while, and they wondered at the perversity of a man who had made nigh a fortune. "Ay, mor'n a fortune if the truth were known, leaving Boulder Point for bits of diggins and new-fangled rushes and places." But when it became known somehow that he would return before long, Mr. Dodd shook his head despairingly, and said it were all along of his brain being 'withered with that Melbourne trip. They might tell him it was the shootin' an' the fever made him rave; but he knew better—it were the dazin' streets of Melbourne and the lock-ups.

"I heard," spoke a voice from a pickle case that was back in the shadow, "that Grant was knocking about Bendigo, not working, but inquiring about, and hunting up Government papers after some dead man's friends."

"Who told you that, Richard?" inquired the widow, quickly, who knew all the voices.

There was silence in an instant. It was not often Mrs. Blane asked a question, and if a stranger had come in just then he would have thought the store deserted.

Mr. Richard Holly recovered his composure sufficiently to say, "My wife's sister had a letter from Tom Murdoch's wife, ma'am. You will mind Murdoch, that you used to cure of headache. Well it was him what said he told him he was searching after a dead man's friends that were."

"I knew his brain were muddled," said Dodd, cheerfully. "That ain't the way to go about it. I once had a missing relative here, but I did not go to Government papers for him. I just advertised and offered a reward of £5."

"Did you find him?" from Mrs. Blane again.

"No ma'am, leastways, I did, that is, I were sent word of his death, signed and sealed and all that; but it cost me nigher £10. I had to send it to a respectable attorney—a respectable attorney, ma'am!"

Mr. Dodd laughed grimly.

"The document is somewheres in my box now."

Mrs. Blane asked no more questions. There were no candles lighted in the long evenings; and the men spoke to each other through the shadows, making themselves suddenly visible when their pipes required lighting, or when an impatient pull caused a spark to burn. The widow's face was almost in darkness. Those present could see little more than the light shade of her figure in the obscurity. There was a new expression with her, however; an expression which one might wear who saw some unlooked-for revealment. When the twilight had slumbered into night, she sat writing, and the little servant moving past the door in the darkness stood, half hidden, to wonder at the look of youth that had fallen upon her mistress. She wrote, and moved buoyantly about the little apartment as if in search of words to convey her thoughts; and, when near midnight, she had written two letters to her satisfaction, she stepped out among the perfume the dew was sending upward from the withered grass and the banks of the silent stream. One letter was addressed to Young, Jenkins and Co., solicitors, Melbourne, and the other to "The Australian." The latter contained the following notice for publication:

"£50 Reward.

"The above reward will be paid to anyone who will give reliable information to Messrs. Young, Jenkins and Co., solicitors, Melbourne, concerning Captain Morrah, who was last heard of at Whipstick rush on the Bendigo goldfield, in the year 1853-54. On the receipt of information given personally or by letter a deposit on the amount will be paid or forwarded as a proof of *bona fides*. Anyone capable of affording such information must, however, convince the advertiser by such proof as will leave no room to doubt the reliability of the informer. In the case of death, the above reward will be increased to £100 for such documentary or other evidence as the law may deem sufficient. Further particulars can be obtained by applying to Messrs. Young, Jenkins and Co., or to M. M., Post-office, Boulder Point, Yarraberb."

The notice was but a short one, but it took Mrs. Blane a long time to put it into the above form. The writer moved rapidly with the letters to the little post-office, and when she had heard them fall into the almost empty box, she ran home hurriedly, with her hand pressing against her heart to stay its beatings. Once committed to the course she felt restless and ill at ease.

It appeared to her that she had laid her secret bare to the world. It had been kept so long and so well that she outlived the sharpness of the pain, till the old sad, or glad, story began to weave itself in her history once more.

The love she had felt once was distant and dim, and woven with a pain that was merciless and a prospect that was darker than night. She had not felt the touch of sunshine, and the joy that is better than the sun, when the cloud came that left her groping in the dangers of a world that was strange—all the crueller that she was fair to look at. All the more expectant of the wreck that she knew the gentle life, and had known and loved its luxuries. She had left the world that knew her. She was brave to leave it with her child upon her breast, and when, with the surroundings and her slender purse, she first saw the weary and toilsome roads that led upward and on over hazardous hills, and away to a country that seemed wild and habitless, she had nearly wept her strength and her courage away. She struggled on, and the effort brought hope back to her again and, with it, strength.

When the advertisement had been in the papers for at least a fortnight, and no letters reached the widow upon the subject that now engrossed her thoughts, she began to droop. The solicitors had replied in their business way, but held out little hope. The waifs of the early digging days had been so numerous, and the times were then so unsettled, that no note had been kept of arrivals or departures. Men, in those days made their fortunes and left the country to rejoin their friends and build up homes elsewhere. There was scarcely a month passed but some such application had been made to them to interest themselves in tracing the whereabouts of those who had disappeared, or in obtaining proofs of the death of others. The only chance lay in the course which Mrs. Blane had taken; and if Mrs. Blane did not hear from some who know Captain Morrah in those early days, the chances would be greatly against the sought-for information being obtained. The passage of the weeks was slow. When the post arrived and was barren, there was the waiting and the hope for the next, and with it a like disappointment, while hope grew fainter. She did not know whether Morrah had worked at the mines under his own or an assumed name. If the latter, the chances were hopeless and she, with the prospect of happiness beside her, with the certainty of the light being glad upon her path throughout the years that were to come, must remain in the outer darkness. Sometimes she sat brooding with her hands clasped, rebelling against the desolation of her life. The voice of Grant and the voice of her daughter had gone from it; the softened sounds of labour from the creek below, that used to soothe her, irritated with their monotony. She tried to break from her thoughts as from a feverish dream that had surrounded her, and an unhealthy light began to flicker in her eyes and upon her face. When the men came in from labour and spoke in her store of the events of the day, they brought some sort of human companionship with them, and she came to long for the glooming of the dusk, to hear the voices, to know that there were friends around her, and to feel that she was not bereft of all life and companionship. When her daughter left, after staying with her for the day, she felt the desertion keener; and so the hours and days moved with terrible slowness, while the uneventful weeks went on.

Mrs. Blane knew that Grant had some intention of trying for a short period his fortunes at Nerrywon, in company with Alick Robbie, and when she saw the latter enter the store, she waited nervously for what he might say, expecting to get some news of him or, it might be, message.

One afternoon, when Robbie entered the store, earlier than usual, she noticed that the big miner was embarrassed. He spoke with some constraint, and appeared to be busy with a new thought that had present-ed itself. Mrs. Blane, as patiently as she could, answered the skirmishing remarks of the stolid Robbie about the weather and the rise in the creek, till he plunged into the business on his mind. Drawing forth a well-used paper, he folded and unfolded it tenderly, while his rough fingers rasped the newspaper, as he inquired, almost with trepidation, if she were a good pen-woman.

"I mean by that, ma'am, if you could write a long scroll proper like. I know it ain't much the work for ladies but more for clerks; but then you are so clever, Mrs. Blane, and it wouldn't be the first time by many a score, you hev done me a service."

"I will write a letter for you, Alick, if that is what you mean."

"That is what I mean, Mrs. Blane. I can use the pen myself, you know; but when a fellow has to explain mor'n half-a-dozen words his head gear gets out of order."

She took up writing material and asked him to follow her. It was the first time Robbie had been in the little parlour that looked into the shop, and he stopped on the threshold, saying, if it was all the same to her, he was first-rate and comfortable where he was, and would tell her what to say from there by word of mouth.

But Mrs. Blane could prefer a request in such a way that the diggers of Boulder Point never thought of declining. She looked at Robbie and pointed to a chair opposite her without speaking, and Robbie found himself trying to step daintily between the patterns on the carpet, and then to balance himself on the corner of his seat.

"Now, Alick, what am I to say?"

"This here, ma'am."

He took out his paper again, and opened and placed it on the table with his palm.

"It seems there's some sort of a party here what comes to the post-office for letters, with a sort of skeleton name. He calls himself M. M., and offers a reward of £50 for information about a Captain Morrah. It's all here in the newspaper under my thumb. Now I want for to say that I knew this Captain Morrah at the Whipstick rush."

The voice of Mrs. Blane came very faint, and trembling—

"You are sitting in my light, Alick. I can write better if you stand by the door."

Robbie joyfully left the chair and stood against the door-jamb.

"Jest hear all I've got to say, and all what I know first, ma'am, and then you can screw it into writing after."

He was standing behind her, and could see her stooped figure over the table, and her white hair. Seeing also a movement of her head that betokened assent, he proceeded—

"This Captain Morrah, when he was at Whipstick, was the captain of the party. He was the quickest worker among us, and very greedy for gold, to get for his wife, he said, who was used to the great folk life at home, and wanted all the comfort that could be got. Nobody knew what he did with his gold, but he got a lot and spent none, so he must have had a fortune. My own share, of the three claims we worked there, was over £3000; but that went like all the rest."

He soliloquised, digging his arms into his pockets.

"It went in speculations, and so they were specs and nothing more. Howsoever, ma'am, this Captain Morrah had a devil of a temper (excuse me), but he was quick and obliging, and if there were one thing he would not do, it was touch grog. We all knew his ways, an' we all liked him; he was what ye call a good mate till a crawler came among us, the man what stole your gold, by the same token. Ned Groves his name was, an' he got the captain on the spree. He and Groves was away from us for a month, an' when he came back he was just mad. We knew where the two had bin all the time, an' every day. I tried to drag him away once, but I did not try again; he was just a demon, ma'am, when the drink was on him. He came home at last, wild an' dangerous, an' told us he had been at his old diggins, an' told stories of what he had seen about his wife, all lies an' madness, an' what I could not tell you. Some people, I've heard say, when mad with drink, hate them they loved afore; that was the way with him, an' the madness was broodin' into him an' growin' stronger and deeper like silently. All at once we missed him; he had left a note, writ just like a clerk, an' calm as calm. It bid us goodbye, naming me by name, an' said he was going to a better land, which maybe was in India, for he often talked of that place, an' showed us a sword wound on the head."

Robbie paused, as if to collect his thoughts, when there came a low murmur from the widow, bending at the table.

"Go on."

"There ain't very much more to say, ma'am. I happened, by accident, to be in Melbourne about a month after (our party broke up after the captain left) when I saw a crowd down by the pier, and something told me just like a voice inside, that the crowd had to do with the captain. I ran up as sure that I would see him as I stand here, and, sure enough, there he was, with his long moustache an' beard an' long sharp face, like a dragoon officer. When I came to name who he was, and said I knew him, I was made attend the inquest an' give evidence; an' bein' the first time I see my name in print, an' bein' the last like of a good mate what named me by name, when bidding the party goodbye, why, I kept the paper, and it's in my old gold belt hanging up at the hut yonder. What I tell you, an' the paper below, is all I know, but if this M. M. is a poor man, wanting maybe to get property or somewhat that the captain had, or a poor relation, why, ma'am I don't want no fifty pounds; but, if so be that the news is worth a lot to him I'd take the fifty. Why not? An' on this point, as well as on the screed of writing, I want your help. Jest you tell me what to do, an' I'll do it."

Robbie waited. The white head was bent forward on the table.

"Jest whatever you say, ma'am, I'll do, an' much obliged."

The lady did not move. He waited for a long time, but there was no answer. Then stealing a step forward, he craned silently over her shoulder and left the room, with a broad smile upon his face.

"Darn my rag! If I haven't sent widow Blane to sleep with my talk! That will be a joke, if the boys gets to know."

Chapter IX: Making a Finish

When the faintness caused by the sudden shock had passed away, Widow Blane raised her head from the table with the words of Alexander Robbie ringing in her ears, describing the face of the drowned man. She seemed to see the body lifted up by the crowd, and the face examined as it was, being covered up, then the cart with the dead burden, slowly lumbering to its destination. Gradually the picture died away like a mist into the past, where it had so long been buried. It was raised for her by the few words of the miner from a grave covered up by the history of nigh a score of years, and the long deep silence that had lain above the dead husband all that time, closed round the memory again as the waters had closed upon him on the pathway of stars. There was before her soon the light of the present, and the sun of the future. The darkness that was so dark from its loneliness was yielding to dawn, and the solitary years she thought coming had the sounds of life and companionship in them. This picture had warmth and light; there was brightness in the foreground, and a peaceful happiness in the middle distance. Away beyond the mellow sunset was over the sombre valley, where rested the shadow of death. In that evening's twilight when the miners came and talked, none saw the widow's face, and her voice was seldom heard; but it was a face lighted with hope, and the voice was soft and tremulous, as of one who had risen from the struggle of a life, and was entering upon peace.

The passage of a few more days, which now appeared to her like panoramic pictures guiding her on to the future, that was looked forward to with welcome, carried to her two letters, which she found waiting for delivery, one to M. M. and one for Mrs. Blane. They seemed to make the time brighter, and to smooth away the traces of years and of care. There was an atmosphere of happiness about her soon that lent fascination to her race and grace. In the moonshine and in the cool she settled herself down, and read:

"Sandhurst, Thursday, March 18.

"To M. M., Post-office, Boulder Point.

"I do not know whether the M. M. who advertises in the 'Australasian' asking for particulars concerning a Captain Morrah, is a lady or gentleman. I wish to state that I write to you not with a view to the reward, but because I have in my possession some papers and other articles which belong, or belonged, to a Captain Morrah at one time digging at a Bendigo rush. Owing to valuable information which these papers contain, I am anxious to find the widow if she is still alive or, if not, his next of kin. It was partly this object that took me to Sandhurst from Boulder Point, of which place I am a resident. My search however has been unavailing. I met a few who had a remembrance of the captain, but none who knew anything whatever about the family. The time during which I intended being absent from Boulder Point has expired, and I purpose returning at once. I shall be happy to meet M. M., at say the Phoenix store on the 29th instant. The lady who keeps the store will give you such information concerning me as may be necessary.

"I have the honour to be, &c,

"JOHN GRANT."

The second letter read as follows:

"My dear Mrs. Blane,

"The period of my separation from Boulder Point, and from one who makes the memory of it dearer to me than any other place in Australia, has expired, and I am about to return with the first and most important object of asking you the question which is always present with me. There is another reason. Someone, who evidently lives near the township, has advertised under the letters M. M. for information respecting a Captain Morrah, and as I have reason to think I can afford the advertiser very valuable information, have requested him or her to meet me at your store on the 29th. I can reach the Point by 3 o'clock, walking over from Hinton, where the coach will leave. The two thoughts that drive all others from my mind are, am I coming too early? And what will the answer be? There is such happiness possible to us in that corner of the world that seems to me to be always so beautiful and so peaceful. Life such as that which sur-rounds me now has no charms for me, and when I think of you, alone and struggling with the world, I cannot rest. Always remember that if the fates are against us so that we cannot journey for the remainder of life together, it is I who must finally take my departure, having then the consolation of knowing that you are amongst those who respect and love you.

"I am yours always,

"JOHN GRANT."

Mrs. Blane cast a rapid glance round her. From the door where she sat (the day was fair and silent, except for the movements of the old bough, brushing its leaves softly) she held up the letter and kissed it, and put her hands upon her face.

On the afternoon of the 29th March, Mrs. Blane sat by the window of her parlour; her assistant was moving softly across the joists of sun that stretched through the dark store, and her pleasant voice rippled over the airs of songs that were intimate with memories. The widow looked out upon the hills, across the breast of one of which a broad white road lay stretched like a shoulder belt; it came out from the shadows, where the still trees and the haze of heat were, and it was dusty and white with the sun upon it. The grassland lay brown and bare, and in the silence of desertion. The sun crept in to Mrs. Blane's feet, and seemed to bestow its light to her as she rested and watched. She was dressed so quietly that she would not have attracted the curiosity of any digger, or digger's wife or daughter on the settlement; but she would infallibly have rivetted the attention of a duchess anywhere. The exquisite taste shown in the quiet colours; the soft peculiar stuff, and the harmony of its folds to her figure, in which a nameless but strange elegance lived, were in themselves causes of envy. These would have been detected at once by an eye practised to the refinement and the mode in a world where such things were worshipped with more fervor than Mammon, and more sacrifice than Juggernaut.

Waiting thus, Widow Blane irresistibly reminded one of the Court beauties of past times. The same flashing charm was over her face and her eyes, contrasted by the hair powdered white with suspense and trial. It was a strange contrast to see that woman dressed in rare Indian texture with a few things near her, speaking of a luxury that had grown out of a hundred centuries of civilisation, yet surrounded by parties of miners and the sound of their toil. It might have been the fashion that powdered her hair, for there was trace neither of suffering nor sorrow in her face now. Looked at in the sunshine, waiting and watching thus, she looked startlingly like the subject of some picture that had left the canvas in search of the times when the stately minuet was trodden in ruffles and rapiers, none the less ready that they were sheathed in velvet.

By-and-bye a little wall of dust arose above the road at its farthest part. It disappeared, and again rose and died like a pennant fluttering indistinctly, but always advancing, till, out of it, as out of a cloud, came the figure of a man, moving steadily in the direction of Boulder Point. There was no fringe of trees to hide it from the watcher, as it grow more distinct, leaving the belt of road stretching out behind it.

The face of the woman who was watching caught such expressions as her heart was speaking, reddening or paling in response; and in her eyes was light; then the road lay bare and silent as before, and there was nothing but emptiness, till a herald of dust rose upon the nearer hill. There was no mistake to be made now in the tall figure and the long stride. Twenty minutes thereafter there was the sound of footsteps on the threshold, and a voice that had lived long through Mrs. Blane's dreams, asked if she were in. In reply to the girl, the well-known walk approached the parlour, and John Grant was standing at the door. He was flushed and dusty with his travel, but the old freshness was in his face, and the old patches of grey in his crisp hair. He came to where she sat with the sun climbing up her figure and its light upon her hair. He felt half embarrassed and almost trembling as he saw her there—better than he expected, better than he had dreamed. Maybe a paler shade came to his face as he put his hand upon her arm, as he saw the brightness and happiness in her look, and her whole expression, as he bent down and kissed her, then softly, and partly through tears, she spoke low words of welcome.

"Back at last, John Grant?"

"Back again, Mrs. Blane," seating himself near to her, "on the business my letter indicated—you received it?"

"Yes, about M. M.?"

"About what is dearer to me and more urgent by far than the inquiries concerning M. M. No one can tell the beauties of this place till they have lived away from it; nor can they realise its peace till they have felt the fret and fume and seen the impurities of cities. You have taken time to think, and I know you have thought charitably of me, and pardoned the haste I have shown to know what you will say. If your thought is unfavourable to me now, take further time: you will give me rest before I start out upon a pilgrimage that looks from here so lonely."

Mrs. Blane's head was bent, waiting on the words, and marking the tone of sadness.

"We will speak of this another time, John," she said, looking at him with the same look that he had seen when he first entered, and still unshaded by thought or pain.

She saw the flush of hope that came to him, and it thrilled her with a keen joy.

"This, which you have made your first business should have been taken last."

"As if," he interrupted, with a ring in his voice, "it is not, and always will be, the first business of my life, Mrs. Blane."

"My name is Margaret."

He stopped, as to understand the interruption, and its meaning dawned upon him. He rose from where he sat, and coming a step forward took her hand.

"Thank you."

It would be impossible to describe the feeling in his words, or the calm that settled in his eyes and face. With him soon there was the bearing of a triumph that was greater than joy.

"You can see how unbusiness-like it was to bring on this business first, John Grant; the advertiser, M. M., should be here by this time, and—and this is not the time to ask me for my answer. It is an answer that embraces both our lives."

"It will be an answer, Margaret, that will give shine to our lives till they meet the eternal sea. As for the advertiser. Well, Heaven forgive me! I was going to say it made no matter to me whether he came or not; and yet I trust he will come, or she will come. It involves a good sum of money to some unfortunates who may be nearly starving. I wish the business were closed up. It is now about the time—"

He stopped and walked over to the chimneypiece, where was hanging the picture of the decorated general officer he had seen in his dream, and the lady's face, of which the counterpart was in the Indian casket. He put his finger upon the portrait, solemnly, and turned to the widow—"Who is this, Margaret?"

"I will show you."

There was a strip of dark material on the table hear her, and with it she tied the bands of the hair above her face, thus hiding the effect of the white tresses, and stood before John Grant the lady of the picture.

"Give me the keys of the hut, Margaret; I will show you something more."

He was back in a quarter of an hour with the Indian casket, and laid it on the table before her.

She at once slipped her hands behind it and pressed the bosses.

"Then you are not Margaret or Mrs. Blane but M. M. I mean that you are not—that is—"

"That I am Margaret and M. M., or Margaret Morrah, but not Mrs. Blane—and yet Blane is my maiden name, daughter of the grim Major General Blane, you see yonder, widow of the unfortunate Captain Morrah. You will understand, John Grant, how jealously I have kept the secret. You will understand the fear, the terror which your question gave me near a year ago, and that my only defence was of a kind I have deeply regretted—it was insolent. There are the clothes and letters. I remember them well, and yet it is so long ago; and here, too, is the rajah-stone," as she held up the pin, looking flushed and anxious. "I understand this to be of great value—worth, I was told, a couple of thousand pounds."

Grant slowly placed the letters and the confession before her.

"These have been written by you, Margaret. This letter contains the ravings of a madman." Unfolding the deposit receipt—"I have made inquiry concerning the gold this represents. It can be obtained without any difficulty. Mrs. Blane, you are rich."

She looked at him suddenly, and her lips trembled at his saddened face.

"You were right, Mrs. Blane. I understand the business today in an unbusiness-like way."

Mrs. Blane came to where he stood, and placed her hand upon his. She was excited, but the light he loved to see was on her face.

"You will leave me with the past until this time tomorrow, John Grant."

The digger took the hand from his and pressed his lips to it, and was gone.

The warmth of the next day was passing, and the purple of the hills was fading, when Margaret Morrah and John Grant walked over to the ravine where the trees and ledges of rock wove their shadows together, and where fragrant breath was rising from the waters in the river bed.

"This time last year you were wounded nigh to death."

"And this time last year," Grant made reply, "we considered your daughter's marriage at the coming Christmas. It was well you decided as you did. There is, you say, no happier household or happier prospect than Rosevale Farm. How could it be otherwise; they commenced their life together from the season of greatest blessing and of special rejoicing. A new life and a new hope was given to the world when the angels sang by night in the old Judean fields; and so, Margaret, let us start the life together under like auspices."

With all the love and devotion of her nature lighting her, with all the strange beauty she possessed upon her and around her, she looked with her large grand eyes at the speaker. She could not have spoken what she looked and felt, but he could read it all. Her hand was stretched out to him, and he took it.

"It is to be made mine forever this coming Christmas time, Margaret?"

"You are always right. If you will, so let it be, John Grant."

Gold-Quest:
A Christmas Tale of the
Early Digging Days

Lancelot Booth

Chapter I

"A merry Christmas, and a happy New Year. Please will yer give us a Christmas-box?" Thus a little urchin—thus in many an English town other urchins chime their peals. I use the word 'urchin' in a liberal sense, as a boy of tender years not yet contaminated by rude fellows.

A little urchin then—a pale-faced, light-haired boy, whose blue eyes seemed glossy beneath the sickly glare of a lamp light—thus accosted a gentleman who was hurrying on through a blinding storm of fine snow.

Scene: The main street in the town of D___, in a midland county, England. Time, Christmas Eve, in the year 1859.

"A merry Christmas, and a happy New Year; please will yer give us a Christmas-box."

The gentleman hurried on; he didn't notice the boy; perhaps he wrapped his Inverness cape more closely around him to repel the storm.

The boy, whose clothes bore traces of some feminine hand's repairing, leant his head against the railings that protected a cheerful-looking house. A cheerful-looking house, indeed, for the lights shone from the bay windows obliquely; and across the little stretch of snow-covered grassplot that intervened occasional bursts of laughter, joyous yet subdued, flittings hither and thither of mysterious shadows on the curtains, all betokened a cheerful house.

And the boy leant his head against the railing, unconscious of the drifting flakes, tired, worn, weary. The words he had used were merely to ask alms, and there was no Christmas ring in his voice. His Christmas-box was 'bread.'

His little fingers clasped the cold iron. Lower and lower those little fingers slid, till, like Enoch Arden, he at length 'fell prone;' and still the flakes of snow kept falling, falling. And there stood the cheerful-looking house, with comfort at every turn.

***

Inside that house, in a cosy room, were grouped about the fire that crackled in the grate a happy family party. An elderly lady sat on one side in an easy chair, and on the other a gentleman, perhaps a year or two older. It was easy to hazard that these two were man and wife—that from the likeness to them both in separate features the bright boy of ten that half-lounged on the hearth-rug gazing at the yule log that surmounted the coals was their son; that the fair-haired girl, who lovingly leant over the old gentleman's arm-chair, was a daughter. Two others sat a little apart, nearer to the recess of the deep-curtained window, a handsome young man of twenty-two, and a dark serpent-looking girl, just budding into womanhood; these last conversed in a low tone, the gentleman's words, though subdued, seemed earnest—the girl's, commonplace, inattentive, as though her thoughts were far away.

Mr. and Mrs. Martindale were people in comfortable circumstances. Mr. Martindale was senior partner in the firm of Martindale, Watkin, and Co., merchants. They were philanthropic people, and no deserving poor went from their door unrelieved. Their family had once consisted of a daughter and six sons; but Death, with fell typhoid in his grasp, had swept away three, and now Rose, a sweet girl of seventeen, Arthur, the boy we have seen lolling on the rug, and Ralph were the only ones left. Ralph, whom we shall presently hear of, and later on see, was the eldest, a young man of twenty-five, and at the opening of our story is far away in Australia, the great antipodean land that lies under the Southern Cross.

Ralph Martindale became enamoured of the medical profession, worked like a Trojan, and at twenty-three was a M.R.C.S. He, too, had been attacked by the fell disease before named, but his robust constitution had successfully combated it, and, following the advice of a brother student, he had taken a passage to Australia as surgeon of one of Green's passenger ships. Then the gold discovery burst like an avalanche upon the great island continent, just at the moment of Ralph's arrival in Sydney. People went mad with excitement—shops were deserted—ships forsaken —everyone was bound for the 'diggings.' Ralph Martindale, like others, caught the gold fever—the adventurous quest pleased his fancy; he threw up his engagement, and made for the fascinating spot.

The two in the recess of the window are Reginald Teale, Ralph's brother student and chum, who had advised him to try a voyage to Australia and back, the other Ada Watkin, Mr. Martindale's niece. I will not describe the characters I am presenting, further than by the few hints I have dropped. Let my reader picture to himself his fanciful portraits— perhaps taking the ideal from loved ones of his own. None so far introduced are ugly—far from it; so dispense with description of eyes, nose, mouth, teeth, or hair (description at times nauseating in its elaborate detail in many writers). Form a picture from the actions, and listen to the conversation. We shall get a start now.

***

"Father, I hate gold." It was Arthur who spoke, and a tear followed the words, spoken with an emphasis that was more striking through breaking an unusual silence of some minutes, in which all had been gazing abstractedly at the yule log. There was no answer, except a half murmur, accompanied by a sigh from the window, "So do I."

Reginald Teale caught it, though, and whispered to Ada, from whom the sigh and the words had come, "Why do you hate gold ?" "I don't know," she replied, in a dreamy way; "except," she said, recovering herself, "that gold is a source of much ill; for men will go to such fearful lengths to get it, nor stop at murder, theft,—nay, in our easy social life, deception in trifles—to secure the dross."

Ada was an heiress—the words come strangely from her. She was an orphan—an only child—and at twenty-one would have supreme right to a thousand a year.

"Yet poverty is terrible," urged Reginald.

"No doubt to some, especially to those who have known what it is to possess all that gold can buy to make life happy. Still, gold cannot purchase happiness any more than it can purchase health."

"Father, I do hate gold," repeated Arthur, annoyed that his first assertion had passed unnoticed.

"Why, Arthur?" inquired Mr. Martindale, as he playfully patted his son with his slippered foot.

"Because," replied the boy, "if it hadn't have been for this gold they have found out in Australia Ralph would have been home with us this Christmas; and look, too, he promised to bring me a kangaroo, and a parrot, and some bees that would not sting."

A general laugh followed upon the boy's words, and Rose, his sister, rallied him about a wasps' nest he had stormed some months back. Arthur rose from the hearthrug and sat down at a table, turning over a large atlas till he came to the map of Australia. In this he became absorbed, his finger tracing over the paper, evidently hunting for some particular spots.

"Do read us Ralph's letter again, father. I could listen to it again and again." This from Rose.

From Ada: "Oh do, uncle. Mr. Teale has not heard it read yet."

"I should like to hear Ralph's letter very much," said Reginald.

"I think I should like to hear it once more tonight, Mark," murmured Mrs Martindale.

"And I am never tired of reading it," put in Mr. Martindale, "though I have to wipe my glasses so often as I read the dear boy's—Well, here goes for the fifth time since it came this morning." So saying he took the letter from his breast-pocket, adjusted his spectacles, spread the sheets of thin foreign-looking paper before him, and read:—

"RALPH'S LETTER.

"Fiery Creek, New South Wales,

"July, 1852.

"My Dear Father and Mother,—Prepare yourselves for a surprise. By the heading of this letter you will see I am not on board the Statesman, but far away in the interior, far from the 'rolling sea,' and it is with some sorrow that I tell you I must spend my first Christmas away from home in the Australian bush. It was impossible to resist the temptation to go to the 'diggings.' Every day there are fresh 'finds,' business is at a standstill in the coast towns, and the bush roads leading to the locale of the discoveries are thronged with bullock-drays and swagmen on foot, pushing forward in their thirst for gold. I have thrown in my lot with an American named Reuben Grant, or 'Rube,' as he prefers to be designated. He is an old Californian digger, and we are what they call here 'mates.' We have pegged out a claim, and have sunk about 6ft., but no signs yet of the precious metal. A claim but little removed from ours has got out some fine nuggets, and we are in hopes. Oh, it is a fascinating quest—this gold-quest! What a scene! There are 4000 men here, and the cry is 'still they come.' And what a *pot pourri!*—lawyers, doctors, even clergymen, habited in moleskins, shirts, and slouch hats, baring their arms and blistering their hands delving for gold. There are storekeepers who reap a richer harvest than the goldseekers. There are loafers, idlers, blackguards, and the scum of time-expired convicts. They have a system here of letting out some convicts to service. Scores of these fellows have taken to the bush and diggings, and lead lawless lives. Police protection is perfectly inadequate; brawls are of hourly occurrence; and the sharp crack of a pistol-shot sounds ominously enough at times. Every man is armed, for life and property are not safe. Only this morning four scoundrels assembled at our claim, and made a bullying effort to jump it; but Rube was equal to the occasion. 'Look 'a here, you darned skunks, Rube Grant ain't agoing to stand nonsense from sich as you. See here,' he said, and he took a short clay pipe from his pocket. He threw the pipe up high in the air over his head, and with remarkable rapidity drew a revolver from his belt, fired, and the pipe was shattered into a thousand pieces. Without pausing he threw a half-crown piece in the same way, and the bullet, from a second discharge, sent the coin reeling from its downward course. 'See that,' he coolly said. By this time others of a better stamp had gathered round, and had applauded the exhibition of his skill. 'Now, jest listen—yes, your ears are big enough; guess Darwin would fix your ancestors sure,' this to the premier bully. 'Wal, if you and the other three black-looking sons of sin come fooling round here, I'll jest serve you as I served that 'ere pipe and half-dollar piece. Here's four left,' pointing to the remaining chambers of his piece; then to each in turn he said, 'I'll chip a slice out of your ear, close to them big bumps of destruction at back on it; and I'll jest carry away that lump of a nose o' yourn that makes you squint so bad—you would be obliged to me, you would; and you that's showing your teeth, wal, I'll shift the top row for you.' The diggers gathered round were enjoying the scene, when the fourth man, whom Rube was on the point of addressing, uttered an oath, and drew a revolver; but before he had time to pull the trigger Rube fired, and with a howl of pain the blackguard dropped his weapon. 'Reckon you won't use that digit any more to draw a barker. Say! you've got yours in advance.' Rube had smashed the ruffian's forefinger. I had been a silent and astonished spectator of the scene, albeit prepared for an emergency. The four drew away, using frightful language; he with the destroyed finger vowing vengeance. Rube only retorted with a laugh and a characteristic reply. But I anticipate trouble. These are common episodes in this great canvas town. Men bent on getting gold, and not a woman's softening face in the mass."

"What a scene!" murmured Rose.

"I hate gold," chimed in Ada.

"I love that American," cried Arthur.

"I fear for my dear Ralph," sighed Mrs. Martindale.

"Ah!" said Arthur, "Rube Grant will stick to Ralph. Papa, he could chip them away a little piece at a time, couldn't he?" And the boy's eyes sparkled.

"Go on, Mark," said the wife and mother, her voice slightly broken; "go on."

The letter was resumed—

"By the time this letter reaches you it will be Christmas, or thereabouts, and you will be all seated round the fire thinking of me, the absentee. Before that time I may make a fortune, and then 'Ho! for England.' At any rate I shall give it a fair trial. I have met here a Captain Eltham, a fine handsome man of thirty, captain in the Mounted Police, a soldierly-looking lot of men told off to escort gold, scour the country in pursuit of bushrangers, and the like. I dare say cousin Ada will be with you at Christmas time. Well, she won't have me to tease. Perhaps she will give Reginald a 'turn.' What will Rose say to that?"

Rose coloured up to the roots of her hair, and hung her head. Reginald had paid her some attention, and the girl in her heart loved him— but when the more attractive Ada came on a visit, and he saw her, his manner changed. For Ada, she amused herself with him, but this night she was 'out of sorts,' and her little coquettish heart was throbbing at the mention of the name of her cousin over the seas.

Reginald, too, felt some qualms of conscience—he felt he loved Ada Watkin, while he knew he would be wronging his friend Ralph, who had set his heart upon making his cousin his wife. Did he advise Ralph Martindale to go to Australia for a trip in order that be might have a clear field? It looked like it.

However, the reading of the letter proceeded uninterrupted by the thoughts of the listeners.

"Tell Arthur I have quite a menagerie in my tent—an emu that can pick bread from the top of my head, a tame wallaby (a small species of kangaroo), a cockatoo, and my staghound Bruce make an imposing collection. Rube says, 'Guess we'll go into the show business if we can canoe these critters over the pond.' It is uncertain when I may write next, as ships are detained for want of hands, most extraordinary wages being paid down beforehand for the run home. Goodbye, my dear father and mother, and God bless you all. I shall pop in upon you unexpectedly one fine day soon, with £50,000 at my back. Nothing less will satisfy me. Love to Rose and Arthur, and last, though not least of all, to my tantalising cousin Ada.—Believe me, ever your affectionate and dutiful son, RALPH MARTINDALE.—Give my respects, &c, to Reginald. The mailman is waiting, and Rube is singing out at the bottom of the hole like a lunatic, so I must close this, and, in his language, 'hurry up.'—R.M."

Mr. Martindale put the letter back into his pocket-book with a sigh. "Ralph is sanguine," he said; "nothing but £50,000 will suit him. Ah, well, I have had to work hard for what I am now worth, still I would not begrudge him a stroke of luck; he is a good lad, and I don't think his head will be turned by good fortune."

"Why doesn't he say what Rube wanted him for?" cried Arthur.

"The mailman was waiting," said Rose.

"Yes, and I suppose," said Reginald, "they are not like ordinary mailmen, but have many a weary mile of riding through the bush."

"I shall be anxious, most anxious, till I hear from him again. I wish he had not told us about those four wicked men," was Mrs. Martindale's plaintive remark.

There was just then a smart knock at the room door, and a trim parlour-maid, in neat cap and apron, entered.

"Please, sir," said the girl, "there's a poor boy lying outside the railings, a'most covered up with snow. Jane thinks the poor soul is froze to death."

"Good gracious!" cried Mr. Martindale, as he and Reginald rose from their seats, "Let us go at once and see."

"O bring him in here, papa," exclaimed Rose.

"Be sure, Rose, your papa will not leave anyone to perish," said her mother.

The two gentlemen went out into the night together, and presently returned, Reginald carrying in his arms the inanimate body of the boy we saw in the opening of this story. There was no sign of life in his frail form, his hair was wet, and his little jacket and trousers were covered with the snow, which in the heat of the room quickly melted and dripped upon the carpet. They laid him gently upon the handsome couch, regardless of the injury his wet clothes would do it, and the tender women gathered around him, murmuring "Poor child," "Poor boy," "Is he dead?" They removed his much-worn boots, and chafed his feet and hands, while Mr. Martindale took from the sideboard a decanter of brandy, and poured a goodly quantity down the lad's throat. This was effective, and presently they had the satisfaction of seeing him open his eyes, and draw a deep sigh.

"Where am I?" he asked feebly.

"With friends, my poor boy," replied Mr. Martindale. "How came you to be lying there in the snow?"

"I dunno, sir," said the boy. "I must be agoing, sir. Poor mother will be awful cut up cause I'm away so long. She's sick, sir, and hungry, and"—the boy burst into tears.

"You shall go to her, my boy, as soon as you have had something to eat to strengthen you," said Mrs. Martindale, and she despatched the servant to the kitchen with a whispered instruction.

"I ain't 'ad nothing to eat since yesterday, ma'am, but I couldn't touch anything till mother 'ad some."

"But as soon as you are recovered and have a little food you will be better able to take something to your mother; and some of us will go with you; and if she is in want of anything it shall be got for her," kindly said Mr. Martindale.

"God bless you, sir. What a funny taste there is in my mouth! Have you been giving me physic, sir?"

"No, child; only a little brandy, which did you good."

"Brandy, sir!" cried the boy, as he raised himself on one arm, "O, why did you give me that brandy? O, lor, I'd sooner have died than had brandy. I knelt by mother's bedside, sir, when littler than now, and swore that drink should never pass my lips, never; and now I've broke it—and mother, sir, she prayed to God to give me strength to keep my pledge. O, why did you give me brandy, sir?"

"Nay, child," said the old gentleman, "it was not your fault—you have not broken your pledge; besides, it perhaps saved your life."

"No, sir, I can't believe it saved my life. O, sir, if you knew the curse of the stuff! Brandy sent my father across the sea a convict to Australia. Nothing but the drink, sir, made him do what he did."

At the mention of Australia the little group were interested.

"Yes, sir," the boy went on unasked, "we was pretty comfortable, father working in a fittingshop; but he got into bad company, and took to drink. He got out of employment, and things went awful bad. Father he got reckless, and didn't care how things went so long as he got drink.

He went from bad to worse, and he got mixed up in a burglary. They took him, sir, and he got ten years, and was sent out to Australia. He's done about six now. I was only five year old, then, but I shan't forget it, sir, never; and it broke poor mother's heart, a'most. Now she's sick, and we ain't got fire nor food. O! it was all the drink. O, why did you give me brandy, sir?"

They cheered him, and diverted the conversation, asking him his name, and where he lived. His name he said was Stephen Bland. "Mother," he went on, "always calls me 'Stephen;' but the boys calls me 'Stiff-un,' or 'Stiff'—I mostly gets Stiff—and we live in a room in Chancery-lane."

Just then the girl entered with some soup which had been made hot, and bread, Mrs. Martindale rightly thinking that something light would suit the boy's empty stomach. 'Stiff' was with difficulty persuaded to partake of it, and then only when he was assured that a basket of food was being prepared for him to take home. Then he greedily devoured it as if in a hurry to get away with the promised gift. A basket plentifully stocked was speedily prepared, and a suit of Arthur's put in to replace 'Stiff's' wet things. He stubbornly refused to change till he got home. Mr. Martindale and Reginald proposed going with the lad to his home, and donned their overcoats. Rose and Ada wanted much to accompany them, but were denied; they would go on the morrow.

'Stiff' expressed his thanks for all this kindness in his characteristic way, and the three set out for Mrs. Bland's room in Chancery-lane.

Chapter II

"Coo-ee, coo-ee; hurry up, hurry up! Hi, Ralph! Ralph! What in thunder keeps yer? Reckon you were born in bits, and put together by contract. Shoo! this is a 'find,' and no darned bunkum. Blame me ef I can get it out. But here, hold on, Rube Grant—Snakes! You'll have to pop the break on and go slow. 'T won't do to let these ere coons know this, or, by Jerusalem, our lives ain't worth a popcorn. Shoo! Guess I'll jest cover this up again for the present."

The reader will rightly judge that we have moved the scene to Australia, back to the time of Ralph's writing his letter introduced in the last chapter; and that the speaker is the genial American Reuben Grant.

Rube covered this up, scrambled out of the hole, and walked in the direction of their tent. The mailman galloped away, Ralph Martindale came out of the tent, and the two mates met each other.

Ralph Martindale was a young man of medium height, strongly built, with nut-brown hair that curled and festooned about a handsome face. Reuben Grant was a tall lean man, with light straight hair, sharp features, small deeply-set eyes, and wore upon his chin only a tuft of stumpy beard that looked as if it had been chopped.

"What were you singing out for, Rube? I was just finishing my letter for home, and it's on the way now, old man, for Peter was late, and he's putting on steam!"

"Wal, I've got some news for yer," replied Rube, "that might have gone in that letter that would make the old folks' hair curl, I opine. Guess, Ralph, my lad, we're in it right up to the chin; O, yes, we're soused, sure."

"What do you mean? What are you talking about?" queried the other.

"That's it; I don't know. But jest come along o' me, and we'll investigate. But keep a sharp lookout none o' those devil's imps are squinting around. I might as well have the six."

So saying, Rube proceeded to load the chambers of the revolver he had discharged in his exhibition of skill in his 'finger trick,' as he called the destruction of the ruffian's digit.

Arrived at the hole, Rube jumped down—it was only some 6ft. deep—and let his tongue wag to the following strain:—"Say, Ralph, have you got a brace of goggles? Blue or green ones would be best, because you'll go stone blind when you cast your optics on this—I swear by Jonathan's eagle. See here, but jest cast a look round. Don't let any o' those skulkers spot us; so give 'crow' if you see any of 'em smelling about; guess we'd have 'em round us like blowflies. You dangle your feet over the edge and sit unconcerned-like, as though you didn't care a tinker's curse whether you struck gold or not."

Ralph obeyed, wondering and expectant, for he began to have an inkling that Rube had some great surprise in store for him. Rube quickly threw aside the dirt, and displayed to Ralph's astonished gaze a massive nugget embedded in the earth.

"Look at that!" quoth Rube. "Just gaze—jest regard it! I can't move it. See! we don't see it all,' and he cleared the soil away round it and showed that the huge lump expanded as he got down.

"By Jehoshophat, there's a hundredweight if there's an ounce!"

Ralph had dropped mechanically into the hole, and was literally mute with astonishment. He stooped down and examined the irregular block. It was almost entirely of gold.

"Now see here, Ralph, we must just be spry; I tell you I ain't been in California for nothing. Do you just take the shotgun with a sack; you'll find some black swans up by Blood Creek; jest you knock over a couple or so, put 'em in the sack, and make tracks back here. Now, don't stand shilly-shallying, but go right off; we've got four hours' daylight. I'll stop here and play 'possum.'"

Used to his mate's ways, Ralph did as directed—got the gun and sack, and set out, first commanding his dog Bruce to keep guard over the tent. Meantime Rube remained at the hole. A digger or two passed and stopped to say a word or so, such as "Got any colour ?" "Any luck?"

"Colour! Nary a colour," Rube answered snappishly, savagely striking the sides with his shovel. "Luck? Freeze me, but luck has deserted this chicken ever since I left San Francisco." Once more alone, he continued,

"But now it has come in a big dose to make up for it."

In about an hour Ralph returned with three black swans in his primitive game bag.

"You see," said Rube, "you are going to stuff these for the old folks at home, Ralph. Pitch down the bag and let's have this out quick. You keep a lookout."

Rube quickly had the block of gold cleared round, and, prizing it up with his pickaxe with an effort, it rolled over. If the two friends were astonished before, they were electrified now. The nugget weighed fully 1¾cwt.—subsequently they found it weighed 2345oz., consecutive figures. It was as much as the two men could do to lift it into the bag. This done, Rube threw a black swan in after it, and, shouldering the burden with Ralph's assistance, walked as quickly as he could to the tent.

"Jest get back to the claim, Ralph; I'll plant this."

Ralph, with mixed feelings of wonder and delight, obeyed. Rube thereupon dug a hole inside the tent large enough to contain the treasure, deposited it therein; then spread the sack over the place, with the swan lying on the sack. But when Rube got back to his mate it was his turn to be surprised. Ralph was down on his knees groping about with his hands.

"Say, Ralph," cried Rube, "fossicking? Ain't that enough?"

"Enough!" rejoined Ralph: "why, Rube, there's a regular nest—look!" He lifted his hat, which was lying on the earth, and displayed a nugget weighing, as was afterwards found, 22oz.

"By thunder!" exclaimed Rube, "that'll be useful for a blind."

"But this is not all either," cried the excited Ralph. Nor was it. It appeared as though a massive rock of gold had been severed into seven different pieces of nearly equal sizes—one, the weight of which has been given, and which Rube had planted in the tent, and no less than six others, which the now half-demented men unearthed and transferred to the tent with a black swan as before; and, as before, Rube disposed of it, leaving Ralph in the hole with the smallest nugget as Rube's 'blind.' Partly exhausted with his labours and excitement, Rube on his return leant his back against the side and gave vent to his feeling. "Wal, I guess those beauties we grubbed up last will turn the scale at 2000oz." It proved afterwards that the six nuggets weighed respectively 1800oz.—a monster in truth—286oz., 150oz., 147oz., and 22oz, the blind; though why Rube called it the 'blind' Ralph could only conjecture. Thus the grand total of this unparalleled find amounted to 4850oz.—a fortune for each.

"Guess, Ralph, this is Aladdin licked; say, isn't it all a dream? No, damned if it is; there's the black swans, sure, and there's the 'blind'."

"What do you mean by the 'blind?'" said Ralph.

"Well," replied Rube, "you Britishers are obtuse. 'Taint in reason to suppose that this hole's got any more like this. Anyhow, we've got enough, I reckon, and 'twill be best for us to 'clear.' Now, don't you see, we can let it be known we've got this nugget, 'cause they'll know we can't shift without the 'chips.' Wal, don't you see, we can fossick a bit longer, sell out cause you want to get home to your people—that's our yarn—and I, wal, I'm sick of the business, you see. We'll sell the claim for a good figure, and the next thing's to get them lumps safe down to Melbourne—see?" Ralph nodded in the affirmative. "Now, listen; we'll just skin them swans you're going to take home; so let's get back to the tent. Bruce is holding guard there, and I reckon he'll give tongue if anyone's skulking around."

At this moment a digger came on the scene, a good-natured open-countenanced fellow, and bade them "Good evening, mates; what luck?"

"Guess we've got a start," said Rube, and he held up 'the blind.' The digger's eyes sparkled as they only can when the virgin gold is found.

"Phew! a good start, too," he cried. "There's a pound and a-half, if there's a pennyweight." He sang out to a mate, who came up; the news spread, and very soon quite a crowd collected round the friends' claim.

Many good offers were made to buy right off, but Rube affected caution. "Look here, mates, this 'ere youngster he's anxious to get home to his mam—leastways he was—'cause the old man's getting shaky, and likely to pass in his cheques. We were getting disgusted, but I reckon we'll try this a bit longer now."

Ralph and the American were popular on the field, and were known as 'The Jack-Stripes'—probably given in the sense of the two national flags, 'The Union Jack' and the 'Stars and Stripes.'

Well, a day or two passed on; the swans were skinned, also a kangaroo, possum, native bear, &c. Ralph and Rube worked with apparent industry at the claim, and found a small nugget, weighing about an ounce and a-half. This Rube considered a favourable opportunity for moving. He gave out that "the youngster was homesick and tired of the game; that the old man had plenty of coin, and there was no good in his wasting his time here. The old man wanted to see him 'afore he died. Guess we'll come back again and try our luck." The explanation was satisfactory. The claim was purchased for a good sum, and repaid its purchaser next day, at which Rube pretended to be awfully cut up.

The 'blind' nugget was sold to a storekeeper, and now every preparation was made for departure. It was the evening before in their tent; and Rube and Ralph were discussing their plans. A dray was going down to Melbourne on the morrow, and they had agreed with the owner to accompany him. Many a digger in those days preferred to carry his own gold with him in preference to entrusting it to an escort—for it was no uncommon occurrence for the escort to be attacked and overpowered by the lawless bands that infested the country; again, too, many a poor fellow had perished whose fate never became known. Ralph and Rube had sold their tent and gold-digging implements, &c, and a couple of chests and their blankets constituted their luggage.

"You see," said Rube, "we'll stuff them nuggets into the swans, and sew 'em up. We must be careful to let 'em down easy, as if they was light."

This had been the substance of the conversation throughout the night, spoken in whispers—their plans—and they proceeded to put them into execution. Very cautiously the precious lumps were sewn strongly into skins, first being surrounded with sacking; and Rube practised carrying them so an not to betray their weight. They were finishing their task, when Bruce raised his nose from the ground, and gave a low angry growl. Rube laid his hand on his revolver, and started to his feet. Presently the dog laid his nose down, only to raise it quickly again with a growl more angry than before. Rube and Ralph lifted up the canvas, and peered out into the night. It was dark as Erebus, and nothing could be distinguished.

"Bruce don't talk for nothing," said the American.

"Some late night-bird staggering to his tent after a booze, or maybe only a possum," remarked Ralph.

Soon the circumstance was dismissed, and the two friends lay down, their revolvers handy, with the faithful staghound nestling his honest snout to his master's breast.

***

If the reader had, about an hour after Rube and Ralph had settled down to rest, visited a lonely spot, rock-bound and tree-bound, about two miles from the outskirts of the goldfield, he would have seen seven men lying or sitting round a small fire, smoking but engaging in conversation, at times loud, at times low and fierce, but throughout liberally bespattered with oaths. Four of these men we have seen before, and one especially can be recognised by his bandaged finger. Rube had done his work well, and that finger was not likely to pull trigger more. Two others, beetle-browed and heavy-bearded, are the premier scoundrels—the 'Simon pure,' who dictate, and swear, and bluster, who are ready to cut a throat at a moment's notice, who have the life instinct of brutes, for their lives are priced; they are outlaws—'Black Ben' and 'Devil Jack.' The seventh man is of a much milder type—nay, there was something gentle at times in his manner, though he appeared to be under the thumb of the rest, looked down upon, and treated with contempt.

"I tell you," said he of the finger, "I was close to the tent. I saw them sewing the gold up in the black swan skins—as much as they could lift— and the Yankee (here a frightful anathema on Rube's head) practised how to carry them without showing up."

"How much gold was there?" asked Black Ben.

"They could scarcely lift it, I tell ye; there were three skins full, bulged out, and they'd got a rope round it inside, holding it up and passing through to the legs. There must ha' been over 2cwt. and more."

More oaths followed this announcement.

"When do they start? Which way do they go?"

"They start tomorrow with Hurworth's dray; they'll go down the old track, sure, till they come to Bill's, of Bang Bang."

"He's right," put in Devil Jack.

"One of us must go ahead right off to put Bill up to it, and spoil the dray," said Black Ben. "How many are there of 'em?"

"Hurworth, the Yankee, and the young fellow."

The leaders laughed.

"Easy game," cried Black Ben.

"The Yankee is a terror (more oaths), and can hit a pin's head. D—n him, I'd like to 'pink' him for that," holding up his finger.

"You'll have a chance," sneered Devil Jack: "but look—Steve here must go right away and see Bill"—Steve is the quiet seventh man described—"and look here," the speaker added with a savage oath, "if you play false, I'll have a look at that white liver of yours," and he drew a knife that had murder in its very sheen.

"What do you take me for?" retorted Steve, with well-feigned indignation, though the colour left his cheeks at the threat.

"We take you for a cur that's greedy for gold, but gets sick at the sight of the ruby," cried Black Ben; "but, curse you, if you peach I'll cut your wagging tongue out, and make you eat it with salt and mustard; I will, by—"

The man said he would perform his part faithfully, and with many additional oaths and threats his instructions were given him, and he took his departure. An hour later the six ruffians left their encampment and dispersed.

What their plans and movements were will be explained in proper time.

They might well doubt Steve. Bad he was and had been, but he owed Reuben Grant and Ralph Martindale a debt of gratitude—nothing less than his life. He had been accused of stealing gold—things looked bad against him—the miners were furious—many robberies had been committed, and no redress could be obtained. A very great number of Californian diggers were on the ground, and the cry of 'Judge Lynch' was raised. Steve was seized, the rope put about his neck, and he was just about to be swung off, when Rube Grant stepped forward, followed by Ralph, and said he "warn't quite satisfied about it," and begged for a quarter of an hour's wait. It was a question of the time when this robbery was committed. The principal witness swore positively to the time and hour when he was absent, and during which the property had been stolen.

"Wal," said Rube, "I wasn't quite certain of the man, but I guess I ain't far wrong. Say, stranger," this to Steve; "you asked me to loan you a knife to cut some tobacco on that day at Dead Man's Gully, just about that time too, I reckon."

A gleam of hope shot into the man's eyes as he quickly answered, "Yes."

"Wal, I was kind o' bothered at the time, and didn't take much notice, but you might ha' returned the knife. Have you got it about your clothes?"

Steve dived into his pocket and produced a large dagger knife. The American took it, and said: "Guess that's the toothpick, 'Reuben Grant' on the handle. See, gentlemen, that was at Dead Man's Gully, twenty miles away, and my mate here can prove it."

Of course Steve was let loose, not without some expressions of discontent from a few bloodthirsty ones. Steve then owed them his life, and he was determined to foil his associates, though their threats were yet ringing in his ears.

***

Our two friends had proceeded on their way for some forty odd miles without anything extraordinary happening. Hurworth had a good team of horses (eight), a valuable property in those days, when bullocks were the usual draught animals used. Watch and watch had been kept during the night. Rube and Ralph were not going to be robbed of their treasure for want of precaution. Hurworth was not aware of the value of his passengers' property. They determined to suitably reward him on safe arrival in Melbourne; but, although the man was thoroughly honest, they deemed it more prudent to say nothing, for, doubtless, he would be alarmed at the risk. However, an event occurred which necessitated their taking him into their confidence. They had approached a spot where the road wound round a hill studded with huge boulders.

"Likely spot this," said Rube, "for bushrangers."

"You may say that," said the teamster. "It was just here that 'Bloody Jack' and his gang were wiped out."

"Where are we going to camp tonight?" asked Ralph.

"We'll make Billy's, at Bang Bang, about sundown," replied Hurworth, "and camp about two miles further on, where there's good water. I can't say I care much about Billy. I fancy he's mixed up with a lot of these characters, and I am always glad to get away with the horses from his neighbourhood."

As he spoke a man stepped suddenly from behind a boulder and advanced towards the team. It was Steve.

Rube laid his hand on his revolver, and accosted the new-comer: "Wal, mate, what's your game now? Guess I seen you afore, when you were likely to dance on a floor as no boards could make. You had a nasty feeling about your neck that time."

"And that's why I'm here," returned Steve. "You saved my life, and I want to save yours now. Turn for turn. Oh, I know you are incredulous. I've been a bad un. I once was a good man, with a loving wife and child—they may be living now; I hope to God they are: and please God if ever I see them again they'll find Stephen Bland a good man again." He then briefly recounted the plan to rob and, if need, murder them, adding, "my life is not worth an hour's purchase if I desert them, but I don't care. I shall desert them. I'm going to start good from this hour. I've got my ticket-of-leave with three years to run, so if you gentlemen—for you are gentlemen—will accept me I'll make one on your side."

The man spoke calmly, and carried conviction to his hearers, but Rube was not quite satisfied. Hurworth was intensely surprised when he heard of the wealth, and seriously alarmed, too; but he was a brave man, nevertheless, and the three set about concocting some plan to defeat the ruffians. Steve said the attack was to be made after leaving Bang Bang, and that he was to instruct Bill to lame the horses, take out the pins of the wheels, &c.

Ralph advised that Steve be trusted, and Rube at last consented, though he quietly told him that the slightest appearance of betrayal would be followed by instant death.

"So they know that the gold is in the swan skins, do they?" asked Rube. Steve answered in the affirmative.

In reply to Rube, Steve said he had a revolver.

"Wal," said Rube, "look here, boys, jest lend me a hand, and we'll shift this stuffing, and put some good-sized stones in instead; there's no time to lose." The gold was removed, and placed in the chests. The teamster was thunderstruck, and Steve's eyes glistened so as to draw a remark from Rube.

"Don't feel satisfied, eh? Wish you'd a kept to your mates, eh? Good haul, eh? By thunder, if you show false I'll put the first bullet through you, so don't forget it."

"You shall have a good reward, both of you," said Ralph, "if we get all right to Melbourne."

Heavy stones were put inside the skins, and they were sewn up more carefully and strongly than before. All this took time. Hurworth was asked what was the best course to be pursued, to touch at Bang Bang or strike off.

"Well, I wonder," said Hurworth "at Black Ben or Devil Jack venturing near Bang Bang. Eltham and his troopers have a notion that they're hereabouts, and are running them up. They've got two smart trackers with 'em; and they'll be worth nabbing; there's £500 offered for Ben, and the same for Jack. The escort will be down this way tomorrow, too."

"By thunder," exclaimed Rube, "let's go right on; blame it, we'll fool 'em yet. I don't see we can do better—these darned wheels will show tracks like a line o' rails. See here, jest follow my advice. I've got a spare pair of revolvers, so've you, Ralph; jest load them up, and plant the others handy in the dray, out of sight. Guess if these fellows are worth £1000 we might as well box them if we can."

This was done, and they proceeded on their way. Suddenly Rube gave utterance to an oath, a thing he seldom did.

"Cuss me, he's gone;" Steve had slipped unperceived off into the bush. The men looked blankly at each other. What was to be done ? The transfer of the gold would be known. Rube bit his lip; they were but a mile from Bang Bang. A halt was called, and the dray taken off the road into the bush. Presently Steve reappeared, and explained that for the safety of his own life he could not venture near Bang Bang, but would assist from the outside when least expected. He said he had taken a short cut through the bush, and had approached close to the shanty to *reconnoitre*; the men were already there, concealed in the house. He swore he had had no communication with them, but had gathered that they were in a flurry, as the troopers were scouring the country all round. They were in a hurry to get the job over.

"Well, darn me if I know whether to trust you or not, but, anyhow, we ain't going to be stopped, so come on."

Steve assured them that he would be there in the time of need, and disappeared once more.

"Look here, these fellers will be in a hurry to get, so if they demand our arms jest give 'em up innocent like, and play skunk. We've got the others planted handy."

They approached a deep gully, with dense bush on either side of the track. Rube had scarcely spoken when seven men sprang simultaneously from the bush, and covered the three with their revolvers. Indeed, so taken by surprise were they that Rube's instructions were superfluous; they were completely at the mercy of the ruffians; Steve was not there; the seventh man was Billy.

With a volley of oaths their arms were demanded and given up, the American saying, "Wal, I guess we're euchred this time."

"Aye, and here's change for your spoiling my hand you—," cried the man whom we may style 'Finger,' raising his revolver.

"Stop that!" shouted Black Ben; "the traps are not far off; do you want to bring them down on us? Fetch them horses, smart, now!"

The horses were quickly brought from their concealment, the black swans lifted out of the dray, and, placing them in front of them, the bushrangers rode rapidly off into the bush, leaving a swarm of oaths and threats behind them. Rube, Ralph, and the teamster looked at each other for a few minutes. The gang were far off by this. A broad grin spread over Rube's countenance, and simultaneously the trio burst into an uncontrollable fit of laughter.

"I'd like to see them rip up them birds," said Rube. "Say, won't they chew. Guess the coon that told them about it'll get snakes."

"They'll return when they find out their mistake," said Hurworth.

"That' so; but we'll get a good start," cried Rube.

"And we may drop across Eltham and his troopers," put in Ralph.

The horses were put to their best pace, and about a mile further on they came upon Steve, who said that the gang had taken to the ranges, and would not stop to examine their booty till they had reached one of their lairs, of which he knew.

This proved to be correct, and good progress was made during the next two days. They were beginning to think they would be no more troubled. Steve felt sure that Black Ben would not give up the chase—his savage nature would be roused to fury. Hurworth confirmed the opinion.

"Wal, boys," said Rube, "we've got to fight this time, anyhow; they'll think we're unarmed, so won't be so particular in coming down on us."

Rube instructed the others what to do in case of attack. What follows took less time to enact than it takes now to describe.

They had emerged from the ordinary gum-studded bush into a little open ground, when they heard the noise of horses' feet behind them, and saw the seven ruffians coming at top speed towards them, shouting and brandishing their weapons. The four men sprang from the dray and made for a clump of trees a few paces away. Hurworth's team stopped dead, and remained so during the whole of the scene. Rube's conjecture was right. The gang, thinking them defenceless, came up with a shout of triumph, and flung themselves from their horses, but scarcely had 'Finger' put his foot to the ground, when he fell, pierced through the heart. The American's bullet had struck home. Three other shots followed in quick succession, and two more ruffians bit the dust—one dead, the other badly hit on the knee. Devil Jack rushed forward with a savage oath, firing his revolver rapidly at Steve, who was not so well protected by a tree as his companions. Steve fell with a heavy groan. Devil Jack was hit on the elbow, and dropped his weapon. At this moment a stentorian voice shouted, "Surrender in the Queen's name!" Half-a-dozen troopers dashed up. The bushrangers were ridden down and securely handcuffed, and all in the space of a few minutes.

"Smart work! How are you off for black swan? Say, mate, how did yer enjoy the stuffing?" said Rube to Black Ben, who was foaming at the mouth like a wild beast.

"Thank you, Captain Eltham," cried Ralph, holding out his hand to the leader of the troop, a fine military-looking man of thirty; "thank you. Your assistance was well timed."

"What, Martindale!" exclaimed the officer, "This is a pleasure, to think I should be of service to you. I'm delighted. Well, yes, perhaps it was just as well we struck you, but," with a glance at the two dead out-laws, "you don't seem to have been doing very badly."

"Guess we'd ha' pulled through, Cap'n," cried Rube. "Say! This poor fellow is hit bad," pointing to Steve, who was half sitting up, supported against a tree, while the teamster was giving him a drink from his water-bag. The officer approached Steve, and scanned him closely.

"I know this man," he said. "He must have recently joined the gang. Fool! I thought there was a chance of reformation for him. He's got his ticket, and would soon be a free man."

They explained the part Steve had taken in the scenes described, upon which Captain Eltham said, "Then I'll see that his pardon is recommended to the proper quarter."

"Wal, I reckon he'll get his pardon from a higher court, Cap'n," quoth Rube. "I surmise he's got notice to quit."

"Nothing of the kind," said Ralph, examining the wound. "The bullet has struck the chest, missed the lung, though, and passed out at the top of the shoulder."

True enough, a small hole in the man's coat showed where the bullet had made its exit. Here Ralph's professional skill was of good service.

Ralph gave the Captain a particular account of their leaving the diggings, and the two mates were censured for being so foolhardy.

"However," he added, "you'll have a safe escort now. I shall take these men right on to Melbourne, where they can be identified. I've been after them for some time."

The two dead outlaws were buried without ceremony, and the party encamped for the night after seeing to the two wounded men.

At daybreak a move was made, and after easy travelling Melbourne was safely reached. The great find of the two friends, coupled with the capture of the desperate outlaws, made a great stir in Melbourne, and Ralph and his mate came in for a vast deal of attention. The teamster and Steve, too, were not overlooked. The latter recovered, and the Governor was advised to recommend the Crown to pardon him. There was much delay about this, Sydney having to be communicated with, and finally the Home Authorities. Ralph wanted to take him home with them, but was impatient of delay. The teamster was handsomely rewarded. Ralph and Rube sold their gold, and each had a draft on London for over £10,000. They refused to participate in the rewards for assisting in the capture of the bushrangers, who were all hanged. Ralph made Steve promise that the moment he was pardoned he would make for England, where honest employment would be found him.

The two friends had to wait some months before getting a suitable vessel, and what with getting dismasted, becalmed, and other casualties, another Christmas will be close upon them before the reader sees them at the conclusion of this story.

Chapter III, and Last

We left Mr. Martindale and Reginald Teale departing on their errand of mercy with 'Stiff' to visit his mother. They found the poor woman in a pitiable condition, but it was evidently weakness caused by want of proper nourishment. There was no fire in the grate on this bitterly cold night, and a single blanket (and that a thin one) was her only bed-covering. 'Stiff' threw himself on his mother's breast, and poured out his grateful heart in praise of Mr. and Mrs. Martindale's kindness. The delicate woman brushed the hair from his forehead, and printed a kiss there. Then he told her about the brandy, but said, "Mother, I never knowed;" and she, smiling, consoled him. Hanging fondly about her, 'Stiff' watched her eat a few slices of bread and butter—long privation had made her stomach too weak for strong food. A little soup seemed to put a new life into her. Mr. Martindale sent 'Stiff' down for the landlady, who came up all smiles to the "gentlemen". She commiserated the "poor dear"—not two hours ago she had threatened to turn her out into the street. Mr. Martindale told her to light a fire in the grate directly, and, after inquiry, paid a month's rent, telling her that she was to look after her till she got strong. Mr. Martindale and Reginald then sallied forth with 'Stiff,' and returned with that now happy urchin laden with groceries, candles, and many comforts, not omitting to mention blankets. Mrs. Bland thanked her benefactors with tears of gratitude, and the gentlemen took their departure, promising to send the ladies on the morrow— Christmas Day. The promise was kept, and the poor mother and son were happier than they had been for many a long day.

Mr. Martindale took 'Stiff' into his office as a messenger, and the lad's heart throbbed with gratitude. Neither did he betray the trust reposed in him. He proved himself sharp, willing, and was a favourite with all. So nearly a year sped away, and no news came from Australia. It was getting near to another Christmas.

Reginald Teale made no progress with Ada, whose heart was over the sea. Rose pined in secret, grateful even for a smile, and ready to throw herself into the arms of the man she loved. But there came a day when a fearful commercial storm burst with fury over the great merchant princes of London and Manchester. The rotten trees went down like ninepins, the sturdy ones that had stood many an angry blast trembled and tottered, and some even fell with a mighty crash, crushing and tearing others in their fall. The house of Martindale, Watkin. and Co. felt the hurricane in all its power, and was staggering—was falling. Heavy bills were falling due, and nothing could save it. Its utmost resources were taxed—the banks were paralysed, and refused their aid.

More than this, Mr. Martindale and Mr. Watkin (another uncle), as Ada's trustees, had invented large sums in the firm's speculations, and should the house fail there would ensue dire loss, and a vast curtailment in the young lady's fortune. This caused great grief to Mr. Martindale.

He and his wife were seated in the library; he had taken her into his counsels. She, poor soul, felt the coming crash keenly; but, like a true woman, soothed her husband with cheering words of hope.

"Never mind, Mark, we can live quietly as we did in our happy honeymoon days."

"My own true wife!" was all that the heartbroken man could utter. There was gloom throughout the erstwhile pleasant home; the very domestics seemed to be aware of the nearing calamity, and in the kitchen many a homely sentence of genuine sympathy was spoken for the poor master and mistress. The morrow would come. The morrow would see bills for £15,000 presented to be dishonoured—an amount that a month ago the firm could have pitched into the street and never missed it; but now all were holding on, and heavy losses through others' failures had shaken Martindale, Watkin, and Co. to their foundation. Yet there was vitality enough in it to rise Phoenix-like and be stronger than ever could £15,000 be but raised by tomorrow's morn.

It was 7 in the evening, quite dark, for it wonted but a few days to Christmas. Mr. Martindale sat alone in his library; his wife had gone to look after her children, and keep the sad news from them as long as possible. They would know soon enough.

The garden at the back of the house extended a long way, and was terminated by a high wall. Over this wall two figures cautiously clambered.

"Come on," said one, "there's a big drop here. Look out you don't go through the cucumber frame."

"Guess I don't want to," said the other. "I reckon it'll take me some time to pick the glass out of my pants. Great Scott! what do they sow broken bottles on stone walls for?—they're darned inconvenient. Great Caesar's ghost!" The speaker flopped right upon the cucumber frame. A hearty burst of laughter greeted his mishap. "Consarn you, you laughing jackass—it's painful."

"So it is, *pane*ful," retorted the other, with another laugh.

"Say! this is worse than mosquitoes, and soldier ants are a fool to it. This comes of burglarising."

Of course Rube and Ralph are recognised. Ralph had persuaded his friend to spend the Christmas with him, and his joyous mischievous nature had prompted him to enter thus stealthily to give his relatives a happy surprise.

The pair stole softly down the walks, Ralph leading the way, past the familiar wicket-gate, past the outbuildings to a door which he opened, and they were at the foot of a flight of stairs that ascended from a spacious lobby. Through this lobby Ralph moved quickly, beckoning his companion to follow. There was no sound in the house; Ralph knew that the family would be gathered in the cheerful rooms at the other end of the house, and made his way along the passage. He had to pass the library, and he softly opened the door and peeped in. The light was turned down a little, but he could see a well-known form seated at the table with his head buried in his hands on the table. He quickly stepped inside. Rube following. Ralph walked rapidly but noiselessly to the table—his father was sobbing. In an instant his arms were round his father's form.

"Father! Father! It is I, your son Ralph."

The old man bounded to his feet, and with a cry "My son! My son!" fell upon his breast. Reuben Grant stood in the background, a quiet but not unmoved spectator of the scene.

In a moment or so Mr. Martindale regained his composure. Ralph turned up the light. Rube was forgotten.

"But, father," said Ralph, "you were weeping. Mother—"

"Is well—all are well; but, my boy, tomorrow will see the old firm of Martindale, Watkin, and Co. posted as bankrupts."

"Is that all ?" cried Ralph; "what sum will save it?"

"Alas! more than I can raise. Vast failures have shaken us, and £15,000 alone can carry us through this unparalleled commercial storm."

Ralph pulled out his pocket-book, and took from it some bills, which he placed and spread on the table before Mr. Martindale.

"There, my dear father," he cried, "are bills for over £10,000. Take them."

"And if that won't do, old man, jest add another £10,000 to it, and you'll confer a favour on yours truly, Reuben Grant;" and the great-hearted American thumped his bills on the table.

Ralph grasped his friend's hand.

"There, Ralph, none o' that; bless yer, I don't think nothing on it. It's jest as well invested in the old man's concern, and God bless him, too!"

How can we describe the joy of that Christmas gathering? Mr. Martindale went gaily into the sitting-room, where all were assembled, and surprised his wife by his altered manner.

"Who do you think is here?" he cried.

"Ralph!" came from every throat.

They had just been speaking of him. Ralph bounded into the room, and was besieged and overwhelmed with kisses and tears of joy.

Poor Rube stood in the background as before; and a tear glistened in his eye. It was many a long year since he had sat at the 'old man's' fireside.

Mr. Martindale, when matters had settled a little, introduced him as Ralph's dear friend and his benefactor.

"O, go slow, Mr. Martindale; reckon I'm not used to this sort of thing—it kinder brings the water up about my eyes. I ain't seen my folks for many a long year—maybe they're passed out. But I guess after this I'll go and hunt them up."

Arthur clung to the American with boyish pride as his brother's noble friend,

"Mr. Rube," said the lad, "tell me, please, did you 'carry away the bridge of that man's nose?'—and did you 'shift the top row of the other's teeth?'"

"What do you mean, youngster?" kindly answered Rube.

Ralph recalled the incident, and explained that he had mentioned it in his letter; whereupon he laughed, and said, "O, no, but they got rubbed out by-and-bye. Ralph has got a lot to tell you about black swans, too."

"Father," said Ralph, "Rube wants to know why you sow broken bottles on the top of your wall?"

"Come, Ralph, that's too bad!" and the scaling of the garden wall was recounted to the infinite amusement of them all, for the American kept putting in some dry remark that added to the merriment. Presently there came a knock at the door, and little 'Stiff' entered, and respectfully stood hat in hand.

"Well, Stephen," said Mr. Martindale, "what is it?"

"Please, sir, I wasn't quite sure whether you asked me to come here first thing before I go to the office?"

"Yes, Stephen, come here on your way."

"Very well, sir; good night, ladies—good night, gentlemen," and the smart healthy lad turned to leave.

Rube had fixed his eyes on the boy as soon as he heard the name, and when he spoke he never took them off.

"Hold on, boy! Hold on! Hang me—excuse me, ladies—but, say, boy, what's your name ?"

"Stephen Bland, sir."

"Darn me if I didn't think so. Say, your father's in Australia, ain't he?"

The poor boy burst into tears.

"Nay, youngster," and the genial Rube placed his hand upon his shoulder; "nay, I didn't mean to make you pipe, my poor lad, I've got some—say, take me—your mother's alive."

Mr. Martindale answered for the sobbing boy.

"Wal, take me right away to her. I've got some news for her that'll add ten years to her life, and I ain't going to waste an hour. Come along. Excuse me, I'll see yer again; but, darn me, I want to make this wife a trifle happy."

And he did. He told her how her husband was to be pardoned, and would shortly be home again, a changed man. How Ralph and he were going to get him something to do, and many other things that carried comfort to that half-widowed heart.

"It was the drink, sir. Stephen was a good husband, and I don't believe he knew what he was doing when he was taken."

Martindale, Watkin, and Co. stood the storm; their credit was enhanced; and soon the firm, like a staggered vessel, shook the angry seas from her sides, and sailed into smooth waters with a fine breeze to the haven of increased prosperity.

Reginald tacitly resigned Ada when he saw his cause was hopeless, and began to see beauties in Rose. Poor Rose was too happy to have him once more; and so matters were going smoothly.

Rube spent the Christmas with his friend Ralph, and then ran over to America to hunt up "the old folks," promising to return in a twelve-month's time "or sooner." Arthur was much distressed at his departure.

Little is left to tell. Ralph and Ada were married; Reginald and Rose, too. And so we will leave all happy and contented.

Steve came home, and Mr. Martindale gave him employment as a porter, and he lived an exemplary life. Rube found the old folks dead, and his only sister married.

Poor Rube was lonely. Ralph wanted him to settle down near him, but Rube could not stand a life of inactivity.

"Guess I'll try Australia again. You're married and settled, and got your profession—you won't come. But I can't keep still; must keep moving." And so Reuben Grant went out once more to Australia.

I intend to follow the fortunes of 'Stiff' in a future story, and perhaps we may drop across the kind American once more.

My story is told. This I may say: The incidents of Reuben Grant's 'bouncing' the four ruffians, and the escape of Stephen Bland from lynching, are perfectly true, and occurred about the time stated. I only wish I had my poor brother's letters now that I have heard read as a boy thirty-three years ago. They were life-pictures of the 'diggings' in those far-away days.

Gentle reader, *adieu*—or, let me hope, *au revoir*. I wish you "A Merry Christmas, and a Happy New Year."

A GOOD PROSPECT

The Adventurer

John Arthur Barry

"Out of darkness come the hands
That reach through nature, moulding man."

Chapter I: The Prospectors' Camp

It was a wet drizzling day in the Mount Lofty ranges, and the Onkaparinga ran bank-high, red and turbid. In a tent, pitched between a couple of she-oaks, two men lay on their stretchers and listened to the roar of the river and the soughing of the wind in the branches overhead.

Presently, one turned and spoke. His voice was low, and he was evidently far from well. "Bob," he said, "I wish you could get as far as the township. They've had plenty of time to write, and there may be a letter from home now."

The man addressed sat up. He was a good-looking fellow of thirty-five or thereabout, with features not unlike those other wasted ones, regarding him wistfully out of a pair of soft brown, dog-like eyes.

"I'll go, Will," he replied cheerfully. "Might just as well be outside as lying loafing here. And I hope I'll bring you back good news, it's a long time since you heard from your people?"

"A long time," repeated the other wearily. "Nearly thirteen years now. And I've never had any luck since I left. I don't think, somehow," he went on, weakly, "that I'm very far from pegging out. I feel regularly used up, as it were, and tired, dead tired of the fight. And that's why I wrote home—not that I said anything to frighten the Mater, but because I felt suddenly hungry to hear of them. You've been a good mate for nearly three years, Bob, old chap. If anything should happen, I can trust you to send the news to them. You know what my life out here has been almost as well as I do myself. I never told you why I left home so young, though.

But it doesn't matter. If I live I may tell you some day. I think I'll try and get to sleep whilst you're away. No, don't bring any medicine. I'm not medicine sick. It's rest I want; I'm tired. Besides, we're not millionaires."

Robert Osborne put on an oilskin coat, looked thoughtfully down at the pale face of his mate for a few minutes, then, with some parting words of encouragement, went out into the rain.

It was evening when he returned, and the sky had cleared. "Letters, old man," he cried, as he fumbled with the tent-flap.

But all was silent inside, and a sudden misgiving seized upon him as he called again, then entered. It was too dark to see distinctly, so he lit a candle. His mate lay just as he had left him, his pale face pillowed on a rough overcoat. But the pinched and soured aspect of the rather weak features had disappeared, giving place to a calm look of quiet content- ment that Osborne never remembered to have seen there before: and instinctively he felt that the tried spirit was at rest. Uttering an exclama- tion of surprise and grief, he held the candle close to the lips. But there was no stir in the flame; and Osborne felt very lonely as he drew the blanket over the corpse, and sat on the edge of his stretcher, considering what he should do.

"Poor old chap!" he muttered, taking a couple of letters out of his pocket addressed to "William Egerton, Esq." "We've done some heavy roughing it together. And now the end's come! And here's the home let- ters he expected so anxiously. Too late! I suppose I may as well see what they've got to say."

He felt no scruples at breaking open the letters in view of his mate's last words to him. But, in any case, as yet, Osborne was a man untroubl- ed by scruples. The first was from Egerton's mother, and, after expressing her delight at hearing from one she had given up as completely lost, she adjured him in the most loving words to come home at once.

"Your uncle John," the letter went on, "has been dead two years now.

So are very many of those who ever heard the story of our misfortune. The remainder must have forgotten it by now. And oh, my dear, you were so young then—a mere boy—whom anybody but John Egerton would have forgiven. A hard and cruel old man; although, at the last, I think he was sorry, for, in his will, he left us this house, you remember, in Edwardes-square, together with a large sum of money, which I have invested so as to bring us in an income of about fifteen hundred pounds per year—amply sufficient for our small household. Have you never seen the advertisements and appeals that we sent to the newspapers for years, until we gave the case up as hopeless? Isabel is getting quite an old maid now—she is twenty-eight—but an unspeakable stay and comfort to her mother. Dorothy, who was a baby almost when you left, is a big girl of twelve. Come home, my son—my son, come home at once! Here are the means."

Enclosed was a letter of credit upon an Adelaide bank for two hundred pounds.

Osborne pondered long over the letter before opening the other, reading and rereading it with care and attention. The second one was from Egerton's sister Isabel—affectionate scoldings for the enduring silence, loving appeals to return home. Both letters were such as hardly any man receives more than once in a lifetime.

"I wonder," thought Osborne, as at length he folded them up, "what the 'misfortune' she speaks of was? I expect that's what he alluded to just before I went for the mail. Well, poor chap, it doesn't matter to him much what it was now."

And with a sigh, for he felt lonely, he rose and went outside and threw wood upon the fire smouldering under its bark shelter, and mechanically put the billy on. He was thinking deeply. Those letters and the money had set his brain working with plans and schemes, shapeless yet, but perhaps unconsciously to himself rapidly taking concrete form and power. It was a beautiful night, and he did not go inside again, but paced to and fro on the hard clayey ridge until the moon rose and flooded the hills with her pale light. The cry of the mopoke echoed loud and clear, and the roar of the river sounded more distinctly than ever as the time passed unheeded; but the solitary figure never stopped. And it was near midnight when, entering the tent, he relit the candle, and, taking a small looking-glass from the head of his stretcher, turned the blanket down over the dead man's face and compared his own with it in rapid alternate glances. Dim as the light was he seemed satisfied.

"Everybody has noticed the resemblance wherever we've worked," he muttered. "I'm older, I know. But it should be safe enough, allowing for the wear and tear of such a life. I wish I knew that little matter of the 'misfortune.' However, it's not likely anyone will refer to that. Poor beggar! Rest from future toil and worry was his at last—a safe refuge for the balance of his days. Now he's resting everlastingly. Why should I not have what he cannot take? Am I not, too, worn and weary with unavailing struggle. I should be mad not to take my chance now it has come!" and he went out to make the tea.

But he had put the billy on empty, and the bottom had long ago burned out of it. With a laugh he kicked the useless thing aside, and went on scheming.

Osborne's was not an uncommon case of a colonial youngster having had early to shift for himself. Whilst still quite a child, his mother died. His father, a licensed surveyor in Brisbane, shortly afterwards went down in the Ly-ee-Moon, a wreck that brought mourning to many an Australian home: and, when matters were wound up, there was found only enough left to keep the lad at school for a few years, and then to pay for his articles in a lawyer's office. Both his parents had come of good old English stock; and, until the death of his father, young Will had known a comfortable home, maintained by one who, living well up to his income, adhered to the traditions of his own and his wife's young days in such matters.

After a year of the desk he became tired of the monotony and ran away, not to sea as the English boy invariably does, but to that refuge of the colonial one—the bush. Nobody troubled themselves about him, and he roamed pretty well all over Australia; and out of it to Sud-Est, the New Guinea mainland, and New Zealand, mostly "following the diggings."

As before mentioned, he was not unlike his dead mate. Both had the same cast of features, both wore beard and moustache of the same shape and colour. In the eyes lay the difference. Egerton's had been of a soft brown, with a sort of beseeching look in them, contrasting strongly with the others, which, although of the same colour, were sharp and piercing, with, at times, a sparkling flash of passion in their depths that spoke to the close observer of an undisciplined nature as well as a strong will.

The two had first met on the Palmer; and although during the time they had been together their luck was of the worst, no hint had ever fallen from one or the other of a dissolution of the partnership. Egerton was content to follow submissively, and Osborne had ever reigned supreme in camp, claim, and on the "wallaby."

For over a month they had been camped in the lonely depths of these South Australian hills, sometimes getting enough gold to pay for rations, at others scarcely even that.

At first Osborne had thought simply of cashing the letter of credit, and nothing more. But he at once saw that such a course could only lead to inquiries being set on foot which would probably end in gaol. So, ere sunrise, he had fully made up his mind to follow out, step by step, the plan upon which his brain had been so busy all through the midnight hours.

Only on one point was he undecided—whether to bury the body and destroy every vestige of the camp by fire, or to leave all standing as it was.

Nobody in the small decayed mining township, eight miles distant, knew of its whereabouts; and save, perhaps, the butcher and the baker, no one there knew him personally. Egerton himself had never even been there.

After much hesitation, he decided to let things, including the body, remain as they were, leaving even his blankets, spare clothing, and the dozen and one little necessary articles that the poorest nomad considers indispensable. An old red leather pocketbook belonging to Egerton, and containing miners' rights, tradesmens' bills, &c., was the only article he took with him, and in this he carefully placed the two letters and the money. Then, once more turning the blanket down, he stood and gazed for some minutes at the calm, placid features, covered them carefully up, and, without a backward glance, walked away on his adventure.

Could he have foreseen another day, not so far distant, on which he was also to go forth, leaving all behind, but followed by the bitter reproaches of an awakened conscience and a hopeless love, he might, even yet, have hesitated. Doubtless he was sorry, after a fashion, for the loss of his three years' companion. But, so far, his nature was not one upon which sorrow of that kind makes much demand. He had made his plans, and was thoroughly satisfied with them. Of course he had read in books of such things as he was doing, and of the inevitable overtaking punishment. But that fact did not weigh with him one iota. It was his chance, the only one, probably, that he would ever have to get rid of the dolorous poverty of such a life as had been his for many years, and, without an effort, to take in exchange that one of comfort and ease such as he dimly remembered and felt himself eminently fitted to enjoy. Deeper into the matter at present he did not go.

In a tin match-box be carried some six or seven pennyweights of gold, which he knew would last him until he could get the draft cashed at the bank. He knew exactly what he had to do; there was no vacillation in his mind, no notion of turning aside from the furrow. And he felt perfectly contented, and presently caught himself whistling in response to the magpies as he tramped through the dew-laden grass towards the main road, where he knew he could catch the Adelaide coach.

At the bank there was some little difficulty. But, with the help of an affidavit and the old pocket-book, the question of identity was at last satisfactorily settled, and the £100, which was all he asked for, paid over. The balance he left as a current account.

His next step was to send a cable—"From William Egerton, Adelaide, to Mrs. Egerton, 23 Edwardes-square, Kensington, London. All is well; leaving for England shortly."

He was not more explicit, because he did not wish to be met on his arrival, as he was pretty sure would otherwise be the case.

At the shipping company's office, when the clerk, struck by his air of thorough colonialism and brand new rig-out—in which, with his tanned and bearded face, he looked the ideal squatter or lucky digger just running over to the Old Country for a trip—asked whether he would not take a return ticket, he hesitated for a minute, then did so. And he went second-class.

The passage passed without incident, and so completely, by the time he reached London, had he identified himself with his part that he felt altogether as if he were the real William Egerton returning home after long years of exile: and almost was able to persuade himself into the belief that the shrouded form, lying there in the far-away ranges, at the mercy of crows and dingoes, was a myth—a thing he had dreamt of years ago. Oblivion of this sort comes to but a few of us, and, as a rule, is not lasting. Osborne, without being especially conscious of it, possessed the power in a very high degree, and its possession enabled him to appear cool and unconcerned in matters that others would have marred or ruined altogether by unwelcome but involuntary efforts of their memory.

Chapter II: "Home"

Without further warning, the Adventurer, as we shall now call him, arrived at Edwardes-square. And, though feeling at first just a little awkward under the caresses showered upon him by the mother and sisters, he soon learned to take these signals of affection as a matter of course, and as his by right.

Mrs. Egerton accepted him wholly and completely from the very first for what he was not. And so also did Dorothy, a pretty child, whose great brown eyes (for a moment) reminded him of others he had once seen somewhere, so like were they, only lacking their sadness.

But Isabel, the stately elder sister, the first excitement over, became at times reserved and silent in his presence. And often, looking up, he would find her calm regard fixed on his face with an expression in them that made his cheeks glow again under the sun-brown.

Isabel, in appearance and nature, different altogether from her mother and her sister, and although not nearly so pretty as Dorothy, bade fair to be. Still, with her perfect figure, regular features, a complexion of the hue of old ivory, great masses of brown hair coiled over a broad forehead, and a pair of blue eyes, deep and dark, through which looked the pure and spotless soul of a noble and maturer womanhood, she was to the Adventurer a perfect revelation of refined and gracious femininity. And it was the first bitter in his cup that she, of them all, should regard him with distrust.

She had very dearly loved the boy who in a moment of temptation had gone astray and expiated his fault so heavily. And she totally failed to accept, all at once, this stalwart bronzed man with the abrupt manners, and eyes in whose depths she saw stern passions lurk, so unlike Will's. But as time passed and her close scrutiny discovered many traits of a nature such as she imagined should have been her brother's had life's course run smoothly with him, her suspicions became lulled. And though she at times often found herself asking incredulously whether this indeed could be the outcome of the pale-faced delicate boy whom she last remembered as sobbing out his grief on his mother's breast in the cabin of the ship that was bearing him into exile, she ceased to examine the Adventurer with that calm scrutiny that hurt him, but accepted him—only with reservations.

The Egertons belonged to the middle-class of Londoners; hardly the upper middle-class, but, for all that, the one that goes to make up much of the strength of the empire—the large tradespeople—always the first with money, and if needs be, blood, in defence of their hearths and homes. Loyal, if perhaps bigoted, believers in the axiom of "England first in everything," this class, hating the French with the old traditional hatred; and submitting to be taxed to within an inch of their lives as long as new men-o'-war were building, or a "little war" pulling through with credit.

Such a one was the late Mr. Egerton, who carried on the brass-founding establishment in dingy Soho that had been in the family for over 300 years. But, in an evil hour, impatient at the slow yet sure returns of a quiet business, he speculated and fell. The crash broke his heart, and, dying with his family almost totally unprovided for, he had, with his last breath, implored his brother John to see that they did not want.

John promised; he was the senior partner of a large and flourishing city firm, a bachelor, and had plenty of room in the old house in Edwardes-square for his brother's wife and her family. Will he put at a desk in his own office, and, although he never "took to" the lad, he intended fully to push him up the commercial ladder if found deserving. But poor Will was weak, and easily led by the fast city clerks with whom he associated—youngsters whose haunts were the "Cri," and the Alhambra, and favourite drink "Scotch, cold."

The outcome in Will's case was inevitable—the pilferings from the cash-box—the marked money—detection. And on his uncle's part, no forgiveness. The lad was not seventeen at the time, but nothing less than expatriation would serve the stern old man, who, by this, had taken an abiding dislike to the boy, which, however, was returned with interest. The first feeling of despair in Will's heart had gradually grown into one of settled bitterness against kith and kin. And he never so much as touched a penny of the annual remittance of £50 which the old man made him. But he swore to himself that someday he would return with a fortune of his own—man-grown, independent. Dreams, alas! dreams! We have seen how they were realised; first, years of misery and privation, and now dead, without sepulture, in the heart of the wild Australian ranges, whilst another holds his rightful place in heart and home. As for the Adventurer, in these early days he fairly basked in the sunshine of domestic peace and quietude, so novel, yet grateful, to one weary with much work and wandering.

Considering the life he had led, he possessed surprisingly few vices. And it was in his favour that, to the wonderful adaptability of the native-born Australian, he added the gift of good blood, which perhaps was the reason that things long forgotten, pertaining to those minor morals of civilisation, and which some people think of the first importance in life, came back to him as by instinct. Although not carriage people, the Egertons lived in good style, and the ease with which he accommodated himself to what must have been such a radical change from the rough and wandering life that he at times described to them, struck Isabel with as much surprise as pleasure.

She had expected to see she hardly knew what, but certainly not a personage who took all the petting and attention lavished upon him by the mother and Dorothy as quite a matter of course, and who seemed, to her astonished perception, to fall into rank and dovetail with their lives as if he had never been absent. Not only that, but as time went on, the Adventurer, in a quiet, pleasant manner, dominated the house, and his was the one will in it to which all were supposed to defer. The mother, even, trusted him with the disposal of her investments, and took his advice on almost every subject with an implicit confidence, often justified by results, and, in fact—rather to Isabel's bewilderment, who felt herself ousted from a position so long held—began to look up to him as her main support and comfort. Isabel's nature was too noble to feel any jealousy at the implied preference, but she would have felt more at ease had she been thoroughly satisfied in her own mind that this re-turned wanderer was, in very truth, what he claimed to be. Always there was a lurking doubt in her soul that caused the Adventurer's morning and evening kiss to thrill her frame with an emotion she felt it difficult to analyse, so curiously compounded was it of attraction and repulsion. And, unsuspected by himself, the Adventurer's character, nay, his very nature, was undergoing a radical change. He grew by degrees to love the calm, grey old lady whose one thought, apparently, was how to make life pleasant for him; and he grew very fond of little Dorothy, who never seemed tired of his company, and would stick close to his heels all day, when she was not at school.

But it was to Isabel that the transformation was chiefly owing. And it would have been indeed curious had not daily companionship with a woman so much above the average as was Isabel Egerton produced the effect of a liberal education upon a brain as receptive and a mind as clear and appreciative as the Adventurer's.

Doubtless he was a scamp, this middle-aged fraud, who had descend-ed lawlessly upon the quiet family in Edwardes-square, and taken unto himself a dead man's shoes. But, doubtless, also, he had some good points about him well becoming a better man. These Isabel was quick to discov-er and put to the credit side of the account.

But the great thing in his favour was that, although most liberally supplied with money, and having every chance, had he so wished it, of becoming acquainted in a certain set, and partaking of their pleasures and dissipations, he seemed never so happy as when at home. Certainly the people who visited at twenty-three were not much to his mind— elderly friends of the late Mr. Egerton, and younger ones of the girls, who came to afternoon tea, and bored him with inane gossip in which he had no part. Still, had he sought it, the reputation of a "fortune in Australia" would have made him a welcome guest at many houses, whose sons would have been only too pleased to show him what their middle-class notion of "life in London" was like. But he did not please, and scored accordingly with the three women. Perhaps if Isabel had not been there he would long ere this have felt hipped to death after the long years of change and vagabondage, in such strong contrast to the sober atmosphere by which he was now surrounded.

As the months went by Isabel's bewilderment and distrust, despite her utmost efforts to vanquish them, would not be laid. Account for the feeling she could not; and at times she blamed herself severely. Thus the Adventurer was surprised by sudden bursts of affection, succeeded by periods of coldness and suspicion. He was far too clever a judge of character to put this hot and cold behaviour of Isabel's, as many would have done, to the score of jealousy at the partiality shown him by Mrs. Egerton. But, all the same, he was troubled by it. For the first time in his life, half unknowingly, he was deeply, passionately in love; a love the depth and intensity of which he did not suspect as yet; and which, so far, was satisfied with brotherly caresses that their object sometimes accepted, but more often put calmly aside.

A seeming thorough unconsciousness in the Adventurer's manner, an implied sort of silent intimation that he was only receiving his due, and had nothing specially to be grateful for, was what, in particular, exasperated Isabel. He ought, she considered, to have returned a little penitent, if not for his original lapse from the path of honour, then, at least, for the long and cruel silence that had born so hardly on their mother. But he appeared neither thankful nor penitent. He was, in fact, masterful, and not a bit penitent. She would have rejoiced beyond measure to have had him cry "*peccavi*" and would have taken him to her arms and condoled with and wept over him, and forgiven him. But now—!

Still it was, without a doubt, far from unpleasant to have someone to take them about to theatres and concerts and other amusements, somebody, too, who dressed well, looked well, almost distinguished indeed, and was in every way thoroughly presentable and *comme il faut* as "our brother Will, from Australia."

To the something hinted at by his dead mate, on that last day in the tent, as the cause of his leaving home, or to the allusion in the mother's letter to a "misfortune" of years ago, the Adventurer had, since his domestication, hardly given a thought. The matter was recalled to him with the suddenness of a bolt from the blue, and with a result—that of causing him to feel shame, if only vicariously—that a short time ago he would have scouted as an utter absurdity. One night there had been a little dinner party in Edwardes-square.

Finding matters rather dull as the evening wore on he stole away to his own smoking den for a cigar. The gas had not been lit; the window, looking out on the garden, was open, and some of the guests were strolling up and down.

He had taken the box of Havanas from its place when voices, close to, struck on his ear.

"Yes, Miss Scott, I can assure you," one was saying in a high-piping tone that he recognised as belonging to an old lady who lived a few doors away; "I heard the story at the time. In fact, I knew him as a boy. And a very wicked, bad boy he was. He stole a lot of his Uncle John's money.

I knew John Egerton too, a nice man, my dear, but hard, very. And this William Egerton, the big brown man you saw tonight, my dear, he's the boy. I knew him at once, although he didn't seem to remember me. He's the same boy, or rather young man, he was when John Egerton gave him the choice of being tried and sent to gaol as a thief, or leaving the country for ever and ever. It nearly broke his poor mother's heart with the shame of the thing. And he never wrote for years and years. And now he's come home with a fortune, and so big, and really not bad-looking, after being amongst savages such a time. He hardly spoke to me; but I used to give him apples when he was in petticoats; and I'd know him anywhere."

As he listened, the unlit cigar dropped from the Adventurer's fingers as if it had been iron at white heat, and he wondered to feel himself blushing fiercely; and, curiously enough, his thoughts at once flew to Isabel, whilst a fine feeling of hot indignation ran through him at having to suffer in this way for the sin of another.

It did not strike him, just then, that his own offence might, by many, be considered by far the heavier.

Chapter III: "Where is my brother?"

Henceforth, the Adventurer moped, avoided the members of the family as much as possible, and especially Isabel. He also went out more, smoked more, and drank rather more whisky and water than was perhaps good for him. His crest was lowered; he grew morose and self-absorbed, a radical contrast to his usual jovial, pleasant manner that was quick to attract notice in such a household, and that brought them—even, in a measure, Isabel—around him, vying with each other in little attentions and thoughtfulnesses. They never dreamt that all the while the shadow of two sins, only one of which he had committed, was looming large betwixt himself and them, spoiling his appetite and taking away all capacity for enjoyment.

Such a state of things irked him mightily, for the reason that he was not at all sure what had happened to him. It was, however, only the working of a new conscience, made raw and very susceptible through love, equally novel, that made him feel as if he were going to be ill.

But worse was to come.

One afternoon, sitting moodily smoking in his room, Dorothy came and coaxed him with winning words and caresses to take her and Isabel to the Military Tournament, then in full swing at the Agricultural-hall, Islington.

Mrs. Egerton was ailing, and could not accompany them. Of late, indeed, she had been far from strong, and obliged to keep her bed for days together. But she was always anxious that her children should enjoy themselves; and the change in her "big boy" as she was fond of calling him, had both puzzled and disquieted her. Therefore, she was sincerely pleased at the proposed expedition, it being the first occasion for a long time on which the three had gone out together, as formerly used to be a matter of course.

After the spectacle was over, and the trio were wandering about amongst the paraphernalia of guns, armed men, horses, and saddlery in the huge basement, a man in the uniform of a New South Wales lancer approached, and after a long look, came up with outstretched hand, saying in loud, cheery tones, "How are you, Osborne, old chap? What in the world brings you here?"

The two girls were a few paces off; but well within hearing distance of the Guardsman who had just ridden in. But they turned at once on hearing the salutation.

For a moment the Adventurer thought of point blank denying all knowledge of the man. But the next question, before he had time to speak, made him change his mind.

"And," went on the other, grasping the mechanically extended hand, "how's that old mate of yours—the chap people would have was like you, only I could never see it? Didn't bring him with you, eh? I thought you were inseparable. Don't you remember," he rattled on, "the arguments we used to have o' nights on the Normanby and the Palmer. Let's see, what was his name again?" and the speaker paused, whilst the other stood impassive, but with his heart beating furiously.

The girls were looking hard at the smart trooper, who seemed to know their brother so well by another name, Isabel white as the lilies of the valley at her breast. "Come and have a drink," said the Adventurer, huskily, breaking the momentary silence with the old formula. "Can't, old man, now, thanks," replied the other, as a long trumpet call sounded down the building. "There's boot and saddle for us! But what was that chap's name, eh?" he continued, with devilish pertinacity. "Surely you haven't forgotten? Everton! That was it. Always used to think of toffee when I heard it. Come and see me. Staying with an aunt, 40 Lupus-street, Pimlico. Off duty to-morrow; any time through the morning. Ask for Mrs. Miles—my name, you know. Don't forget. So long," and, with a sweep of his plumed hat to the two girls he made a rush for his horse, stalled nearby, mounted, and clattered away over the stones.

"Shall we wait to see any more?" asked the Adventurer, presently, by an effort recovering his usual tone and manner.

"I think not," replied Isabel faintly, instinctively recoiling as he came near her; whilst Dorothy, with all the insouciant abandon of youth, said, "Will, who was that nice man with the pretty feather in his hat who called you Osborne?"

"An old acquaintance who used to work close to me on the diggings, dear," replied the Adventurer. "You know we take the first name that comes handiest there."

"Yes but, Will," she insisted, "what was it he was saying about Everton toffee? I couldn't quite understand. That's what they used to call me at Madame's, you know, when I was quite little—'Sticky Everton.' Not Egerton but Everton. You remember—the place where all the best toffee used to be made."

"Only his joking, my dear," replied the Adventured turning cold, and stealing a glance at Isabel, walking like one in a dream, with wide-open despairing eyes staring straight ahead. "Miles was always a terrible fellow for barracking and poking fun at people over yonder."

And then came an explanation including ones he had just made use of. By that time they were at the 'Underground.'

But Isabel never spoke. She was saying to herself, over and over again, lest she should forget, "Mrs. Miles, 40 Lupus-street, Pimlico."

During the brief journey the silence was unbroken except by Dorothy, and to her, at last, the Adventurer returned such cross, curt answers that the child's eyes filled with tears, and she, too, was silent. As for himself, he began now to realise, rather dimly as yet, what the deeper consequences of his act might be, helped each minute to a clearer under-standing as he glanced at Isabel sitting with that stony tense look on her face—the face he had learnt to love above all things.

And all night long he tossed and turned restlessly, whilst before his eyes came and went the vision of a still shrouded form, and in his ears was the sound of rain pit-patting on the calico, and the hoarse roar of the river as it surged amidst the nodding ti-trees.

Isabel's mind was in a whirl with mingled feelings of hope and de-spair, and almost the only thing that seemed to stand out plainly from the hurly-burly was that name and address—forgotten, if, in that supreme moment, ever marked, by the Adventurer.

If he were not her brother Will, who then was he? Where was Will? She knew, now, the meaning of those conflicting feelings that had been such a burden to her—the natural wish to believe in and love, kept back by instinctive doubt—realised now this latter to the full.

Yet, deep down in her heart of hearts, even whilst the darkest suspicions swept across her mind, there sprung into being a tiny bright flower of comfort and hope in the thought that, if it were well with her brother, then, in spite of all appearances to the contrary, the mystery might be cleared up so as to, in some sort, extenuate the Adventurer.

At the breakfast table next morning the latter's face showed such traces of the battle fought during the long and silent hours of the night that Dorothy cried out at sight of it, and even Isabel could not refrain from sympathetic inquiry, repented of the next moment as treachery. The mother, in these days, seldom appeared before noon.

After the meal, unable to bear the strain any longer, Isabel called a cab and drove to Lupus-street, finding the place without any difficulty.

Mrs. Miles, it seemed, kept a boarding house, and, although she was not at home herself just then, her nephew was. And, if rather surprised at such a visit, having nothing to conceal, he told what he knew willingly. But, except as confirmation of long-held fears and doubts, it amounted to little.

The trooper was, it appeared, Berkshire born, but had been in Australia for many years, and now, with his brother, held a large selection on the Richmond River. In '75, or thereabouts, he had been on the diggings and his mate, Egerton—yes, of course, that was the name—owned, indeed, the adjoining claim, and worked next to them for some months. Egerton was often a bit "off colour," and would have to lay up with fever and ague. But Osborne was a good mate, and always looked after him well. Everybody on the rush took the pair for brothers, although, for his part, he thought the resemblance of the slightest. Still others said it was very strong. No; he had never seen either of them since, until the meeting at the Hall yesterday. Was he quite sure, perfectly certain, that the person he spoke to there was Osborne, and not Egerton. Yes, he was certain. The difference, to him had always been plain; one look at the eyes even was enough for him. And here the young man glanced at Isabel as if he would very much like to know the reason for all these questions. But there was a misery in her face that deterred him. So be simply contented himself with hoping that he had been of use, as Isabel, hardly daring to trust her voice, thanked him for his kindness.

And, as he looked after the departing cab, he muttered to himself, "Well, it's no business of mine, of course. But if that beggar Osborne's been up to any of his larks with that young woman I'd like to kick him. I thought that yesterday he looked wonderfully put out at sight of me. Couldn't understand it at all. I expected, seeing him togged up and with ladies, that he was just one of those swells we see such a lot of over yonder, coming and going, diggers today and dukes tomorrow, as it were. But I fancy there's something more in this affair, if looks are to count for anything."

And Trooper Miles was right.

That evening a servant brought word to the Adventurer, moodily smoking, as was his wont in these days, that Isabel wished to see him in her own room—the one she used for working in when she wished to be alone.

He went upstairs, feeling as a man might do who is about to receive sentence of death—a sensation in no way diminished when, as he shut the door behind him, Isabel advanced and said—

"Robert Osborne, where is my brother?"

For several minutes Isabel and the Adventurer stood and faced each other.

Drawn up to her full height, in spite of her pale cheeks, grief-stricken aspect, and eyes in which doubt and terror seemed striving for the mastery, he thought to himself that he had never seen her look so beautiful. Presently his eyes fell before hers, as at the last moment he made up his mind, with a pang that turned him as pale as herself. Numberless excuses and subterfuges, more or less specious sounding, flashed through his brain in that minute. Not so long ago he would have used them without scruple, holding his ground till the last, using every stratagem and fence to discover how much was really known, fighting for existence inch by inch, confident at least of support from Mrs. Egerton.

But now, as for the second time that stern question fell on his ears, he only grasped the back of the chair near which he stood more tightly, and answered hoarsely—"Dead."

There was silence in the room as the fatal word fell from his lips. The ticking of a little clock upon the mantel sounded like thunder in his ears as he stood and stared at Isabel, who had sunk into a chair, and crouched there with her face bowed on her clasped hands.

At last, after what seemed an eternity of waiting, Isabel looked up and asked—"Did you kill him?"

"God forbid, poor chap!" he answered simply. And then, in reply to the mute questioning of her shining eyes, he told the whole miserable story, concealing nothing, extenuating nothing, speaking low and distinctly, but with a curious feeling as if a voice not his own was making use of his body.

He ceased; and Isabel, whose tears had been quietly falling for some time, now sobbed passionately. "How could you? Oh, how could you leave him like that, and come and impose upon mother, upon all of us as you have done? Cruel, cruel! Unburied, too! Go, for God's sake. It would kill our mother. I will make some excuse for you. Poor Will, my own dear brother! If you could but see the man you called your friend usurping name and place!" And she thrust out an arm as in the act of repulsing some loathsome thing—a gesture that cut the Adventurer to the quick.

"I'll go back," he said brokenly, as she again hid her face in her hands, as though to shut him out of her sight. "I'll go back," he said, "and bury him, if that will give you a little comfort. But don't think that I haven't suffered, too. For these last few days I've been like a man in hell! Look at me for a minute, Isabel—it will be for the last time."

A shudder ran through her frame, but she made no answer, neither did she raise her head. And, after one long, lingering look he went softly out of the room, and downstairs, and into the street, feeling wan and dazed, and not his own man.

Then Dorothy, returning home, met him, and, frightened at his distraught face and bearing, caught hold on his arm, crying—

"Should I call Doctor Bartlett? You mustn't go out. Come back with me!"

Controlling himself with a ghastly attempt at a smile, the Adventurer, gently putting her on one side, said, "I'm all right, little woman. Bad news from Australia. Must go out straight away. Not even time to see the Mater. Give her my love when she gets up. Goodbye," and kissing her passionately, he strode along the street eastwards, walking very swiftly, but unable to escape his thoughts. So, on a day not quite a year old yet, had he left his dead mate lying in the lonely camp beside the river, but taking with him then a cheerful spirit that whistled to the birds as he went forth on his adventure, stout of heart and without misgiving.

Now, as, by degrees, his steps lagged, and he glanced around with vacant stare at the roaring bustle of the great city, it became borne in upon his soul with sickening certainty that behind him he was leaving all the gladness and beauty that his life had ever known; leaving, too, a memory that would never die, of a bowed head crowned by a wealth of dark brown hair, and the sound of bitter weeping that he knew would remain with him always.

Chapter IV: Coolgardie

It will be remembered that, on his departure from Australia, the Adventurer, perhaps because fearing disaster, had not only taken a return ticket, but left a portion of the stolen money behind him in the bank at Adelaide.

Also, when he walked away from the house in Edwardes-square, despairing, and with only the one settled idea in his mind of escaping more shame and more disgrace, he had ten pounds in his purse.

To his newly-aroused sensitiveness, the making use of this money seemed wrong, to say nothing of the balance of the two hundred pounds. But there appeared no help for it. Besides, had he not promised the performance of a certain matter, impossible without means! And, changed man as he might be, there was nothing foolishly quixotic about his views. Only, as he went to the branch bank in Old Broad-street, and sent a cable for the money, he swore that if it ever lay in his power the whole sum should he restored, ay, if it took years of labour to do it. To tell the truth, he felt all broken up, morally and mentally, for a while, and now and again caught himself wondering at a scrupulousness he would once have thought the height of absurdity.

As luck would have it, one of the great liners sailed in a couple of days, giving him just time to put a few things together in the shape of an outfit.

The trip out was as uneventful as the passage home had been, but, to the Adventurer, suffering from the tortures both of conscience and the memory of a hopeless love, the time seemed endless before the big ship brought up in Largs Bay. Actually it was a record run. From port to city, thence to the site of the old prospecting camp in the ranges, took but a few days. Not a sign of the tent remained. The fire-shelter, with its bark roof supported by four uprights, still stood, so did, also, the forks of the stretchers. And up a blind gully a short distance away was a caved-in shaft with the wreck of a windlass lying upon it.

But no sign of a grave or of human remains could the Adventurer find anywhere. And he searched high and low. It was a dry season, and the river only murmured now over its rocky bed under the shady ti-trees that, when he saw them last, were wildly whipping its red current with their wind knotted crests.

He stayed there all night, and the place brought back memories that he could have well dispensed with. But the mystic touch of "the hands that reach through nature moulding man" was upon him, and their power was not to be denied. He had done a shameful thing light-heartedly, fearing, nor caring, nor believing in any retribution. And now it had come upon him at the hands of his love.

In the morning he made inquiries at the little township, unchanged and dreary as ever. But no one knew or cared. He had promised himself that, when his task was finished, he would write, telling her, and bidding her a long farewell. And now even that poor consolation was denied him.

Returning to Adelaide, he remained there some days, uncertain whither to direct his steps. He shrank, with something almost akin to fear, from beginning the old too familiar struggle again, the wandering life of disappointment, and failure, and hardship every turn and twist of which he knew so well, had learned with such long and bitter experience—that of the luckless digger. And he had no reason to believe that there ever would be any difference. Once he could have "faced back" with a light heart and ready for every hap. Now he had lost confidence in himself, seeming to care little what became of him.

Whilst in this frame of mind Coolgardie blossomed forth into a golden notoriety, drawing men from all quarters into the Western desert. The Adventurer, carelessly joining the human stream, presently found himself at the front, behind a few, but in advance of the many.

He began the same old story that he knew so well—failure everywhere. Other men made fortunes where he had to slave for mere bread on the adjoining ground.

His money, too, was getting low, and, as he pondered, one day, worn with toil, half smothered with the dust that swept over the plain in clouds, he suddenly threw down sieve and shovel and returned to his camp, determined on one last supreme effort in which failure should also mean death.

Next day he bought off Hassan Ali, the Afghan carrier, a pair of camels, a saddle animal for riding and one for pack. He bought also a condenser and a good stock of rations. Then he set out due east into the desert, determined to return no more unfortunate. He had parted with his last shilling, and, as he headed out of camp in the early morning he felt more tranquil in mind than he had done for a very long time.

A day's rapid travelling took him clear of the last outpost. Then, journeying more leisurely, he prospected the country, but for a time in vain.

For many days and weeks past his listless apathy had given place to a fierce desire to make money—to find gold. With time and reflection had come the assurance that some explanation of the disappearance of the tent and the body of his mate must be sought. To his practised eye it was evident that someone must have taken the tent away. It certainly had not been carried off by a storm, for there was not a remnant left. Of course, it was just possible that other prospectors had found the camp, and buried the body, whilst taking possession of the property. But the latter was of little value, and their first proceeding in that comparatively settled neighbourhood would probably have been to notify the police. Still he had inquired closely, if guardedly, in Adelaide and the township without success. And now, o' nights, lying on his back and looking up at the stars shining in the cloudless blue, he turned these matters over in his mind again and again, whilst his camels cropped the spinifex and scrubby bushes that grew scantily around, the noise of their eating the only thing to disturb the absolute silence of the desert.

It became apparent to the Adventurer that he had not done as much as he might to keep his promise, and he swore to himself that, should fortune favour him in this—the last attempt, he would return, and, telling his story in the face of all men, if necessary, spare nothing to find the remains of Will Egerton, and make good his last words to that sister on whom, even now, were his thoughts always bent.

One day, camping in the heat on a barren, unlikely-looking ridge, he discovered shortly after starting that he had left his pocket-compass behind him. Returning to the spot, he searched long without success amongst the lichen-encrusted boulders. And at length, in the depths of a crevice, he saw the dull gleam of the brass case. But his strength was insufficient to turn the big stone over, and he was obliged to cut a sapling to use as a lever. Sure enough, the instrument he sought was there, but the bottom of the mass of quartz and ironstone was thickly studded with gold, that glistened as it saw the sunlight. And in the pocket were lumps of nearly virgin ore; and, better than all, just below the surface, was the cap of a well-defined reef, which, as he broke great flakes off it, seemed bound together with threads of gold. This was the spot he had not thought worth a second look, as he had sat on the big boulder and ate his tinned fish and biscuit!

Every successive hour proved that the find was no ephemeral one, but one out of which, if he so wished, he could very soon take away many thousand pounds' worth of gold by doing little more than surfacing.

So fortune had come to him at last! And by what a mere fluke! Had he not dropped the compass he would ere this have been plodding on through the dreary sea of spinifex that, from the isolated ridge on which he stood, stretched far away to the horizon—a wild and savage outlook that he had plunged into with a hopeless sensation at his heart when recalled by his loss to wealth sufficient for a dozen men.

A short distance away lay a large salt lake, and on the edge of this he made his camp, after carefully pegging out his legal allowance of ground as a prospecting claim. Then, as rations were getting short, he set off on his return—a four days' journey in a straight line. To follow his own tracks rambling hither and thither would have meant a week.

On the third day, making for the usual morning spell towards a clump of acacias, he saw a man lying, stretched just within their shade, at full length upon the bare red ground, face downwards. High in the air circled an eaglehawk: a crow watched from a branch; close by lay an empty water-bag.

Only the old, old story over again—the rash intruder, unprepared, unequipped, and the punishment of the wilderness. The Adventurer had learnt of such matters, and saw at a glance that there should yet be life in the quiet form, or ere this the birds would have been at their foul work.

Lifting the unfortunate up, he caught sight of the pale face, with its closed eyes, cracked lips, and dry protruding tongue. One wild stare of horror and dismay, and with a shout he let the body drop and rushed away towards his kneeling camel. Then, suddenly stopping, he ran back again, stared again with fiery disbelieving eyes: and then, in a very paroxysm of frantic haste, he tore open the coarse blue shirt and placed his hand on the traveller's heart. It beat, but very faintly. Racing for his water bag with wild gestures of astonishment, he poured lavish streams over the body, and a few drops mixed with brandy down the parched throat.

And after many minutes a little colour came into the wan cheeks, and with a deep sigh the man sat up and sipped mouthfuls of spirit and water, opened a pair of big, brown eyes, stared hard and long at the Adventurer, and then said feebly—

"Why, if it isn't Bob! Where have you been ever since, old man?"

But at the sound of the well-remembered tones the other's heart became too full to speak just then, and the strong man's frame shook with hardly-repressed, big, dry sobbings, and his breath came thick and fast as he bent like a reed before the intensity of the shock of mingled feelings of shame and joy, whilst Will Egerton looked on wondering.

"I suppose you thought I was dead, Bob," he said at length, gazing at the Adventurer with affectionate eyes. "And, for my part, I couldn't make out at all what had happened to you. I remember you going over to the township to see if there were any letters. Then I fell asleep, and must have slept a long time, for when I got up, very weak and ill, the fire was out and the ashes cold; the 'possums had eaten all our rations, and the place looked as if it had been deserted for a month. I wasn't strong enough to do anything but just to stagger back to my bunk again and lie there, hoping and watching for you. But you never came, and I should have pegged-out right enough, only a camping party, shooting and fishing, came along from the city, and when they saw how bad I was they sent me to the hospital, with all the traps—tent and things, you know—in their buggy.

"When I got better I overhauled our swags, looking for the pocket-book and the little bit of gold, but I never found them. The gold would have been acceptable, because I hadn't a penny. I was in the hospital three months. Then I got odd jobs about the wharf. I wrote to the postmaster at the township close to where we camped that time, asking if there were any letters, or if he could tell me anything about you. But he said he knew nothing. And, as the people at home don't seem to care about writing, I never troubled again. Then this place broke out, and I came over, worked my passage as steerage steward, knowing pretty well that, if you were alive, you'd be somewhere around the big rush. Of course I've had the same old luck! It's almost a pity you came up so soon. Very little more would have played out the game. That's all my story. It's simple enough. Now, Bob, let's hear yours. Something very serious must have happened to stop you from coming back to me, I'm sure."

"I can't tell you just now, Will," replied the Adventurer, regaining his self-possession, although some things in the short history had made him wince with pain. "But," he continued, "please God, I will tell you the whole story—let us say this day week."

And Will Egerton, although mystified, was content. Always in presence of the stronger mind he had been submissive, and satisfied to follow the lead.

Supporting him, for he was still very weak, to his riding camel, the Adventurer placed him in the saddle, and himself bestriding the pack, they set off, arriving in Coolgardie on the evening of the next day.

There the Adventurer established Egerton at the best and most comfortable house he could find, and bidding him rest and recover, rode away to Southern Cross, whence he sent a cablegram, paid for by a small nugget from "The Isabel," as he had already, in his own mind, named the golden claim on the edge of the desert. The message was nearly a facsimile of the one he had sent before, but under a very different signature and changed circumstances, that ran:—"William Egerton to Mrs. Egerton, 23 Edwardes-square, Kensington, London. All is well. Shall be home shortly." Then back to Coolgardie again, to find Will looking well, and completely recovered from his so narrow escape of a desert death.

And, presently, the pair rode away in the darkness towards El Dorado, Will, as yet, knowing nothing, but, as usual, obediently following the lead.

Great as was his amazement at sight of the apparently endless richness of the find, it was greater still when, one night, lying close to the margin of the salt lake, deceptive in its calm, fresh beauty under the stars, with the shadow of the bedded condenser casting a long black streak across the water, the Adventurer told his promised story, keeping back nothing, extenuating in no degree.

His companion listened in silence, never interrupting by word or motion. And, as the Adventurer's voice ceased, there was for a time silence still.

But, as he sat with drooping head, presently a hand stole out of the darkness, grasping his, and Will Egerton's voice said, "Never mind, old man. The temptation was strong, and God knows it's not for us to judge each other. Never speak of it again. I can dimly realise what you have suffered since. You said a while ago that half of this claim is mine, or more if I wished. I accept a share of it, and in return will go home and explain things, and plead your cause with Isabel. And I am more than hopeful." And they wrung hands again in the darkness.

Shortly after this, for the Adventurer hurried him away, long ere "The Isabel" had yielded a quarter of its riches, Will Egerton sailed from Albany for England. The Adventurer was the last man to leave the deck of the big mail steamer when the bell rang for "all ashore." "You won't forget, Will," were the parting words he whispered to his friend at the head of the gangway. "Trust me," replied Egerton, as the screw began to slowly revolve, and the ship's bows to turn to the open sea.

And, one day, a desert-stained man, coming into Coolgardie from the world-famed claim known as "The Isabel," had put into his hands a cable message "From Isabel Egerton to Robert Osborne," containing two words only. But they were "Come home."

A Chinese Nurse

Thompson's Claim

Carl Feilberg[1]

Chapter I

We had been introduced in Brisbane, had travelled to the North together, and had to some extent become intimate. "Just the man to show you round the goldfields," my friend had told me; adding, in a confidential aside, "and to put you on to a good thing, if there is one going."

The first part of the recommendation was in course of being justified. My companion had taken me quietly in hand, and had devoted much of his time to the task of showing me what to a stranger were the most interesting features of the busy active scene I was visiting. In the course of our acquaintance I had found much to respect and admire in him. He was not what he himself would have called a "swell." His large hands told of the toil, his rugged weather-beaten countenance of the hardships, he had endured. But, although evidently possessed of that wealth which in these crude colonial societies is the main basis of social distinction, he was free from pretentiousness, and maintained his natural simplicity of speech and manner. It is true that when speaking calmly and without excitement he evidently tried to choose his language with some care, yet when excited and moved he dropped unconsciously into the simpler and more rugged speech of his fellow-miners. In repeating the tale he told me I have endeavoured, as far as possible, to preserve the language in which it was conveyed.

We had just gone over the quartz-mill in which he was specially interested. The thunder of twenty stampers hard at work pounding lumps of quarts into fine sand still seemed to fill my head. We had inspected the

---

[1] Original text: By the Author of "Dividing Mates."

appliances for catching and saving gold, the new kind of ripple-tables, the latest variation in blankets, and the machinery for treating the tailings so that not a speck of metal should be left in the heaps accumulated outside, and I left the mill with a slight headache, and a doubt whether my sense of hearing would recover the shock it had received.

"It is an unusual name for an important mine—'Thompson's claim'— isn't it?" I queried.

"Yes," he replied with a smile. "They generally give the claims fancy names, such as the 'Who'd have thought it?' 'Just in Time,' 'Erin,' 'Vulcan,' 'Homeward Bound,' and so on. But this was called 'Thompson's claim' at the first, and it never got any other name. The machine inside is called the 'Ethel'."

"That is an unusual name too, isn't it?"

"May be; but it's a pretty one. We never altered either name. Perhaps the luck hangs to them."

"It has been a lucky mine, this one?"

"Ah—you may say so. A hundred thousand ounces it has given first and last and there's plenty more where that came from."

"Have you been long connected with it?" I hazarded.

"Me?" and he glanced at me. "I put the first pick in the ground, before a tree had been cut down."

He paused for a moment, wrapped in thought, and then went on:

"It was a most wonderful thing how this reef was found. I didn't find it, you know," he continued, seating himself on a bit of timber under the shade of a portion of the shed covering part of the workings, and cutting up some tobacco. "In fact I had nothing to do with finding it. Joe Thompson was a friend of mine, and we came here to this field just when it opened ten years ago. Joe and I weren't mates, although it always seemed to me that we ought to have been, for we were generally working on the same fields, or near about it. Perhaps Joe thought my luck was too bad—just as bad as his own—and that if we went mates it wouldn't run to tucker between us. Not that it did much more anyway. We'd come to a new field—Joe with his mate and I with mine—and we'd peg out as far away from one another as possible. Sometimes I'd bottom first, and sometimes he would; but, as sure as death, he'd come over to my claim.

"'Well, Bill, have you bottomed? I have.'

"'What's it look like, Joe?'

"'Just about the colour, and precious little more.'

"'Same here,' I'd say, and 'blank it.'

"The boys used to call our parties the Jonah crowd; I never could stick to a mate long.

"'Bill,' they'd say to me, one after another, 'I like you, old man, but darn your luck. I think you are enough to frighten the gold out of the Bank of England.'

"But Joe stuck to his mate. I don't think the poor beggar could have found another if Joe had given him up. He was a weak sickly young chap. Been a clerk in a London office, I think, and got all the marrow sucked out of him by late hours and penning up in an office. He had taken to digging, Joe said, because he had read in a book that the diggings were romantic. So he came out to Australia, and Joe picked him up on one of the fields down south, with his hands all blistered into sores, very sick, without any money, and trying to sell a new-fangled revolver, a bowie knife, and a dagger, that he'd brought out to keep off the bushrangers. The poor fellow hadn't thought about bringing out anything to keep off an empty stomach, and he was about to try to make his way down to Melbourne, and to beg or work his passage home again. But Joe told him if he would stop he might go in with him as his mate. So the young chap stopped, and stuck to Joe wonderfully close. Not that he was ever much good at work, but he was willing, and he was a fine scholar, and played the concertina beautifully. The boys liked the young fellow, and he was all there to play for the dancing when there was a spree at night. Joe's mate stuck to him, and Joe seemed very fond of the young fellow. So when we came up here, and the young chap got the dysentery, Joe was very bad about him. He nursed him like a woman would have done, but the young fellow got worse. I think he had been on the spree and drunk bad grog, so that the dysentery laid hold of him. By-and-bye he got worse, and then they called it fever. Mostly up here in Northern Queensland, when a man gets very bad with grog, or dysentery or what not, they call it fever. Anyway, the young fellow got worse and worse, and last of all he died, and they buried him on the other side of yonder ridges where the old workings are.

"I never saw a man cut up so bad as Joe. You know we diggers think a lot of our mates, and we stand by them in any trouble. Naturally when your mate dies you are cut up. But Joe took on worse and worse, instead of getting better, as time passed after the funeral. He never went near his claim, and any man might have jumped it. Not that any man on the field would have jumped it, seeing how it happened to be left. Besides, being Joe's, it was bound to be no good. However, time passed and Joe never showed up, so I went over to his hut.

"'Joe,' said I, 'this won't do, old man, you've got to shape.'

"'I know it Bill, but I can't.'

"'Oh, that's nonsense. Frank was a good fellow and a good mate, but you ain't a woman, you know, Joe.'

"'Ah, you don't know what's the matter," says he. 'I never told a living soul but poor Frank that's dead and gone, and it's got to come out now.'

"'Good heavens! Joe, you haven't been doing anything, have you— not shooting somebody on the sly?'

"'Not that, old man, but it's near upon as mean.'

"'Well, if it's any comfort to you, out with it. You know me, old pard, and if there's hanging in it I'll stand to you.'

"'You are right, Bill; I know that. I'll tell you all about it; though how you are to help me I don't know.'

"With this he began fumbling about in his swag and pulling out old letters.

"'Did you ever hear I'd been married, Bill?' he asked.

"'No.'

"'Well, I was then, just when I first went digging. That was my wife.'

"He handed me an old photograph in a gilt frame with glass over it. The frame was bruised and the glass was cracked, and the picture was dirty, as if Joe had been handling it too much, and perhaps trying to clean it. But the picture was that of a sweet pretty face, and a real lady.

"'Why, she was a lady, Joe!' I said.

"'So she was, God bless her! She had come out to be a governess, poor thing. There is a lot of old fools in England who sends out poor girls, educated like ladies, and not used to hard work and hard living, telling them they will get on in the colonies. What becomes of the poor creatures—some of them—I don't rightly know, but I can guess. I found my poor darling at a boarding-house, her money all spent, and nearly desperate. I made love to her—as what young fellow wouldn't who saw her!—venturing only because I saw she needed someone to help her. She saw what I meant at once. There had been plenty anxious to make love to her—God forgive them!—after their fashion; but I was ready to kiss the ground under her feet. She didn't love me. How could she, a dainty sweet creature like her, and me just a common fellow? But she married me. "Take me if you will, Joe," she said—she called me "Joe," old man, and ever since I've thought it was the prettiest name there is—"Take me if you will. I fear I don't love you as I ought to do. But you are a brave good man"—she said it, Bill, true as I'm sitting here—"and I'll try to be as good a wife as I can, though not so good as you deserve." I was only too glad to take her. I thought she might love me afterwards, you know,

Bill, after she got over the roughness and had seen how I loved her. And she did. Rough as I was, mind you, I wasn't quite so rough then as I am now. She was frightened and shy at first, and there were times when she would sit looking straight before her, and her brown eyes would grow softer and deeper, as if she saw far away. But she got fond of me, and I think—yes, I think I might have grown to be good enough for her, if she had stopped. But she didn't. She sickened and got weak, and soon after our baby girl was born she drooped terribly. I did what I could for her. I think she was happy. "Joe," she would say, "I was a silly girl not to fall in love with you when you first came courting, for I love you dearly now. But I was too silly to know my dear old rough diamond then." Oh, wasn't it maddening to lose her just when we could have been so happy! But she died. Just before her death she seemed uneasy, and I begged her to tell me what it was. "Joe, dear," she whispered, "you are a brave good man, and you are strong enough to fight your way into a good position in this strange wonderful land. Try and bring up our little Ethel to be a lady." And I swore, holding her hand in mine, by the Heaven she was going to, that I would. And that,' he continued, breaking off, 'is my trouble now.'

"'Why, Joe,' I said, 'what a close chap you are! Did you ever tell any-one?'

"'He knew,' he answered, pointing over his shoulder to the empty bunk where his mate used to sleep.

"'And where is the child—is she alive?'

"'That's just the trouble, don't you see.'"

Chapter II

J oe fumbled about a good bit before he went on again.

"'The child is alive right enough,' he continued at last, 'and she is a grown girl now seventeen last birthday. That's her.'

"And he handed me another picture. This one was a very different sort of thing from the last; prettily got up and freshly taken. It was the picture of a very handsome girl. She looked like a lady; anyone could see it at a glance. And she had her mother's sweet face too. I handed back the picture to Joe.

"'You have kept your promise, old man. Where is she?'

"'In England. There was an old friend of mine, the wife of a steward on board one of the big ships sailing from Melbourne, who took the baby to England and left her with an aunt of my wife's, who kept a boarding school, where she has lived ever since. I send home what money I can, and, although my luck is very bad, it does. England is a cheap place anyhow.'

"'Do you always know how she is getting on?'

"'Always. First, when she was a little thing, the old lady used to write and send me photographs. But when she got bigger she wrote herself. I've got them all here, letters and photographs.'

"'And do you write to her?'

"Joe didn't answer for a while; then straightening up a bit he said:

"'That's where I feel so mean. You see, old pard, I wanted my little girl to be a lady, as I promised my wife she should be, and I was afraid she would despise her father if she knew what a poor scholar he was. I ain't a scholar, you know, Bill. These hands,' and he spread them out, 'they are all there for hard work, but they never were any good with the pen. So I've been putting a trick on my little girl all these years. I made out what I had to say, and Frank, that's dead, he used to write it out all proper for me. That's what's troubling me, Bill. That little girl of mine has been pouring out all her innocent heart in these letters, and I know her, bless her!, just as if she was with me every day of my life; but she doesn't know her old father from a crow. It did seem mean to me at times, but I thought it would all come out right. Maybe the luck would turn, and

I might strike it rich, and then I was going to send for her. Her mother knew I was no scholar, and she learned to love me, and I thought my little girl would do the same if she saw me, and heard me talk instead of seeing my writing. And now, it isn't me she knows at all; it's Frank. She will think it's all a hoax if I write, and perhaps she will turn against me. Look here, old man, if she does that I'll jump down a shaft. It's been a hard life with me, but I've never lost hope. All the time I was working away I kept on thinking it was just with me like one of those showery days in the wet season. In the morning there's a blink of sunshine, and then the clouds settle down and the rain falls regular and steady all day. But near evening it generally clears up a bit, and the blessed sun shines out all the more welcome for having been so long missed. I've been happy, and I had hoped I was going to be happy, and I didn't care for the bad luck between. Look at this!'

"He threw me over a letter. It was the last one he had received from his daughter. I am a rough working man, as you see, but we diggers know a lady when we see one, and we take off our hats to her. So I read that letter, looking over to Joe between whiles, and wondering how he could be the father of the girl who wrote it.

"'You are right, mate,' he said, seeing me looking; 'that's just it. I ain't fit to be her father—any more than I was fit to marry her mother. But she mightn't have known it if she had got to be fond of me. Just look at the end of her letter.'

"I did so. It ran:—

'Do you know, papa, I think you must be living in the loveliest country in the world. That description of the Scrub Gully—why do you have such horrid names in Australia?—has made me so anxious to see the place. What wouldn't we give to have those beautiful creepers and ferns and flowers growing here! I tell Aunt Martha I am so proud of being an Australian-born girl, and I read to her all the bits in your letters describing my beautiful country. Oh, how I wish I was there with you! Do you know, dear papa, I think you must be a little bit of a poet. I know how good and brave and strong you are, because mamma tells me so, in that farewell letter she left for me to read when I was old enough to read it. I keep it as a sacred relic, and I often read it, though it always makes me sad. But I cannot understand what she means by saying that she did not appreciate you enough, and warning me not to judge by outside appearances. I have no fear that I shall need any warning of that kind, or that I shall not honour and love you as I ought. Do I not know you thoroughly from your letters? although you cannot get a photograph done in the far-off diggings where you work so hard, poor dear papa. Never mind, I am seventeen now, and I shall soon be sent for, shall not I? You will not keep me here after I am eighteen—you will not, dear, dear papa. I love Aunt Martha. She is very good to me. But she is not the dear papa whose constant society is the one thing most longed for by his loving daughter,

'ETHEL'

"'There,' said poor Joe with a groan, 'you see how I am fixed. That poor young chap used to work in some of his pretty fancies, and she takes them for mine. Believes I am a bit of a poet! Good heavens!'

"Well, you know I could almost have laughed, looking over at Joe, in his working clothes, his rough hair and his two big hands one on each knee of his patched clay-stained breeches.

"'It's no laughing matter, mate,' he said reproachfully.

Chapter III

"I told him I would try to fix up a letter, so he got out his dead mate's writing things, and we fixed a board on the bunk for a desk just as he had done. Then I picked out a sheet of paper and the best pen I could find and made a start. It was hard work, you know, and worse because

Joe stood over me looking so terribly anxious, and I had only just started when he knocked my elbow and made a blot. However, we got out another sheet and began again.

"'Dear Ethel,—Your father writes to you by another hand,' I began.

"'Hold on, Bill!' Joe cried. 'It won't do, mate. I can't let on what I've been doing by letter. Can't you make it somehow that she will come out and see me. If she could only see me, perhaps she wouldn't mind.'

"There was no getting him from that, so we went over it all again. First we agreed that we would go mates. His show was as good—or, for the matter of that, as bad—as mine, and I was without a mate. So I agreed to go in with him. Then we cast up to see what money we had. Joe always kept a few pounds saved up, and as for me I generally had an ounce or two stowed away against a run of worse luck than usual. I said that Joe had better bring the girl out. It was a poor place, a digging camp, for a girl like that, but it would have to come to it sooner or later. And perhaps if she came the luck might turn. As for the letter sending for her, I thought how to do that. I would write, making out that Joe had hurt his hand or something. There would only be need for one letter, and when that was sent away, why, we would just have to work as hard as we could. Joe was on a reef with gold in it. Not much—nothing like the reefs men were working all round us—but still the stone was payable, and by working hard and living close we reckoned we could make out a crushing big enough to give Joe a start in housekeeping somehow. For the rest we had to trust to luck. Not that it troubled us much. Six or eight months is a long time ahead for a digger, and he always expects that he may be a rich man before it is over.

"So we settled it that way, and Joe and I went to work at his claim. It turned out better than we expected. The stone was easily got out and soft to work, and when we tried a prospect now and again it looked like two ounces.

"We had a crushing before the answer came to the letter, and the stone went better than we had calculated. There was 120oz. banked, and the reef looked well. And the camp was growing. More women came, and the storekeepers built good houses. It wouldn't be so bad a place for the young lady after all.

"'The luck has turned, old man,' Joe said to me, 'I don't like to be over sure, you know, but it looks like it. Those were good specimens we picked out today.'

"At last the letter came. Joe read it tremblingly. It was all right, though. She was coming, and mad pleased to come. Her aunt Martha was going to put her on board a ship that was to sail in a month or two. Joe let a contract of a little cottage to be built near the claim, and it was known on the field that Joe Thompson had a daughter, and that she was coming out to live with him.

"I never saw a man take on so about his daughter. If Joe had been expecting a sweetheart he couldn't have been more fidgety. I think, may be, it was a little of both—the girl that he was expecting was to him the old dead sweetheart coming back from the grave. Anyhow, he would sit smoking his pipe and watching the rafters of his new cottage against the sky in the moonlight, without ever a word. How he did worry that builder! And he wanted a garden all at once, and got into a regular rage with me for laughing at him when he asked if there was no way of buying ready-grown flowers to put in it.

"At length the time came for him to go down to the port and wait for the vessel. The cottage was finished and painted, and there was enough money in the bank to furnish it. The reef too looked pretty fair—not a pile, but a living. And nothing would do Joe but that I should go down with him, putting on men to work the claim. So I agreed, not being unwilling to have a bit of a spell, especially as things were going on fairly right with us.

"The night before we had fixed to start Joe was more restless than ever. We weren't living in the cottage—Joe wouldn't have anyone live in it till he had furnished it for his daughter but he took me with him and rambled over it with a candle. Then he came out in the verandah and sat down on the edge of it, talking about what his girl would do.

"'There she will sit, bless her, of an evening, and talk to her old dad. And maybe it'll run to a piano by-and-bye if the gold in the stone holds. She won't want to leave her old dad yet awhile. They aren't of much account, the young chaps out yonder'—pointing over his shoulder to the main township—'not fit to hold a candle to her. She won't look at them, no fear! Of course she will marry some time. But she's got to have a swell. A banker may be—that is if he don't play too much loo and isn't likely to come to grief. Or, maybe, a P.M. or a warden. Perhaps a lawyer, though there's not many of them any account. Perhaps she might'—he went on, as if he was thinking—'marry you, Bill, and stop with me all the time. She would have married Frank fast enough, poor chap; that is mainly what I was keeping him for. But I'm afraid you won't do, Bill; you are too old and not good-looking enough—for a young girl, mind you, Bill, a very young girl.'

"'What a blamed old fool you are, Joe!' I laughed. 'Hadn't you better turn in? I'm off.'

"'I believe I am an old fool, Bill. But it seems too good to be true—it's enough to turn my head.'

"In the morning Joe got up early. There was a little mare of his running with some other horses out at the edge of a big scrub, seven or eight miles from the field, which he wanted to get in. She was a gentle little thing, and he thought if he took her down to town he could break her to carry a lady during the time we would have to wait for the ship. We reckoned to make a start in the afternoon and get over a short stage the first day.

"I wasn't in any hurry that morning. We had settled all our business, and I had only to get ready to start. Naturally, too, I wasn't as fidgety as Joe. However, when dinner-time came, and Joe not back, I thought it a bit strange. There really wasn't anything in it, for the mob of horses might have got into another pocket of the scrub, and away from their usual feeding-ground. But I couldn't shake off an uneasy feeling. I broke my pipe, and cursed over it the same as if I had lost something that was valuable. As time went on I got worse, and mooned about saying to my-self over and over again, like the words of a song, 'Luck's turned—luck's turned.' I swore at myself for a fool, but it was no good. The same words kept making an infernal sing-song in my head.

"'Thank God!' I said at last, jumping up as I heard the sound of a horse's feet near the hut. I ran out. It was Joe right enough, but he was galloping like mad, and there was no mare with him. He hadn't even brought back the bridle he took with him to lead her.

"'What the d—l has kept you—and where's the mare?' I sung out as he pulled up. I noticed he looked strange. There was a regular glare in his eye, and he sat unsteady in his saddle, and made a clumsy mess of it taking his foot out of the stirrup. I saw also that the horse he was riding looked vicious and was showing the white of his eyes. 'Take care, Joe!'

"There—I can't tell you now rightly how it happened, but in a min-ute the horse was galloping off, dragging Joe along the ground with his foot caught in the stirrup. He wasn't dragged many yards, but when I had reached him he lay still as death, and bleeding from a score of gashes.

"It wasn't long before I had carried Joe into the hut and sent a man who had caught and brought up the riderless horse for a doctor. There was only one doctor on the field, and he was mostly drunk, but when he was right—not sober, mind you, but with just enough liquor to steady him—he was a first-rate one. He came and looked Joe over very carefully, feeling his head.

"'It's a pretty case,' he said, speaking to himself, 'a very pretty case. It's most likely the man will die. I wonder if I have the nerve to save him? Gad, I'll try. Look here you—what's your name?'—this to me; 'just you stick to me like wax. Let me have just six nips a day of rum—no, brandy will be better. Not a nip more. If you see me trying to get any more stop me—knock me down if you can't stop me any other way. Don't lose sight of me for the next week, and I think I'll save your mate. It's a splendid chance,' he went on, rubbing his hands, 'to see if I've lost my old form.'

"'So it is, doctor,' said I, humouring him, 'and I'll see you through.'

"'And now,' he went on, taking off his coat, 'before we begin work I think I'll take a nip. I see you have a bottle in the corner.'

"'No you don't, doctor. You have just got about enough for work. There will be a nip before supper time, and another after.'

"'Oh, nonsense. I didn't mean that,' he answered, moving towards the bottle.

"'Don't drive me to it!' I said, jumping up and squaring.

"He stared at me and swore to himself. Then he made as if he would put on his coat, flung it down, and turned to where my mate lay. It was pretty to see how he rigged up the bunk, with me helping, so as to make a comfortable sick bed, sending some of the men who had come round to hear the result for the things he wanted. When everything was snug and comfortable I went to the bottle and poured him a good three fingers of brandy.

"'That's right,' he said as he tossed it off; 'my hand was beginning to tremble. Beg pardon for swearing at you just now, but you were right not to let me have the grog. You'll do.'

"'Look here, doctor,' I said; 'you may say what you like or do what you like if you'll only pull Joe round—and you needn't be frightened for your fee.'

"Well, to make a long story short, the doctor camped at our hut; I watched him, and he watched Joe. Any other patients he had were bound to come for him or do without; for I wouldn't let him go from the place. And he pulled Joe round. That is, he kept the life in him.

"'He will be safe now, Bill,' the doctor said, 'if looked after a bit. I expect he will be as strong and hearty as ever he was, but he's gone here,' touching his forehead, 'and he may never be right again.'

"That was just it. Poor Joe lay there weak still, but getting better fast, and as silly as could be. He knew me, but as for his daughter he had forgotten all about her. He just rambled on in a weak voice about one thing and another, but as for anything that had passed he might as well have been a new-born baby.

"It was with a sorrowful heart I took horse for the port, where I expected the ship would be in before I could reach it. As I rode out of the camp I came across the doctor, sitting at the foot of a big stump, without his hat and waving his hand to me.

"'Wasn't it shplendid op'ration, Joe's mate?' he shouted. 'Show me the man in N-thern Queensland could have done it but me. All pack of … quacks—every mother's son. But he's cracked, you know, cracked. Can't mend that. Can't minister to mind disheased, eh?'"

Chapter IV

"I had been expecting to see a pretty girl and a young lady, but I was flurried when, having asked for Miss Thompson, my old mate Joe's daughter came across the deck to me. These were just the words which I kept saying to myself—'my mate's daughter'—so as to keep me up, for there wasn't a grander lady in the town than the tall slip of a girl who stood before me. Not grand by reason of her clothes, which is what many of the ladies seem to depend on, but the sort of girl who would make a man take off his hat to her whatever dress she wore.

"'Where is my father?' she asked, opening her big brown eyes very wide.

"'He's all right, miss—at least he isn't, he is very ill.'

"She turned very white, and clasped her hands.

"'Not dangerous, miss, by no means. But he had a fall from his horse and was very bad.'

"'So he sent you?' she asked.

"'I came. He wasn't fit to send anyone.'

"'I beg your pardon. You are—?'

"'His mate—Bill—at least William Watson.'

"'Tell me the truth, Mr. Watson—the real truth,' she implored, suddenly stepping forward and taking one of my hands; 'is my father dying or dead?'

"'Lord bless you, my dear—at least, miss—no. It's the solemn truth I'm telling. He was fairly out of danger, the doctor said, and mending fast. But not well enough to talk much.'

"I put this last in because I wasn't ready to tell her that her father was silly. It took me some little time to get accustomed to her, but by the time I had got her few traps ashore we became better acquainted. She was very gentle and good, only sad because afraid for her father. I could see that she looked upon me as a good honest sort of fellow that her father might have picked up for a mate, but who could not be evened with him. I'm not a coward but it frightened me when I thought of what was coming.

"However, there was no holding back. They had started a coach to the field and we took it. The booking office was the best hotel there, and Mrs. Slattery, the wife of the man who kept it, was a decent kind sort of a woman, but with a free tongue of her own. She came out as the coach drove up. I jumped down, and she asked me in a whisper loud enough for everyone to hear:

"'And who's that purty gurl ye've got in the coach wid yez, Bill?'

"'Hush! That's Miss Thompson.'

"'And who's Miss Thompson at all?' she asked still louder.

"'Joe Thompson—confound you.'

"'And is it Joe's darlin'? Come out wid you, poor thing; and yer poor father as wake and silly as a baby. Come out wid ye, my dear. Faith ye're a foine girl, and it's welcome ye are, and mighty glad I am to see me ould friend Joe's darter.'

"'This is Mrs. Slattery, Miss Thompson,' I said, helping her out; 'a decent woman,' I whispered.

"'None of your joking, now,' she shouted still louder; 'I don't want you coming between me and poor Joe's daughter now that he's in trouble.'

"The girl went on very quietly with Mrs. Slattery into the hotel, the confounded woman chattering away like a magpie. I got down the boxes and things, hardly knowing what to do next, out she soon came, out to where I was standing.

"'Take me to where my father is,' she said very quietly. 'I believed you, and you have deceived me;' and there was something like a choked sob in her voice.

"'I said nothing but led her over to the hut; the men we met staring at her, and she not minding any more than if she had been blind. I opened the door of the hut. The old man I had paid to look after Joe was there, and Joe himself was sitting up looking a bit weak but quite well. I hoped for a minute.

"'Oh, Bill—that you?' he broke out. 'Where have you been ? Ain't it work time now? Seems as if I've been idle. And who's that gal?'

"She went quietly over and knelt down by the bunk.

"'Father!—papa!—don't you know me—your daughter?'

"'Don't cry now, pretty dear,' said I smoothing her hair: 'Don't cry.'

"'Don't you know me—papa? Oh dear darling papa—your own daughter Ethel!'

"'What pretty eyes. Where did I see eyes like them?' he said—puzzled like for a bit; then, shaking his head, he went on, 'Take her away, Bill—take her away, and don't let her cry.'

"She remained kneeling, and then sank slowly on the ground. I rushed forward.

"'It's all right, boss,' said the old man, 'she's only fainting.'

"She was some time before she recovered, and, when she came to with a shivering sigh, she sat upon a stool and seemed to be pulling herself together. Joe kept on talking away about all sorts of things.

"I asked her if she would go back to the hotel. Without heeding me she asked:

"'Was he—was my father always like this?'

"'No, certainly not,' I answered, not making out what she meant, 'there was no more sensible man on the field.'

"'I don't mean that. I know he is not right in his mind just now; but did he always talk—talk like that?'

"'I saw then what she was aiming at. Poor Joe was no scholar, and it showed plainly enough in his talk. I tried to tell a lie, but I could not.

"'Yes—he always talked like that.'

"'Did he write much?—did you ever see a letter?'

"There it came—the whole trouble was come. There was nothing for it but to tell the truth, and I told it as well as I could, poor Joe rambling on all the time. She grew white again as I went on, and thinking she would faint I stopped.

"'Don't stop,' she said; 'Don't stop; I won't be foolish again.'

"So I finished my story—thinking that hanging would have been better. She heard me right out.

"'Thank you. Will you be good enough to get my things for me from the hotel?'

"'But surely you won't stop here!'

"'Where else should I be but with my—my father?'

"I said nothing, but went over to the hotel. Mrs. Slattery got hold of me and made me tell her what had happened.

"'Poor dear cratur,' she said; 'I'll just step over and see her comfortable.'

"And so she did, I carried over her traps, and Mrs. Slattery brought over a bit of something to eat.' The girl seemed glad to see her, and I left them.

"After that she took things into her own hands. She turned away the old man who had been nursing Joe, and took care of him herself. To me she would say very little, and would sometimes repeat what questions she put in a way that cut me to the heart, for it was plain she doubted what I told her. To Mrs. Slattery she took very kindly, and it was wonderful how that woman, with all her free way of talking, kept her tongue to herself about this girl. 'Miss Ethel' she called her—and I don't think she would have put 'Miss' before the name of any other young woman in the country—no, not the Governor's daughter. If the boys had anything to say about her new friend she shut them up. 'Is it yerself that would go coorting her, Mick? Let me tell ye, me boy, that it would be too good for the like of ye to ate your victuals off her dirthy plate.'

"Of course there was plenty of chaff about her. 'Lady Thompson' the boys called her; 'Biddy Slattery's princess,' and names like that. Not that the meanest of them would have said a word or done a thing to anger herself, and if ever any of them met her out about the field they made way as respectfully as diggers always do for a lady. But men will talk, and they talked aggravatingly. So it seemed to me; and I got into a bit of a quarrel with the 'Jumping Peddler,' a flash sort of fellow who kept mostly on the outside diggings, and wasn't altogether a square man.

"'What's the gal to you?' he asked; 'mayn't a man speak—as good a man as yourself, and maybe better?'

"It was said in an aggravating sort of way, and I felt nasty. So I thought to get even with him by casting up something he had done to one of his mates; and, before I could say 'knife,' there he was with his coat off outside the shanty, and threatening to dance on my grave before morning if I was game to go out to him. Of course I went out, and it was hard work licking him. The worst was that the boys got talking about me and Joe's daughter, and of course Biddy Slattery told her. That was, I reckoned, what made her more stiff with me than ever.

"One day she asked me suddenly:

"'What was Frank Smithson like?'

"'He was a nice quiet-spoken young fellow not much good for work.'

"'He wrote all the letters that I thought came from my father?'

"'I think he did—at least so Joe told me.'

"'Will you show me where his grave is some day? It is'—she went on to herself like—'where my dead father lies.'

"This was too much for me. 'Don't say that, Miss Ethel. You don't know your own father; you don't know what a good brave true man he was before his wits were shaken. You don't know how he spent his whole life working hard for your sake, and looking on to the time when you might be with him. You are forgetting what your dead mother told you.'

"'How do you know what my mother said?' she flung at me; 'how dare you speak of her?' Then after a bit: 'I beg your pardon, Mr. Watson. You are right; I am a hard-hearted girl.'

"Then she left me to go into the hut, and before I was out of earshot I could hear her sobbing, and Joe's voice mumbling: 'Poor dear! Never mind, don't cry.'

"She came to me soon after that and said, 'Mr. Watson, I should like to see Frank Smithson's grave.'

"I took her over to the place where Joe's mate lay. It was a quiet spot, away altogether from the workings, and Joe had put him at the edge of a bit of scrub, under a tree—I don't know its name—with dark glossy green leaves and large flowers like yellow cups at the ends of the little branches. It was shady and damp under the great tree, for the branches hung low and kept the sun away, in different fashion from the trees that grow in the South, so that a few pretty little flowers grew round the grave even at that time, which was near the end of the dry season.

"'It was a favourite place with poor Frank, Miss Ethel,' I said; 'he used to come and sit here on Sundays when the sun was hot; so Joe would have him laid here, though it isn't where they are making the regular burying-ground for the field.'

"'I can understand it," she answered quietly, looking round with a little shiver. It did seem almost as if Frank had got the best place in the cool shade, for around the earth was dry and dusty and baked, and the few tufts of grass that hadn't been eaten by the half-starved horses were white and dead, just, as the poor boy had once said, like the locks of hair on the head of a feeble decrepit old man. And it seemed worse being a sandy flat, for even the bushes looked burnt up, and the trees hung as if they were tired of the hot dry sun pouring down upon them all day long, without a cloud to give them a rest. Besides, all that were any good had been cut down; and bare stumps are not pretty.

"Seeing her stand, leaning on the rough fence round the grave, I thought well to go aside a bit, making as if I wanted to chip some rock. But I saw her stoop and gather one or two flowers carefully and put them in her bosom. When I went up to her again her eyes were full of tears— she had been crying quietly.

"'Oh, isn't it ugly?' she said under her breath, shuddering as she looked over the dusty flat at the dusty trees and the bare unsightly stumps.

"'Wait a bit, Miss Ethel,' it came to me to say; 'wait till the rain comes, and then you will see more pretty things in a square yard here than you will in an acre in the old country. There are some now,' I went on, stopping at a mean-looking tree from which one of those queer-looking things—orchids I think they call them—was hanging. It was a string of flat round green things, looking just like bits of leather stamped out to a size, but growing on it was one of the prettiest and most delicate flowers you ever saw.

"'Oh, how perfectly lovely!' the girl cried when I pointed it out to her.

"'Yes, Miss Ethel; but, mind, you have to look close if you want to spy such pretty things as those.'

"She glanced sharply at me, and then walked on without saying anything.

"To make things worse the reef began to duffer out. We had made some fair crushings out of it, but the stone was getting poorer and poorer as we went down. And there wasn't much money laid by to pay wages. We had spent most of what had been made before in building the cottage, and in expenses and one thing and another. So it came to this at last that I had to throw it up. What to do about keeping Joe and his daughter I didn't clearly see. There was a pound or two left, however, and wages ran high on the field; so I hired out at £4 a week. Mrs. Slattery kept me as a boarder at her hotel for 30s. a week, seeing after my clothes and all. The rest I paid over to Miss Ethel, making out it was dividends from the claim. In this way I kept on well enough till I got down with a bit of fever, and went off my head.

Chapter V

"It wasn't much of an attack, but it takes a man down, does colonial fever. Seems as if all the world somehow was pressing down on you, and mighty sore it makes your head. When I was round a bit Joe's daughter came to see me. I was lying back in a canvas chair, and tried to rise.

"'Don't try to get up, Mr. Watson,' she said, standing by me looking, it seemed, more beautiful than ever. 'I have come to make a confession to you. Mrs. Slattery has told me what you have been doing. No—please don't speak yet. It has opened my eyes. I have been a very, very wicked hard-hearted girl.'

"'That's not true,' I would say.

"'It is. I have found out for myself what my mother tried to teach me, what noble and generous hearts may be found under a rough cover. I won't say how I thank you, dear Mr. Watson; I think I begin to know what sort of man you are. But I will be a different girl, and I want you to help me.'

"'And I always will do it, my dear—that is, Miss Ethel.'

"'Please don't call me Miss Ethel; call me Ethel, or what you will. Treat me as if I was your—your—'

"'I'll call you my niece, dear; your father and me were old friends.'

"'Please do—think of me as your niece,' she said eagerly. And do you know it didn't seem quite so pleasant as I thought it would be. You see I wasn't much over forty—not really, though maybe I looked it.

"'Well then, dear,' I went on after a bit, and feeling a little as if some more lead had come down and was pressing on my head, 'you won't make a fuss over me paying in my wages same as I have been doing. I shall be all right directly, and there is lots of work to be done on the field.'

"'It shall be as you like, uncle,' she said, and when she said it again it seemed to hurt me more; 'but I have been thinking that poor papa would be better at work too. He always seems restless, and he gets his pick out and makes holes about the hut. Couldn't you help him to make a hole somewhere, and perhaps you might find some more gold. I could cook and keep house for both of you, and we could live very cheaply.'

"'We'll see about it when I get about. Anyway, I think you are right about his working.'

"Then we fell to talking about her father.

"'Please, uncle,' she said, 'tell me about him. I want to learn to love him, and I know so little about him.'

"So I told her all about Joe, and all the good I knew of him in all the years we had known one another. She sat by me, leaning forward, her big brown eyes fixed on me taking in every word.

"'Thank you, uncle,' she said very simply when I had done. 'If I had only known this sooner it would have been better for me.' Then she rose to go, and, promising to come back soon, she put her little hand into my great big fist.

"'I'll do all I can for you, Ethel, and never even ask for a thank you. But I'd like it better if you didn't call me uncle.'

"'Why? I wished to call you uncle because next to my own father I wanted to love you,' she said very seriously; 'but I will not if you do not wish it.'

"'I wish you to love me, Ethel, and perhaps, after all, it's the best way.'

"When I got about again I went over to see Joe, and found him as his daughter had described with pick and shovel busy sinking a hole. All round the hut were holes as thick as if it had been a rich pocket on a good alluvial field. It had been all done since I had fallen ill, but Joe was a quick workman and never lazy. He came up out of the hole with a dishful of stuff, and began to wash it. Of course there was no gold, but he washed steadily to the end, and didn't seem to mind when he found nothing. After he had done I spoke to him. He knew me, as he had always done.

"'Come along with me, Joe,' I said; 'I'll take you to work at a reef where there is gold.'

"He looked at me, nodded, and made ready to start without a word. When first he had gone silly there was no stopping his tongue, but now he was quiet, and had barely a word to say. They made no difficulty about putting Joe on at the claim where I was working, and he earned his wages. He worked just as well as ever he had done, only he had to be told what to do always.

"Between us we earned a good bit, and I gave in to Ethel and came to live at the hut, building myself a bit of a lean-to against one end of it for a bedroom. The cottage that poor Joe had built had been sold—at least the timber had. He used to get terribly excited when he was taken near it, so there could be no idea of going to live in it. But you wouldn't have known the hut. Ethel got me to fix up first one thing and then another, and she was always busy with odds and ends of little things to ornament it, till it became the prettiest little place in town. We had a Chinaman to do washing and job about the hut, and Ethel cooked and kept it tidy.

"I don't know that I was rightly comfortable at that time. It seemed as if the hut where Joe and I had sat each on a bunk and smoked was gone, and this was a place where rough men like me had no right to be. Ethel used to get her father to dress tidy when he came home from his work. There was always a big tub of water—warm water—and he, being as obedient as a child, would go into his bedroom and wash in it and then dress in a nice clean Crimean shirt and thin woollen trousers, with a loose coat over all. After supper he would sit outside, under the verandah Ethel had made me put up, and smoke, she sitting by his knee on a little stool. Sometimes he would look at himself, at her, and around him in a strange puzzled way; but for the most part he smoked quietly and without talking.

"Of course I got into the same way. There was a tub of water for me too, and I got into the way of tidying up.

"'Took to dressing for dinner, I'll be blowed if he ain't! Say old man, won't you get me an invitation!'

"It was the younger son of a lord who said that, and a dirty, flash, jeering blackguard he was. I believe the boys did chaff about us considerably, but not much in my hearing. I was sore about it, mind you, but I would rather have gone against the whole camp than against Joe's daughter.

"As time went on I took to the quiet life amazingly. Mrs. Slattery came in on some of the evenings, and Ethel was always glad to see her. It was wonderful how quiet she seemed to be and how fond of the girl. Living in this way we spent very little money, and began putting away savings till it seemed as if we were going to save up our rise—that rise which poor Joe and I had been expecting to make all our lives.

"It went on regular, as could be, month after month, Joe just as well as he had ever been, and even stronger and younger looking, though no nearer his right mind. And when the break came it was just the simplest thing. I wasn't there when it happened, being on top for something, but I saw a lot of people running to the mine. So I ran too, and the first thing I heard was:

"'Joe Thompson is killed.'

"The words seemed to strike me faint and sick, and I pushed through the crowd to reach the top just as the bucket came out of the shaft with two men, and what looked like poor Joe's body. They laid him out on the floor, and sure enough he seemed dead.

"'It was only just this little bit of a stone hit him, and it hadn't fallen far,' said one of the men. 'I saw it come down and strike him, and he dropped flat.'

"But I had been kneeling by him and could make out his heart beating.

"'Send for the doctor,' I shouted.

"'All right, Bill; the doctor is very tight and they are pouring water over him to sober him.'

"By-and-bye the doctor came—it was the same one we had before— looking very wet and silly.

"'What! Joe again—and Joe's mate!' he exclaimed. 'Wasn't once enough?'

"So he knelt by him and felt him, and shook his head.

"'Is it a case, doctor?' I asked; but he wouldn't answer, and got some of us to carry Joe over to the hut.

"Ethel—poor Ethel—stood there very white, but ready to do what was wanted. Mrs. Slattery, good soul, had run over and broken the news to her. So they undressed Joe and laid him in his bed, breathing so that you could just make it out, but still a corpse. The doctor went over him again very carefully; Ethel waiting in the next room.

"'Look here, Joe's mate,' he said after a while, speaking very low. 'I can't make this out—at least not to my satisfaction. It doesn't seem as if there was sufficient cause for the state he is in; the blow was not a bad one but it's touched the old trouble. Hark ye!,' is a whisper, 'He may live or he may die, but it is my belief that he will live or die sane.'

"Are you sure of it, doctor?' said I, gripping him tight.

"'No, I ain't, but I think so.'

"Then he went on giving directions what to do, and I stopped him, asking that he would tell Ethel.

"'I can't,' he said, looking down; 'I can't face her. Maybe you don't understand, but she is a lady, and I—I was a gentleman once.'"

Chapter VI

"When the doctor left I told Ethel what was to be done. He came again and again, and he kept sober. To be sure Mrs. Slattery took him in hand, and, being up to all his dodges, when he wanted liquor managed to keep him straight. We waited one day, two days, three days, and the change came.

"It was evening. I was sitting outside in the moonlight; Ethel was with her father. Suddenly I heard her step, and turned round. She was standing in the doorway, holding to the side, with big eyes staring. I jumped up and went to her.

"'Go-go-in,' she half sobbed; 'he is awake, and I frighten him. Go in, and I will run for the doctor.'

"I ran in. There was Joe, trying to raise himself in his bed, and looking all round as frightened as may be, but not silly. I could see at once he wasn't silly.

"'Is that you, Bill?' he said, sinking down. 'Thank God! I couldn't make out where I was, and there was my dead wife—my dead wife, Bill, as sure as you're alive, standing by the bunk.'

"'It's all right, Joe,' I said soothingly, not knowing what to say; 'lie down.'

"He lay still a bit looking round him. 'Where am I, Bill ?' he asked. 'I don't know the place.'

"'You are all right, Joe; just keep still.'

"'Oh yes, I'm all right now you are here, but I was frightened.'

"Then again after another rest.

"'I think I remember. I suppose the horse slung me. Say, pard, you'll have to go to the town without me; it won't do to risk missing the ship.'

"Then another quiet spell.

"'How long have I lain here? Perhaps you ought to be gone now. Don't stop for me.' As he said this he began raising himself excitedly.

"'Lie down, Joe. I'll take care about the ship; don't you be afraid.'

"It was getting too much for me, and I was very thankful to hear footsteps. I got up and went to the door.

"'Don't go, Bill; don't go!' he cried feebly. I was just able to mutter, 'He's sane' as the doctor passed. Joe used to know him.

"'Ah, they've got you for me, doctor,' he said feebly. 'I expect I had a big fall.'

"The doctor made him swallow some medicine he had brought, and remained with him a little while. Then he came out to us.

"'I have given him a strong sleeping draught,' he said, 'and he is quiet.

I'll come again in an hour. He is quite sane, and I think he will get round.'

"The doctor went, and when he was out of sight Ethel threw herself upon me and began sobbing. I drew her to me, and she cried on.

"'Let me cry,' she begged, as I tried to soothe her.

"After a bit she gathered herself up.

"'Forgive me, dear uncle,' she said, her sweet face all lit up through her tears; 'I won't be so foolish again. But I am so, so happy!'

"Joe did not wake that night. When the doctor came back he found him sleeping, and told me to sit and watch, and not to let him see his daughter when first he awoke. The sun was high overhead, and I was sitting beside him nodding with sleep when I noticed his eyes were open. He lay very quiet, looking around him, and I spoke, asking if he felt better.

"'Aye, mate,' he said, 'I am better, much better, and I'm trying to make out how it all happened. But there's the ship, Bill. Won't you make a start now, and let me follow when I can travel?'

"'You needn't trouble about the ship, Joe; she's come and gone long ago.'

"He turned towards me. 'And my daughter?'

"'She's here, Joe, all right. It's a year and more since your horse threw you, and you have been out of your mind ever since.'

"It didn't seem to excite him; he just lay quietly without speaking.

"'Then it was not—not her dead mother! It seems to me I've been dreaming all the time, mate, and her mother came to me always in my dreams.'

"I didn't know what to say. Presently he began again:

"'Where is she?'

"'Here, father;' and Ethel passed me and knelt by the bed. Joe stretched out his arm, and laying his hand on her head looked steadily in her face. I got up and went outside.

"I was frightened, mind you. It was not what the doctor said should be done, and very glad I was to see him coming again. He listened to what I had to say, and then went softly to the door of the room. In a minute he came back rubbing his hands.

"'It's all right, Joe's mate. They didn't see me, but I saw enough. The man's right. Wonderful cure, ain't it?' he continued; and I nodded; 'wonderfully successful cure "due to the skilful treatment of our esteemed fellow-citizen, Hugh Mafiddy, Esq., M.R.C.S., &c, &c.;" that's how to put it, my boy. No it ain't, old man. Though I'm sober I will be honest. It isn't my cure at all, and it's a better job in consequence. And now, my friend, I'm very thirsty; don't you think that—eh? I shan't have another chance, for you won't want me anymore.'

"I gave him the bottle and a tumbler, and he nearly filled the glass. But he deserved the drink. After he had gone Ethel came out looking—I can't say how she looked. And she came up to me and kissed me in the joy of her heart.

"That afternoon Joe was up and walking round the hut leaning on his daughter's shoulder, and as the sun sank in the west he sat outside, just in the place where he had sat and smoked so many evenings, and his daughter sat again by his knee. A short distance from the place was the stump to which we tied our horses and near by the spot where he had been thrown, that terrible day when our troubles began. He kept looking at it and asking about the fall.

"'Don't keep bothering about it, Joe. It's all over now.'

"'No it ain't, mate. There's something on my mind I'm bound to remember, and I can't yet. It will come to me.'

"Then he made me go over the whole story again, questioning about every little thing that had happened, till I was tired of answering. At last he straightened up suddenly and put his hand to his forehead.

"'I have it, Bill; at least I think I have.'

"From that he went on to ask me about the claims that had been opened since he could remember, and where there had been prospecting. I told him all I knew, and as I spoke he kept on stroking the thick brown hair of his daughter.

"At last she put in a word:

"'This won't do, papa. You have had enough talking now with uncle Bill. You shall go to bed, and I will hurry Ah Ching and bring some nice tea in to you.'

"'All right, my darling,' he said, stooping over and kissing her fondly; 'but I want you to do something for me, Bill. Get me a quiet horse to-morrow, and one for yourself. We have got to take a ride in the morning.'

"I told him I would do nothing of the kind, and that it was only foolishness in him talking of going on horseback so soon. But he insisted on it—begged of me to humour him—but wouldn't tell me why. All I could get from him was:

"'So many of the dreams I have been dreaming, old friend, have come out true that I can't rest till I see whether one more I haven't told you about yet isn't true also.'

"There was nothing for it but to promise to do as he wanted, and he went to bed."

Chapter VII

"In the morning Joe was quieter in his manner, and seemed quite strong.

"'I don't think that last little crack did me any harm at all,' he said. 'It was just a rough way of putting me straight.'

"Ethel was very pale and anxious-looking. 'You won't go out for that ride today, dear papa?' she said.

"'I must, darling I've got an idea here,' he went on, tapping his head, 'that burns like fire. Maybe it's only a fancy, but I can't rest till I have settled it, for the more I think the more sure I am that it's a memory, and not a dream. You say that I was excited and wild looking when I came galloping up that morning?' he asked, turning to me.

"'That's so, Joe,' I answered.

"'My horse wasn't bolting with me?'

"'No, you had it in hand right enough till you began to get down.'

"'Well, then, what was I excited about?' he cried in an almost angry voice.

"'I can't say, Joe. I've thought you might have had a touch of the sun—a stroke, you know.'

"'Ah! I never thought of that. They say that people who are struck have fancies, don't they, Bill?' he went on sadly, 'so maybe mine's all a fancy too. Never mind, I must go and see.'

"There was no use trying to stop him, so I went out to borrow two horses. They were easy got. The boys were all very curious about Joe, and there was a man getting up an address and a testimonial to the doctor. I don't remember the fellow's name, but he was going to run for Parliament as the miner's friend, and he was always looking out for a chance of making speeches. He would have been a big man now, I reckon, only he died after a great burst at Mick Flannigan's one time that the barmaid there got married. Anyway, there was no trouble in getting a loan of two horses. Joe wanted a ride, I said, and I was going to look after him.

"Ethel looked rather miserable when she saw the saddled horses, but she tried to be cheerful.

"'Cheer up, darling,' her father said as he kissed her, 'maybe I'm only going to get rid of a dream. But if it isn't—if it isn't—and he held her back from him for a while, looking at her sweet troubled face. Then he kissed her again and again, and mounted his horse.

"We started off quietly, Joe taking the lead, and for a while he seemed not very sure as to the way he was going.

"'Blessed if I'm not puzzled,' he said, 'they have been cutting down trees and changing the look of the place.'

"But he quickly picked up the track and went jogging steadily along. I soon saw that he was making for the scrub where he went to look for his horse that morning. He had very little to say as we went along, and made straight for a pocket of the scrub, a bit of grassland running into the thick wall of trees. There was a mob of horses there and he looked at them.

"'That's just how they were,' he said, 'and I swore because the mare wasn't among them.'

"Then he rode out and along the edge of the scrub some distance till we came to another pocket, but with worse grass.

"'That's right,' Joe said, 'I came here, but there were no horses, just as there are none now. I wonder if there is the same track.'

"He rode in close to the scrub that rose up, trees and bushes all tangled with vines like a green wall, and he searched. I could see he was terribly excited, and I was getting uneasy.

"'By G—d!' he cried, 'here it is.'

"Sure enough there was a little opening, just like what a mob of wild cattle or horses might make travelling in and out of the scrub, and Joe pushed his horse under the vines and into it. I followed. Fortunately Joe's horse was a steady one and went slow, for he was too excited to pay much heed to the branches that closed over him. Indeed he was nearly jerked off the saddle by a vine which hung low. But the old horse went very steadily, and, except a few tears in his shirt, there was not much harm done.

"After going maybe half a mile, I could see the light through the trees ahead, as if we were coming to an opening in the scrub, and I could feel my horse slipping and hear its hoofs striking on stone underfoot. Up to then the ground had been soft and spongy, but we had come on to stones, and soon after we rode out into a wide opening of the scrub, where nothing but a few trees were growing. It was a terribly lonely place. Some big grey kangaroos hopped out of sight, and there was a great chattering of cockatoos in a clump of tall gum trees.

"'Help me down, Bill,' said Joe, 'or I'll fall.'

"I was off my saddle and lifting him down in a minute.

"'There's been no one here—eh, Bill?'

"'No one, I think, Joe; but why have you brought me here?'

"He was grey looking, and his lips were dry, and he answered feebly and hoarsely:

"'Maybe it was only a dream, Bill, but it looks very real. Tie up the horses and I'll sit down yonder—on that flat stone.'

"I did as he told me.

"'That's right, Bill. Now you see there what looks like the cap of a reef. Pick up one of the loose stones and chip it.'

"I did so, he watching me with staring eyes.

"'Well?'

"I shook my head.

"'It's quartz, Joe, and likely looking, but there's nothing in it.'

"'Try again, Bill—for my sake try again.'

"I looked at the reef for a good place to chip with the little prospector's pick I carried with me, when my eye fell on a lump that seemed to have rolled off the cap. I put my hand on it and tried to raise it, and was surprised to find it fast. I looked again. It was lying loosely, and did not seem too big a bit to be lifted, but it was terribly heavy. Then I chipped a corner off, and it was my turn to start.

"'Great heavens!' I cried, 'it's half gold.'

"I turned round, and Joe had fallen on his knees with hands clasped.

"'It's true—my dream is true; it's my little girl's fortune!'

***

"That was how Joe Thompson's claim was found," my companion continued, "and you would hardly believe that the township around you is built on the desolate empty-looking scrub opening Joe and I rode into that day. There isn't much of the scrub left either, is there?" he continued, looking around. "We all found that where we had been reefing before was the wrong place; it was in the scrub that the richest veins lay. But there was no claim so good as ours. No more talk of the 'Jonah crowd' for Joe and me."

"And how about Miss Thompson—the Ethel you have told me about?"

"Oh, of course she was glad when the claim was found, and her father took her down south soon after the reef had been fairly opened and we had made sure that it wasn't all surface-blow. It was a pretty sight when she christened the new machine; I don't think there was a man on the field who wouldn't have punched even his mate's head if he had spoken a disrespectful word of her."

"And after that?" I persisted.

"She lived with her father down south till she married."

"Then she is married? Who was the fortunate man?"

"A swell, of course," he answered, a little roughly. "Joe was bound to see the thing through. But he is a fine fellow, and when I went to see them this last trip I found that they had christened their little boy 'William,' and his mother told me that she would teach him to call me uncle. But come along. We have had quite enough yarning, and dinner must be nearly ready. I expect one or two men in this evening, and maybe we'll have a quiet game. I have plenty of company sometimes. The married men say they like my bachelor's quarters. 'Liberty hall' they call them."

The Christmas Reef

James Crozier

Chapter I

"Certainly, my dear young lady, certainly. Of course I accept whatever apology you think necessary but some years ago—a good number now to be sure—I should have stood for half-a-day with a pretty girl perched on my favourite corn. Gout and rheumatics make a difference that I hope you will never know from experience but even now it is not very hard to forgive a soft tread on a captious toe."

I had been really very inconsiderate, and my mother would have told me, "unlady like." Though my manners never will have the repose "which stamps the caste of Vere de Vere," I doubt I shall be a hoyden, as mamma put it, until the end of the chapter, and brother Will says he pities the man that will get me—as if I should care for any man for whole years and ages yet! I like old men, I really do. They are much more kindly and gentle and courteous than conceited donkeys like the men!!!—I would fill up the whole line with the marks but it would hardly look nice—that Bill brings home for tea from Ormond or Trinity College. Half of the innocents should wear petticoats, or at least, take to bloomers. But I like old men, not too old, but old enough to have got rid of conceit. They are very nice. In Victoria they have the look of having done something, and of having done it well. And they look too as if they could do more yet, and do it well also. What a pity it is I can't express all I think in words. It is really a great shame for me to tell this true story, for there—even at the beginning—I have said something I don't quite understand myself, and how am I to expect others to understand?

But, as I said before, I like nice old men, gentlemen, of course I mean, and you can fancy how disgusted I was when running up to the railway carriage—first class—at Spencer-street, I rushed in over an old gentleman's feet, and would have come to an ignominious collapse on the floor if he had not caught me as I was on the point of falling. That's always the way with me. I never seem to have time to do anything right, and I am always in a muddle trying to catch up with something ahead.

When I get over the rush I usually take things easy, and on this occasion I quickly subsided, after profuse apologies, into a comfortable seat, and now I have a chance of quietly letting you know who your humble servant is, and why on this 23rd day of December I am a passenger in charge of the guard of the afternoon train for Maryborough, which leaves so exasperatingly punctual, and made me make such a hoyden of myself.

Well, I am just at that delightful age which poets long ago used to rave about—"sweet sixteen," and my name is Millie Walton. It is the fashion now-a-days to overlook young ladies of my age—that is when we allow ourselves to be overlooked, which, thank goodness, is not often the case—and we are duly put down—as pert and forward minxes, no good but for getting into and making trouble. There is a good deal of truth in the indictment, I confess, but not all the truth, Mr. Censor, and if we are more troublesome to papas and mammas and stern older brothers than were our grandmothers at the name age, the reason is not hard to find. We really know more than they did when they were in the teens or even in the twenties. Our education is higher, and we can fight our own battles with the boys in Latin, and French and Mathematics, and those delightfully horrid chemistry and physiology and things. In fact, we *fin de siecle* girls are an improvement on the "sweet sixteen" of the beginning of the century. Perhaps we know it too.

I doubt I am troublesome to my papa and mamma, and, as for Bill; he says I am the plague of his life. But I know they were all pleased when I did so well in the last Matric. Examination and actually took honours in French. I thought "no small beer" of myself, as Bill had the impudence to say, and fancied myself a "grown-up," and at once let down my dress at least two inches as the outward and visible sign of growth and gravity. My dear, dear friend, Jessie Maitland, asked me to spend Christmas with her, and, if I was proud before, I was actually "puffed up" when papa gave his consent to my travelling all the way to Maryborough by myself, and with a nice little purse well stocked with bright new sovereigns and crisp bank notes. Some of the latter, I am sorry to say, turned out to be of little use, because the nasty bank took that very time to fail, and I could not get the notes changed for a little while even at the most polite grocer's in the whole country. I doubt Madam Perambost would not pass that sentence, but since I have "grown-up" I find far kinder critics of my English than she was.

Well; I reached Spencer-street late as usual, and had just time to shake hands with Bill and implore him to look after my portmanteau— there was a duck of a gown in it that came right down to my toes—when the train whistled, and I had to run in the most undignified manner into the first carriage handy, and into the arms of the nice elderly gentleman, whose reply to my apologies I have already written. O, dear me, what must he have thought of me?

The train travelled slowly at first, and I had time by thrusting my head out of the window to see brother Bill waving his handkerchief, and telling me in violent pantomime, that the big portmanteau was safe in the guard's van. What guys men can make of themselves, to be sure! but then I think with all the worrying I give him, Bill has a good stock of love for his little sister. I notice quite a number of men are now-a-days devoted to their sisters. Poor fellows, I suppose a wife is a luxury too big for the dimensions of their purse.

The old gentleman was sitting in the seat opposite mine, and there was not a passenger in the compartment but ourselves. That is quite a comfortable thing when you have a long journey to go. I mean that the compartment ought not to be crowded on a hot, musty day. People can be so disagreeable and when there is a baby and a fractious child, it is simply unendurable.

Of course, I had had no time to lay in a stock of literature, and I began to repent of my pet sin, unpunctuality, in this instance at any rate. What a sweet thing it is to read while you are in a train of some great long-legged hero with a marble brow and fierce black moustache, making frantic efforts to win the love of a slim waisted heroine, always ready to fall into a faint or a flood of tears at the shortest notice! We don't meet either the heroes or heroines on the "Block," but they might exist in some undiscovered island, or might have existed on that big continent which they say has been sunk under the waves of the Atlantic. But I had nothing to read, not even a Family Herald or London journal six months old.

My young old friend handed me the "Argus," but that is a stupid lady's paper, unless on Saturday and it soon drooped out of my hands, and I sat listlessly gazing from the window at the long stretches of level plains that we have to cross before reaching the more picturesque scenery of Macedon. Notwithstanding my new "grown-up" importance I was actually getting bored.

"The paper does not seem to interest you much," said the gentleman.

"No," said I, "there is nothing in it but musty, old politics, and I hate politics. It is all fighting, and no doing."

My companion laughed, "Do you know," he said, "that without intending it, you have been getting on my corns again? I am a bit of a politician myself, but I can hardly say I am much good at the fighting."

"So I should say," I said, looking at him, "you are too nice for that."

"Well, my dear, that is a compliment that I should have given much to get thirty years ago, but I suppose I would not have got it so freely then."

"Perhaps not, and perhaps too I should not give it so freely if I had five more of those years myself."

"That is a very shrewd observation, my dear. It is a pity too that the years make us less candid with each other."

The silence was broken between us, and we chatted away in fine style until we reached Sunbury. There was little that I could tell that he did not hear something about, and we found out that there were many people in town whom we both knew. Indeed, when I mentioned papa's name he said that he had had business affairs with him frequently, and was glad to make the acquaintance of his daughter.

From Sunbury to Kyneton the railway runs through a most interesting stretch of country. Viewed from the distance, big Macedon forms a dim but splendid background to Melbourne, against which the churches and domes of the great city stand out like frescoes, when the smoke and mist are blown over the bay by a north-westerly wind. The big mountain seems to have been suddenly sliced away, and by the gap the engineers have run the Castlemaine and Bendigo line. The passenger is awed by the near presence of the huge mass, except when he is delighted by hasty glances of sylvan nooks and glades and ravines where I am sure the Australian fairies must hold their revels.

When we approached Kyneton Station, the gentleman—he had not told me his name—opened the window, saying that he expected to see his son on the platform. We had become quite sociable by this time, and I was rather sorry that our *tête-à-tête* was likely to be interrupted.

"Miss Walton," said my new friend, "will you allow me to introduce myself to you? My name is Allan. We shall have a quarter of an hour here for refreshments and perhaps you will permit me to see that you are not starved. Here we are at the station, and here is Ted waiting for me."

A gentleman came up to the carriage window, and was greeted most affectionately by Mr Allan.

"Ted," said the latter, "Miss Walton allows me to introduce to her my big son. Miss Walton has made the run from town a really pleasant experience, and it is anything but that without congenial company."

"Ted" turned on me the lustre of the two most wonderful eyes I ever saw or I think ever will see. This is not the rhapsodising of a young girl just out of the school-room. There are moments of existence when the whole wealth of maturity is realised is if by a flash, and one of those moments to me was when Ted Allan's eyes and mine met in one first long look. I have always wondered since that moment if his sensations were in any way comparable with mine.

I am not so stupid as to dilate on his personal appearance. He was as I saw him, a handsome man but a strong handsome man with everything about him strong to fit in with his strong personality. I cannot account for the fact that from the very first moment I mentally recognised the man's superiority, and instinctively submitted to it, but not without a struggle. I had had too much my own way to surrender at discretion before even a shot was fired.

Well, you can fancy us returned to our carriage after the halt at Kyneton, where we had a hasty snack. Many people might think I had acted without sufficient reserve, and all I can do is to cry out *"peccavi,"* and throw myself at their feet (metaphorically) and ask for absolution. These are people, however, with whom you assimilate at once, with whom every chord of your being is at once in harmony. The string of the piano remains mute until its own peculiar sound is produced, and then it echoes at once. Perhaps after all we are only musical instruments ourselves attuned to the music of the spheres.

"Well, Ted, have you succeeded?" asked Mr Allan, when we had settled down for the run to Castlemaine.

"No, father, I have not, I am sorry to say. The person I went to see was an unbeliever."[1]

---

[1] The word 'unbeliver' has been inserted to replace a line of indecipherable text in the original.

"Then shall we have to give up the scheme?"

"By no means. We want power, and power is only to be had in this world by one thing. It is not for our own gratification. If it was I should hesitate about the step. But there is nothing selfish in either your mind or mine. We have tried to do good, and no one knows better than we do how much need there is for good. When one thinks of the dens of the city reeking with sin, and the sin made habitual by want, there is no room for selfishness, and selfishness will have no part or parcel in anything we do."

I suppose my look of astonishment at these words made Mr Allan all at once remember that to me they must seem passing strange. With a smile he explained—

"My dear Miss Walton, I must tell you that my son and I are two of those people who believe that while man should be man's chief study, we should not confine ourselves to study. There are not many problems in life that we might stand aside and only wonder and despair, but while we are here we have time for neither wonder nor despair. Ted and I"—he looked fondly at his son as he spoke—"have been trying to work, but we find our very best efforts stopped by what we have to regard as the God of the world. Whatever favours we had at his hands we have passed on to others, and our work is in danger because our means are most limited."

"Tell her all," said Ted looking at me with a strange glow in his dark fathomless eyes. "Tell her all; she is one of the elect."

The old man continued with a kindly smile lighting up his benevolent face—

"We have undertaken a great work in the final regeneration of mankind. The atmosphere of the slums, we think, is not congenial or natural, and so our scheme is to carry the unfortunates away from the breeding places of contamination and give them a chance of cleanliness of body and soul. That is all we aim at, but money is wanted, and unless we can continue to get it our work must go.

"We belong to the cult of theosophy, and theosophists regard every phase of human thought or life as eminently worthy of human examination. They do not assert facts nor repudiate anything as illusory because it does not chime in with things that we regard as facts. They simply recognise the illimitable, as well as the illimitable responsibilities of life.

"It is rather unfair to bother your young head with these speculations, but you must blame Ted, and not me. Theosophy recognises immediate influences beyond ourselves and superior intelligences operating on human life, some for good and some for evil. There are certain individuals who by temperament or by natural organisation are more susceptible to these foreign influences than others. These individuals possess a power of prescience not granted to others, and at times they can convey the will and perhaps wishes of higher intelligences to us who are clogged by the hebetating shackles of the earth."

"Some of these higher intelligences have taken an interest in our work, and it has been intimated to us that at a certain place near Maryborough there lies only a few feet from the surface a quartz reef of extraordinary richness. This, if we can find it, will solve all our difficulty at once, but we require a "sensitive" of the very highest class to help us. We are conscious of the integrity of our own purposes, and that makes us bold, but of others we cannot be sure. Gold can be a curse as well as a blessing. There are those who are dominated by malign influences—"

"That," said Ted, "is what is checking us. I was told that I should find one at Kyneton who would fulfill all the requisite conditions, and came to Kyneton to see a person of whom I had heard. She was everywhere surrounded by the aura of earth, of gross selfishness. Whatever gifts she possessed were desecrated to the purposes of sensual, earthly desires. Have you ever seen anything like this?"

He took from a case a little box strongly clamped with brass. The box he proceeded to open with a key which hung from his watch chain, and within it there lay a ball of pure, bright crystal. The father took the ball from its nest with the greatest care.

"Just look at this for a moment," he said, coming over to the seat beside me. "Take it into your own hands and place that little drop 'of purest ray serene' in this direction."

There was what seemed a drop—tear shaped—in the solid ball, and this he adjusted towards the north. I took the ball in my hand with considerable trepidation.

"That which you have in your hand is Cagliostre's Crystal. To those who know what it is, it is invaluable, but we got it for only five hundred guineas. In some hands it is useless; in others it is instinct with a life of its own."

At first there seemed nothing very remarkable—only a ball almost like glass. Transparent, but with a misty opacity in its depth which seemed, however, to spread and shift and change like the morning haze over the sea when the newly risen sun begins to scatter the fading vapours.

Then—good gracious—the filmy clouds condense and gather into consistency forming flitting images which come and vanish in a twinkling, but always more and more distinct, always taking form against the pure cold background of the translucent crystal field.

So absorbed was I in watching the flitting shades that I had not noticed we were approaching the long tunnel at Elphinstone, and suddenly, with a roar and shriek, the train was buried in the black cavern. The light of the sun was cut off as if by a knife, and we were in a darkness that could almost be felt. Then my eyes unconsciously turned to where the Crystal had been left in my hands.

A pale ambient light floated around it, spread and wavered until it crept into the interstices of the carriage, advancing and retreating like a lavender halo of flame.

"Look!" I heard the young man say, "Look! it is not given to many to see as you see."

I did look. I saw a form of divine beauty glow out of the radiance. The thousand prismatic colours and shades now permeated the grey mist which had been all I saw before, and each lent its charm to paint with mystic distinctness the face limned by, yet glorified by their rainbow splendour. It was a god-like face, full of divine majesty and compassion. Then with a rush of the wind we were again in the open air, with the bright prosaic sun flooding the landscape with his garish brilliance. I looked at my companions; they were smiling at my wonder and amazement.

"Yes child, you are gifted," said Mr Allan.

Ted said nothing, but I could feel the intensity of his look thrill to my soul. Surely I was but then the young, perhaps fickle, and careless maiden who a couple of hours before entered that carriage with a narrow circle of facts, dull facts, as her only mental horizon. No! I had grown the growth of years within the limits of minutes.

The young man lent forward and placed his hand over mine, which still held the ball.

"Pray, look again," he said, "You have seen what proves you to be one of the gifted. The gift is for use, not abuse."

I looked. The opacity I had noticed before was now more distinct and centralised with blackness, but the edges becoming attenuated, shaded off into the crystal transparency.

I saw myself—my own self—walking in a field with a queer stick or wand in my hand. Mr Allan smiled significantly when I told him this. Then the figure changed and I saw a man lying on the ground with his drooping head supported on my knee. Again the figures faded and I could see a bright landscape of waving corn, a village nestled amongst orchards and vineyards with wealth producing mulberry trees lining the long stretches of the vista.

Then—well then, I blushed and put down the mysterious crystal—

for I saw myself a proud and happy mother with children playing on a trim lawn, and a man standing by my side—the same man that sat before me in whose beautiful eyes I could catch a gleam of the birth of love, which once cherished by that strong nature must live for ever.

At Castlemaine we changed for Maryborough, and only when we were in a crowded and uncomfortable carriage—the Victorian railway Commissioners must think that only city folk care about comfort—Mr Allan asked me to whose place I was going when I reached Maryborough. He was much surprised when I told him that my visit was to Mr Maitland's.

"Why we shall be going to Mr Maitland's tomorrow," he said. "Indeed it was entirely for the purpose of seeing him we came up. You might tell him we shall be with him tomorrow morning after breakfast. Of course he knows we shall be there, but you might mention the matter to him."

There was no opportunity for conversation during the dull journey. I think I must have fallen asleep at times, but I was always watched with wonderful care by both the gentlemen, who although they conversed in undertones most earnestly never relaxed in their constant and faithful guardianship.

At length we reached Maryborough and on the station platform was my dear friend and ally, Jessie. She received me with all the spontaneous gladness of youth. My luggage was escorted to the pony carriage by Mr Allan and his son, whom I introduced to Jessie.

"You and I," said the younger gentleman as he shook my hand, "You and I have known each other in other ages, this is only a renewal."

I did not understand him at all—only—only—when we drove away, the portmanteau in which was the dress that came down to my toes, was not nearly so important in Maryborough as it had been a few hours before in Melbourne.

Chapter II

Although I am very much tempted to do so I must refrain from enlarging on the hearty welcome I received at Jessie's from all the family. Mr Maitland was a thorough specimen of what is the colonial ideal of Father John Bull—bluff, kind, hospitable, and trustworthy. Mrs Maitland was a lady from the crown of her silvered head to her foot, well shod and small. There was a little army of brothers and sisters, and for a wonder they could get along without much tramping on each other's toes. The house was a big one, and the family fully occupied it. Mr Maitland was a large land owner, and of course he was deeply interested in every mining adventure about Maryborough.

He spoke of the Allans at breakfast several times, and seemed to think them a pair of Quixotes with more money than common sense. They had started, he said, a philanthropic scheme up in the Wimmera, but he evidently thought little of the prospects of success.

Yet they were received when they drove up after breakfast with the utmost cordiality. The gentlemen retired to the study immediately after the introduction of the strangers, but during the short time they were with us I felt that the eyes of the younger Mr Allan were always following me wherever l went about the room. It gave me quite a strange sensation—very pleasant, undoubtedly—but utterly bewildering to a young girl who had always been on a perfectly unembarrassed footing with all the men she had hitherto met, and had never dreamed of what is called love. It was a revelation.

After about an hour I was asked to the study, and Mr Maitland laid the case before me. The gentlemen were thorough believers in rhabdomancy, or the power of discovering certain metals by the wand. I had never heard of the thing before, and I suppose expressed my wonder in my face. Mr Allan explained.

"There are certain persons—and you are one—who possess this power. We shall only ask you to take a walk with us and your friends and hold a little stick in your hand in a certain way. You know," he said in a lower tone, "what depends on it. We have purchased a large tract of land, and we know there is a rich reef below the surface. We want you to bring us as close as possible to it to prevent unnecessary expense. That is all."

"I have never heard of minerals being discovered by this means," said Mr Maitland, "but I know that it has been tried with the greatest success for water. If the young lady likes to make the experiment, I shall take a great deal of interest in it."

What else could I do than say it would give me the greatest pleasure to be of use, though I doubted if I could do much good. Ted—I always thought of him as Ted—bent over and said—

"Surely you cannot have forgotten what occurred only yesterday."

I had not forgotten what had occurred, and Ted read his reply in the quick flickering glance I threw into his smiling and earnest eyes.

Christmas Day was fixed for our experiment, and I confess the ordeal through which I had voluntarily promised to go prevented me joining in the Christmas Eve jollity with the vivacity of my age or spirits. Jessie rallied me on my unwonted quietness, and said it was all through the magnetic influence of young Mr Allan. Of course it was, but I was not going to confess it to her or anyone else.

Christmas Day came, and the whole party of us started out on our adventures, some on horseback and a big load in Jessie's pony carriage. What I had to endure in the way of "chaffing." I was the witch of Endor at the very least, and Jessie would have it that I wanted nothing but a broomstick and my place in the carriage might be taken by Mr Allan. I was demurely silent under it all. An impromptu picnic had been suggested, and the good things provided.

About half an hour's driving brought us to the scene of operation.

I was impressed by the experience of the day before, but I must say the company generally looked on the whole thing as more of a "lark" than anything else, and the young Maitlands, all home from school, did not hesitate to express in plain terms their heretical ideas. But Mr Allan and his son seemed to have no doubt on the matter, and treated the scepticism of the others with quiet disregard.

It was a pretty spot where we halted. The woodmen had long forsaken the glade between two swelling hills, but had left behind them the great stumps of the trees they had felled, and round the trunks had sprung up small thickets of shoots crowned with the soft, green foliage that contrasted with the silvery pliant branches. The soil was encrusted with tiny quartz pebbles, barely leaving room for the stunted bush grass and vagrant orchid.

"Now, my dear," said old Mr Allan, "all you have to do is to take this rod by these two prongs and hold it out before you."

The rod was V shaped, with what may be called a long stem. I really did feel ridiculous, but I had promised, and was determined to go through with it.

It was a trying time. At first they all came after us, and we had the full benefit of their opinions, and these not very complimentary, but gradually even Mr Maitland got tired of the experiment, and they all went off to see about the contents of the baskets, except, of course, Mr Allan and his son.

Up the hills and down their sloping sides and across the gullies, where here and there we saw the little holes of the prospectors of the old digging days, with the tiny heaps of "mullock" at the side. Notwithstanding all my determination I was getting tired and discouraged myself, when suddenly—

A tremor shot through the rod and quivered through my arms. The point of the stick twisted and curved and wrinkled, and actually bent itself in the air until it formed almost a semi-circle, and nearly forced itself out of my hands. I was frightened—so, much so, that if I had possessed sufficient presence of mind, I should have dropped the wand to the earth. It reminded me of Aaron's rod, which turned into a serpent.

"I knew it," Mr Allan almost shouted. "Go for Mr Maitland, Ted, and bring the pick and shovel. Ten minutes' work will reveal everything."

Ted went away at the double, leaving his father and me, the one exultant, the other amazed.

He returned in a very short time with Mr Maitland and all the rest. In a minute he had off his coat, and seizing the great pick with his brown, sinewy hands struck it into the earth. We all stood round in a circle wondering what we should see next.

The steel point dug deep in the stubborn soil at every stroke, and rooted up the great boulders of quartz from their ancient bode. Then the strong man bent to the shovel, and swept away the loosened earth from the excavation. Suddenly he knelt down and seemed to examine the spot where his last stroke had fallen.

"There is a reef here," he said, "and right beneath where I am standing. I can't judge of its thickness, but this," continued he, "will show what its value may be."

We gathered round him, and he held up a little cornered mass of white crumbly quartz, evidently broken away, and all along the blueish seams were tiny specks of shining yellow metal, which centered in a mass of leaf-like gold, that filled a little cavern in the body of a fused rock. It was gold—gold indeed, and expectation was justified.

I need not repeat all that was said in the way of wonder by Mr Maitland and his children. Jessie was more than astonished. Like myself, she was half frightened, and thought it was a bit uncanny. As for myself I was actually bewildered, and could not help wondering at the change which the experience of two days had made in the character of a young, inexperienced and fickle girl. One can easily guess what was the topic discussed at our *al fresco* luncheon.

When we were leaving, Ted came to me and said—

"There is no one here, perhaps, who will retain a more vivid remembrance of this Christmas Day than you will, but you must have a memento. This piece of quartz is yours. Keep it. I may become the owner of it again, but no one has a better right than you to the first fruits of the 'Christmas Reef.'"

I had dreams, rather pleasant dreams, that Christmas night in the dear little room, with the room festooned with honeysuckle and blush rose. The days melted into weeks, and the weeks into months, and still I lingered at "Iara." The schoolgirl friendship between Jessie and I broadened out into the communion which lasts a lifetime. I was at home at "Iara," and loved it.

Perhaps I have become accustomed to look forward to the presence of one, to make up for the gaiety of the town and compensate for the dullness of a country house.

Ted Allan was a constant visitor at "Iara." With all the energy of his strong nature he threw himself into the work of developing the "Christmas Reef," which promised to become one of the wonders of the country. His father's trouble about the future of his great scheme was at an end, and he soon left for town to carry out his philanthropic ideas—which completely absorbed him. Ted came constantly to see us all at "Iara," but although he and I were frequently thrown together and although I instinctively knew that I was more to him than anyone else, yet he never allowed the preference to be betrayed to me or any one of the Maitlands. I think he thought me too young for such things, and I am sure I had no idea of the extent to which he monopolised my thoughts and my existence.

One evening he mentioned incidentally that he was going to explore the next day an old shaft about half a mile from the place where we had discovered the reef.

"It looks," he said, "as if it was on the same line, and I should like to see how the country makes. Joe Perrian and I will have a look. It is just on our borders and it will be interesting to see how the people who sank it failed to get the gold."

Jessie and I knew where the shaft was, and half playfully she proposed that we should walk over and see Mr Allan and his mate at work. He seemed delighted at the proposal, and we promised, unless something else turned up, to meet him on the condition that he came back to "Iara" with us. We knew Joe well—a big, blue eyed Cornishman, with the strength of a giant, and the sunny kindliness of a child.

Next day we did walk over in that direction. The shaft was at the foot of a little hill with a great mound of yellow earth raised beside it, and near it an old waterhole made years ago for mining purposes, and now partially silted up with big tree trunks stranded in the thick, muddy waters, and throwing their gnarled shadows over its dim surface. When we came to the top of the little hill, we were surprised to see a man running rapidly round the great heap in the direction of "Christmas Reef." He saw us and began gesticulating furiously and shouting for us to come quick.

"There is something the matter," said Jessie, "that is Joe Perrian."

My heart leaped to my throat, but I gulped down my emotion, and seizing Jessie's arm, I ran with her towards the shaft. Perrian was at the mouth of the shaft when we reached it.

"Mr Allan has fallen down," he shouted, "are you girls strong enough to lower me? The air I thought was bad, but he would go down. It must be bad yet, but there is a chance it is disturbed, and I shall take it. Something has to be risked. I should go down hand over hand, but have no knowledge of the depth."

The moments were precious. If there was a chance it must be taken, and at once I felt every muscle in my body become strained and tightened, every energy and force wound up in tension.

"Go down, Joe," I said, "and we shall see."

There was a windlass bridging the black square hole. When we knew it, it was covered over with a number of planks, and we used to take girlish delight in looking between the interstices and calculating the depth to which the gulf extended. The rope hung loose over the cylinder.

Perrian caught the rope and placed his foot in the loop. We then lowered him away into the darkness. I could not even at that moment of intense and agonising uncertainty help thinking what a brave man this was. Without comment and without demur of any kind, he simply offered himself to death in the way of duty. There was no mock heroism there.

The scanty light of the candle he held in his hand was soon swallowed up in the overwhelming blackness, and then we heard a shout—a shout of something like gladness—not the shout of horror or despair.

"Don't lower much further. Easy, easy, that will do."

We stood there wondering and wondering what was happening so close beside us yet so far removed from us. In actual distance it was only a few steps, but what a change that distance made! We had noticed that Joe had a long, small cord wound round his body when he went down. We heard nothing from him, but we saw the windlass rope tighten, and in a few minutes—perhaps they were only seconds, but time was an awful laggard just then—Perrian's face appeared at the surface.

"He is still alive," he said. "When he fell he caught between a plank and the wall of the shaft. The plank had been left near an old drive. He was far below it when he told me to 'wind up.' The air is not very bad. Something must be done, and at once. He is fastened to the rope, but someone must be below to guide, and you two girls could never raise the weight yourselves."

"I'll go below," I said, grasping the situation at once.

"You will," said Perrian, "Well you are a brave girl, indeed."

I don't know about being brave. I could have thrown myself down on the yellow ugly soil, and wept in an ecstasy of hysterical frenzy, but I knew that that would be real madness.

"I'll go," I said, "if you will tell me what I am to do. I have often enough climbed a rope and slid down a rope in the gymnasium."

"That was in fun, but, this is in grim earnest. Remember your life and his depend on your courage. Give me your hand."

I held out my hand and placed it in his. It was small and brown, but I know not a tremor betrayed the awful struggle that was going on in my soul.

"It will do. You will have to slide down the rope not more than twenty-five feet. You must stand on the plank and take the cord which I have tied about Mr Allan's body. When you are ready we shall haul up. Shout to us. What you have to do is to guide. Do not allow the body to swing against the side. That is all." Then with a gleam of light in his kind face, "He will owe much to the courage of a brave woman."

I said nothing. I dared not speak.

Heaven! what a sensation it was when I swung myself over that yawning abyss of horror! I gripped the rope with the tenacity of steel. My fingers clutched it as if they would bury themselves in its tough fibres. Then I went down. The cold walls, ugly and blotched, sprang up past me and shut out the light of day until I travelled through a twilight into almost palpable darkness. It seemed an age, but was in reality only a few seconds when my foot touched the plank and I knew that the first part of my work was completed.

There, huddled up, was the form of the man so dear to me. His head was resting against the wall of the shaft, and his body was doubled up between it and the plank. Heavens! if that plank were to fall. Down, down, far down I could hear the sullen echoes of water when the stones which

I could not help disturbing whirled through the awful void. But I must not indulge in fancies or fears.

I saw at once that the big rope was securely fastened. Joe was not a man to do things in half. The cord was partly coiled on the plank, and the end trailed down far below.

Now I could see. My own body had shut out the light, but now a square patch of sky was cut out above me and I could see Joe looking down.

"In God's name haul up," I shouted. The face was withdrawn. The rope tightened and I felt the plank shake and quiver and rock as gradually the tension increased, and slowly the body rose and set out on its awful journey. I think I did my duty, although even now those awful seconds seem buried in a cloud like the ghosts of a frightful dream.

Up the awful burden went, and again darkness was all around, but I kept steady, and at last I could see the load taken from the rope and drawn in by the Cornishman's strong arms.

Then a great loneliness descended on me. There was a dreadful consciousness of being forsaken, and for the first time I myself became the subject of my own thoughts, and the terrible possibilities of my own position almost shattered what little there remained of my courage. "Are you strong enough to tie yourself to the rope?" Perrian shouted down. "If you place your foot in the loop, you will be up here in no time, but the excitement may have been too great, and I am afraid to trust you. Will you tie yourself to the rope?"

"I will, I will," I cried. "Send down the rope."

The rope descended, and I wrapped the cord round it and my body again and again, and tied it as fast as my hands could, now trembling with excitement, and bruised and torn by the chafing and the unwonted work.

A few minutes, and I was in the free open air of Heaven again, and the breeze kissed my cheek. What a difference between that glorious freshness and the stagnant and sluggish atmosphere below!

"I shall run for assistance," Perrian, said. "Miss Maitland has gone already towards the reef."

Now that the excitement was over I felt the reaction. I felt the hysterical struggle and tottered to the spot where Mr Allan lay stretched out as if he were dead. Sitting down I lifted his head on my lap. An awful gash had torn the scalp, and there was a dreadful suppleness in the arm bent beneath him. He groaned when I touched him, but he was evidently reviving. His eyes opened, and there passed over his poor, bruised and wounded face the smile of welcome recognition. I bent down my head and caught the words as they struggled through his feeble lips—

"My wife for the ages—I knew it."

Yes, and at that solemn moment I knew it too. The clouds of fate were rent, and I could catch a glimpse of the soul life of the past.

It was no longer a girl they found there bending over the senseless body—it was a woman with a woman's soul vivified into a new life and a larger existence.

***

I am contented. The magic crystal was right in two instances. I can trust for the others. At any rate, I feel transfigured, and feed my soul on the ether of hope.

ON THE WALLABY AGAIN.

Gold Thirst:
A Queensland Tale of Adventure

John Westgarth Ellerman

Chapter I: The Escort Robbery

It is noonday. There is a blazing sun right overhead. The atmosphere is smoky with intense heat. Birds are silent. The cicada in his leafy abode exercises a vocal monopoly; and through his unceasing stridulous scream comes the ring of chain bits, the occasional clang of stirrup-irons, and the rhythmic hoof-beat of horses. It is the gold escort from Clarefield to Rockhampton. Sub-Inspector Lee rides ahead, beside him Trooper James Blacklear; next comes the pack-horses; behind these, four black troopers riding two and two; and Sergeant White, riding alone, brings up the rear. And so, with a wake of red dust behind it, the cavalcade swings along the narrow bush track which serpentines among ravines and gullies, and through dense brigalow scrubs. Just where a natural rocky escarpment causes, a slight deflection of the track, a voice rings through the sultry stillness.

"Halt!"

The black troopers mechanically rein in their horses. Sub-Inspector Lee is in the act of raising his hat to wipe his brow. He turns in surprise; finds himself confronted by Trooper Blacklear's revolver; and promptly dashes the hat in Blacklear's face. With an oath the latter fires. Lee falls forward on his horse's neck with a gasping cry, and then rolls heavily to the ground. Three men occupy the rocks and cover with their rifles the remainder of the party. The first, who has evidently constituted himself leader, is a coarser and heavier duplicate of the renegade trooper, and is in point of fact his brother. Both are dark-haired and swarthy featured. The second is a powerfully built red-bearded man who answers to the name of Rufus. The third half crouches behind the other two, and contrasts strangely with his companions. He is short in stature, and round-shouldered almost to deformity, but strongly built withal. His hair and eye-brows are a dull sandy-brown and his face is mottled and colourless.

"By God, I've shot him dead!" says James Blacklear.

"Damn him, let him lie! Head those horses back. Take it easy, sergeant, I've got you under my rifle. Rufus, shoot the first nigger that shows fight. Sam Dexter," this to the sandy-haired man, "you collect their shooting irons. Begin with the sergeant."

So, Richard Blacklear. Sergeant White bites his lip as he complies with the order to disarm. One by one the blackboys unsling their rifles and dismount. The fire-arms are strapped on the pack-horses; and the robbers with a mocking farewell, strike into the bush with their plunder, leaving the Sergeant and his black contingent afoot and unarmed.

Sergeant White stands for a few minutes as if stunned by the swift shock of disaster. Then his eye rests on the fallen leader of the escort, and with the assistance of one of the native troopers, he carries the body into the shade and covers the face.

It is only on the stage that tragedies with purely heroic surroundings are enacted. In tragedies of real life, the common trivialities of existence sooner or later find their way; they will not be denied. Perhaps it is in accordance with nature's law of compensation. The blackboys have gone to the creek for a drink, and, tempted by the shaded coolness of the water, are swimming, diving, and splashing each other in play as though the sticking up of escorts and the shooting of sub-inspectors were quite ordinary episodes. Presently they return, and lounge luxuriously on the grass, smoking. The sergeant addresses one of them.

"Know this country, Paddy?"

"Little bit." The answer comes with a puff of smoke.

"What name this creek?"

"Redwater."

"Where's the nearest station?"

"Cattle station ten mile up the creek—I lose'm name." And the black-boy lazily indicates the direction by a barely perceptible motion of his leg.

"Ah," says the sergeant reflectively; "we might get horses there."

"Might," assents Paddy with uncompromising brevity.

"You shall take a letter to the boss of the station, Paddy;" and the sergeant produces his note-book. In Paddy's mind some rudimentary installations of discipline struggle for a moment, but succumb to the levelling influences of a common misfortune. He abandons the attitude of half-attention evoked by the last speech, and mutters sulkily.

"Station close up twenty mile, I think. Might be no water longa road. Might be nobody sit down there. Might be all hands out mustering. Might be—"

But what other dire potentialities existed in Paddy's imagination are lost to the world, for an exclamation breaks from one of the boys: "Yarraman!"

The sergeant springs to attention. A column of dust is curling over the treetops, and slowly advancing. Soon is heard the tramp of horses, and through it a sharp interchange of voices. Through the timber the sergeant has caught a glimpse of a uniform, and his eye lightens. The approaching party swings round a bend of the road, and Sergeant White utters an ejaculation of relief. Chance, fate, or Providence, or all three, have sent a goldfields bound detachment of four white troopers with a native contingent to his rescue.

A council of war is held, and a pursuing party speedily organised. Two picked native troopers prepare to accompany the expedition. Among those left to await its return is the recalcitrant Paddy. The sergeant has not forgotten him in his report. The officer in command of the newly arrived force calls him out. Paddy shuffles uneasily forward.

"Salute, you dog!"

Paddy salutes. Next comes a brief order.

"Tie him up to a tree with a surcingle! Not that one—the next." Under the next lies the dead body. Companionship with the dead is the Australian aboriginal's pet aversion: and herein lay the punishment of Paddy.

***

Some twenty miles lower down its course, Redwater Creek witnesses another tragedy. A sudden atmospheric change has occurred; it is a moonless night, and cold, and the glittering stars look down upon the scene with frozen serenity. A tongue of red flame in a thick clump of bauhinia disperses the shadowy gloom under the trees, only to make deeper the obscurity immediately beyond its radius. Grouped in various attitudes round the camp fire, all unsuspicious of an immediate pursuit, are the gold robbers. Suddenly, Richard Blacklear grasps his rifle and bounds to his feet. His example is quickly followed by his brother and Rufus. Almost simultaneously a voice peremptorily calls upon the party in surrender. Dexter throws himself at full length on the grass; the other three stand their ground, and fire at random into the surrounding gloom. From the darkness comes a flash, and an answering volley. James Blacklear and Rufus fall dead—both shot through the heart. Richard Blacklear staggers back with a bullet through his right shoulder, and the rifle falls from his damaged limb. He bestows a contemptuous kick upon the prostrate Dexter, and roars defiantly:

"Blaze away, and be damned to you!"

A rush from behind overpowers him, and crippled and unarmed he fights to the last gasp of breath with the fury of a wild beast at bay.

As a sequel to these stirring incidents comes the trial and subsequent sentence of Richard Blacklear and Samuel Dexter each to a long term of penal servitude. The gold is recovered, all but one plant of about one thousand ounces, the hiding place of which baffles the most scrutinising search. From time to time in after years treasure seekers return from the fruitless quest. Only two men know where lies this lurking yellow hoard, and on that subject they are dumb, moreover their secret is immured with them in the prison island of St. Helena. And so the missing gold slumbers harmless in its lair like a fettered devil until the hand of fate shall have cast it once more amongst men to work some new evil.

Chapter II: At Redwater Creek Again

Ten years have elapsed. Scattered upon the western bank of Redwater Creek is an assemblage of habitations ranging, in progressive styles of architecture, from the grey weather-beaten solidity of the rough slab hut that hints of pioneering days to the garishly finished and yellow-painted product of later times. Taking a long, low verandah'd structure which announces itself as the Redwater Hotel for a centre, these lie around promiscuously in open defiance of the law of alignment. They suggest, on a large scale, the unpieced fragments of a child's puzzle. Collectively they are known as Redwater township.

Down by a rocky crossing in the creek, Lizzie, a half-caste girl, had just finished her washing, and patiently awaited the drying process. She lay in the shade with her arms under her head, her eyes blinking languidly at the stray sun-motes that pierced the leafy screen above and played fitfully on her face. Most half-castes are straight-haired and smoky-complexioned, but Lizzie was remarkably clear-skinned, and her hair was a clustering mass of jetty curls. She was perhaps eighteen, and looked five-and-twenty. The mingled experiences of her early girlhood had induced a mode of life which oscillated between the galling respectability of domestic service and the freedom—with its questionable morality—of the camp. A love of cleanliness in her surroundings, seconded by a vague sympathy with the refined adjuncts of civilisation, impelled her in one direction; a rooted distaste of set occupations, and an inborn impatience of restraint influenced her in seeking an alternative in the other. In the camp she was the nominally assigned property, chattel, slave, of the aboriginal ex-trooper Paddy; but she usually preserved an independence of action, which was not altogether pleasing to that sable warrior.

Lizzie had lapsed into deep thought, her brows knitted with perplexity, some knotty problem was evidently taxing her crude reasoning faculties. A stupendous secret held her in thrall; a secret that opened up possibilities hitherto undreamt of in her wildest imaginings. An episode which had lately enlivened the immediate sphere of her little world was in some measure responsible for the present trend of her thoughts. Rosalie, a half-caste girl of her tribe, had been married—actually married!—to a prosperous Chinese storekeeper, and wore shoes and stockings. Rosalie was tall, Amazonian, broad-faced, almost Malayan in type, with large dark eyes whose filmy languor hinted of opium. Ah Quoy, her husband, was a shrunken, parchment visaged little Mongolian; Lizzie's lip assumed a disdainful curve as she mentally appraised him. White and black in Australia concur in a contemptuous antipathy for the Chinaman; and this feeling, being in her case doubly inherited, Lizzie perhaps exhibited in a doubly accentuated degree. She was conscious of having finer eyes, more regular features, and a slimmer figure than Rosalie, and she would go one better than that enterprising damsel; she would marry a white man if—

A series of lurking misgivings—spectral reminiscences of the past arraying themselves with contingencies looming large in the future; insignificant considerations magnified to distortion under the lens of apprehensive scrutiny—rose up in hydra-headed hostility to the evolution of her plans.

But then, this mighty secret of hers, involving as it did, the possession of the most potent factor for superlative good or superlative evil that the world has ever known; what countless legions of difficulties would vanish into shadowy nothings at its magic touch. And still pondering in this strain—though in her own fashion—Lizzie rose to her feet, and gathered together the bleaching garments that fluttered, now dry, from some neighbouring currant bushes. These having been neatly folded and balanced in one compact bundle upon the summit of her curly head, she set out along the cattle-pad which followed the many windings of the creek, walking with a springiness of step and a graceful freedom of carriage which would have provoked at once the envy and despair of a silk-clad city dame.

About three miles south of the township, the tent of Jack Elton, kangaroo-shooter, stood on a high cliff overhanging Redwater Creek, and above it a leafy wild-orange tree warded off the fierce afternoon sun. The sides of the tent were looped up to admit the passage of stray currents of air; and within, reclining on a pile of skins, pipe in mouth, was Jack Elton himself. A rifle and a volume of Shakespeare surmounted a heap of leather pack bags in a corner. Outside, against the butt of the tree, were stacked a nest of pack-saddles; a riding saddle swung by its crupper from a limb, and round the smouldering brigalow fire, a few paces distant, were strewn a graduated assortment of flat-sided billycans and other camp necessaries.

Jack Elton had been, during his seventeen years' experience of Queensland, a bank clerk, a stockman, a shearer, a horse-breaker, a drover, a station overseer, a gold prospector, an opal miner, a timbercutter, and a kangaroo-shooter.

He was emphatically a rolling stone, with the proverbial lack of moss, and there are many of his sort in Queensland; men who, goaded by an insatiable thirst for novelty, drift easily from one occupation to another. Mostly Australian natives these; none other possess the adaptability, the confidence, the innate resource necessary for such a kaleidoscopic life. Thirty-two years of age, of medium height, spare, sun-burnt, and wiry, with an alert eye, and a supple elasticity of limb, the kangaroo-shooter was a fair specimen of an Australian native. As he lay dreamily watching the apparently aimless hurryings to and fro of a colony of ants, the retrospective workings of his mind might have been clothed thus:—

"There is a lamentable want of finality about my undertakings. I slide too easily out of one groove into another, and don't seem to advance in any given direction. I have either no definite aim, or so many indefinite ones, that they become mutually destructive. Balance the experience gained during the last ten years with the time expended in its accumulation, and how do I stand? Somewhere about in status quo. Altogether there is something wrong with the scheme of existence in general, and that of the Queensland bush in particular. I conclude that ambition is stultified within me by the very monotony of living: or if I have any left, it lacks direction, so I might as well be without it. I ask myself solemnly: 'What is the chief aim and ambition of Jack Elton, kangaroo-shooter?' and I reply, with less solemnity; but with all truthfulness, 'Hang me if I know, and hang me over again if I care!'"

At this stage-of his reflections came an interruption from without. There was no sound of approaching footsteps, but a crisp clear, voice vibrated in the sultry atmosphere.

"You in there, Jack?"

"Yowi, Lizzie."

"Why don't you speak English?" returned the voice half petulantly.

Chapter III: St. Helena—A Discharge and an Escape

St. Helena Island frowns over the wide expanse of Moreton Bay. In prehistoric days it may have smiled; but as it now appears—its natural beauties seamed, corrugated, and blotched by unsightly quarries, grim walls, and ugly rectangular blocks of solid masonry—its sole claim to benignancy of aspect is confined to one verdant patch of cultivation. This unexpected relief to the eye hangs on the slope which trends pear-shaped to the east, and when the sun rises out of the distant waters, gleams in its sombre setting like an emerald. In the distance large ocean-going steamers move in slow majesty, behind them long undulating pennons of smoke darkly pencilled between sky and water; sailing yachts, and a variety of smaller craft dot the dusky-green waves, their broad tense sails dipping to meet the curling billow-crests; but none approach the lonely shores of St. Helena. A girdle of warning buoys delimits the jurisdiction of the island; intruders from the outer world within this doomed circle are fired upon by sentries stationed on the walls.

Down on the western beach is a boatshed and a stone jetty a quarter of a mile in length—a long gaunt arm which the island thrusts far into the sea to grasp fresh victims and bury them in its stony heart; or to extend a menacing *adieu* to those who have expiated their crimes. The main building occupies an almost central position on the island, and in this human hive are huddled together whites, aborigines, half-castes, Chinese, Malays, and Kanakas. *Crimen æquat quos inquinate.* All nationalities, grades, distinctions, find a common level in this republic of crime. Here a man loses his identity with his name. Whatever he has been, whatever he might have been but for one fatal step, here he is regarded as a living antagonism; a force to be controlled; a creature to be fed, watched, worked, and caged.

The sun rose out of the eastern waters and warmed the stockade into activity. The morning parade; the drafting into gangs; the sharp word of command; the sullen march; the daily toil; and, again, the gloomy cells and soundless corridors; in all this soul-quenching routine had good-conduct man No. 45 participated for ten years. Now he stood apart, experiencing the mixed sensations which regained freedom inspires, dim aspirations, shadowy anticipations, long crushed and fettered, struggling into life and form, taking new shape and meaning; and withal the vague sense of helplessness which, after many years of captivity, the boon of liberty confers. It was the day of his discharge.

Later, he stood on the deck of the Government steamer, looking back at the prison island fast dwindling in the summer haze, and a cunning leer overspread his mottled features as he thought of No. 50, who was not a good-conduct man, and who had still two years to serve, while he—no longer No. 45, but Samuel Dexter—was free—free!

The sun set behind the western hill-tops and No. 50, a swart Hercules striking in the blacksmith's shop, flung down the heavy hammer, and brooding silently during the homeward march over the discharge of No. 45, muttered to himself: "It must be tonight or never."

Three hours later a warder lay half-strangled, bound, and gagged in a corridor, and a naked fugitive sprang from the shadow of the boatshed where he had divested himself of his prison-garb, and plunging boldly into the sea, struck out for the distant shore lights. He was a strong swimmer, and, as he clove the comparatively smooth waters of the bay, his mind rapidly traversed the incidents of his fortuitous escape. The abandonment of a long-matured scheme in favour of a bolder stroke; its consummation indebted to an unlooked for chance; the momentary inattention of the locking warder; the furtive step into a vacant cell, left open pending repairs, adjoining his own; the sweating suspense while the unwitting gaol-official shot the massive bolts with mechanical precision, and left his refuge unheeded; the breathless waiting for a favourable opportunity; the cat-like spring; the warder's choking cry as the desperate hands clutched hard at his throat; the hurried search for the keys; the stealthy progress to the outer wall, taking advantage of shadows; the successful negotiation of the wall itself under the star-lit night, every moment apprehensive of the crack of the sentry's rifle; these dangers were passed, but there was yet another—an imminent and deadly one, clothed in all the hideous repulsiveness which a stimulated apprehension lent it. He was a strong swimmer, but against this ugly peril the strongest swimmer is powerless; the bay was infested by sharks!

Nevertheless he swam steadily on. He had been figuratively up to his neck in risk since the inception of his bold bid for liberty, and this last, with all its uncertain horror, must be taken with the rest. A buoy afforded him a few moments rest, and an opportune elevation to reshape his course. Then on again, changing his stroke to lessen fatigue; but presently he steadied. A suspicious sound had reached his ears; a sound that was like the dash of oars. He listened painfully. No, it was only the lip-lipping of the waves on the friendly buoy he had just left. Still onward, and a large steamship passed across his course; her towering bows rising darkly and steeply out of the water; her ports ablaze; and a seething flood of foam scintillating in her wake. Then he knew he was near land, and when the steamer had ceased to obstruct his view, could just make out the dark line of mangrove scrub. Nearer and yet nearer it appeared. A few-more strokes and—

Suddenly a dark object rose out of the water in front of him. In imagination he saw the cruel rows of gleaming saw-like teeth; he closed his eyes and shuddered expectant. The object touched him; it was a drifting log, and he breathed again. Then he struck out vigorously; one crowning effort, and he sank exhausted on *terra firma*. While he lay panting he caught the glimmer of a light through an opening in the underbrush, and, as soon as he begin to feel cold, rose and made straight for it. A hut stood in the centre of a cleared patch; through its open doorway the light flickered fitfully. In his nude condition, none but heroic measures could avail him, so he advanced boldly and entered. A chained dog gave a startled yelp at the unusual apparition, and slunk bristling into his kennel, whence issued from time to time low uneasy growls. The hut—a fisherman's evidently—was untenanted. A heap of nets occupied one corner; a fire burned in the rude full-width chimney place; at the further end was a wooden bunk, and above it, depending from a row of nails, an assortment of wearing apparel. No. 50 or to reinvest him with his name—Richard Blacklear, made a rapid inspection of the latter, and as rapidly clothed himself. A pair of old boots dragged from under the bunk, together with an equally time-honoured felt hat, lent a finish if not a grace to his costume. Then he bestowed his attention on a camp oven, lifting its lid and appropriating the contents—lump of beef and half a damper; snatched a blanket from the bunk; and, passing swiftly out, vanished into the darkness.

Chapter IV: A Momentous Question

To return to Lizzie and Jack Elton. The girl handed him a pile of clean shirts and moleskins, and received a silver coin in exchange, which she poised reflectively on her forefinger. She looked skyward, then earthward for inspiration, and finding none, approached her subject tentatively.

"What would you do if you had plenty of money, Jack?"

This was a conjecture which from its exceeding remoteness the kangaroo-shooter had given little attention to, and he answered briefly: "Don't know."

"You might do almost anything you liked."

"Yes, almost anything."

"You might marry some girl."

"Yes, I might even marry some girl," he replied, absently repeating her. He was far away in the region of retrospect. Lizzie's words had lightly smitten the sepulchre of some long buried memories, and in a flash they leaped forth to life again. He remembered—it was five years ago—a garden; the heavy odour of violets mingled with the subtle perfume of roses;

an open window, and the witchery of music stealing through it; a fair-haired girl; a soft interpressure of fingers; an interchange of whispers—

"Would you marry any girl if she gave you plenty of money?" Lizzie continued, with a kind of intuitive divination of his rapt silence.

Banished once more were those fleeting phantasies, their spell broken by the voice which had evoked them. They had come with an audible sigh, and fled with its echo; and the kangaroo-shooter laughed somewhat irritably as he replied: "Oh, yes, I suppose so."

"Yes, but any girl?" timidly persisted his inquisitor.

"Why—Damn it, yes—any girl, always supposing she would have me. What are you driving at, Lizzie? What does all this catechism lead to?"

Lizzie made no verbal answer, but from the knotted corner of an old red handkerchief—the usual receptacle of coins and other stray articles of value that came in her way—she extracted a small cylindrical tin match-box and unscrewed the lid. Jack Elton drew a long breath as he examined its contents.

"Well, I'm damned!"

The girl watched him curiously.

"It's gold right enough," he muttered to himself: then aloud; "Why Lizzie, where on earth did you get this?"

"Not far—somebody make a plant long ago I think—plenty more there—can't know how much—might fill that big billycan, close up," answered the girl lapsing, as she sometimes did under excitement, into pigeon English. Jack had caught her enthusiasm.

"Well I'm—; where did you say it was, Lizzie?"

Lizzie's eyes sought the ground during an embarrassed silence. She was balancing herself on one shapely bare foot, and with the other nervously tracing and effacing figures in the sand.

"I didn't say where it was," she said slowly: then hurriedly; "I'll give it all to you, if—" Another awkward pause.

"If what, Lizzie?"

"If you take me away with you, and"—here a swift glance from under her drooping eyelashes—"and marry me."

Lizzie had played her trump card, and now stood with averted eyes, suddenly conscious of the awful enormity of having reversed the generally accepted order of things. There was much she would like to have said. Chiefly, that realising her inability to cope with the *embarras de richesses* that had been thrust upon her, she had determined to bestow its responsibilities, together with herself, upon someone in whom she could trust; and that she had singled out the kangaroo-shooter from a motive of partiality as well as confidence. But she discovered an overwhelming trepidation in setting about these explanations, and so bit her lip hard, and said nothing.

When a man has lived many years in the bush, working chiefly at occupations below the level of his attainments, his finer sensibilities become more or less blunted. When a man is in a "don't care" frame of mind, momentous questions lose half their significance. Preference flatters vanity, and flattered vanity is almost as wilfully blind a love itself.

This claims to be a non-digressive story, so no further remarks of an axiomatic nature will be inflicted upon the reader. The foregoing are merely intended to throw some light on the converging forces that influenced Jack Elton's decision. With regard to the hidden treasure itself, though he was already smitten by the *auri sacra fames*—the accursed gold thirst; yet something jarred slightly in the notion of its forming the sole basis of such a compact. Without it she would not have sought him; without it he would not have entertained the idea of marrying her. Such a compeller of destiny is gold. Some other considerations lent their weight.

He was a fairly temperate man, but one night he had succumbed to a particularly deadly brand of Redwater whisky, and falling from his horse, half-way between township and camp, had lain in the middle of the road blissfully unconscious. It was Lizzie who found him thus, and who, after a vain endeavour to arouse him, carefully "went through" his pockets, in order to anticipate a similar procedure with felonious purpose. The next morning she had presented herself at his tent door with an intricately knotted red handkerchief in her bosom, from which she produced a considerable sum in notes, gold, and silver, remarking simply as she handed it over: "I didn't keep any of it."

The kangaroo-shooter, lying half-dressed on his bunk, nursing a sick headache, and viewing his surroundings with a pessimistic eye, had rewarded her with a half-sovereign, bestowing the remainder in his pockets without counting it. He had known she was speaking the truth. Then Lizzie from the serene altitude of her moral superiority, had improved the occasion by giving him a brief lecture on the evils of drunkenness.

"When a man gets drunk, he gets wicked," she had remarked as a final synoptical statement, and with the air of one who has arrived at an incontrovertible logical conclusion. And Jack—an amused appreciation of the humour of the situation stealing over him—had replied with a nervous airiness: "Quite so, Lizzie; and wickedness is sin, and sin is damnation. I am in a parlous state."

Nor was this the only obligation Lizzie had imposed on him. He probably owed his life to her unwearied and not unskilful nursing during a severe attack of fever and ague, and gratitude for this service was not yet extinct within him.

She had probably broken but one of the ten Commandments in her life, not even knowing it to be a transgression: still less knowing that what it regards in man as trivial escapade, the seeming-virtuous world condemns as an unpardonable sin in woman. He of all others could scarcely cast this in her face. So it came to pass that the kangaroo-shooter, after the first brief shock of surprise, turned to Lizzie and said simply: "So be it."

And she inquired artlessly: "Does that mean yes?"

"It means yes."

"All right."

And Lizzie's "all right" was honest, if unromantic.

Chapter V: Two Victims of Social Prejudice

About twenty-four hours after the ratification of the treaty detailed in the previous chapter, a solitary one-horse traveller slung off his swag and other gear, and hobbled out on the creek, a quarter of a mile above the kangaroo-shooter's camp. He looked around him carefully, as though searching for landmarks; then after a brief hesitation struck into the thick brigalow scrub. A ten minute walk brought him to a small tributary of the creek, and just where it narrowed into a rocky gorge, he stopped and looked suspiciously about him. No one was in sight. A few moments search among the boulders, and he stooped over a flat slab of rock. To his consternation it betrayed indications of a recent displacement. He lifted the slab, and realised his worst fears. Beneath was a natural cup like well in the rock. It was empty! He dropped the heavy slab with an oath.

Two distinct tracks were visible on a clean sandy patch close by: one the vigorous imprint of a man's boot: the other, the less clearly defined impression of a bare foot. He followed them in a retreating direction for some distance, then lost them on a stony ridge; and, after a series of detours to make a recovery on more favourable ground, found himself back on the main creek. Looking across the channels, he observed, for the first time, a tent, and close by it, two figures—a white man and a half-caste girl; and the girl's feet were bare. Here evidently lay the solution of the tracking difficulty. Yet in order to strengthen assurance, he crossed the creek; exchanged salutations with the man; lounged carelessly up to the fire, and lit his pipe with a cinder; and made a few remarks about the scarcity of water and grass, furtively taking in all the details of the kangaroo-shooter's belongings. Then he returned to his own camp, where he consumed the rest of the day in profound meditation, with intervals of profane mutterings.

Towards evening another traveller arrived on the scene. He was mounted, and led another horse, carrying an overlander pack. As he approached, the first arrival stared in mute amazement, and a flush of annoyance tinged for a moment the mottled pallor of his countenance. Was he dreaming, or was that, indeed Blacklear?

Blacklear it was. He seemed to read a series of questions in the other's eye as he advanced, and anticipated them.

"Yes, Sam Dexter, I'm here. How did I get out?—Never mind; I got out, and it's a long story. Where did I get the horses?—Duffed them out of a squatter's horse paddock. Which way did I come? Across country mostly. How did I get on for tucker?—How does any man get on in the bush without money? I didn't starve. Think I'm the sort of man to starve? Give me some tobacco."

When he had hobbled out his horses, he filled his pipe in a leisurely manner, eyeing Dexter curiously meantime.

"You don't seem over and above pleased to see me," at length he remarked.

Now Dexter's plan at the outset had not included the possibility of this unexpected meeting; but in view of the turn affairs had taken, it was just as well to have a mate, though his choice of a coadjutor would certainly not have fallen on Blacklear. He feared him, and hated him with the impotent hatred of cowardice. But his reply was given with a forced geniality.

"Pleased, my dear fellow?—I'm delighted; which you won't be when you hear what I have to tell you."

It was now Blacklear's turn to look inquiringly.

"The plant—"

"Well, the plant?" burst from Blacklear.

"Is gone—that's all," concluded Dexter lamely.

Blacklear's face took on a darker tinge, and his language for the next few moments was lurid. He turned fiercely on his companion.

"Answer me one question, Sam Dexter. Did you have a hand in shifting it?"

"No—square and all—I hadn't; but I've got a pretty good idea who had."

Dexter then related his experiences in the earlier part of the day, and the two sat late into the night conspiring.

With the first blush of morning, even as the Moslem faces Mecca, so did the anxious regard of Dexter turn in the direction of the tent, where lay, as he believed, the rifled treasure. But no tent was there. The kangaroo-shooter had mustered his horses during the night, silently packed up, and decamped. A blackfellow turning over the littered debris with his nullah-nullah was the only occupant of the deserted camp. By-and-bye he sauntered over to the white men in that desultory, zig-zag fashion which characterises his race. He endeavoured to initiate a conversation by recounting a grievance.

"Some dam white feller bin take away Lizzie. Which way that one yan?"

The two treasure seekers, absorbed in their own perplexed affairs, and scarce heeding his words "didn't know," and "didn't care."

Their visitor then informed them that his name was Paddy, and casually drew attention to the depleted condition of his pipe. This hint passing unregarded, he reverted, with greater odiousness of detail, to his former subject. When it came out that the "dam white feller" alluded to was none other than the kangaroo-shooter, and that "Lizzie" was a commodity in whom Paddy professed to exercise a proprietorship, Blacklear, sitting in moody meditation, looked at the speaker reflectively.

Here, he thought, was a possible ally not to be despised under the circumstances. He would be useful in tracking, and would have the additional stimulus of serving his own interests. Yes, Paddy's co-operation must be secured.

Accordingly, negotiations were entered into with Paddy, who at first demurred, suggesting as the essence of the contract: "Money and tobacco first time," which was amended by Blacklear to "Tobacco first time, money by-and-bye."

However, with a present supply of tobacco, and Blacklear's munificent promises of countless sums of money to dream upon; Paddy was finally prevailed upon to accompany the expedition, and preparations were made for an immediate pursuit.

Chapter VI: With the Pursued—A Misunderstanding

It was night—the third since their departure from Redwater—and the kangaroo-shooter and Lizzie were encamped upon a long waterhole of Bauhinia Creek. They had accomplished that day a dry stage of about twenty miles, and the horse bells now jangled industriously on a neighbouring ridge where the grass, though dry, was abundant. The atmosphere was still and heavy. Dark masses of clouds overhead seemed to promise a long expected downpour of rain. A neglected fire smouldered at the butt of a stump, and Jack Elton sat silent, staring in mental isolation into its dying embers.

There is no more unsatisfactory process of thought than a futile comparison of what might have been with what actually is. He was thinking of the various roads to fortune that had been open to him, and the many turnings back on them; of opportunities neglected; tides not taken at the flood; enterprises abandoned through lack of capital. Now, he had a small fortune at his disposal; but a fortune *per se* is one thing; a fortune hampered by conditions, quite another. These bonds that he was forging for himself—there was something so hideously unpoetical in their nature; and if he thought so now while the roseate blush of novelty tinged them, what might they not appear later on. He almost wished the gold back in its hiding place undiscovered, and Lizzie and he back in their old uneventful grooves. If he could only summon up the requisite cold-blooded villainy it would be easy enough.

But no, he could not entertain the idea of playing her false. Such treachery would be too revolting. Besides, he owed everything to her—fortune, life itself.

"I know what you're thinking about, Jack." Lizzie had been sitting, nursing her knees, and regarding him intently. "You're thinking about that other girl; that's one thing. Another thing: You're thinking you'd like to get rid of me."

The kangaroo-shooter started from his reverie, flushing slightly, and somewhat staggered by the facility with which she read or guessed his thoughts, not knowing or forgetting the acute aptness of love in translating facial expression. That very afternoon, while riding behind the packhorses, she had surprised him in a similar manner; and then goaded by a strange impulse to revel in self-torture, had extracted from him some unwilling particulars of a former love episode in his career. On this occasion she had favoured him with a bit of her own naive logic, as thus:

"Look here, Jack, I like you; perhaps that other girl doesn't like now. You know all about me; you don't know all about her. You know altogether how bad I am. You don't know how bad she might be." A mode of reasoning which, though rude and unpolished, the kangaroo-shooter had recognised with tempered amusement, as not altogether devoid of point.

He was casting about in his mind for a suitable reply to this singularly direct accusation, when Lizzie spoke again, and the unusually level tones of her voice betokened a hidden depth of emotion.

"All right. Jack. You can leave me if you like. You can take all the gold; I don't want any of it. You can go to that other girl. I don't care—I don't care." And she bowed her head to her knees rocking slightly to and fro.

Jack looked at her in silence, smitten with a feeling of remorse. What in his case was the fever and fret of brooding over unfulfilled aims, compared with the blank desolation of her life if he abandoned her? For he was beginning to partly guess at the strength of her affection for him, though as yet unaware of its self-sacrificing intensity. A new sensation stirred within him. Something that seemed to partake of admiration, gratitude, pity, and yet distinct from all three; an undercurrent below their depths.

"Lizzie," he touched her arm softly as he spoke.

But Lizzie had passed, into another mood. She had misinterpreted his silence. She had taken it to imply a calm acquiescence; and every fibre of her passionate nature rebelled at the heartless injustice of it all. She sprang to her feet; her eyes flashing through a mist of tears.

"Don't touch me," she said repulsing him angrily. "Don't come near me, I hate her, and I hate you! I'm going to sleep." And she withdraw hastily into the tent.

Surprised and vexed by this unwonted outburst. Jack Elton judged it wiser to defer reconciliation until the morning. The girl was no doubt overwrought, and tired by the unaccustomed horseback journey. After a good night's rest, a few words would set everything right again without the risk of an emotional tableau. So he threw himself on the ground, and sought consolation in a pipe; and while lazily smoking, and watching the gathering clouds overhead, fell asleep.

When he awoke it was within an hour of daybreak. He listened for, but could hear nothing of his horse bells. The horses were most likely camping, he thought, but at any rate it would be daylight shortly, so he might well start after them at once. He looked into the tent. Lizzie evidently was fast asleep, her head pillowed on a leather pack-bag. He picked up a bridle, and went whistling up the ridges.

Chapter VII: With the Pursuers; the First Death

The two treasure-seekers, aided by Paddy's skill in tracking, had lost no time in the pursuit: and on the evening of the third day halted at the long waterhole soon after the kangaroo-shooter had hobbled his horses out. Having ascertained—unperceived themselves—the position of the latter's camp, the pursuers took up their quarters in a thick patch of scrub at some little distance from the water, letting their horses go in hobbles, but without bells. The kangaroo-shooter, they knew, was well provided with firearms, while they were practically unarmed. It was necessary therefore to employ strategy in recovering the gold. A plan had been determined upon, and it was agreed that a blow should be struck before morning. Paddy was getting uneasy with each remove from home, and Blacklear himself—the dominating spirit of the party—exasperated at the mischance that had wrested the treasure almost from within his grasp, was in no mood for delay. He was developing a dogged moroseness of demeanour which increased with each little contretemps, and on occasions flamed forth in such ungovernable spasms of fury as almost to terrify his companions. Of the latter Dexter was perhaps the more uncomfortable. A wild idea had darted through his mind: "Why not effect a desertion to the enemy's camp, and make terms on his own account?" But a glance at the man sitting glowering at him in the darkness was enough. His half-formed intention died in the shadow of fear.

A small fire which had served to boil a billy of tea threw evanescent flickerings upon the group.

Paddy had finished his supper, and was smoking in placid rumination. He sat on the ground with his feet tucked under him, humming choice scraps from his repertoire of corroboree vocalisation. Presently, looking at each of the white men in turn, he broke into a secretive chuckling laugh.

"What's amusing you Paddy?"

It was Blacklear who asked the question. He had been contemplating the black-fellow for some time in sullen silence.

The Australian aborigine, following the bent of his chief characteristic —indolence—had constructed (or modified the construction of) his language with a view to rapid enunciation with the least vocal effort. He avoids hard consonants and harsh syllabic combinations, and his mutilations of the English language are merely attempts to soften its asperities. Without attempting to follow literally the idiom of Paddy's speech, it will be sufficient to say that the ex-native trooper had been turning over in his mind the incidents of the escort robbery of years ago. It had been slowly dawning upon him that he was again face to face with two of the participators in that famous raid, and now he was sure of it. He laughed in complacent approval of his own superior sagacity, and, as he detailed some of the events of that fatal day long ago, he laughed again at the evident effect he had produced upon his listeners. The two whites exchanged a significant glance, and Blacklear's hand sought his belt.

"Do you see that bright star over there, Paddy—that one yonder?"

Paddy turned his head in the direction indicated; and it was his last look with mortal eyes on things either celestial or terrestrial, for then and there Blacklear's knife solved the riddle of futurity for him.

A gasp, a moan, a quiver of the ebony limbs—and Dexter staring in amazed horror at the awful suddenness of the deed!

"I won't take any risks," said Blacklear, as coolly as though he had merely crushed a centipede in his path. "Lend me a hand to carry him out of this."

The request took the tone of a command, and Dexter complied in quaking silence. Paddy, whose retentive memory had done him a fatal disservice, found a hastily improvised grave in the sandy river bed.

"We can do without him now, and he's just as well out of the road," commented Blacklear, when the interment was accomplished.

The summary wiping out of Paddy necessitated a reconstruction of their scheme; so the following plan was arranged:—Blacklear to hunt the kangaroo-shooter's horses well away before the latter was stirring; Dexter meanwhile to bring their own horses back. This would ensure the protracted absence of the kangaroo-shooter, during which it would be easy enough to surprise his camp—there would be only the girl to reckon with; secure his firearms, and regain possession of the gold. Accordingly, about two hours before daybreak, the two separated on their different errands. When, however, Blacklear came up with the kangaroo-shooter's horses, he discovered that his own were among them. He caught and bridled one of these, and creeping silently among the rest, removed all the hobbles, and muffled the bells. Then he vaulted on to the horse he had caught, and drove the whole mob back along the road they had travelled the day before. After driving for about five miles, he blocked them, intending to cut out his other two horses, and then, by making a slight detour with them, to regain his camp unperceived. But while thus engaged his horse went shoulder deep into a hole, and falling, threw his rider heavily. Blacklear must have lain stunned for some considerable time; for when he recovered consciousness it was broad daylight, though the sun was obscured by the heavy clouds that still mantled the sky. The horses had kept on along the road, and he followed their tracks in the hope of overhauling them when they stopped to feed. But hour after hour crept by, and still the tracks kept the road, and still he pursued them, until he arrived, tired and thirsty, at a small waterhole which he remembered passing the day before. It was dry, or as good as dry. A mob of cattle had been through it, and churned it into a slough of mud. And the horses—not a hoof of them to be seen; they had halted there and gone on again, and would probably never pull up until they reached the next water, twenty five miles further back.

Blacklear threw himself on the ground wearily. There was but one course now open to him: to rest first, and then retrace his steps to the waterhole he had left fully twenty miles behind him. While he lay anxiously watching the darkly-impending rain-clouds that so tantalisingly withheld their relief, another thirsty pedestrian arrived on the scene, and limped slowly towards him. It was Dexter, who during a fruitless quest for the horses had got bushed, and who, after accidentally striking the track, had followed it in the wrong direction, having no sun to guide him, and being at the best a poor bushman. Still later, another victim to the torture of thirst was added to the list; the kangaroo-shooter himself, who emerged from the scrub, and stood looking doubtfully at the two former arrivals, evidently connecting them in his mind with the free leg his horses had got.

Chapter VIII: The Stage is Cleared

When Lizzie awoke, somewhat later than usual, she hastened to light a fire and make preparations for breakfast, expecting every minute to see Jack Elton returning with the horses. But the minutes lengthened to hours, and the hours succeeded each other, and still she waited, and waited in vain. Towards midday she began to grow uneasy. She knew that the kangaroo-shooter was too good a bushman to get lost; therefore either something must have happened to him or else the horses must have cleared out during the night. She made an excursion back along the road far enough to observe that the horses had gone that way, and also noted the fact that they were out of hobbles. Somewhat puzzled, she retraced her steps, and on her way back her attention was arrested by a thin wreath of smoke curling upward from a dense patch of scrub on the further side of the waterhole. She approached the spot, looking around her cautiously, and listening. In the heart of the scrub she came upon a smouldering fire, two riding saddles, and a general scatter of blankets, billycans, quart-pots, and other camp fixings. No living creature—neither man nor horse—was there: but near the fire was a dark stain in the sand that looked like blood. Lizzie returned to her own camp and resolved on a course of action. Anything was better than the idle suspense of waiting. First she scraped out a hole in the yielding sand of the creek; then carried down the bank, one after the other, the two pack-bags containing the gold and buried them; afterwards carefully obliterating all traces of her work. Then she filled a waterbag, and was about to start, when another idea came into her head. She had remembered seeing a revolver in a leathern case among some other shooting fixtures. She found it, and slipped a cartridge into each chamber; and, after putting things ship-shape in the camp, with the waterbag in her hand, and the revolver slung from her shoulder, she started bravely on her doubtful quest. When she picked up the horse tracks again, there also was Jack Elton's bootprint right enough; but a few miles further on she observed another, and further still, yet another, all three quite distinct from each other, and all three evidently following the horse tracks. She thought of the strange camp she had seen earlier in the day, and though regarding the circumstances of travellers camping unseen within coo-ee of them as a mere coincidence, yet she felt glad that she had brought the revolver with her. The afternoon had been fairly advanced when Lizzie started; it was now shaping towards evening. She had walked about ten miles, chiefly over heavy sand, and was beginning to feel tired and a little thirsty. She sat down to rest on a cypress pine ridge and wet her lips with the water, but drank none, not knowing how far she might yet have to travel, nor where, or in what condition she might find Jack.

She had scarcely risen to her feet to pursue her journey again, when, in the gloomy half-light of the forest, she caught a glimpse of the figure of a man lying at the butt of a tree. She sprang forward with a cry of joy, and realised all too late her mistake. It was not Jack Elton, but a mottle-faced man with unkempt sandy hair, who tore the water-bag from her grasp. The next moment, another man—a swarthy giant—appeared from the other side of the tree, and the two fought like wild beasts for the precious fluid. In the struggle the waterbag fell to the ground. Lizzie picked it up, and fled in an agony of fear. Blacklear started in pursuit: but the other still clinging to him in a blind frenzy of despair, he struck at him savagely with his knife. Dexter relaxed his grasp, and fell with a groan, and the thirsty sand drank his blood.

Lizzie in her flight had scarce covered a hundred yards, when she came full upon another figure lying on the sand. Jack Elton at last!

"Here's water, Jack—water!" she cried breathlessly.

Water! The sound of her voice fell on the kangaroo-shooter's ears like rain upon a parching wilderness. He staggered to his feet and took a long deep draught. He had raised the waterbag to his lips again for another drink, and Lizzie stood close beside him, forgetting, in the joy of discovery, her own thirst; forgetting also for a moment their dangerous neighbours. It was now the dusk of evening. Neither of them saw or heard a dark stealthy form that came swiftly and noiselessly over the sand. It was Blacklear, who, brandishing his deadly knife—the madness of thirst in his eye, and the lust of murder in his heart—leaped suddenly upon them with a hoarse tigerish snarl. Lizzie saw him first, and, too late to use the revolver that hung at her side, too late even to utter a warning cry, she flung herself between the man she loved and the descending blade. The blow fell, and she sank backward into the arms of the kangaroo-shooter, who, in a delirium of fury, tore the revolver from its leathern case, and fired once, twice, thrice, into the huge bulk of his assailant. Blacklear fell dead, riddled with bullets.

In the momentary mist of bewilderment and grief that followed, Jack Elton hardly know what he did; but, with the partial recovery of mental equipoise, he found himself kneeling by the side of the dying girl, one arm supporting her head, examining the open wound, hoping wildly, fearing, despairing.

"No use," she said; "quick—listen—Jack!"—the words came from her in broken gasps—"I buried—the gold—in the sand—"

"Oh, curse the gold!" broke from Elton.

She tried to speak again, and failed: but the questioning look in her eyes—so intense in its mute agony—scarce needed words.

"No, Lizzie, no; I thank God that I never meant to leave you!"

Then her eyes grew calm, and her lips moved towards him in dumb entreaty. He bowed his head, and kissed them passionately—then reverently. For she had smiled on him, and died.

The last breath of wind died away. The clouds gathered blacker overhead. The gloomy cypress pines seemed to stand in a shuddering expectancy. Then at last, drop by drop, fell the rain, and still the sole survivor of the tragedy knelt motionless. At length he laid the dead girl's head on the ground, smoothing the hair from her face, and crooning a kind of broken lullaby. He gazed around him with eyes from which the light of reason had flown for ever. He stared stupidly, and wonderingly at the dead man lying face downward on the sand, and then throwing up his arms, laughed wildly up to the streaming heavens.

***

The flood waters of the Bauhinia had subsided. A turgid yellow stream now raced between its banks. A party of cattle musterers reined in their horses on a pine ridge, and contemplated with wonder the spectacle of two dead men lying on the sand within a hundred paces of each other. A mound of earth covered with branches that looked like a rude grave furnished further food for speculation. While searching the neighbourhood of this ghastly scene for some tokens that might tend to an explanation, they came across a man busily engaged in digging in the sand with a sheath knife. His clothes were torn to rags, his frame emaciated with starvation; but he scarce heeded the horsemen who formed a questioning circle around him. At length he spoke, suspending for a moment his labour.

"There's gold in the sand; there's gold in the sand! But where—where?"

The appealing look on his face was piteous to see. And this was the mental and physical wreck of what had been Jack Elton, kangaroo-shooter.

And the gold—the shifting sands of the Bauhinia River still guard their secret.

A CHINESE SWELL

The Surveyor's Ghost

Spinifex[1]

The tents of the survey camp were pitched in line—the cook's, the dining tent, and these of the four chainmen. Forty yards off was the Government tent, where the surveyor in charge, Harry Gifford, camped alone. A light burning on his table was surrounded by a host of winged insects. A butcher-bird was stumbling about with badly-singed feathers. The surveyor himself was in the tent of Burt, the head chainmail, listening to what the dying man had to say. Outside, with his ear to the canvas, close to the head of the stricken man, knelt Simon Price; his tent mate.

"Doesn't your wife know that you have the money?" asked the surveyor.

"Until a moment ago not a soul but myself knew. In another five minutes no one but you'll know. I can't tell why I kept it a secret even from her. I've been a close beggar, and, I suppose, a selfish one. But I've never let her or the kiddies want for anything. I carried it about because I didn't trust banks. You promise, sir?"

"I have promised, but I'll repeat the promise."

"She's a good little manager, and will know how to make it spin out. Make no mistake about the stump, sir. It's the one you always used to sit on when we were camped there. It's a bit charred but a lot of the roots are alive, and have sent up saplings. The storekeeper dries his towels on them. Dig for about a foot at the root of the stump—it's been tunnelled by ants—and put your arm up. You'll find the box stuck a bit perhaps."

"Two hundred and eighteen sovereigns, you say?"

"Yes. When will you go for it, sir?"

"The first thing tomorrow."

---

[1] Pseudonym of the editor of *The Goldfield Courier* and *The Coolgardie Miner*, Alfred Chandler.

Burt moved his head and arms uneasily. The surveyor noted the sign, and said:

"If it has been safe so many weeks it will keep one more night."

"If anything happened to you tonight my wife and children would he beggars."

Gifford laughed as he replied:

"No; I'd come back from the grave to straighten things. But if it's any comfort to you, I'll get to the Soak tonight and get the money."

"God bless you, sir—thanks."

"And now cheer up, old man. You may not be so badly hurt as you think. Price ought to be here with the doctor from the Cross soon. You have no pain?"

"No, sir. My back's broken. There was a fair lot of timber in that tree, and I got the whole weight of it. If you'd give me a drink?"

He drank, and in the act he died.

Gifford drew the grey blanket up over the dead man's head, and smoothed it over the body, then went outside and walked up and down in the heavy darkness before the line of tents. The sound of men's heavy breathing was a relief to him. He listened awhile, then went into his own tent, and tried to resume work till the doctor should arrive. But the horror of another's death was on him. The fine lines of the plan drawings took the shape of falling trees; the groups of figures lost meaning; the snarls of half-wild cats hunting food around the camp had a sound as of human groans; the smell of singed feathers and roasting insects stank in his nostrils. Gifford put out the light, walked forth into one of the tents, and shook the sleeping cook by the shoulder.

"Bob."

"Yes, boss; a'ri."

"Here, listen a minute. Burt is dead. I'm going over to the Punic. If the doctor comes, shove him into my tent."

Gifford got on to the track, and pressed forward through the flawless dark under the towering gums.

The four-mile track to the Punic Soak ran for part of the way by the edge of an old-time watercourse. It was a deep, narrow gully for the most part, but in places shallowed and broadened out. Gifford had just got abreast of the ordinary crossing track when there reached him the sound of heavy feet stumbling through the scrub, and a voice sang, whistled, and coughed in turns.

"Hullo, there!" called the surveyor.

"Hullo-loo-oo-o," returned the voice in cheerful diminuendo, and a little later, Price, very surprised, stood by his employer.

"Where's your horse, man? And where's the doctor?"

"Horse dead lame, boss; had to leave him at Max's Dam. That's why I'm so late through hoofing it. Doctor can't leave the Cross till morning; he's got some awfully bad cases."

"Well, Burt's dead, so it doesn't matter. I'm off to the Punic. Suppose the caretaker will be awake; it's only 10.30. Goodnight."

"If you like to do a short-cut trick, you'll be there in a few minutes. You see this gully winds and turns on itself."

"How's the short cut done?"

Price faced round and led the way for a few hundred yards through the denser scrub to where a mighty gum grew slantwise from the bed of the ravine.

"This is how it's done."

He took hold of a slender branch, and drew it carefully towards him, till he could grasp the heavy wood of the main bough; then giving himself an impetus forward, he swung to the opposite lip of the hollow.

"Good," said Gifford, as the man swung himself back in the same manner: "but I'm heavier than you, and—?"

"Well, if you fell, boss, you'd only drop eight feet into soft scrub and sand. Wait, I'll hold the limb taut for you. Have you got hold? It's so dark. You needn't spring; say 'Ready' and I'll let fly."

He held the creaking bough with all the strength of his left hand, and with his right drew something from the back of his belt.

"Ready," said the surveyor.

Price let go the branch, and at the instant, struck with his right hand below Gifford's upraised left arm. The murderer stood holding his breath in check as he listened to the crash of branches, the snapping of twigs, and the displacing of scrub, as the body clove its way to the sandy bed twenty feet below. Then the violent oscillation of the swing-branch lessened, ceased, and all was still.

A little later, Price mounted his horse, where it had been tied in a hollow at the back of the survey camp. "Keep your promise," said he, looking up to the sullen sky; "come down and wash our tracks." And as if in response, the Heavens were split by a jagged elbow of fire. Behind that clanged the thunder, and the clouds burst with their weight of rain.

Price rode into camp.

"How d'ye manage to get so much pace out of one hoss?" growled the cook, peering forth. "He must have grown another four legs since today."

"Is Burt any worse?"

"No; he's dead."

Price said a few words of sympathetic profanity, then asked: "Boss in his tent?"

"Gone to the Punic."

"Well, I'll leave those letters on his table, and then get under canvas with the other fellows. I don't fancy Burt's company tonight."

The morning broke clear and hot. While the staff waited for their chief, they fashioned a coffin for their dead comrade. When it was finished, and breakfast eaten, a chainman went to the Punic Soak for news of Gifford. He returned with no news, which was bad news, meaning lost in the bush, and the search began. All the survey party except Price turned out. He was left to drive the body of his tent mate to Southern Cross. By noon every dam and soak and bore within twenty miles of Gifford's camp had been spoken to by as many searchers. Not a track was visible after the sweeping rain. By sundown the office of the Public Works Department at Coolgardie had notified the head office at Perth that Gifford had disappeared—lost, it was supposed, in the dense scrub. The head office waited a few hours, and learning that the lost was not found, it made a number of memos, did a quantity of telegraphing, authorised the employment of black-trackers, and reprehended the practice of men in a West Australian wilderness leaving camp unprovided with a compass.

The trackers by-and-bye picked up a false trail, and followed it to the ranges, where it was lost. By day the search never wearied. By night streams of odorous smoke trailed skyward from signal fires of salmon gums and sandal wood, and night hawks and butcher birds awoke and flapped away on frightened wings from the frequent sound of gun-fire.

On the fourth day of Gifford's disappearance, a young woman, with eyes tear-drowned, sought a Public Works official in his private room at Perth, and laid a letter before him. The official read and re-read it, retained the letter, and dismissed the woman, then talked through the telephone to his friend the Superintendent of the Police. Next morning the official search for Harry Gifford was transferred from leagues of sand plain and murmuring scrub to open roadways, railway termini, sea ports, and passenger lists. A letter from Burt had been found in the dead man's breast. Among other things, it told of his hoarded money, and that Mr. Gifford, to whom alone he would confide its whereabouts, should see that she received it safely.

Gifford, it was understood, had had a long private talk with Burt in his last hour.

Some hours after the civil and police officials at Perth had exchanged telephonic opinions on Gifford's rascality, five men sat round a fire at the Punic Soak for the night, after the manner of West Australian nights had followed chill upon the day-time heat. The men had begun to keep their Christmas holidays. For the next few days traffic of teams and swampers would be light and infrequent on the road. As the men sat, they talked of the search, and told each other at intervals that never a finer fellow than Boss Gifford had ever set foot in this unspeakable country. And they strengthened their statement with many a slaughterhouse adjective, and frequent adverbial use of a sacred name, and drank to its truth in pannikins of illegitimate whisky.

The Punic Soak is a mighty mound of rock, forty acres in extent and about eighty feet in height. During rain the water drips from it at all points, and is collected by channels into a dam. All round the desolate landscape looks as if the sea had but recently receded, and scrub and eucalypti had sprung up. The prefix Punic was the evolution of the name and nickname of Soak's first caretaker. His name was Hick, but not only did he call himself 'Ick,' but wrote himself so. To the passing teamsters and swampers he was 'Puny Ick,' for he was a small, slightly deformed man. One night, after having drunk to above par, he saw the full moon's reflection in the conserved water.

"I'll lose my billet," quoth Hick, "for letting that sun-struck rascal spoil the water."

He got a rope and a grappling iron, and, trying to remove the phantom corpse, became a *bona fide* one himself. A Perth newspaper, in reporting the occurrence, corrected what it considered its correspondent's imperfect spelling of a classic name. It had been wired 'Puny 'Ick's Soak.' People laughed, and the Soak was henceforth known as the 'Punic.'

The permanent population of the Soak sat on two stools. They were Hallick, the present caretaker, and Brown, the storekeeper. The former was host. He was a tall, thin man, with a long jaw and a prominent tan moustache. His expansive, discontented mouth, high conical head, and low-set flap ears gave him a certain resemblance to an aged cocker-spaniel. He wore his coat loose on his shoulders, with his sleeves tied under his chin. His visitors were a teamster, camped for the night, one of Gifford's chainmen, disheartened from the fruitless search, and a 'swamper' en route for the field. They sat on stumps which had been cut to within a few feet of the ground, and worn smooth by friction. Each man had a pannikin, and at intervals the swamper went round with two pannikins filled respectively with water and whisky. A bucket of each stood near the caretaker.

"Spare the water and punish the other," he would say as the swamper came up for a fresh supply. "Not that I grudge the water"—looking anxiously round on his guests—"because there's eight feet of it in the dam, but just because we're drinking to the luck of the search, to say nothing of Christmas being only a day off."

The chairman and the teamster were playing cards, using as a table a fourth stump much higher than the others, and at arm's length from either player. Outside the wide circle of firelight gloomed the thick night.

The caretaker took up a blazing twig of sandal wood and held it close to his watch, studied the hands intently for five minutes, then asked the swamper: "D'ye know that it was ten when we had our last drink?"

The swamper laboriously drew a silver watch from his clothes, laid it on his knee, and consulted it, keeping his thumb-nail on the lesser hand while he traced the whereabouts of the larger with a shaky forefinger.

"Well," he replied, his words staggering, "it's only thirteen past now."

"What 'f 'tis," came in tones of liquorish indignation from Hallick.

"If yer don't like yer billet o' barman, get out. D'ye hear? Yer spoilin' the fun. I'll kick yer out."

He rose, put his pannikin down carefully, and went a few paces towards the swamper, sliding his feet along like an amateur actor doing a sleep walking scene; then suddenly changing his mind, he sat down again and began to cry.

"What's the matter?" asked his friend the storekeeper, hastening unsteadily to his side; "did he hurt yer feelings, or have you gotter pain?"

"No," wept the caretaker, jerking his thumb towards the card table; "the sight o' them cards on the stump remembered me o' Boss Gifford. D'ye mind how he used to come and sit there like this?" The caretaker threw himself well forward, crossed his feet, and clasped his hands between his knees—"and have a pitch with you and me, and read his letters when the coach came in, and his old collie Rosy lyin' near him all the time?"

Hallick dried his eyes, emptied his pipe, fumbled through several pockets, and finally brought forth a box of liver pills, from which he filled the bowl, capped them with a live coal, and continued:

"Cook from Gifford's camp told me old 'Rosy' is tracking with the rest—leastways, she's away all day, and rolls up at night to howl."

The 'swamper' was going his rounds with the two pannikins. "Say when," he droned before each firelit visage, as he poured from the pannikin in his left, then 'right,' as he filled up from the other under the impression that he was diluting the spirit, and had not dipped both pannikins from the whisky bucket.

The nauseous odor of burning podophyllin was sobering the caretaker.

A night hawk had begun to hoot, and waked up a magpie, who started carolling. Hallick remarked to the storekeeper that the "blessed birds was a-givin' us a Christmas yim in advance. When I came through with Bailey," continued the man, "two years ago there wasn't a bird had ever been here. Now there are swarms, because there's water. They follow the dams."

The chainman, with folded arms, and chin sunk on his breast, was reciting the 'Sick Stockrider' into the bosom of his shirt, and the teamster was entreating the others to listen to the piece, which "wouldn't be so bad if it wasn't so damn badly said."

"Hark!" said the storekeeper. And all listened, sitting silent and upright, to the sound of nearing hoof beats.

The rider dismounted, and brought himself and his horse's head into the nimbus of light. It was Price, a short, broad-shouldered man, with arms as long as an ape's, a white face that no sun or wind ever tanned, and deep set blue eyes, with a genial expression. He had been detained at Southern Cross, first by the inquest on Burt's body, then by having his horse stolen. And in order to allay anxiety about the safety of certain hidden money, he felt it necessary to drink frequently. Now, he was disgusted to find so many men at the Soak, but he noted with satisfaction the state they were in. Deep sleeping must follow deep drinking.

"No news of your boss?" asked the caretaker, after Price had tethered his horse.

"Yes, plenty. The 'traps' want him on their own account. It seems old Burt had a pot o' money, and before he died gave it to the boss to send on to his wife. The news was wired to the Cross just before I left."

The shock of the news half sobered the drinkers. They talked in angry chorus, repelling the implied accusation; but out of the tangle of sound the words spoken by the thin, high voice of the caretaker could be heard as a shriek is audible above wind. He was imprecating all who spoke the lie, and all who listened to it, and avowing his intention to cut out Price's most important vitals, and grill them as soon as he was sober enough to move from his stool: "Gifford steal the money that a dead man left to his widder?" he foamed, thrusting his tan muzzle into Price's face. "Why, even if he was dead that yarn would fetch him back here to defend— Why Godlemighty! what's the matter, man?"

Price's body had stiffened midway in the act of seating itself; his wide-open eyes, gleaming like blue fire, were fixed at a point above the stumps on which the cards had lain. One shaking hand was stretched in the same direction; the pannikin in the other rattled against the buttons of his coat.

"He has come back!"

The five men stared where he did, bound hand and foot, and mastered by a horror that thickened the mists of their overcast faculties, and seemed to give pause to their very heart-beats. A bunch of scrub growing beside the stump waved and cast shadows, a lizard rustled through the foliage of the tap roots; but the six men gazed at an imaginary seventh, and in their mind's eye saw the surveyor as they had seen him twenty times in reality—the lithe, compactly-knit figure, clad in rough grey tweed; the dark, closely-shorn head, with its incipient patch of baldness; the clear-cut outline of the lowered face, as the figure sat well forward with loosely-clasped hands between its knees. For a minute there was no sound but the laboured breathing of the living as they gazed on the memory of the dead; then the teamster fell forward, swooning on to the edge of the fire; the half-filled pannikin, dropping from his nerveless fingers, spilt its undiluted contents over the embers, and shot up in ghastly flame.

The tension of horror was eased. The men dragged the teamster away into the dusk the other side of the fire; he stood up and gazed with them across the blaze.

"We're all drunk," said he, through chattering teeth: "maybe we only think he's there?"

"Yes, that's it," whispered Price; "you're all drunk."

"Well, you ain't," said the caretaker, softly. "You hadn't more than time to show the liquor the way it ought to go when I seen your eyes glarin' like the headlights of an ingin'. You fetched him here with your tradoocin." He turned to the others. "Boys, let's sing a hymn, or do something religious, then we'll go over and—?"

"No, Hallick, for God's sake; you'll drop dead if you do," and Hallick quailed before the terror in Price's tone.

"We'll do the hymn," said the storekeeper. "I don't think I see anything there now. But the hymn won't do any harm."

But, upon consultation, the men discovered that though they knew the airs of several hymns, none of them remembered the words.

"Would it do if we all whistled 'Rocked in the Cradle of the Deep?'" quavered the 'swamper.' "Whistle it soft, you know; only my tongue's like a bit of stringy bark."

He began to whistle just above his breath; the others joined in, and gaining courage from the sound, finished full volume.

"Now, boys, you back me up," said Hallick, much heartened. "I'm going over to see if the boss is there."

He stumbled round the fire, glancing over his shoulder to see if the others were following. Price rushed to where his horse was cropping the scrub some yards off. Hallick pulled up a safe distance from the stump.

"Mr. Gifford," he began, vainly trying to stop the chattering of his teeth, "we're all damn glad to see you safe back, sir."

The saplings rustled again, and the fire gave little sportive crackles.

"Go over, Bill," whispered the storekeeper, "and feel the log."

A horse and rider dashed out of the formless scrub, shone for a second in the fireglow, then swept into the night, leaving only a memory of a terror-stricken face and wildly-galloping hoofs.

Price never tightened rein till the few drowsy lights of the Cross shone before him. He secured a room, and passed some hours persuading himself that he was the victim of overwrought nerves, too much drink, and too little food. As for the other ghost seers, he told himself that they were also the fools of drink, and the victims of thought transference from himself. When day broke he was sleeping heavily.

The news from the Soak spread with sporadic swiftness. In the morning the chainman arrived at the Cross with it. All along the road to Coolgardie the teamsters told it. The 'swamper' had been detained at the Soak for extra companionship. Price came out of a prolonged sleep, and scoffed with the scoffers at the ghostly news, and gave an exaggerated and humorous description of the condition of the ghost seers at the time of his visit. But the remarks made warned him that neither he nor the treasure stump must attract further notice. He was anxious to settle his business and get out of the country, and his anxiety unnerved him.

That night was Christmas Eve. He again set out for the Soak, timing his arrival late in hope that the two residents would be asleep. There was a light in the storekeeper's tent, and voices and laughter. Price cursed his bad luck, as he dismounted and tied his horse amongst thick scrub. The night was very dark. Another horse which Price knew not was nibbling amongst the saplings. He pulled a pair of thick woollen socks over his boots, and trod softly towards a rough hut, where Hallick kept some tools. Through the tent's open entrance Price saw the Punic's visitor, a trooper named Fitzgerald, taking a hand at cards. The recognition was another shock to his overwrought nerves. He got a spade, and crept towards where the spent light from the store tent gave a white haze to the circle of stumps, arguing with himself, and entreating himself not to be the fool he was the night before. He paused to wipe a cold sweat from his forehead and neck, then knelt and began to clear a spot for digging round the base of the stump. As he groped with frantic fingers over the sandy soil, there grew before his eyes, right where his hands moved, the form of two crossed feet. His arms dropped to his sides, and he shut his eyes for a second, arguing desperately against his folly. Nerve returned, and the man forced himself to look upwards. It was not self-control, but terror, that kept him dumb as he rose and sprang backwards, stumbling heedlessly among camp debris as he backed away from a vision of his own brain-coinage. He swerved as if to flee towards the tents and humanity, but at sight of the trooper hastening forth he turned and fled towards his horse; but the trooper's voice was calling in his rear, and the trooper's spurs were jangling behind him. He cast the reins free, but ere he could fully mount the trooper's hand was on his shoulder, and he was recognised.

"What are you running from? Seen the ghost again?"

Price nodded. The caretaker and his companions bustled up with a lantern. They chaffed him good-naturedly, then pressed him to come in, have a drink, and stay the night. "Come along, old man," seconded the trooper, his pressure on the murderer's arm emphasising the invitation, and his eye on the socked boot still in the stirrup.

They went back, towards the tents, something holding Price's eye in passing as the eye of a rattlesnake might that of a bird. Within the tent they set a full pannikin before him, and the night was growing old ere the trooper ceased refilling it or the men stopped wishing each other a merry Christmas.

Price slept helpless and senseless. The trooper rose softly from his shake-down, went to the sleeper's bunk, and felt over his body. A white glimmer of dawn filtered through the eastern side of the canvas; by its light the trooper picked the charge from Price's revolver, put in empty cases, then restored it to its place. The knife he took from the inert waist he transferred to his own belt.

The light widened and brightened. The trooper stepped without the tent, and walked round the circle of stumps. He stopped where the spade lay, and bent to examine the trail of fingers on the sandy soil; then he dug rapidly till the great roots lay bare.

"What a time to start choppin' wood," grumbled the caretaker, coming to the door of his tent and blinking out into the pearly light. The trooper was splitting the stump with an axe. He had struck but twice, and the sound outer wood was rent. At the third blow the splintered lengths flew apart, and from the hollow centre a tin box fell with rattling noise into a bed of wood dust.

The trooper beckoned the caretaker, and without a word they opened the box and counted its contents. It contained two hundred and eighteen sovereigns, and the will of Jonas Burt. The profuse command of language possessed by the caretaker was reft from him; his jaw had dropped, displaying his fangless lower gums. By gasps he indicated his astonishment and delight, and, as he was in his scanty night drapery, executed a few steps of some frantic dance. Then by signs he intimated that it was too early to be up, and went back to bed, taking the box with him.

The trooper saddled his horse, and with the intention of following out some train of reasoning, started for the survey camp, where a successor to Gifford was now in charge. He had crossed the gully by the worn track, and was well into the bush beyond when he was met by a collie dog. The dog gave the trooper a casual glance, but did not pause in her jog-trot pace. He had not seen her before—he did not know her ownership—she was not in his programme; but so well did she seem to know her own business that the trooper turned and followed, desiring to know it also.

Trooper Fitzgerald had not ridden far from the Punic before Hallick's numbed faculties reasserted themselves. He could not sleep. It would be rank selfishness to keep the news longer. He dressed himself, and after placing the box of money open among the splinters of the log where it had been found, he started screaming to the accompaniment of a fantasia beaten on a tin dish. Out came the storekeeper, and, after an interval, out came Price.

"Where's the trooper?" asked the latter, after he had looked for a while at the gold, and waited for Hallick's music arm to tire.

"Gone to the survey camp. He reckons he'll lay Gifford's ghost before he eats his Christmas pudding."

Price poured the black liquor that remained on last night's tea-leaves into a pannikin and drank, then walked away from the camp. His brain was spinning; his thoughts, chased each other in circles. A blind instinct, something stronger than will, directed his feet till they paused on the brink of the gully at a spot that he alone of all the bushmen knew well. He looked above at the branches of a great gum that slanted up from the bed of the fissure, then below at the dusky foliage of the stirless scrub, and wished, in a spasm of dreary misery, that he could recall the past week, or that he that he had never given the place a secret to keep. He stood still, as the still life round him, the rose of the Christmas sundawn faintly flushing his pale face.

Out of the unseen depths below came the sound of a man's voice. The murderer bent forward, his erstwhile stagnant blood racing through his veins. Again the voice spoke as if in entreaty. He crouched, listening, staring. At the back of either eye a pulse began to throb, till each glistening eyeball was thrust forward under the dry lids. Something was climbing up from the ravine by the trunk of the gum. The sandal bushes stirred, the tops of the tall saplings swayed, and a lean, sinewy hand and sunburnt wrist reached up and caught at a branch. Price gazed in a trance of terror, never doubting but that the hand and voice were Gifford's. And when the back of a closely-cropped dark head shoved through the foliage his breath stopped for a second, then came in such whistling-gasps, as one hears in the diphtheria ward of an hospital. The hand reached still higher, square shoulders heaved themselves after the dark head, which, turning, showed the stern eyes and set, white face of Trooper Fitzgerald.

Price reeled where he stood, then realisation burst full upon him. He drew his revolver and pressed the muzzle to his temple. The trigger snapped once, twice, then the weapon was pointed at Fitzgerald. The trooper sprang to the ground.

"If there's any shooting to be done," said he, "I'll do it. Throw up your hands. I arrest you for the wilful murder of Harry Gifford."

The Baby Saved Them!

"Why? What have you got here, Tess?"

"It's the tail-board out of the dray, Tom. I've got to barricade Daisy in with something. Leave it there, Tom, the door will shut as well with it down, and I am afraid this little puss will crawl out and fall down a shaft before we wake in the morning."

"What a very lively imagination you must have, Tess."

"Ah yes, you men don't know what it is to feel a mother's anxiety. Where would you have been now if your mother had not looked so well after you?" retorted his wife with a wise little air of conviction.

"Perhaps I should not have been here at all, and some other fellow would have owned you, and this little terror"—putting his arm around her and giving her cheek a gentle pat,—

"Don't call her a little terror," said his wife preparing with caution to reinstall the baby limbs in their proper place beneath the covering.

"For goodness sake, let her alone," whispered Tom, "she may take it into her head to get up."

"Don't speak that way of her, you know she brought us good luck," said his wife.

"How do you make that out, Tess?"

"Well, you didn't exactly get gold the day she was born, Tom, but you wouldn't have had the claim but for her."

"This is news to me, Tess."

"Don't you recollect you were complaining to old Scotch Peter that you could not go to the new rush at the Five Mile because you could not leave me, and he was in the same predicament with regard to his wife when you concluded to give the wet claim another trial."

"Oh, I see!" said Tom.

"And now," continued his wife, "we are to leave the wretched diggings for ever, and I am so glad, for the fear of Daisy falling down a shaft haunts me day and night."

"But what sort of a settler will I make? I always hated cockatoos, and nothing will content you but I must be one."

"Don't speak that way, Tom, you know that if we stay here you will be tempted to try new ground and will lose all the money you have made, and we will be as badly off as we were before Daisy was born."

Some thought gave Tom's face a very tender expression for he again put his arm round his wife's shoulders and said feelingly, "Yes, little woman, we were indeed badly off, but you never would own it, would you?"

"Why? What was the use of owning it Tom, you were miserable enough on my account without my adding to your trouble by complaining. No, I'd work my fingers to the bone before I'd murmur when I saw you doing your best."

"And you did," said Tom, taking up her little hand and looking at it affectionately. "To think that these little fingers that I could crush up in my hand, made and washed the diggers' shirts,"—

"Now don't hurt my fingers, Tom," said his wife withdrawing her hand and stooping to caress Daisy.

"Now don't go and wake her up," said Tom, as his wife stooped again to kiss the little one, "she'll start crawling all over us, and perhaps want to get up for a couple of hours, and I want to be up early in the morning and off; it is not safe to have so much gold in the hut." So they closed the door—never bolting or barring it, for the very good reason that huts in the bush and on the goldfields seldom boast of an inside fastening. How long they slept is not known, but sometime towards the small hours, the stillness was suddenly broken by a loud clatter of chains and a heavy fall, and upon the two starting up, they found the door wide open and a most unwelcome visitor, who afterwards proved to be a notorious bushranger, painfully picking himself up from the white-washed floor. It took Tom but a second to take in the situation, and, reaching his gun, he took steady aim, and not wishing to take life, shot the robber through the leg, laming him and preventing his getting away to give further trouble to the police in particular and quiet folks in general. His comrade seeing his leader fall, concluded he was done for and left him, and so soon as Tom could calm his wife and induce Daisy to cease yelling, assistance was summoned, and after waiting for daylight, aided by a faint stream of blood they discovered the wounded man, under a bush not far off, who coolly confessed that he and his mates intended to have the gold even if it cost the owners their life. He also complained of the disadvantage under which he laboured saying that Tom had the clear moonlight through the doorway to help him make a true aim, whereas he had nothing but pitch darkness at the end of the hut to fire his random shot into.

The robbers had quietly unfastened the door which opened from the outside, meaning to steal in and secure the gun which they knew Tom always kept loaded within reach while sleeping, but did not bargain for the noisy trip-up caused by Daisy's barricade.

When all the trouble was over and they were alone, Tess said, "You see. Tom, it's just as I told you about the luck. If it hadn't been for baby—"

And Tom stopped her with a kiss saying, "Yes, old woman, I knew I had one Mascotte, but now I see I've got two of you."

A Chinese Nurse